PRAISE FOR MELISSA FOSTER

"With her wonderful characters and resonating emotions, Melissa Foster is a must-read author!"

—*New York Times* bestseller Julie Kenner

"Melissa Foster is synonymous with sexy, swoony, heartfelt romance!"

—*New York Times* bestseller Lauren Blakely

"You can always rely on Melissa Foster to deliver a story that's fresh, emotional, and entertaining."

—*New York Times* bestseller Brenda Novak

"Melissa Foster writes worlds that draw you in, with strong heroes and brave heroines surrounded by a community that makes you want to crawl right on through the page and live there."

—*New York Times* bestseller Julia Kent

"When it comes to contemporary romances with realistic characters, an emotional love story, and smokin'-hot sex, author Melissa Foster always delivers!"

—*The Romance Reviews*

"Foster writes characters that are complex and loyal, and each new story brings further depth and development to a redefined concept of family."

—*RT Book Reviews*

"Melissa Foster definitely knows how to spin a tale and keep you flipping the pages."

—*Book Loving Fairy*

HOT MESS SUMMER

SEASIDE SUMMERS

Seaside Dreams

Seaside Hearts

Seaside Sunsets

Seaside Secrets

Seaside Nights

Seaside Embrace

Seaside Lovers

Seaside Whispers

Seaside Serenade

BAYSIDE SUMMERS

Bayside Desires

Bayside Passions

Bayside Heat

Bayside Escape

Bayside Romance

Bayside Fantasies

THE STEELES AT SILVER ISLAND

Tempted by Love

My True Love

Caught by Love

Always Her Love

Wild Island Love

THE RYDERS

Seized by Love

Claimed by Love

Chased by Love

Rescued by Love

Swept into Love

SUGAR LAKE

The Real Thing

Only for You

Love Like Ours

Finding My Girl

HARMONY POINTE

Call Her Mine

This Is Love

She Loves Me

THE WHISKEYS: DARK KNIGHTS AT PEACEFUL HARBOR

Tru Blue

Truly, Madly, Whiskey

Driving Whiskey Wild

Wicked Whiskey Love

Mad About Moon

Taming My Whiskey

The Gritty Truth

In for a Penny

Running on Diesel

THE WICKEDS: DARK KNIGHTS AT BAYSIDE

A Little Bit Wicked

The Wicked Aftermath

Crazy, Wicked Love

The Wicked Truth

His Wicked Ways

THE WHISKEYS: DARK KNIGHTS AT REDEMPTION RANCH

The Trouble with Whiskey

Freeing Sully: Prequel to For the Love of Whiskey

For the Love of Whiskey

A Taste of Whiskey

SILVER HARBOR

Maybe We Will

Maybe We Should

Maybe We Won't

BILLIONAIRES AFTER DARK SERIES

Wild Boys After Dark

Logan

Heath

Jackson

Cooper

Bad Boys After Dark

Mick

Dylan

Carson

Brett

HARBORSIDE NIGHTS SERIES

Catching Cassidy

Discovering Delilah

Tempting Tristan

STAND-ALONE NOVELS

Chasing Amanda (mystery/suspense)

Come Back to Me (mystery/suspense)

Have No Shame (historical fiction/romance)

Love, Lies & Mystery (three-book bundle)

Megan's Way (literary fiction)

Traces of Kara (psychological thriller)

Where Petals Fall (suspense)

HOT MESS SUMMER

MELISSA FOSTER

Published by Montlake, Seattle

www.apub.com

Amazon, the Amazon logo, and Montlake are trademarks of Amazon.com, Inc., or its affiliates.

ISBN-13: 9781662507939 (paperback)
ISBN-13: 9781662507953 (digital)

Cover image: ©alanadesign / Shutterstock; © Dean Drobot / Shutterstock

Printed in the United States of America

For anyone coming out of a relationship and wondering if you're enough.
Don't wonder. Believe. Take time to heal, rediscover yourself, and create your happiness.
Your vibe really will attract your tribe. I am so thankful for mine.

Chapter One

NICOLE

"Who needs a sex life, anyway?" I say semi-jokingly to my besties as we cruise toward the small New England fishing town of Chatemup, Massachusetts, where for some godforsaken reason, I thought it was a good idea to buy a cottage. Not rent, like a normal thirty-eight-year-old who had never been to the area, but purchase after a twelve-minute video tour with a spunky real estate agent who probably isn't much older than my twenty-year-old daughter, Mackenzie. It's been almost three years since my divorce, and I've been so busy writing, time flew by. *Finally* taking charge of my life and giving myself a summer to start over in a place where nobody knows me seemed like a spectacular idea at the time, but as we near the bridge that separates my new summer home from the rest of civilization, I'm not so sure.

"*What* did you say?" Rachel's green eyes nearly bug out of her head. "You have been out of the game for far too long if you're entering an I-no-longer-need-sex phase." Her fiery red ponytail swings as she spins around in the passenger seat, gaping at Dani, thumbing out something on her phone. "Dani, are you hearing this?"

"*Yes.* It's worse than we thought. We need to get her some action, *stat.*"

"No, we do *not.*" I scowl at Dani in the rearview mirror. Her blond hair is piled on her head in a messy bun, and she's crammed beside our suitcases in the back of my *other* post-divorce, new-start purchase: a red convertible VW Bug. Fitting all our crap in my little car with Rachel the fashionista and Dani the shoe hoarder was a feat in and of itself. Luckily, Rachel is ridiculously good at packing, because nothing was going to stop them from bringing every little thing or stop me from going on our annual girls' trip. Lord knows I need it this year.

Dani's eyes narrow. "Girl, don't scowl at me. You've seriously lost your mind if you think you can go without sex. Sex is rejuvenating. It makes everything better."

"Romance writer on deadline here, remember? I need to get words on the page, not *D* in my *V.* I told you my frigging muse ran for the hills last month during Kenzie's mini crisis."

Dani rolls her eyes. "Don't get me started about Kenzie and her crisis."

My daughter is having a hard time grasping the concept of being a responsible young adult. "Can we not go there right now? I'm stressed enough over my deadline." My manuscript is due at the beginning of October, and I haven't even started it yet.

"Well, it's no wonder your muse ran away. She needs inspiration," Rachel chimes in. "You need *D* in the *V* to get steamy words on the page. You're a successful single woman. You should be out there having fun and experiencing life as your inspiration, not living vicariously through your characters."

I eye her skeptically. "Hello, Pot, meet Kettle."

"What are you talking about?" She looks between me and Dani, wrinkling her nose, which makes the spray of amber freckles across its bridge more prominent against her fair skin. "I go out. I just broke up with Jack three weeks ago."

"She's kind of right, Rach," Dani says, pecking away at her phone again, probably setting up dog-walking and grooming gigs for three months from now. She's always booked. "You went on, what? Three dates with him and then blew him off for a month before finally ending things?"

"I was busy."

"Binge-watching *Emily in Paris* and *Schitt's Creek* for the third time is not busy." Honestly, I don't blame Rachel. Nobody can compare to her late husband, Lucas. He was a loving husband and a friend to everyone. We were all devastated when we lost him six years ago. "No judgment here, babe. You know I'm all for flying solo. I'm finally happy with who I am and where I am in my life. I worked really hard to get here, and I don't want to chance messing that up for some guy who's just going to let me down." They know this, of course. They supported me through the devastating months of mourning the end of my second marriage, gave me tough love when I needed it, and cheered me on as I rebuilt my sense of self with a stronger foundation than I ever had before. But even good friends need a gentle reminder sometimes.

"So have a little fun and let *them* down," Dani suggests. "We're not saying you need to sleep with a bunch of guys or get married again. What happened to the bold teenager we met in cheer camp who convinced us to sneak out in the middle of the night to go to a party and hooked up with—"

"Brad with the abs!" we chant in unison, then crack up.

"He *was* fun," I admit. "But it's not like I'm trying to live a sex-free life. It just hasn't happened yet."

"Really? How weird," Dani says sarcastically. "You mean a steady stream of hot eligible bachelors didn't come knocking on your office door in *Buzzkill*, Virginia, over the last two years? Seriously, Nic, if you refuse to use dating apps, then you have to leave your writer's cave to meet men."

The last thing I need is dating apps. I'm done with drama, and after two failed marriages, I'm pretty much done with relationships, too. "You guys, come on. I was drowning with Tim. I had no social life—no *life*, really—and he lied about everything. I need to figure out how to *have* a life outside my office and find a community I connect with a lot more than I need to get laid. Besides, I have my battery-operated boyfriends, and I'm quite happy with them."

"We get it," Rachel says. "We're glad that you're finally happy, and after all you've been through, we totally get that you want to protect your peace. But you have to admit, you tend to lock yourself in your office and never come out, and we don't want you to lose out on having a really great life."

"I know, and I appreciate that. I'm looking forward to starting fresh and refilling my creative well in a place where nobody has heard Tim's lies."

"That ass really did a number on you," Dani says. "I still think you should bring me as your plus-one to Nolan's wedding."

I give her a wry look. Nolan is Tim's son. I helped raise him from the time he was twelve, and although I'm not looking forward to seeing Tim and his girlfriend, I love Nolan, and I'm not going to show up at his wedding armed with Dani's hatred for his father. She knows the demise of our marriage wasn't one-sided, but these are my ride-or-die girls. We've had each other's backs through cheerleading mishaps, first loves, painful divorces, and heart-wrenching losses, and I don't want to chance lighting a Tim-bashing fire.

"She's *not* taking you to the wedding," Rachel says emphatically. "Let's focus on how great this trip is going to be."

"Damn right it is." Dani pats my shoulder. "I know you have to write, Nic, but I've been manifesting all sorts of goodies for you. You'd better not camp out in your office."

She has been manifesting every aspect of her life forever, and the woman has it down. She envisions the impossible, and it always seems to come true. I believe it's the incredible quirky woman doing the manifesting that makes her dreams come true, and I don't expect her magic to carry over to my personal life. Don't get me wrong. I think I'm pretty amazing, too. I'm making my professional dreams come true. It's just my personal life that's lacking.

"You'll be happy to know that I plan on getting up early to write and getting in three or four hours before you're even out of bed. Then I'm all yours."

"Perfect," Rachel says. "We've got a busy week ahead, and with a little luck, you might find some horizontal inspiration along the way."

Don't hold your breath.

"I can see the title of your next book." Dani moves her hand like she's reading a sign as she says, "*Nicole Ross Gets Her Groove Back.*"

"I'd settle for *Nicole Ross Gets Words on the Page and Puts Her Toes in the Sand.*"

As we start across the bridge, I gaze out at the surrounding water and clear blue sky, both of which seem endless and peaceful. I roll down my window, breathing in the warm New England air, and feel a gust of something invigorating that I can't quite place, except enough to know that once upon a time, I felt it often.

Rachel and Dani are singing along with Lizzo's "About Damn Time" and dancing in their seats, as carefree as we were as teenagers. Their enthusiasm is contagious, and even though I can't carry a tune to save my life, I join them, belting out the lyrics and wiggling my shoulders to the beat, and realize I never let go like this unless I'm with them. That's when it hits me. The unfamiliar sensation seeping beneath my skin and billowing inside me as we cross the bridge is the feeling of *freedom*. The realization makes me feel sucker punched by life.

No, not by life. Sucker punched by my own poor choices.

I try taking a page from Dani's playbook, imagining the weight of my most trying years falling away like a snake shedding its skin. When we reach the end of the bridge, I envision leaving that skin behind, and I'm surprised to feel lighter as we follow the GPS to a two-lane road lined by tall pitch pines and sandy grass, so different from the overpopulated streets of Virginia.

Suddenly Chatemup feels like a really good idea again.

Chapter Two

NICOLE

"We're here!" Rachel exclaims, whipping out her camera to take a picture of the sign announcing my new summer town. "*Welcome to Chatemup, Massachusetts, where gossip is ripe, fish are plentiful, and no one is a stranger for long.* Gotta love a place that tells it like it is."

"We'd better keep our shenanigans on the down-low so Nic doesn't become the talk of the town," Dani suggests.

"That's going to be difficult. A gorgeous author is a hot commodity." Rachel waggles her brows at me and Dani.

I roll my eyes. I'm not too proud to admit that I pale in comparison to my beautiful friends. Growing up with a houseful of brothers put being attractive low on my priority scale. Beating my brothers in everything I could? Now *that* was right up there at the top. I'm more tomboy than feminine, a little thick around the middle despite consistent exercise, and my curly auburn hair is frizzy and unruly on good days. But I've got a great personality when I'm not working. Or at least I used to.

I hope I haven't lost it.

"Smile, Nic!" Rachel turns the camera on me, and I hold up a two-fingered peace sign and grin as she takes a picture, then turns the camera on Dani, who lifts her hand to wave and promptly gives her the finger. Rachel, a professional photographer, catches both the flip of the bird and her laughter before taking a selfie with her signature open-mouthed excitement. She's been documenting our trips since we started taking them together what seems like a hundred years ago.

I spent the last several weeks learning everything I could about the sleepy little town where salt-of-the-earth fishermen have lived for hundreds of years. There are no big chain stores or fast-food restaurants, which suits me fine, and the Chatemup Market has been owned by the same family for decades. There are plenty of cute mom-and-pop shops, a couple of restaurants, a movie theater, a new *and* a used bookstore, and best of all, the Rise and Grind coffee shop is within walking distance of my cottage. That was a big selling point for me. I've always wanted a special place where I could hunker down while writing and blend into the background, watching life unfold around me. Talk about inspiration.

As we drive through town, there are a few people window-shopping and not many cars on the road. I'm glad it's not swamped like a tourist town. Every street corner boasts enormous planters bursting with summer blooms, and the sidewalk is lined with waist-high wooden bollards with thick nautical rope strung between them. Rachel's taking pictures, and I'm smitten with the cute shops that look like houses, with pretty awnings over the doors and display windows. After writing about small towns for more than a decade, I'm excited to immerse myself in the culture of this one.

"Am I dreaming, or is this place even cuter than the pictures?" I glance down the streets to our right and catch a glimpse of the late-afternoon sun glistening off the water at the bottom of the hill.

"There's nothing like the old-world charm of New England." Rachel is looking through the lens of her camera. "It's beautiful. I can't wait to explore."

"This place definitely has potential," Dani says. "Check out the cutie by the pub."

Rachel and I follow her gaze to a gray-haired man walking a dog. "He's good-looking, but since when are you into older men?" I ask. "He looks at least sixty."

"I meant the dog," Dani clarifies. "But sixty or not, that guy's got it going on, doesn't he? Nic, how do you feel about a little Daddy action?"

I glance in the rearview, choosing to ignore her question. "Please tell me you wouldn't call a guy Daddy in bed."

Dani laughed. "Normally I wouldn't, but now I'm going to *have* to call Bennett Daddy in bed just so I can remember that look on your face." Bennett is her boyfriend of the last few months. He's a little uptight for my taste, but she seems happy.

"The poor guy will think you're laughing at him," Rachel said. "I have to pee. Let's stop."

"We're almost to my cottage."

Rachel deadpans. "Seriously, Mom? Can you please join the party?"

"You sound like Lucy." Lucy is her twelve-year-old daughter.

"Where do you think her mini me learned it from?" Dani asks. "There's your coffee shop. Let's check it out."

I see the Rise and Grind on the corner up ahead. "*My* coffee shop. I love that."

I park, and we make our way past people chatting at tables out front. Once inside, we're greeted by the heavenly aroma of fresh-roasted coffee and the din of music and conversation. There's an eclectic mix of distressed wooden booths and tables and cozy nooks lining the front and side windows with inviting upholstered and leather chairs, and the walls are full of colorful paintings and pictures of the town.

"I'm digging this old-school fishing town meets big-city coffee-house vibe," I say as we step into line.

"I'm digging the hot barista," Rachel says quietly.

The guy behind the register is cute, with wavy blond hair and patchy scruff, but he looks about a decade younger than us. "I bet you'd like to be twenty-five again, wouldn't you?"

"No way. Life was so confusing back then. Society wanted me to fall in love and get married, my brain wanted me to make something of my life, and my body wanted great sex *all* the time."

"Mine still does," Dani says. "And Nic could use it. Younger guys like older women, so it's a win-win for her."

I give her a look that I hope will shut her down.

"While you convince Nic to seduce the man-child, I'm going to the ladies' room," Rachel announces. "Will you get me a vanilla latte?"

"Sure," I say, checking out the display of freshly baked breads, muffins, and other goodies.

"I have to go, too," Dani says. "Nic, I'll take a chai tea latte with a side of hot young thing for you."

I roll my eyes, and they head in the direction of the bathroom. The line moves quickly, and when I step up to the counter to order, the barista looks me up and down. "This must be my lucky day. I haven't seen you in here before."

Is he flirting with me? We've been driving all day, my eyes are tired and probably bloodshot, and I didn't wash my hair this morning since we left at the crack of dawn. There's no way he's flirting with me, and for some reason that makes me breathe a little easier. That worries me. I'm not afraid of flirting. *Am I?* I shake my head to clear those ridiculous thoughts.

"This is my first time in the area. I just bought a cottage around the corner."

"Cool. I'm Matt, and I'm glad you came in. What can I get you? Wait, let me guess." He gives me another appraising once-over. "I bet you like it sweet with a touch of *spice*, right?" His brows rise on *spice*. "I can sense a cinnamon coffee lover a mile away."

I notice the female barista at the next register eyeing him with amusement. Yeah, he is definitely flirting, and damn, cinnamon coffee sounds just my speed. I contemplate ordering something else to discourage his flirting but decide to throw caution to the wind and put myself out there. Not that I'd ever consider being with a guy his age, but it's been so long since I was single, it can't hurt to brush up on my flirting skills.

"You're *very* good at this, Matt." It takes more effort than I'd like to admit to muster the flirtatious tone I've long ago forgotten. "That sounds perfect." I order my friends' drinks and pay.

"I hope these are for here. Or are you going to break my heart and take them to go?"

"I wouldn't want to break your heart. We'll drink them here." As he goes to make our drinks, excitement flickers inside me at being flirted with. Although from the look on the female barista's face, she's used to whatever vibe I'm giving off, which makes me feel silly, and I school my expression.

Matt returns with our coffees. "How long are you here?" He tosses a handful of napkins on the tray.

"For the summer."

He pushes the tray across the counter, and his fingers very purposely graze mine, throwing me for a loop. His voice goes low. "I hope that means I'll be seeing more of you."

Holy crap. He's seriously flirting, and I'm so out of practice, my nerves get the better of me. "Oh, yeah, sure. Okay. Thanks!" Feeling like a bumbling teenager, I pick up the tray and spin around, smacking into a wall of stone and splashing coffee everywhere. Scrambling to still the cups, I look up, registering the irritated gaze of a rugged man with windblown black hair, salt-and-pepper scruff, and *oh no*, a broad, coffee-drenched chest.

"Oh my gosh. I'm so sorry. Why aren't there lids?" Balancing the tray in one hand, I grab the napkins and start patting his shirt dry. His chest is hard and thick, and my writer's brain takes off running. *He's not muscular like Thor, just thick or maybe brawny, like a lumberjack or a—*

He lets out a long, loud breath, as if he's had a *day*, and grits out, "It's fine," in a deep, craggy voice.

"No, it's not," I insist, trying to dry the spots on his shirt. "I'm really sorry."

He flattens a large, calloused hand over mine, pinning it to his chest. "I *said* it's fine."

As I process his authoritative tone, he flashes a boyish grin, bringing out killer dimples that soften his bite and cause an unexpected flutter in my chest. He arches a brow. "Don't you think he's a little young to get you all worked up?"

My jaw drops. The nerve of him. "I wasn't . . . I'm not . . ."

"Right." His eyes sparkle with amusement, the skin around them crinkling.

For some stupid reason, I notice those wrinkle lines are whiter than the rest of his tanned skin and think about how he must spend a lot of time in the sun. *Shirtless?*

What in the actual hell is happening here? Forcing my brain into gear, I yank my hand away. He chuckles and steps up to the counter, like he didn't just infer I was too old and too eager. I hear Matt say, "Declan, my man. Were you flirting with my girl?"

Great.

I spot my friends making their way toward me and stomp over to them, giving them what is left of their drinks.

"Wow, he's super cute," Dani says in a hushed whisper. "There was a lot of touching going on, and did you see those dimples?"

"We leave you alone for five minutes and you pick up a Jeffrey Dean Morgan look-alike?" Rachel sips her coffee. "Color me impressed."

"Yeah, well, I don't know if you should color me annoyed or embarrassed. He basically called me a cougar. Let's get out of here."

Chapter Three

NICOLE

We swing by the liquor store to pick up wine and hit the market for groceries. Chatemup Market is a far cry from a chain grocery store, with only six aisles, a small deli, and a massive fish counter. But the farm-stand-style vegetable and produce area, fresh-baked goods, and self-serve coffee bar give it a quaint feel. Everything is pricier than back home, and there's not much variety of anything other than fish, but I'm enjoying the process of finding the ripest fruit and the freshest vegetables instead of having them delivered to my door like I usually do.

"Are you going to inspect every piece of fruit?" Rachel asks, tossing oranges into a plastic bag.

"I forgot how much I enjoyed this."

"Grocery shopping?" Dani asked. "You can do mine weekly if you'd like."

"I'm serious. I used to do all my own grocery shopping and cooking and loved every second of it." I got pregnant at eighteen and married my high school sweetheart, Jay. We lasted only five years. I moved in with my parents after the divorce, but after a few months, Mackenzie and I moved into an apartment, making ends meet on a shoestring budget.

"And then you married Tim, the egotistical butthead," Dani says.

"We were careful at first. I still grocery shopped and cooked. It wasn't until the kids got older and our careers took off that we started taking the easy route. Ordering out too much and buying everything on a whim, which I didn't realize until right this second meant nothing was longed for or, in many cases, even necessary."

"In *all* cases where he was concerned. I mean, really, who collects *cars*?" Rachel tosses another orange in a bag.

Tim earned a good living selling high-end real estate, but collecting cars became his hobby after I started earning six figures. As my income climbed, so did his penchant for pricier cars. "I'm glad to be done with all that nonsense, but I got stuck in that easy mode, and I forgot that grocery shopping can be satisfying."

"Let's get out of this aisle before she asks for an apron," Dani says.

As we make our way through the store, I wonder how those easy-mode changes have affected me, and my mind travels back to the coffee shop. Why was I so nervous around Matt and Dimple Dude? With the exception of Dani and Rachel, I've always gotten along better with guys than girls, and I miss having guy friends. Maybe I have been in my writing cave for too long, because being flirted with by a younger man would never have thrown off pre-Tim Nicole. It feels good to have caught a younger guy's eye, and I'm not even annoyed about being called a cougar by Dimple Dude. Not that I want to be seen as one, but as his dimples and boyish grin play at the edges of my mind, I think his comment was kind of funny.

"What's that goofy grin for?" Rachel asks.

"Nothing." I head into the freezer aisle as Rachel and Dani double back for toiletries.

I'm perusing the ice cream, in search of frozen yogurt, when I real- ize I don't even really like frozen yogurt. I've eaten it forever because Tim liked that it didn't have as much fat as ice cream. *When did I become a puppy who follows rather than a woman who leads?* I don't have to look far for the answer. It was after I married Tim, because it was easier than fighting.

I thought I had broken out of that mold when I filed for divorce, but now I realize that while I ended the marriage, I lost a piece of myself in it.

That pisses me off. Right then and there I make a decision. This summer isn't going to be solely driven by finishing my novel and refilling my creative well. This is going to be the summer I find all the lost parts of myself. Including the ones I can't even remember losing.

Like the part that loves mint chocolate chip ice cream.

I toss a pint into the cart and go in search of my friends.

"There you are," Dani says as I walk into the toiletry aisle.

She tosses me a box, and I glance at the label. *Large condoms. Ribbed for her pleasure.* "Why do you want these? Bennett isn't here."

"They're for *you*. We're manifesting, remember?"

"Dani." I thrust the box toward her. "I don't need these."

"You're right." Rachel plucks the box from my hand and puts it back on the shelf. "If we're manifesting, we should do it right." She grabs a box of Magnum XLs and tosses them in the cart.

"Yesss." Dani high-fives her.

Their laughter reels me in, and I smirk. "Amateurs." I snag the XLs and put them back on the shelf.

"Come *on*," Dani pleads. "You're not even giving yourself a chance to manifest."

"Shows how much you know. If you're going for size, get the Magnum Ecstasy." I hold up a box of them. "It's four-tenths of an inch longer than the XLs."

"How do *you* know that?" Dani asks, exchanging incredulous glances with Rachel.

"Book research." I toss the box in the cart, lift my chin, and head down the aisle. "I might not have a great sex life, but my characters do."

◆　◆　◆

Twenty minutes later we're driving down Old Wharf Road, which runs along the harbor, and Rachel and Dani are tossing around names for my cottage—"Raspberry Tart . . . Nic's Nest . . . Raspberry Dream . . ." Did I mention the cottage is the color of raspberry sherbet? I love the idea of naming my cottage as a nod to our cheerleading-camp days. Each of the cabins we stayed in had a cute name, and we have great memories from the time we spent there.

I gaze out the window just as a seagull dives into the water. It flies away a few seconds later with a fish in its beak. Can't see that in suburban Virginia.

"Look at those two houses right on the beach," Dani exclaims. "I bet they cost a fortune. Can you imagine living there?"

"The smaller one sold last summer for eight hundred thousand more than mine." Only two houses sold in Chatemup in the last three years, which I took as a good sign that once people move here, they rarely leave.

I turn off the main road and onto the gravel lane that leads to my driveway. We pass Oyster Run, a cul-de-sac of cute cottages, and turn onto the steep driveway I share with one neighbor.

"Hillside Hideaway!" Rachel exclaims.

"That's a cute name," I say.

"*No*," Dani protests. "Nothing with *hideaway*. We're trying to break Nic of that habit."

"I'm always going to be a writer, which means I'll always hide away to some extent." Excitement builds as I pull up to the raspberry-sherbet front-gabled cottage, although the driveway is in the back. "Holy shit, you guys. It's adorable, and it's *mine*!"

We scramble out of the car and stare at the cottage like we've never seen one before. "I still can't believe you bought it," Rachel says.

"Me neither," Dani says. "When you said you did something crazy, I thought you finally put those purple streaks in your hair you're always talking about."

"This is way better than purple streaks." I feel giddy. "Let's go see how the furniture looks." The real estate agent connected me with While You Were Out, a business that helps homeowners with everything from opening and closing seasonal homes to handling repairs, cleanings, and furnishing. It was an amazing feeling to fill the rooms with pieces *I* loved instead of muting my tastes for a husband. The girls even talked me into putting in a patio with a firepit and buying beach chairs and deck furniture, so I wouldn't have to go without this summer. I stretched my budget, but I knew I'd enjoy those things more than the nest egg I'd been tossing money into since my career took off.

Rachel grabs her camera, and we leave our suitcases in the car, running up the seashell walkway and around to the side door. I promptly unlock it and throw it open, revealing wide-planked hardwood floors running through the open living room, dining room, and kitchen. There are two bedrooms and bathrooms upstairs and one bedroom and bath on the main level. A cursory glance proves my decorating rocks. The beige L-shaped couch and multicolored pillows pick up the blues and greens in the throw rug and curtains and go perfectly with the yellow kitchen cabinets. The pièce de résistance, my cream-colored writing desk, is tucked into the bay window off the living room with a perfect view of the water, like it was meant to be.

We squeal like kids and rush inside. Rachel flops onto the couch. "This is perfect!"

"So freaking cool!" Dani runs around the first floor checking out every room. She runs back into the living room. "I found my bedroom."

I can hardly believe I took this chance. This is my blank page. My fresh start. I don't go upstairs or check out every nook and cranny. I have plenty of time to do that. The water is calling my name. I head out the sliding glass doors onto the deck, and my friends follow. There's a second deck above us, off the second-story master suite. A generous name for a cozy room.

I can hardly believe my eyes. I knew the view would be special, but it's literally breathtaking. The flagstone patio gives way to long dune grasses, the roofs of cottages along Old Wharf Road, and just beyond, deep blue water as far as the eye can see. I know the beach to our right ends at the marina, although I can't see it from the deck. A good distance to our left, cottages dot the shoreline of the land as it curls into the water like a finger beckoning us to explore.

"Holy crap, Nic," Dani says. "This is incredible."

I hold out my arm. "Pinch me."

Rachel bumps me with her shoulder. "You really don't need a man. You've got everything you need right here."

She starts taking pictures, and I glance at Dani, her penchant for feng shui taking over as she rearranges the patio furniture. Not for the first time, and surely not for the last, I count myself lucky. With my besties here for the week, knowing I'll see Mackenzie at the wedding later this summer, and a fresh start to look forward to, I sure do have it all.

Chapter Four

NICOLE

After unpacking and putting away the groceries, we post to social media and scarf down snacks, too excited to be there to eat a full meal. Dani insisted we help rearrange the living room, and agreeing was easier than arguing about energy flow versus aesthetics. We're almost done, but Dani and I are having a stare down. She wants to move my writing desk, and I'm not having it.

"Don't you want your chi to flow while you're writing?" Dani pleads.

"I think I know my chi better than you do. It'll flow best with the desk exactly where it is."

"How can you know it's best if you haven't tried it at an angle?" She reaches for the desk.

"Danielle Potter, touch that desk and lose your hand," I warn.

"Dani, let it go," Rachel pleads. "She let you move everything else."

"But one piece of furniture in the wrong position can totally mess up her natural energy." She softens her tone toward me. "Can't you try it my way for a week?"

"Sorry, babe, no can do. You know how I am. I need things to feel right to *me* or I can't write."

She throws her arms up. "Fine. But don't blame me when your words come out wrong."

I'll be happy if they simply come out. "Thanks for understanding." I hug her, and her arms hang limply by her sides, which makes me smile. She's steadfast in her beliefs, but I know her pout will only last a minute. She can't hold a grudge to save her life.

"You know this is all I'll think about now," she says.

Rachel takes her arm, dragging her toward the kitchen. "A little wine will fix that."

It's after six when we finally head down to the beach with a blanket and insulated wine tumblers in hand. We follow a path through the dune grass and kick off our flip-flops in the warm sand. As they spread out the blanket, I can't tear my eyes away from the water. After weeks of buying furniture and kitchenware, curtains and towels, and praying I wasn't making a mistake, I can't believe I'm finally here.

We flop onto the blanket with loud sighs, and I push my feet into the sand. "What feels better than this?"

"Nothing," Rachel says.

"I don't know about that," Dani says. "Remember that trip we took to Myrtle Beach the summer before Nic met Tim, when I met that guy who looked like a young George Clooney and we fooled around on the beach?"

"How could we forget? You talked about him having a face like Clooney and a package like Jon Hamm nonstop." I sip my wine.

"Until you found out he had a girlfriend, and then you wanted to castrate him," Rachel reminds us.

"Oh yeah." Dani's face pinches in annoyance. "You should have let me do it."

We sit in comfortable silence, sipping our wine and soaking in the view. The early-evening sky holds the promise of a beautiful sunset. With my toes in the sand and the salty air kissing my skin, I feel my entire body exhale. This is what life should feel like every day.

I lift my cup. "Here's to the start of another great trip."

"Hear, hear," Dani says as we tap tumblers. "I love my work, but I am happy to be sitting on my ass instead of hitting twenty thousand steps a day with my four-legged friends."

"I hear ya," Rachel says. "I swear work has become a reprieve from my twelve- going on twenty-five-year-old daughter."

"I remember Kenzie testing me at that age. It got worse at thirteen."

Rachel's head drops back with a groan. "Don't tell me that."

"Sorry. I guess I won't mention fourteen, fifteen, sixteen—"

Rachel scowls.

I laugh and lift my drink in another toast. "Here's to parenting. May we all survive it."

"You guys are my built-in birth control," Dani says.

"That's good, because Nic and I are living vicarious sex lives through you and Bennett," Rachel says.

"Be my guest." Dani glances at me. "Listen to us going on about how much we need a vacation, and Nic's the one who needs it the most. By the way, Curly Top, I put the box of condoms in your bag, in case you get lucky while you're out."

"You're nuts. The only way I need to get lucky is with words on the page."

"I don't know how you do it. You haven't taken a break since our trip last summer," Rachel says. "I'd lose my mind."

I run my fingers through the sand, thinking about the last several years, during which I've written seven days a week. "At least I wrote a ton of great books, but I won't do that to myself again. I'm going to change things up after I write this book."

"Hold that thought." Dani whips out her phone and aims the camera at me.

"Don't!" I laugh, waving my hands in front of her phone. I've said the same thing for years, and she has videos to prove it. "This time I mean it, and the video jinxes it."

"Yeah, yeah, whatever." Dani takes a picture of the water. "You won't stop until those voices in your head go silent, and we all know that's not happening."

I wish that were true. My words haven't been flowing lately, but I don't want to be a downer, so I keep that to myself. "I don't want to think about work or real life. I just want to sit on this beach and soak in the view, drink wine with my besties, and pretend like this is my everyday life."

"I'll drink to that," Dani says.

We chat about the things we want to do and see this week and how exciting it is to finally be here after months of waiting. Dani tells us funny stories about the dogs she walks, and Rachel fills us in on a few of Lucy's latest antics as we finish our wine.

"It's scary how quickly she's growing up," Rachel says. "She had a slumber party a few weeks ago, and they put makeup on just for fun. Oh my God, you guys. I kid you not, they looked about fifteen. I don't know if I'll survive it when she's a teenager."

"If I survived Kenzie, you'll survive Lucy," I reassure her. My phone rings, and Mackenzie's name flashes on the screen. "Speak of the devil. She's probably checking in to see if we love it here." I push to my feet and put the phone to my ear to answer the call, but before I can say hello, Mackenzie's off and running.

"Mom, you won't believe what happened last night. Chad and I went to a party, and I was talking with this guy I know from school, and . . ." She's talking too fast for me to get a word in. "And then Chad starts talking with Janie, as if I'm going to get jealous over my best friend? I was like, *ha!* Are you kidding me? So he starts acting irrational and saying *I* was flirting with *Joe*, which I *wasn't*. I've never seen him act like that. It was crazy."

Prickles of anxiety spike in my chest, memories of Tim's passive-aggressive accusations coming back to me. "That sounds really uncomfortable. You're allowed to have male friends, and he needs to understand that. I hope you set him straight." Rachel and Dani implore me with questioning looks, and I hold up a finger.

"I set him straight, all right. I ended things with him. I'm not going to put up with him accusing me of that crap."

I'm stunned. This is the first grown-up decision Mackenzie has made in a long time. "I'm proud of you, sweetheart. I'm sure that wasn't easy."

"It wasn't, but I was so embarrassed, I had to do something. It all went down in front of everyone at the party. Hold on, there's someone at my door."

I hear the door open.

"Chad? What are you . . . *Aww*," she says softly, and I cringe. "Mom, I've got to go. Chad's here, and he brought me Starbucks and a stuffed bear wearing an I'M SORRY T-shirt. Isn't that sweet?"

Damn it. "Kenzie, use your head. That shouldn't be enough to make it all better. He showed you who he is, and you need—"

"*Mom*," she snaps.

I'm not going to argue with her while Chad is standing there. "Fine. In case you're wondering," I say sharply, "I love the cottage, and Chatemup is really cute."

"Oh crap. I forgot you were going this weekend. I'm glad you're having fun. Tell Dani and Rachel hi for me. Love you."

"*Wait*, Mackenzie. You're supposed to be looking for a job. Have you made any progress?"

"I've been spending extra time at the yoga studio, but I'll get on it this week. Gotta go. Bye!" The line went dead.

"*Ugh!*" I fist the phone and stomp back to the blanket.

"What is it this time?" Dani asks as I sit down.

"She broke up with Chad last night because he got jealous and irrational, and while we were on the phone, he shows up with gifts and Starbucks, and just like that, he's forgiven." I gulp my wine.

"Young girls are stupid," Rachel says. "We all were. Remember how in love with Jay you were when you got pregnant with Kenzie?"

"I know, but girls are supposed to get *smarter* as the world progresses."

"Making stupid mistakes with boys is the least of Kenzie's problems," Dani says.

I give her an annoyed glance. She's not wrong, but I don't want to talk about it.

"What?" Dani says. "You know it's true. She didn't call to see how her mom is doing. She called to bitch about her boyfriend."

"Cut her a little slack. She's still healing from the divorce. It took a toll on her."

Dani rolls her eyes. "I hope being here will clear that stubborn head of yours. We all love Kenzie, but she needs to grow up."

"I know she does, but it's not like there's a handbook on the right way to make that happen. Wait until you have kids. Am I right, Rach?"

Rachel nods. "Raising kids is like driving a car with no brakes. It's a crazy mix of fun and being scared shitless as you careen around unexpected corners, and you can't stop or put parenting on hold. You're pretty much holding on for dear life, for the *rest* of your life."

"And Lord help you when you crash, which you will, because we all do," I add. "But it's worth it."

"Like I said, you guys are great birth control," Dani says. "And so are your kids. I'm not ready for all that careening and crashing."

No argument there. "I thought we were leaving reality behind."

"You're right. No more real talk. Let's get our first beach picture." Rachel looks around the blanket. "Damn it. I left my camera at the cottage."

"That's a sign that you really do need this time off. I've got it." I pull out my cell phone and motion for them to lean in close. "Say *ecstasy*." We cheer, "Ecstasy!" and I get a few great shots.

"Hey, Marcus, did you hear that? These ladies like ecstasy."

We spin around and see two men and two women coming off the path.

"We weren't talking about the drug," Rachel clarifies.

"That only leaves one kind of ecstasy," the younger of the two men says with a waggle of his brows. "How's it going, ladies?" He's stocky and looks to be in his fifties, with short sandy hair and vivacious energy. He reminds me of the charismatic jocks in high school who could get everyone to follow their troublemaking leads and who somehow always escaped being caught.

"Great," Rachel and Dani say in unison.

He looks at me expectantly.

I wiggle my toes. "My feet are in the sand. I'm happy."

"There's no better feeling," Military Cut says.

"Are you Jacob's niece's friends?" the older of the two women asks. "He told us you were coming." Blond bangs shade her friendly eyes, and a sheer white cover-up reveals an enviable bikini-clad body. If not for the crepey skin on her arms and fine lines around her eyes and mouth, she could pass for forty. But my guess is she's in her sixties.

"That's not them," the other woman says, straightening her floppy sun hat despite the setting sun. Her long dark hair trails down the back of her blue tank dress, and she looks to be about my age. "Jacob's son is coming this weekend, and the girls aren't coming until next weekend, remember?"

"Oh, that's right." The time-warp blonde shrugs. "I swear my brain is a sieve lately."

"Lately?" The older of the two men winks at her, and her coquettish smile tells of years of teasing. He's tall and lean with longish silver hair. He plants his hands on his narrow hips, eyeing us with a serious expression. "You know this is a private beach, don't you?"

"Oh, no. Sorry." I scramble to my feet, and Rachel and Dani follow.

"If you're not careful, you'll get arrested for trespassing," Military Cut says.

"We didn't see any signs," Rachel says.

"Nic just bought the cottage on the hill," Dani adds. "Shouldn't the real estate agent have mentioned that to her?"

"Don't listen to these jokers." The bikini-clad woman waves a hand, and the guys chuckle. "They think they're funny."

"We *are* funny," Military Cut says.

"As funny as a paper cut." The brunette shakes her head. "I'm Maggie. I share a driveway with the cottage on the hill. Which one of you is the author and my new neighbor?"

"That's me. I'm Nicole, and these are my friends Rachel and Dani. They're here for the week. How do you know I'm an author?"

"Not much goes under the radar in Chatemup." Maggie points to the other woman and the man who had winked. "This is Aspen and Marcus O'Reilly, and that's Russ McLean. They live in the Oyster Run cottages." She leans closer. "Keep Russ out of your place or he'll try to fix everything that's not broken."

Russ aka Military Cut offers his hand. "Head of the beach family welcoming committee. It's nice to meet you."

"Beach family?" Rachel arches a brow. "Are you all related?"

The four exchange amused glances. "We're the family we chose," Russ explains. "So, what're we looking at here? Three single ladies looking to have some fun?"

Rachel says, "Yes," while Dani says, "Two," and I say, "No," all at the same time.

"Aren't you girls just the *cutest*." Aspen giggles. "Let me guess, Dani's got a sweetie, and Rachel and Nicole are single?"

"Yes, but I'm not looking for that kind of fun," I say quickly.

"Yes, she is," Dani and Rachel chime in.

I shake my head, and our new friends laugh.

"*Friends* are more my speed," I explain. "I got divorced a few years ago. I'm hoping to get to know the people and the area, but I'm not looking for romantic entanglements."

"I hear you on that," Maggie says.

"You've come to the right place, baby doll," Aspen says. "Community is important to all of us."

"I've got a great idea." Russ claps his hands. "If you ladies don't have plans later, my wife, Marlo, and I are having a little shindig at our place. Nothing fancy, just cocktails and good conversation. You should join us."

"*Yes*, please do. It'll be fun," Aspen exclaims. "We'll all be there, and you can meet some of our other friends, too."

I look at Rachel and Dani.

"Sounds good to me," Rachel says.

"Awesome, and, Nic, you've got to meet my buddy Miller," Russ says. "He knows everyone and everything about this town, and he's the greatest guy. Ex-military, helps vets, and owns a fleet of fishing boats."

Dani raises her brows. "This sounds promising."

I give her a look that says, *Chill*. "As I said, I'm really not looking to get involved right now."

"That's why you have to meet Miller," Russ says. "He's divorced, too, and he's got so much on his plate, he's not interested in entanglements, either."

Rachel nudges me, her eyes gleeful.

"Okay, sounds good," I relent, more excited about having met nice neighbors than I am about meeting Miller. Although my interest is piqued at the prospect of a male friend who wouldn't expect more. "Where and when?"

Chapter Five

NICOLE

After drying my hair, I spend fifteen minutes trying to tame it. My curls always look best the day I wash them, but it's a double-edged sword, because along with tighter curls comes massive volume. I finally give up.

Crazy hair it is.

I wave a blush brush over my cheeks, put on eyeliner, and curl my lashes, because if I don't, they tangle. No mascara necessary, thanks to my Mediterranean roots. I head into the bedroom to get dressed, which is never a quandary. My style hasn't changed in a decade. I prefer comfort over trends, and even though my friends think I'm crazy, I brought only one suitcase of clothes for the entire summer.

I throw on cutoffs and a maroon shirt with blousy sleeves that ties at the waist and hides my muffin top, and shove my feet into my favorite leather Roxy boots. My phone rings, and MOM flashes on the screen. My parents had me late in life. My mom and I have always been close, but we've gotten closer since my father died. We have dinner every Tuesday night and watch a movie together on Sunday nights.

I head outside as I answer. "Hi, Mom." Cool air brushes over my skin, and music drifts up from one of the cottages below. A lighthouse

I hadn't noticed on the sprig of land to the left casts a spray of light over the water.

"Hi, sweetie. Well? How is it?"

"Incredible. We met some really nice people, and we're going to their house for drinks in a few minutes."

"You've already made friends? That's wonderful, honey, and how's the house?"

"Perfect. It's not too big or too stifling, and the view is amazing. Want to see it?"

"Of course!"

I switch to a video call, and her face appears on the screen, an older version of myself. I hope I look as good at seventy-four as she does, with her bright hazel eyes and thick auburn-and-silver curls that she wears above her shoulders. I show her the view. "It's even better in the daylight."

"Oh, honey. I'm so happy for you. I won't keep you on the phone. I just had to check and see if you were okay."

"Thanks, Mom. How are you doing?"

"I'm great, and even better now that I know you're having fun. Tell the girls I said hello, and enjoy those new friends. I love you, sweetheart."

After we end the call, I take a moment to breathe in the salty air. I have the strange sensation of being far away from the stressors of everyday life, which makes no sense since my responsibilities haven't changed.

But my location has.

I won't run into Tim or his friends here or see people who knew us as a couple. I never realized just how anxious that made me until now, when I don't feel it looming like a villain waiting to pounce. I feel a spark of excitement.

Welcome back, old friend.

I head back inside, take a cursory glance in the mirror on my way out of the bedroom, and holler down the hall, "Almost ready, Rach?"

"Yes!" she calls from behind the closed door.

I find Dani in the kitchen looking over the wine we bought. My perpetually messy-haired friend, who, by her own admission, lives in pet-hair-covered clothes most of the time, looks absolutely fantastic in tan shorts that tie at the waist, a white long-sleeve knit top that accentuates her curves, and strappy wedge sandals. Her hair falls in glossy golden waves down her back, her makeup is flawless, and she's wearing her round wire-framed glasses.

"Look at you, all cleaned up and ready to go. Were your contacts bugging you, or are we going for a fashion statement?" I snag my keys from the kitchen counter.

"Fashion statement. It takes the focus off my mouth." She's always been self-conscious of her wide, toothy smile.

"Get outta here. Your mouth is as gorgeous as the rest of you, you sexy thing."

"I *so* love you." She holds up a bottle of Top of the Island Vineyard wine. "What do you think about bringing this tonight?" We'd taken a tour of that winery when we'd gone to Silver Island a few years ago on one of our summer trips and were thrilled to find the liquor store here carried their wines.

"Great choice."

"Sorry I took so long," Rachel says, hurrying downstairs in a summery sea-blue dress and matching sandals. "I could lie and say I was on the phone with Lucy for twenty minutes, but the truth is, we only talked for a few minutes. I just couldn't decide what to wear."

"We wouldn't have believed you anyway," I say. "You look beautiful."

We head out, and as we make our way down the hill, Rachel says, "I wonder if Miller is as great as they said he is."

"Probably. I picture an old fisherman with a thick gray beard and a paunch," I say.

"And those yellow rubber pants with suspenders they wear on fishing boats," Rachel adds.

"Whoever he is, he'll be thrilled to see Rach in that dress," Dani says.

"I don't want him," Rachel says. "He's for Nic."

"Dani's the one who wants to call someone Daddy." I link arms with them. "I'm so happy to be with you guys, meeting new people, with no pressure to look or act a certain way. I thought I'd be nervous, since I don't go out very often—"

"You mean *ever*," Dani corrects me.

"Okay, yes. The point is, I'm not nervous. I feel great."

"Well, duh," Rachel says. "You were a social butterfly until Tim squashed that in you."

"Again, reality is not allowed on this trip," I say as we walk into Oyster Run. "Look how cute these cottages are." They're cedar sided with two dormers, but each cottage has a different color door and matching shutters. We head to the one with the pink door, which Russ said was Marlo's favorite color.

Russ greets us warmly, announcing, "Our new friends are here. I'm really glad you made it. Come in."

As I step inside, he pulls me into a hug. I'm surprised, but I go with it, and then he proceeds to hug Rachel and Dani.

"I'm glad you made it," Maggie calls out as she fills her glass at a beverage table. She's wearing the same dress she had on earlier.

"Hi, sweeties!" Aspen waves from across the living room. She's with a middle-aged strawberry-blonde who is rocking white capris and a pink top. "Come meet Marlo."

Marlo lifts her glass, and we all say hi.

"They'll be there in a minute, sunshine." Marcus struts over in shorts and a sweatshirt and goes in for a hug. "Nice to see you."

"You too," I say as he releases me and hugs Rachel.

"What warm welcomes," Rachel says.

"We're a huggy group." Marcus embraces Dani. "Life goes quick. Keep your friends close and your enemies out of Chatemup."

"You got that right," Russ says. "Some of our friends are out back by the bonfire. I'll introduce you to them when we get outside." He raises his voice. "Listen up, everyone. This is Nicole, Rachel, and Dani. You've just said hello to my beautiful bride, Marlo."

"Your bride? Are you newlyweds?" I ask.

"We've been married for thirty-four years, but every day feels like the first," he says.

"You stopped earning nookie points for that line years ago," Marlo calls out, and everyone chuckles.

Russ blows her a kiss and doesn't miss a beat as he introduces us to a handful of other friendly people, and finally, he points to the last two people in the room, an elderly couple. "Those fine-looking folks are Evelyn and Claude. They live in the house on the beach with the blue shutters."

A petite gray-haired woman with a pixie cut waves. "It's nice to meet you."

The balding man beside her grumbles loudly, "Who's that?"

"A new neighbor and her friends," Evelyn answers.

Claude lifts his chin. "Welcome. Don't walk on my grass."

Everyone laughs, but I don't think he's kidding.

"So, what are we drinking tonight, ladies?" Russ asks.

"We brought wine." Dani holds up the bottle.

"Nice." Russ looks it over. "This looks great, but how about we put this on the drink table and I make you sophisticates. You'll love them. That's what all the ladies are drinking."

"I've never had a sophisticate," I say.

"They taste like candy. Be careful," Marcus warns as he takes the wine from Russ and carries it over to the table.

"Cool. I'm in," Dani exclaims.

"Me too," I say.

"If it tastes like candy, it's made for me. Would you like some help?" Rachel asks.

"No thanks. I'm an old pro," Russ says. "You ladies go mingle, and I'll bring you your drinks when they're ready."

As he walks away, Rachel whispers, "Do you think they're swingers, or just nice?"

"I don't see any pineapples," Dani says.

"Stop being weird. They're just nice," I whisper as we make our way over to Aspen and Marlo.

"Welcome to the madhouse," Marlo says. "I hear our husbands gave you a hard time this afternoon."

"They were funny, and I'm glad they invited us over. I was hoping to meet my neighbors, so this is great. Everyone seems so nice."

"We're lucky," Aspen says, looking youthful in jeans and a flowy hippie top. "We have a good group of friends, and, Nic, you will be happy to hear that Marlo is an avid romance reader."

"Really?" I'm curious if she's read my work, but I'd never ask. "What kind of romance do you like?"

"Have you read Nic's books?" Dani asks.

So much for being humble.

"I haven't, but I like contemporary," Marlo says. "I looked you up on Amazon, and wow. You've written a lot of books. I've never met a romance writer, and I have some questions."

"Okay, well, I have answers."

"Just how steamy are your books?"

"Very, like between-the-sheets, feel-the-hair-on-the-hero's-legs steamy."

"*Mm.* My kind of romance," Aspen says.

"Mine, too. Do you get inspiration from the people you know and use it in books?" Marlo asks.

"Sometimes. But don't worry. I might use an aspect of someone's personality or a mannerism, but that's about it."

"Whew." Aspen feigns wiping her brow.

"Everyone worries about that," I say.

"What about the sex scenes?" Marlo asks. "Is it true that hands-on research is the best?"

"How is that a question?" Aspen asks.

"She could prefer to do online research," Marlo answers.

"Would you rather have sex with Russ or read about it?" Aspen challenges.

I *love* these women.

"Okay, I get it," Marlo says.

"Well, now I'm curious," Aspen says. "Nic, have you *researched* all your sexy scenes? You don't have to answer if it's too personal."

"It's okay. I get asked that a lot." I notice Rachel and Dani looking at me funny, but I can't read whatever they're trying to tell me. "I've done some of the naughty things I've written into my sex scenes, but not everything, and no, I won't give specifics."

"Well, *damn*. There goes my night of fun."

I cringe at the faintly familiar gravelly voice. *Am I going to embarrass myself every time I see you?* Rachel and Dani grin like fools as I turn to see the brawny guy from the coffee shop's dark eyes twinkling with his devilish grin, those panty-melting dimples bringing tingles of aware-ness. *Damn dimples.* I steel myself against the unfamiliar sensation. I've written moments like these a million times. A devastatingly handsome hero sweeps in, and it's love at first sight. Except it's not. I'm not risking my happiness. Not even for those dimples.

"Miller. Hi, baby doll. Come meet our new friends." Aspen touches his forearm. "This is Nicole, and these are her friends Rachel and Dani. Nicole bought the Jenners' old cottage. She's our new neighbor."

Miller? I thought the barista called him Declan.

Those dark eyes lock on me. "We've already met. Be careful with your drinks around her. She's a spiller."

"You're safe. No drinks here." I hold up my empty hands just as Russ walks over with our sophisticates and hands one to me. As we thank him for the drinks, Miller takes a step back. I shake my head, earning a chuckle.

"I see you met Miller." Russ claps him on the shoulder. "I was talking you up on the beach earlier. I thought you and Nic might want to connect. She's new in town, and she's a romance writer."

"So I hear." Miller eyes me as he takes a drink of his beer.

"She's also a really great person," Dani says.

I start to give her a *what are you doing* glance but stop myself. She knows that as grateful as I am to have a career I love, sometimes I wish people would see me for me and not for what I do.

"I'm sure she is," Miller says. "If you'll excuse me, I'm on wood duty tonight."

"*Wood* duty? Sounds like you have a fun night planned after all." I can't help smirking.

The girls laugh, and he grins, shaking his head as he walks away.

We chat with Aspen and Marlo for a while and learn that Aspen is a Reiki master, and Marlo, a schoolteacher. They're funny and laid-back, and they clearly think the world of their friends.

A little while later the party moves outside, where Miller is busy stoking the fire and chatting with Russ and Marcus. Their laughter punctures the air as we make our way around the yard, mingling with the others. I catch Miller stealing a glance at me while I'm talking with Maggie and a mountainous man with a quiet demeanor. I smile at Miller, and he lifts his drink as if to say *hey*. A little while later Rachel and I are chatting with Evelyn, who is lovely, and Claude, a curmudgeon who wasn't kidding about his lawn, when I feel Miller's eyes on me again and glance over.

He's sitting by the fire and nods to the empty chair beside him.

"Excuse me." I saunter over and sit down. "If you're hoping I'll amuse you by embarrassing myself again, you're out of luck."

"When did you embarrass yourself? We're all friends here. Stick around long enough, and I'm sure you'll hear Marcus and Aspen share their sexual escapades, too."

"Great. I'll be sure to take notes."

He winks and takes a drink. "Nice boots."

"Thanks." I like his easygoing nature.

"No one around here wears boots."

"Is that a hint that I shouldn't, either? Because I'm not really a trend follower."

He shakes his head. "I'd be disappointed if you were."

I'm not sure how to respond to that with anything other than the smile plastered on my face. "So, Miller, didn't I hear the barista call you Declan?"

"You mean your boyfriend?" He leans closer with a tease in his eyes. "Were you eavesdropping, Writer Girl?"

"*No.* It's not like he said it quietly."

"Uh-huh. You can admit it. It's okay."

"There's nothing to admit. I'm not out to pick you or anyone else up. I just heard him say it and wondered why you used two names."

"You're cute when you're riled up. I mean, you're cute anyway, but riled up is even cuter."

"I'm not trying to be *cute*." As I say it, there's no denying that it feels good to hear it. "But thank you."

"Just telling the truth. For what it's worth, I'm not looking to hook up, either. Been there, done that, and don't need the headaches." He kicks his booted foot up on the edge of the firepit.

I breathe a sigh of relief. "Most people don't get the allure of being single."

"Most people are doing what everyone else thinks they should. Get married, have kids, live the fairy tale that's really more of a nightmare, and pretend you're happy until you're on your deathbed, wishing you'd done things differently." He crosses his long legs at the ankles, taking a pull of his beer. "I'm done with that nonsense."

I can't believe he gets it. "Right? After two divorces, and healing from all that went along with them so I don't bring old baggage into my new life, I'm finally happy with who *I* am."

"I remember hitting that point after my divorce and feeling like, *Damn, I like this guy.*"

I laugh. "Me too. It's like, yeah, I'd be friends with myself. Did you ever wonder if you'd get to that place?"

"Hell yeah." He rubs his thumb over the label on his bottle. "People say you're better off without them, and you know you are, but it still hurts to end a marriage."

"Exactly. I asked for the divorce, and I didn't want my ex back, but it was still devastating to lose the person who had been there for a decade, who I'd pinned my future on." I sip my drink. "And then one day it didn't hurt anymore."

"It's like being reborn, isn't it?"

"Yes, and it feels fantastic to know who I am and what I want. I'm ready for new experiences that don't require a life partner. I'm a whole person. Why do I need an *other half*?"

"You got that right." He looks at me for a long moment, and his gaze turns serious. "To answer your earlier question, Miller is what my army buddies used to call me. Russ and these folks have known me for twenty years, so . . ." He shrugs. "But when I meet new people, I tell them my first name, like your young beau at the coffeehouse."

I smile and shake my head again. "As long as you didn't get me in trouble and say I was flirting."

He flashes those dimples.

"So, what should I call you?"

"What do you want to call me?"

I study him for a minute, waiting for a name to hit me the way it does when I'm writing a new character. He's a burly guy, wearing a faded T-shirt and jeans that look like old favorites, worn and frayed at the hems. There's no air of pretense, and I like that. But the only names that feel right are Brawny Guy or Dimple Dude, as I've tagged him in my head. Declan is a nice name, and it fits him, but I use this opportunity to dig deeper. "I don't know you well enough to decide yet, so tell me, who is Declan Miller?"

"Your writer's brain is taking notes, isn't it?"

"Always." I sip my drink.

"I bet that's true."

"If I'm not creating worlds on my laptop, I'm crafting stories in my head. Now stop changing the subject and tell me something about yourself."

"Not much to tell. I'm just a dude who grew up in Chatemup with a couple of brothers, thought I could make a difference, so I joined the army. I saw horrendous shit, met a girl while I was on leave, got married at twenty, had a couple of kids. Fast-forward sixteen years, got divorced, and now I'm a fish peddler, and I do a few other things here and there."

That's a lot to process, and I have questions, but I'm not going to get into all that drama. "A fish peddler?"

"Yeah. I keep the restaurants around here stocked with fresh seafood. No big deal."

I remember Russ saying that Declan owns a fleet of fishing boats. He's humble. I like that. "Have any great fishing stories to share?"

"How much time you got?"

"Depends on how good your stories are. Tell me one, and I'll let you know if I want to hang around for more."

"A'right, Writer Girl. Get your mental pen ready, because this is a good one. My buddy and I were dragging clams in the bay one February. It was cold as shit, and the weather was terrible. We had no business being out there, but kids don't stop eating because it's winter. Gotta put food on the table. The boat flipped, and we lost everything. No cell phone. No way to call for help. We're five miles offshore in thirty-eight-degree weather, treading water. I know we're fucked. My buddy knows it, too. We're doing everything we can to keep our bodies from shutting down. We're numb, we've got ice on our faces, and my buddy starts talking slower, slurring, and I'm barking orders to get his brain to kick in. No way was I going to let him give up. It was awful." He takes a drink.

My heart is racing. "What happened? How'd you get out?"

"Some guy was working on his house along the shore and realized the boat had capsized. He reported it to the harbormaster, who came and rescued us. We were in the water for forty-five minutes. I still don't know how we survived."

"Holy crap, Declan. You must've been terrified. What were you thinking? Anything? Or was your only thought that you had to survive?"

"Nobody's ever asked me that before."

"You don't have to tell me if it's too private."

"It's not. It's just interesting. I guess that's why you're the writer and the rest of us aren't. I just kept thinking about my boys, picturing their faces. I didn't want them to grow up without me."

That tells me more about him than he probably realizes. "I can't imagine what that must have been like for you. You have two boys?"

"Yes. Do you have kids?"

"Yeah. I have a daughter, Mackenzie, and I helped raise two stepsons."

He nods. "Where's your daughter?"

"She goes to college in North Carolina, and she stayed for the summer. What about your boys?"

"Boston and Connecticut. They got the hell out of Chatemup as soon as they could."

"Does that mean you don't think this little town is so great?"

He points his beer bottle at me. "This town is the best, and don't let anyone tell you otherwise. But the sign doesn't lie, and it's a fishing town, which means there aren't very many other career opportunities. Now, tell me a writing story."

"This writer's life is not as exciting as yours. Most of my stories will bore you."

"Give 'em up, Writer Girl. Let me hear one." His cell phone chimes. "'Scuse me a sec." He pulls out his cell and reads a text. His jaw clenches, and he utters a curse as he pushes to his feet. "Sorry, Nic, but I've got to take off." His tone is flat, his demeanor serious.

I was enjoying talking with him, and I'm bummed, but I try not to let it show. "Okay, well, it was nice meeting you."

"Yeah, you too. Thanks for not spilling your drink on me." He tries to sound light, but his voice is riddled with tension. He points at me. "Don't think you're off the hook, Writer Girl. I want to hear your stories next time I see you." He scans the yard, his gaze landing on Russ. "Hey, old man. I gotta take off. Thanks for a great time."

"Everything okay?" Russ asks.

"Same old shit," Declan grits out.

"A'right, buddy. I'm around if you need anything." Russ waves, and everyone else calls out goodbyes.

Declan holds my gaze as he walks away, and there's a definite draw there, but it's not the burn of lust that keeps my eyes on his. There's something much more intriguing simmering between us. A tether of amusement and curiosity. The kind that speaks of two people who aren't done enjoying life and who have no skin in the romance game.

Chapter Six

NICOLE

Five thirty comes too early the next morning. I sit at my desk sipping coffee while listening to music through my AirPods. The breeze coming through the open windows draws my attention. As I gaze out at the gorgeous view, which I still can't believe is *mine*, my mind tiptoes back to last night.

We stayed at Russ and Marlo's chatting around the fire until after midnight and had a terrific time. Everyone was friendly and fun, and they all have their quirks, as we all do. Aspen called everyone *baby doll* or one of a dozen other endearments, and Russ ran around like he was on roller skates making sure everyone's drinks were topped off. I'm not sure that guy could sit still if his life depended on it. The whole group acts more like a big extended family, the way they tease and support each other, and it's no wonder. With the exception of Maggie, who bought her cottage three years ago, they all grew up together. Aspen told us that the cottages in Oyster Run have been owned by their families for generations. She and Marcus were neighbors and grew up with Russ in the Oyster Run community. Most of their other friends who live there now grew up spending summers there and raised their children spending summers there, too. Eventually Aspen and Marcus and Russ and

Marlo moved into their cottages full time. That's the kind of close-knit community in which I always wished I could have raised Mackenzie.

But, as my mother says, it's never too late to find your people.

My thoughts turn to Declan and the story he told me, which put my minuscule gripes into perspective. I really enjoyed talking with him. It's been a long time since I met someone whose life was more interesting than my characters'. *Writer Girl.* I like it, which is weird, since I've always strived to have an identity outside my career. But Writer Girl is kind of fun.

Declan is kind of fun.

I glance at the clock. *Shit.* I've lost twenty minutes of writing time.

I force myself to turn off the social part of my brain and try to focus on getting words on the page. It feels like I haven't written in a month. This is why I don't usually take time off or change my routine when I'm on a deadline. Even taking half an hour in the middle of my writing day can cost me forty minutes trying to get back into the zone. It never used to be like that. My characters would speak to me twenty-four-seven, but that changed over the last several months, and it's beyond frustrating.

It better change back, too, because there's no way around taking time off while Dani and Rachel are here. I don't usually work while we're together, but this was the only week they could both come over the summer, and I need this time with them, so I put my nose to the grindstone, reading the last chapter I wrote, hoping to find the characters' voices.

Half an hour later, I'm still staring at a blank page.

I close the curtains, thinking I'm distracted by the view, and give myself a pep talk. *That's what I needed. I've got this.* I crank the music and feel inspiration coming as I sit down. My story is about a single father of three falling for the attorney his late wife's sister hired to try to take the children away from him. My fingers work their way over the keyboard, crafting the opening scene where they first see each other in the courthouse. After a few minutes, I'm typing faster, feeling like I'm right there with them as they head into the courtroom and she . . .

Spills coffee on him?

Shit.

What is wrong with me? I'm seriously getting worried about my ability to bring my stories to life, but I refuse to give up and force myself to write until my friends stumble into the kitchen in their sleeping shorts and tank tops.

"There she is, working her magic while we sleep," Dani says as she pours Rachel a cup of coffee and hands it to her.

"Just call me the word fairy." I know what I've written isn't great, but they don't need to know that. I'm hoping when I go back to read it tomorrow morning, it'll inspire a better scenario. "Did you sleep okay?"

"Like a baby." Rachel carries her coffee to the living room and plops onto the couch, pushing Dani's sandals from last night under the coffee table. "I've been thinking about *Sneak Attack*."

I save my document and close my laptop. "Who's that?"

"Declan." She sips her coffee. "Do you think Russ told him you were coming?"

"No. He seemed as surprised as I was."

"I don't think so, either." Dani joins her on the couch. "But he took off so fast, I wonder if he had a date."

"He wasn't dressed for a date," Rachel says.

Dani pulls her feet up on the cushion. "Still. He could've been waiting for a Tinder response and went home to change first."

"We have to get in on the gossip here," Rachel says excitedly. "I bet Aspen and Maggie are in the know. We should join them on the beach later."

"Why do you care if Declan was going on a date?" I ask.

They look at me like I've lost my mind.

"Don't pretend you're not curious," Dani says.

I scoff and push to my feet. "I don't care if he goes on a hundred dates. I told you I was excited that he also believes being single and happy can be synonymous. That's all it was." I join them in the living room. "You guys wanted me to put myself out there, and that's what I'm doing. Can you please stop trying to make it into something it's not?"

Rachel's brow furrows. "Sorry. No more sneak-attack talk."

"Thank you." I exhale with relief. "What are we doing today?"

"Beach," they both say.

"Sounds perfect. I'm going for a run. Either of you want to come?" In all the years we've been friends, they've never once gone running with me. They'll walk but never run. Today I need a run to clear the cobwebs out of my brain.

Rachel wrinkles her nose and burrows into the pillows.

"Don't look at me. My legs are on vacation." Dani lies back, scrolling on her phone.

Aspen is a speed walker, and last night she shared her two-, three-, and five-mile routes with me. Opting for a three-miler, I put in my AirPods, crank up my *I'm Done with You* playlist, which I put together when I finally ended my marriage to Tim, and head down Old Wharf Road. Running by the water is much better than running in suburbia, where the only views are tract homes and traffic.

Claude is standing on his porch. I mute my music and wave as I jog by. "Hi, Claude! Beautiful day today!"

"It was, until someone's dog pissed on my lawn," he grumbles.

A few minutes later I hit my stride and lose myself in the music and the sights as I run what Aspen called *the back loop*, which circles around the baseball fields and the library and then loops through town on the way home. The sun beats down on my shoulders, and by the time I hit Main Street, I'm dripping with sweat. I see people saying hello as I run past, and though I can't hear them, I smile. I'm singing along to "Shapeshifting" by Taylor Acorn, when I reach the corner where an old black truck is making the turn. I jog in place, waiting for it to pass.

It stops in middle of the road, and a brawny guy grins from behind the wheel, watching as I process the fact that it's him. I whip out my AirPods and stop singing.

"You might want to stick to writing instead of singing."

He's not wrong. "You think you can do better?"

"I think a dying cat would be better." He grins. "Aren't you supposed to be pounding out all the words?"

"I already did." Or at least I tried.

"Way to go, Writer Girl. Where's your entourage?"

"They don't run."

"I'm not sure you do, either." He nods to me jogging in place. "You know you're supposed to actually gain ground, right?"

Enjoying the banter, I give it right back to him. "Some chatty guy cut me off and won't move his truck."

"See ya around, Writer Girl." He winks and drives off.

I put my AirPods in and jog across the street feeling good all over. "Confident" by Demi Lovato comes on, and I run faster, heading back toward my cottage. I listen to one great song after another and turn onto Old Wharf Road, dancing as I run.

Someone honks as they drive by.

I wave, not caring that I probably look ridiculous, because I feel frigging fantastic. As I near the road to my place, I look over at the beach and spot the backs of a familiar redhead and blonde. I cross the road and walk down the narrow path that leads to the beach. I pull out my AirPods and put them in the zipper pocket of my shorts. Rachel and Dani are wearing shorts over their bathing suits, and Rachel is standing close to an older man wearing khakis and a polo shirt, showing him pictures on her camera.

Dani turns as I come off the path. "Hey, Nic. Come meet Jacob."

His eyes light up as I walk over.

"Hi, I'm Nicole."

"It's nice to meet you." He holds out his hand, and I shake it. "You're the author people are talking about."

"I'm not sure that's such a good thing." I wonder if I'll ever get used to the idea of people knowing who I am before meeting me.

"It's a lot better than the reasons some folks are gossiped about," he says.

"That's probably true."

"This is Jacob's house." Rachel points to the house on the beach that sold last year. "I was taking pictures of it when he came outside, and we got to talking." She shows me some of the shots she took.

"You have such a good eye, Rach. They're beautiful." I glance at Jacob. "You bought last summer, right? How do you like Chatemup?"

"I'm still here. That should tell you something. I've been renovating all winter. Would you like to see the inside?"

"I would love to see it," Dani exclaims.

"Me too," Rachel says.

We follow him into the cottage, which is bigger than mine. It's gorgeous and reeks of luxury, with fancy crown molding, a stone fireplace, and expensive furniture. Not my style, but Rachel is raving about it and asks if she can take pictures.

As she clicks away, I say, "Why don't I give you Rachel's number so you two can connect and she can send you copies of the pictures."

"I'd much rather have your number," he says.

"I guess you can text me and I can pass the number to her, but—"

"You can pass it to her, and you and I can grab a painkiller down at the pub sometime."

The girls' eyes widen. I have no idea what a painkiller is, but I assume it's a drink.

"*Oh*" comes out as surprised as I feel. He's got to be twenty years older than me, and I am not into daddy action. But he's nice, and I don't want to burn bridges with a neighbor. "Okay, sure." That makes my friends beam with delight.

He takes down my number like he's proud to have gotten it. "Great. Painkillers it is. Let me show you the upstairs."

We head up to find three nice-sized bedrooms and a man who looks about my age hanging shelves in a closet. He shoots Jacob a curious look. Jacob makes no move to introduce us, and an awkward silence hangs in the air. I remember what Maggie said about Jacob's son coming to visit, so I jump in.

"Hi. Sorry to interrupt your work. I'm Nic, and this is Dani and Rachel. I just bought the cottage up the hill. Are you Jacob's son?"

He smirks. "Yeah, that works. We'll go with that."

Jacob scrubs a hand down his face and ushers us down the hall to check out the bathroom.

I feel like I've stepped in chewing gum.

When we leave, Jacob walks us out to the porch, and we thank him for the tour. As we leave, he calls after me, "Looking forward to those painkillers."

"Me too," I say, baffled, and we head up the path toward home. Rachel and Dani rush to my sides, and I lower my voice. "That was weird, wasn't it? Was he aggressive about getting my number? Or is it just me?"

"He was a little aggressive, but that just means he likes you," Rachel says. "He's cute, and he's obviously good with his hands. That place is gorgeous."

"Silver fox action coming Nic's way," Dani says.

"*Please.* He's not at all my type."

"So what? You wanted to make friends, and painkillers at the pub sounds fun," Rachel says as we cross the street.

"Did you pick up on a vibe between him and the younger guy?" I ask.

"A buddy vibe. Why?" Rachel asks.

"I don't know. I thought there was something more between them."

"You're nuts," Dani says. "Jacob was totally into you."

"Hey, baby dolls!" Aspen waves from where she's working in her flower bed.

"Let's get the scoop on him." Rachel and Dani rush ahead of me.

Aspen pushes to her feet. "Excuse the dirt." She wipes her hands on the sides of her shorts and tries to brush dirt from her T-shirt, which has a picture of a person lying on a table and a woman dragging a rake down her back. "If I don't get the weeds out, Claude will park himself in my front yard and do it for me."

"Claude's a character," I say. "We had fun last night. Your friends are great."

"They're your friends now, too, sweetie. I hope you'll join us on the beach later."

"We'd love to," Rachel says.

"We just met Jacob," Dani blurts out.

"He's a doll, isn't he?" Aspen says. "He's been working so hard to fix up his place."

"It's gorgeous," Dani says. "He gave us a tour and asked Nic for her number."

Oh God.

"He wants to take her for painkillers at the pub," Rachel adds.

"That's interesting." Aspen's eyes light up. "I hear he's quite the ladies' man, so be careful, Nic."

"I'm not interested in him like that. But I think we met his son."

She peers across the street. "I don't see Billy's truck. I think that blue truck belongs to a friend of his. Or is he an employee? Jacob owns a construction company in Rhode Island, and I think his friend might work for him. In any case, he comes often to help him renovate."

My gut instincts are usually spot-on, but maybe they've taken a wrong turn, like my muse.

We talk for a few more minutes and plan to meet on the beach in a little while. As we head up to the cottage, my cell chimes. I pull it out of my armband and see a text from an unfamiliar number. *Hi, it's Jacob. Looking forward to those drinks.*

"You guys, look." I show them the text.

"Told you there was no vibe between him and that other guy," Dani says.

"Okay, I was wrong, but who texts five minutes after meeting someone?"

"A person who's interested, obviously," Dani says. "This is a good thing. He's too old to play games."

"This is not good. Either I'm giving off the wrong vibes, or there's a serious lack of single women around here."

"Well, you did buy a place in *Chat 'em up*," Rachel says, and we all laugh.

Chapter Seven

NICOLE

Two days later my muse is still playing cat and mouse, so I give up and take an early run. The girls and I spend the rest of the morning hanging out on the deck, reading and chatting, and I field calls from two of my brothers. After a late lunch, we head out to explore. We cruise along the harbor with the music up and the top down, stopping so Rachel can take pictures of boats and houses and check out roadside shops, of which there are many.

When we run out of shops, we circle back to town and set out on foot. As we make our way through the stores, I find a cool serving dish in Pete's Pottery and learn that Pete is the owner's pug. Dani thinks she's found heaven in a tiny shoe shop, where she buys two pairs of cute sandals and some sexy high heels, and Rachel walks out of Peachy Keen with two bags of clothes and accessories. After perusing the shops and galleries around Main Street, we hit the side streets. I buy a Chatemup mug, nautical dish towels, and a pretty doormat for the patio doors on the deck. We buy more fudge than any three women should consume and know we'll eat every bite.

"I need to find something for Lucy," Rachel says as we leave an art gallery.

"Maybe Knotty Sails will have something." Dani points down the street to another clothing store. "I need to get Bennett something, too."

"What do you want to get him?" I ask as we head down the sidewalk.

"I have no idea," Dani says.

"They had funny T-shirts in that shop with the hats," Rachel suggests.

"He's not a funny T-shirt kind of guy. Most of his tees are white." Dani pulls open the door to Knotty Sails.

"What about a Chatemup sweatshirt?" I suggest, nodding to one on a mannequin.

"He's not a sweatshirt guy, either," she admits. "He dresses nice. I told you that."

"You also said he's laid-back," I remind her.

"He is, but he has specific tastes. He likes things *neat*."

I glance at her messy bun, tank top that has a stain from the salad dressing she'd dripped on it at lunch, and funky platform sneakers. Rachel and I exchange confused glances.

"You can get him a magnet for his refrigerator," Rachel says.

"Real nice, Rach," Dani says as we head over to the preteen section.

"Well, what does he like?" she asks.

Dani sighs. "I don't *know*, and yes, I realize we're very different, but we have fun together, and it's not like I'm marrying the guy."

I'm starting to understand why she needs this vacation so badly. "I'm sure we'll find him something."

We pick through racks of trendy outfits for Lucy. Rachel holds up a tiny shirt. "Don't they have anything that isn't tight, cropped, or too low cut?"

"That's what kids are wearing," Dani says.

"I know, and I hate it," Rachel says. "There's so much pressure for young girls to look and act older, and I swear it's twice as bad in the city as it was where I grew up."

"You grew up in Boomerang, Maryland. A town of *what*? Six hundred people?" I ask.

"Thirty-four hundred, thank you very much," Rachel says. "Life is easier there. Kids can be kids, not mini twenty-year-olds."

"That was thirty years ago," I point out. "I'm sure times have changed there, too."

"You're probably right." She moves to another rack and starts picking through the clothes.

The worry in her voice brings me closer. "If you're really worried about Lucy growing up too fast, why don't you talk to her about it?"

"I tried. She just gets mad at me. I get it, you know? She wants to keep up with her friends, and her friends are good kids. But I can see the writing on the wall, and it's all on fast-forward. She's only twelve, and she's a sweet twelve, not tough or streetwise."

"I remember how hard it was when Kenzie was going through that tween stage of wanting to grow up but still being a kid at heart. I wanted to lock her inside for five years."

"That might not have been a bad idea with Kenz." Rachel holds up another shirt. "She's a tough one."

"Yeah, she is. When she was Lucy's age, I didn't want to hold her back. I wanted to teach her to go after what she wanted. But I obviously did something wrong, because getting that girl to take responsibility is harder than potty training was."

"Give me a B. *B*. Give me an O. *O*. Give me a U-N-D-A-R-I-E-S," Dani whisper-cheers.

I roll my eyes. "You're not helping Rachel with Lucy."

"Sure I am. Kids are like dogs," Dani says as she looks over a table of crop tops. "You have to claim the alpha role and set up boundaries."

"A kid's bark is worse than a dog's bite, because you birthed it, and there's always a sliver of guilt tied to saying no or making them do things that are hard for them or that they don't want to do," Rachel says. "Forget it. Maybe I'll just get her a sweatshirt. Let's stick to that no real-life-talk rule. Thinking about Lucy growing up wears me out, and it's been such a great day."

We leave the store empty-handed.

"I'm starved." Dani pulls out her phone. "No wonder. It's six thirty."

"Let's put this stuff in the car and grab dinner at that restaurant we passed down at the harbor," I say.

"Dockside it is," Rachel says, and we head back to the car.

Two hours later, we've eaten a delicious meal, and we catch a second wind, so we head into the bar for margaritas. The bar is busy, and the stools and high-top tables are taken, but Dani spots a little space at the end of the bar and rushes over and flags down the bartender.

He's clean-cut, with tattoos on his arms and hands. "What's the name?"

"Dani." As soon as she says it, the bartender walks away. "Do I have food in my teeth or something?" She shows us her teeth.

"No. That was weird," I say.

He comes back a minute later. "Did you call in your order?"

"Call in a *drink* order? Why would I do that?" Dani asks.

He grins. "You wouldn't." He points up to a Pickup Food Orders Here sign we missed when we walked in.

"Oops," Dani says with an adorable shrug. "Sorry, we're new in town."

"No worries. I'm not going to turn a pretty lady like you away. What would you like? I'll serve it up and you can find another place to stand."

"Thank you," Dani exclaims. "Can you run a tab, please? Three margaritas, and if you have a dog, I'll walk it for free."

"Man, do I wish I had a dog," the bartender says, and goes to make our drinks.

"I've got a dog," a guy says from a few seats down.

"Me too," another guy calls out.

"I'll borrow one if it'll get me your number," a third guy shouts, and practically everyone in the bar laughs.

We move out of the pickup line, and Dani strikes up a conversation with the first guy who said he had a dog. "Hi. What kind of dog do you have?"

"A chocolate Lab. Lottie. She's six." He looks like a Lab owner: outdoorsy, with shaggy dirty-blond hair, wearing cargo shorts and a gray T-shirt.

"Cute name," I say.

He gives me an appreciative glance. "What's your name?"

"I'm Nic, and this is Dani and Rachel. What's yours?"

"JT."

The darker-haired guy next to him leans back on his stool and says, "I'm Mike. Careful giving personal info out to this guy."

JT scoffs as the bartender serves our drinks. After he walks away, Dani says, "Did you guys come here together?"

"First date," Mike says.

JT shakes his head. "Dude, really? And you wonder why you can't get a date."

"I get plenty of dates. You're here with me, aren't you?" Mike puts his hand on JT's leg.

"Shit." He swats Mike's hand away. "We just met twenty minutes before you all walked in."

We laugh.

"Are you guys from Chatemup?" Rachel asks.

"Born and bred." JT takes a drink of his beer.

"I'm a transplant from Boston," Mike answers. "I got sick of the rat race. What about you all?"

"I'm from Virginia, but I just bought a summer place here. Rachel lives in DC, and Dani's from North Carolina." JT asks Rachel about

DC, and Dani starts talking to another guy about his dog. "So, Mike, what do you do for a living?"

"I'm a goat herder," Mike says.

"Oh yeah? Don't tell anyone, but I'm a swamp princess."

"Very cool. I've never met a swamp princess."

"We're rare. In fact, I might be the only one outside of fantasy novels." I sip my drink, and we fall into more playful conversation, weaving a story about swamp princesses and goat herders.

As the night rolls on, we order another round of drinks, and the five of us chat about movies, books, hobbies, and work. Mike is a cop, and JT is ex-military, working as a security consultant. I try to pry more information out of him, asking if he means something along the lines of a bouncer or a security guard, but he just laughs it off. The guys joke about hands-on research, and I don't tell them that I've heard it all before. Let them have their fun.

"I've got my dog in the car. What do you say we all get out of here and take a walk on the beach?" JT suggests.

"Sure, why not?" I say, and my friends agree.

We settle the bill, and as we're heading to the door, Declan walks in, heading to the pickup area. Our eyes connect, and the air between us electrifies. I must be a little high from the drinks. His brows knit as his gaze moves over the five of us.

"Hey, Miller," a guy calls out from across the bar.

Declan looks in the man's direction.

"Tell your old man I'm looking for him," the guy says.

Declan's jaw tightens. "What does he owe you this time?"

"You don't want to know," the guy says.

I wonder what that's all about, but when Declan shifts his attention to me again, his eyes are shadowed by something dark and uncomfortable. Dani nudges me, and I realize I'm staring, and Rachel, JT, and Mike are almost out the door.

As I follow Dani toward them, Declan lifts his chin in my direction. "Don't go giving away my stories, Writer Girl."

He smiles, and it doesn't take away the shadows in his eyes, but *damn*, a thrill zips through me. I have a fleeting thought that I should fight that thrill, but it's pushed aside by my next thought. Does he think I'll repeat the story he told me, or share the ones he didn't get to hear?

"I wouldn't dream of it," I say, and follow my friends out of the bar.

Chapter Eight

NICOLE

I open my eyes to the sound of gentle waves kissing the shore, the mid-morning sun glistening off the water. "The ibuprofen is finally working."

We came down to the beach early this morning, Rachel in her bikini, Dani in her one-piece, and me in a tank top and cutoffs. I gave up bathing suits three years ago, when I got sick of holding in my stomach. My C-section scar has developed a lovely shelf above it. If I ever have a sex life again, at least my stomach will look like it's smiling. I cringe at the idea of getting naked in front of a man who wasn't around for my child-rearing years.

Rachel moans. "I don't think thirtysomethings are supposed to stay out past midnight."

Last night's walk on the beach with Mike, JT, and his adorable dog ended with the five of us sitting on my deck drinking wine and chatting until two in the morning. We were having such a great time, we didn't realize how late it had gotten until I got a text from Mackenzie asking me to transfer money into her account because she'd spent some of her grocery money on a birthday dinner for her friend.

"Speak for yourself." Dani flips over. "I feel great. You guys are lightweights."

I am a lightweight. I almost never drink more than a glass of wine, unless I'm with Dani and Rachel. "I had a good time last night despite the headache. Mike had me laughing so hard I was in tears at one point, but I feel guilty about not writing this morning."

"Give yourself a break," Dani says. "You work like a fiend."

"I can't afford to give myself a break."

Rachel looks at me incredulously. "Says the girl who just bought a summer cottage."

I want to say, *Yes, I make a lot of money, but Kenzie's school is expensive, and so are her spending habits, and while I'm glad I bought the cottage and already feel a thousand times better here than in Virginia, I spent most of my nest egg, which is scary. What if something major breaks, or I break my hand and can't write?* But I can't tell them that, because I'll look like a jerk complaining about financial pressure when I just bought a cottage on a freaking whim, and I'll have to battle about Kenzie, which I don't have the energy to do this morning. On top of all that, there's a certain degree of pressure that comes from being the overly successful friend. Especially since Rachel and Dani are my biggest cheerleaders. I don't ever want to let them down, and even though *that* sounds ridiculous in my own head, it's true.

So I go with the reason I feel guilty and tell them about my writer's block, because that's a normal issue for any writer, new or seasoned, and won't make me look like a jerk. "Yes, I make plenty of money, but I won't get paid if I can't write the books, and I'm really having a tough time writing."

"That's because *we're* here. You'll be fine once we're gone. You always are," Rachel says. "But you have to enjoy your life. Otherwise, why bother working so hard?"

"She's right. It's because we're here. Remember your birthday?" Dani adds. "You had a deadline, but all you wanted to do was spend time with us when we visited. Once we were gone, you got right back to writing."

"I don't think that's what this is," I admit.

Dani shields her eyes from the sun. "Meaning?"

"Meaning I'm worried. I can't get my brain to focus, and it's been like this for a while. It takes me twice as long to write every chapter."

Rachel pushes up on one elbow. "Maybe you're burnt out after writing so many books."

"I've considered that, but I don't feel burnt out. I love writing, and I have stories in my head that I'm excited about. I just can't get the scenes from my head onto paper."

"Well, you're a brilliant writer. Maybe your brain is tired, and all you need is a little brainstorming," Rachel suggests.

"And who better to do it with than us?" Dani sits up and rubs her hands together. "What hunky hero are we creating this week?"

"His name is Liam Roberts, and he's a single dad." I pull a notebook and pen from my backpack and move to my beach chair.

"I love him already. *Rachel Roberts.*" Rachel gets a dreamy expression. "I like the sound of that."

"Do you always picture yourself as my heroines? Because it's going to be even harder to write this book if I'm picturing you getting down and dirty with him."

"Oh no, that's not good," Rachel says. "Pretend I didn't say that."

"Hey, sweetie pies!" Aspen waves as she comes off the path with Marcus, Maggie, and Evelyn. "Want some company?"

"Sure."

They set up their chairs, and Aspen winces as she lowers herself into one.

"I've got you, sunshine." Marcus eases her down.

"Are you okay?" I ask.

"Oh *yes*, sweetie." She lowers her voice as Marcus sits in the chair beside her. "We just got a little too adventurous last night, if you know what I mean. This old bod needs more recuperation time."

Evelyn giggles. She looks like she walked off the pages of *Nantucket Magazine* in sky-blue capris that match her toenails, a white tank top, and a blue-and-white sun visor.

"What's new and exciting, chickies?" Maggie asks as she settles into her chair.

"We were just going to help Nic brainstorm the book she's writing," Rachel says.

"How fun. Can we help?" Maggie puts on a floppy yellow sun hat that matches her shorts. "I love crafting stories."

"Do you write?" I ask.

"Only boring engineering proposals right now," Maggie says. "But when I retire, I'm going to write my women's fiction novel."

"What's it going to be about?" Rachel asks.

"I can't share that," Maggie says just above a whisper. "I don't want to jinx it. I've been manifesting its greatness for years."

"A fellow manifester?" Dani pops to her feet and high-fives Maggie, and we all laugh as she sits back down. "I knew I liked your vibe."

"I'd love to help you brainstorm," Aspen says. "I've got a lot of life experience to share."

"We all do," Evelyn says. "Believe it or not, we were young once, too."

"We're still young, and we have a lot of experiences that might inspire Nic's writing." Marcus reaches for Aspen's hand and says, "Remember when we broke into the observation tower and made love at the top of it?"

"You two are naughty, and I like it," Rachel says.

"That was an unforgettable night," Aspen says dreamily. "We should do it again."

"Says the woman who hurt herself in a bed," Maggie says.

"She never said we were in a bed." Marcus leans in to kiss Aspen.

"It sounds like you have more exciting love lives than any of us." I open the notebook. "Let's do this."

Aspen lets out a little squeal. "This is so exciting. We can give you all sorts of sexy inspiration. We've done it in a train station, on a lifeguard chair, on the roof of our old high school . . ."

I'm scribbling notes as fast as I can.

"And here I thought Claude and I were creative when we were younger, making love in his father's boat in the winter when it was up on stilts," Evelyn says.

"You risky chick!" I write that down and scribble *Risky Chick* as a nickname for a character.

"Maybe you should tell us what the book is about," Maggie says.

"Sure. It's about a single father who falls for the attorney his late wife's sister hired to try to take the children away from him."

"Intriguing," Maggie says. "Have they met yet?"

"No. I haven't found the perfect opening. I've written several, but none of them feel right."

"Could they meet at a bar and then realize they're foes?" Evelyn suggests.

"Yes, but that feels a little too easy," I say.

"What if they meet at the grocery store?" Aspen suggests. "He's squeezing a melon, and she's thinking, *All men are alike.*"

"I like it, but I'm not sure it's right for this one."

"They could meet at a community event, like you and Miller did," Marcus suggests.

"That's another solid meet-cute, but it doesn't really fit the story, since he has kids and she's a workaholic."

"That wasn't the first time Nic and Miller met, anyway," Dani says.

"Oh?" Aspen exclaims. "Do *tell.*"

Dani shares the story in full detail, including the flirtatious barista, and we all have a good laugh. "How about the coffee spill as the meet-cute?"

"I tried it, and it didn't feel right, either." Probably because I kept picturing Declan's dimples and not my hero.

"Do you know anything else about the heroine?" Evelyn asks. "Could she have a fun hobby or something that brings them together? Or a sibling?"

"I haven't fleshed out her hobbies yet, but she has one sister."

"Count me out on sister stories," Aspen says. "My sister is the most aggravating person on earth."

"What if she loves to travel, and they meet when she's on a road trip, then meet again over the legal case?" Maggie asks.

"That's an interesting idea. What are you thinking?" I write down *Road trip?*

"Well, I took a gap year in college, and I went to Antarctica. I wasn't back home for ten minutes before I decided to take my parents' RV across the country."

"That sounds awesome," Dani says. "Did you go by yourself?"

"Yes, and it wasn't easy. The RV was on its last legs, and I ended up stranded in Nevada. It was beyond repair, and instead of coming home, I took a job piloting a rich couple's boat from the East Coast to Spain."

"Wow. I guess you knew how to pilot a boat?" I say.

"I grew up on boats," Maggie says.

"I could never do those things," Evelyn says. "But I admire people who aren't afraid to take risks and see the world. My older sister is like that, but I've always been the careful one. I could never quite measure up to her greatness."

"You don't believe that, do you?" Aspen asks.

"Sometimes, but I wouldn't want to be like her. I like who I am," Evelyn says. "She's never been married, and even though Claude has his moments, I wouldn't trade my life for hers or anyone else's."

"What do you mean, he has his moments?" I have a fondness for curmudgeons, as my grandfather had been one, but beneath that gruff exterior was a heart of gold that you just had to look a little closer to see.

"He never used to be ornery the way he is now. He got sick a few years ago, and ever since, his attitude can go from charming to rude in the blink of an eye. It comes and goes, and it's worse when we're in public. The doctors can't find anything wrong with him except his hearing is going. It's a shame. Claude was a brilliant attorney, and what I admired most was his ability to take charge without being rude. And now sometimes he's rude around our closest friends."

I hear the pain in her voice and can only imagine how much she misses those parts of him. "It could be his age. I remember my mother saying the same things about my grandparents as they got older. If you ever need an ear, or a break, I'm a good listener, and you can come up and hang out at my place anytime."

"That's so nice of you. Thank you." Evelyn shares a thoughtful expression with Aspen and Maggie. "I think we got off base with brainstorming."

"Actually, you've given me some ideas for side characters."

"Let me tell you about some of the characters I met on my travels," Maggie says.

Several hours and lots of laughter later, I've got pages of ideas about characters, meet-cutes, and romantic outings. They're not necessarily right for this book, but I can definitely use them in the future, and I've learned a lot about our new friends.

"You guys have helped me so much. I really appreciate it."

"That was fun," Aspen says. "We should do this again sometime. I know Nic is here for the summer, but how long are you girls in town?"

"We fly out Saturday morning," Rachel says. "I can't believe it's Wednesday already. Time goes so fast when I'm not working or playing chauffeur to my daughter."

My phone chimes with a text and MIKE (MET AT DOCKSIDE) flashes on the screen. I'm a weirdo who always enters how I know people in my contacts. I open the message. *I had a great time last night. Want to hang out again tomorrow night?* "You guys, I just got a text from Mike asking if we want to hang out tomorrow night."

"Do you feel like hanging out with him?" Rachel asks. "He's obviously not asking for us."

"Yes, he is." As I say it, I realize I have no idea if he is or not.

"We all exchanged numbers with them, and he texted *you*." Dani lies on the blanket and closes her eyes.

"Who's Mike?" Aspen asks.

"Who's *them*?" Maggie asks.

"A couple of guys we met last night at Dockside," Rachel says.

"Mike's a cop and he's really nice, but if he *is* asking just me, I don't want to give him the wrong idea."

"You're here to meet people, and you hit it off with Mike," Dani says. "You don't have to sleep with him. Just hang out for a while and have fun."

"Hey, single woman over here." Maggie waves. "Hook a sister up for a few hours of fun."

Marcus holds up his hands. "As the patriarch of the beach family, of which you are all now part, I have something to say. You girls are around our daughters' ages, and I feel a need to set my eyes on these guys and make sure they know you're being looked after."

A pang of longing for my own father hits me. I wasn't prepared for his sudden passing five years ago, and I still have days when I can't believe he's really gone. He would have said something very similar at a time like this, and it feels good to know someone would even want to look out for my well-being.

Aspen pats his hand. "You're such a good daddy."

"Careful, Marcus," Evelyn says. "Or you'll have them clamming up and sneaking out their bedroom windows."

Maggie shields her mouth, whispering loudly, "If you guys sneak out, come get me."

"You know what you need?" Aspen says excitedly. "You need to have a bonfire."

"That's a great idea," Rachel says. "Nic has a gorgeous new patio with a firepit just waiting to be broken in, and you won't give the guys the wrong impression. Maggie can check out the guys."

"You know, that's not a bad idea," I say. "Would you guys be into that?"

"Heck yeah," Maggie says.

"And I know Russ and Marlo would love to join us if they're not busy," Aspen adds. "When can we do it?"

I really want a couple of nights to hang out with Rachel and Dani, but I'm excited about the idea of a bonfire. "How about Friday night?"

"Perfectly perfect!" Aspen says. "We'll bring snacks. Maggie, can you make your seven-layer nachos?"

"Only if Evelyn makes her lemon bars," Maggie says.

"I can do that," Evelyn exclaims.

"We can put lights on the deck, and we'll need more chairs. What kind of music do you guys like?" Rachel asks, and just like that, we're planning my first get-together.

As I zip off a group text to Mike and JT, so as not to give them the wrong idea, I wish I had Declan's number. I consider asking Marcus for it, but I don't want to give him the wrong idea, either, so I let it go and join the party planning.

Chapter Nine

NICOLE

"How do you make a sophisticate?" Dani asks as I put two more bottles of wine in the basket.

"I don't know, but I can google it." I whip out my phone.

It's Friday afternoon, and we're in bonfire-prep mode. I made up for missing my Wednesday-morning run by running two of Aspen's longer routes yesterday and this morning, but I wasn't as lucky with my writing. My brain is still at a creative standstill, but the time with my friends wasn't wasted. It has rejuvenated my spirit, which is even more important than writing. The last two nights we cooked dinners together and ate on the deck, took long walks on the beach, and just enjoyed being together in this amazing new place.

Rachel puts a case of beer in the basket and peers over my shoulder at my phone. "Who's Bellamy Silver, and why would I want her sophisticated look?"

"I don't know. I searched how to make a sophisticate, and all these sites popped up with her name on them."

"Give me that." She grabs the phone and tries a new search. "Here we go. You have to search sophisticate *cocktail*."

"With Nic's recent luck, she'd get a porn site." Dani smirks.

"What does that mean?"

"I'm just saying that after the way Jacob blew you off this morning, your luck with men is changing."

"No shit. What is up with that guy?" I saw Jacob and his friend on his front porch this morning when I went running. I jogged over to invite them to the bonfire, and Jacob looked right at me, turned around, and went inside. "It wasn't like I even wanted to go out with him, but what the hell? First he pursues me like he doesn't want to miss out, and then he totally blows me off. That's weird and rude."

"Almost as weird and rude as the thumbs-up he sent me when I sent him the pictures of his cottage," Rachel says. "Forget him. We need to find vodka and St-Germain elderflower liqueur. I've never even heard of that."

We gather the rest of the ingredients, toss a few other types of alcohol in for good measure, and walk out of the liquor store with our arms full. "I know I haven't thrown a get-together in years, but are you sure this isn't overkill?"

"You've got all summer to use it." Dani stops to adjust the bag in her arms. "I'm sure this won't be your last bonfire."

I set the case of beer I'm carrying on the hood of my car to get my key fob out of my pocket. As I unlock the doors, a familiar old black truck stops beside me, and heck if my day doesn't get a little brighter.

"Hey, Writer Girl, are we having a party?" Declan calls out the open window.

Those dimples should come with a warning. "A bonfire, actually. I would have invited you, but I didn't have your number. If you're not busy, it's tonight around eight."

"Russ and Marlo and everyone will be there," Dani adds.

His expression turns serious for a beat. "I've got to take care of something tonight, but it looks like you ladies are ready for a good time."

"Yeah. Maybe next time." I try to ignore the disappointment tiptoeing through me. "Do you know where we can get some wood?"

He cocks a grin. "From the look of things at the Dockside bar, I'd say you have no problem rustling up wood."

"She sure doesn't," Dani says.

I try to scowl but can't keep a straight face. "Very funny."

He feigns wide-eyed innocence. "Oh, did you mean *firewood*?"

I arch a brow.

"Riled up is definitely a good look on you, WG."

There goes that little thrill again, damn it.

"Swing by the corner of Wilkes and Haverly. There's a self-serve firewood stand there. Bring cash—it's ten dollars per stack. See ya around, ladies." With a wave, he drives off.

"Is it just me, or is he wicked charming?" Dani asks.

"Infuriatingly so." I put the beer in the car. "But then again, most of them are . . . until they're *not*."

We have fun getting ready for the bonfire, stringing lights around the deck railings, choosing music, and setting out finger food and drinks. Russ and Marcus brought up extra chairs and helped us get the fire started. While they were there, Russ made about a dozen comments about things he could "fix," none of which were broken. The guy obviously likes having a honey-do list, but the last thing I need is someone rattling around my cottage while I'm trying to write. I let him down easy, and all was forgiven when he learned we had all the makings for sophisticates. He promptly appointed himself the bartender.

By eight thirty the table on my deck is covered with homemade dishes and desserts, and my patio is buzzing with music and conversation. Everyone showed up. JT brought Lottie, and she instantly became Dani's shadow, and Mike brought his guitar, although he has yet to play. They seem to be getting along well with my neighbors. Rachel is taking pictures as she mingles, and I'm doing my best to be a good hostess and talk with everyone. I'm in the middle of a conversation with Claude about how his family used to own one of the houses near Main Street when he kneels by my flower bed and reaches for a weed.

"Claude, what are you doing? I'll get to those weeds."

"I've heard that before." He yanks a weed.

"Seriously. I'll do it. You don't have to—"

"I'm going to get you the number of my landscaper, but for now I'll handle it."

"No, really. There's no need. I can—"

He waggles his finger at me. "You listen to me, young lady. When there's a weed, there's a need."

Evelyn taps my shoulder. "Just let him do it. It makes him happy."

I step closer to her and Marlo. "I feel bad letting him weed my garden."

"You shouldn't. He enjoys it. He weeds all our gardens when he visits." Marlo sips her drink.

"Sometimes I think he's more comfortable with plants than people," Evelyn says.

"Okay," I relent. "Are you guys enjoying the party?"

"Yes. We're having a great time," Marlo says. "I was just bending Evelyn's ear about the trials and tribulations of having adult children."

"Don't get me started. Kenzie is twenty, and she's supposed to be working this summer, but as far as I can tell, the only thing she's working on is having fun with her friends."

"Sounds like my Larissa. She's twenty-two, and I swear sometimes it seems like she expects the world to bow at her feet," Marlo says.

"I remember that stage," Evelyn says with a shake of her head. "It drove Claude batty. But, Marlo, Kelly wasn't like that, was she?"

"Kelly's my oldest," Marlo explains. "She's as determined as they come, but before she decided on a career in marketing, she wanted to do everything at once. I couldn't keep up with her. One day she wanted to be a cruise director, and the next she was thinking about joining the Peace Corps or becoming an influencer. Russ nearly had a heart attack over *that* idea."

"Be glad she wanted to work," I say.

"I'll toast to that." Marlo taps her glass with mine, and we spend the next half hour comparing parenting stories.

I take a few pictures for social media and post with the caption *New friends. New inspiration*, then make my way around the bonfire. Maggie and Marcus are having a heated conversation about sports, of all things. I skip that conversation and head across the patio to join Aspen and Rachel chatting with Mike and JT.

"How's it going?"

"Better now," Mike says with a smirk, patting the chair beside him. "Take a load off."

As I sit, Aspen gives me an approving smile, and Rachel's is more of an *I told you so*. She looks gorgeous in a green maxi dress that brings out her eyes. I'm shocked Mike isn't flirting with her, but then again, maybe he was before I walked over.

"JT was just telling us that he's a surfer," Aspen says.

"I've got to get you out on a board, Nic," JT says.

"I'm more of a dry-land type of girl, but you might be able to get Dani out on a surfboard the next time she's here."

"Come on. You'd love it," JT urges.

"Don't push her." Mike eyes me. "I bet a hike out by the bluffs and a picnic would be more your speed."

"I like hiking." Although hiking and a picnic sounds a little bland compared to surfing. "At least there's no risk of drowning or getting eaten by sharks."

"We should go sometime," Mike suggests.

"Once Rachel and Dani leave, my life will become all work and no play until the sun goes down."

Mike cocks a grin. "That's when the real fun begins. You know what they say, nothing good happens when the sun's up."

Oh boy. This is not where I wanted this conversation to go. "I think you mean nothing good happens after midnight."

Mike's eyes turn seductive. "Nope."

Amusement rises in Rachel's eyes, and I mentally check myself to see if I'm giving off the wrong vibes. I'm wearing cutoffs and a sweater that has a feather pen on the front. Nothing too sexy there. I replay the things I said to Mike earlier in the night, but I can't remember saying anything flirtatious.

"Have you met Maggie?" Rachel asks, and I'm thankful for the rescue. "I bet she'd enjoy hiking."

"Miller, my man!" Russ hollers, drawing my attention away from our conversation.

I turn to see Declan walking up the side yard with a guitar strapped to his back, and happiness bubbles up inside me. Russ claps a hand on his shoulder, and Declan's eyes find mine as he says something I can't hear. A smile tugs at the corner of his mouth.

"Excuse me." I get up and head over to greet Declan.

"Don't be too long," Mike calls after me.

Ugh. Why can't all guys be okay with just being friends?

"I'll get you a drink," Russ says to Declan, and heads for the deck. "Nic, ready for a refill?"

"No, thank you." I lift my half-empty glass, which I've been nursing all night. "Hi. I'm glad you made it." His gaze slides slowly down the length of me, and I try to ignore the shiver of heat that follows.

"Hey, Boots. I got finished early and figured someone should babysit the girls with the booze."

"Babysit?" I arch a brow.

"You're new in town. You don't know the ups and downs of the locals yet."

I follow his gaze to Mike and JT. "Do you know Mike and JT?"

"I know *of* them."

"Well, they seem like good guys. JT even brought all the makings for s'mores." I lower my voice. "Don't tell him this, because it was really sweet of him to bring them, but I don't like s'mores. If you ask me, all snacks should come in wrappers and include nuts."

His dimples appear. "Seems like I guessed right, then." He pulls a Snickers out of his pocket.

I gasp and snag it from him. "How did you know this is my favorite?"

"I can spot a fellow Snickers fan a mile away."

"Declan Miller, what other secret talents are you hiding?"

His grin turns wicked, and I like it way too much.

"Keep that thought to yourself, and *maybe* I'll share this with you." I tear open the wrapper.

"You'll share it if you ever want to get another one from me." He glances at Russ coming off the deck with his beer, and suddenly his hand swallows mine, pushing the Snickers down between them. "Hide the goods," he whispers conspiratorially. "He's a fan, too."

"Here you go, buddy." Russ gives him a beer. "Are you going to monopolize our friend tonight or play that guitar?"

"This old thing? It's just a prop to pick up chicks."

I roll my eyes, and he chuckles as he follows Russ toward the fire.

◆ ◆ ◆

A dozen songs and several great conversations later, the fire is still crackling, Mike and Declan are strumming out another classic-rock tune, and Rachel and Aspen are singing along. Russ and Marlo are talking quietly and sneaking smooches, and Marcus holds Dani's rapt attention as he tells her a story about a dog he and Aspen rescued when their kids were young. Evelyn and Claude left a little while ago, and I'm glad I had a chance to chat with them. I feel like I've been plunked down in the middle of one of the many bonfire scenes I've written, and I'm loving every second of it.

JT saunters over with a s'more on a napkin. "You've been so busy taking care of everyone else, I thought you could use this."

"That was sweet. Thank you." Not wanting to be rude, I nibble a corner of the graham cracker. My eyes flick to Declan, and he gives me a knowing smile as the song comes to an end.

"Let's hear it for our dynamic duo!" Aspen cheers, and everyone applauds.

Mike beams as they set down their guitars, and Declan gets up and stretches, avoiding meeting anyone's gaze, including mine, as he kneels to love up Lottie.

"I'm so bummed we're leaving tomorrow," Rachel announces to no one in particular.

"Me too. I wish you could stay a month," I say.

"We all do," Maggie says, and agreement rings out.

"Who's going to volunteer to take care of our girl after we leave?" Dani asks.

"I've got her covered," Mike says.

Declan glances at me just as JT says, "Your friends are leaving tomorrow?" drawing my attention away.

"Unfortunately. I'm going to miss them, but I have a lot of writing to catch up on."

"I know you're going to be busy during the day, but I'd really like to take you out sometime and get to know you better."

I feel the heat of Declan's stare and know he's close enough to hear every word. I take a minute to really look at JT. He's handsome, with kind eyes and strong features. I feel bad. He's thoughtful and interesting enough, and being an animal lover says a lot about him, but I'm still not attracted to him. I don't feel a spark of attraction to Mike, either. They're like vanilla ice cream. Good enough to make do but not special enough to fall off the wagon for.

"Well, like I said the night we all met, I'm always looking for new friends, but I'm not really interested in dating." Hoping that makes it clear, I excuse myself to refill the snacks.

When I turn to walk away, Declan is *right there*, guitar in hand. He starts playing "Brown Eyed Girl." His voice is gravelly and too damn sexy. A flutter in my chest catches me off guard, and I hurry around him, trying to tamp it down as I hightail it inside. I throw the s'more into the trash, wondering what the hell is wrong with me. It's like I have a vixen on my shoulder, pushing for something I don't need. I take a few deep breaths, reminding myself that I'm not a silly girl who can't control herself. It's been almost three years since I've been touched by a man. Maybe that's messing with my head. I remind myself there's more to life than the comfort of being in someone's arms. Even someone as adorable and enjoyable to be with as Declan.

The man who took off rather quickly the night of Russ and Marlo's bonfire. Was Dani right? Had he left for a date? A Tinder hookup?

Those thoughts are exactly what I needed to calm my overactive hormones. I don't need those kinds of questions or that type of drama in my life.

Feeling more in control, I head for the door just as Aspen walks out of the bathroom.

"How're you doing, baby doll? Are you enjoying tonight as much as we are?"

"I am." *With the exception of my momentary slip into never-never land.*

We go outside, and I stand at the deck railing, taking in this beautiful night with friends. Declan is still playing his guitar, and he lifts his chin in my direction. I smile, feeling more like myself.

"Look at all these wonderful people you brought together," Aspen says.

"I'm so thankful to have met you all. I'm not a manifester, like Dani or Maggie, but I've been hoping to find community, and I feel like I've lucked into a good one."

"You don't have to believe in manifesting for good things to happen. The universe knows what we need and usually finds a way to provide it."

"Maybe you're right. I did find this cottage, which was totally out of the blue, and that brought me here."

"Exactly. You were always meant to be one of us, baby girl. We were just waiting for your light to arrive."

I look at this woman I've only just met and feel like she's an aunt or family friend I've known my whole life but had never spent much time with until now. "You can't imagine how nice that is to hear. I went through so many years feeling like the only people who really saw me—the real me—were Dani and Rachel. You and I have only just met, and we don't even know each other's life stories yet, but it feels like we do."

"Because we will. A lot of people think *meant to be* refers only to couples, but I believe it's more universal than that." She lowers her voice. "I also have to wonder if Madame Universe knows something you don't."

"What do you mean?"

"For a girl who is not looking for a man, you have attracted quite a few."

"It has definitely been a strange week in that regard. Either there's something in the Chatemup water, or they're just interested in the new girl in town. That interest will fade, and I'm making it clear that I'm not looking for anything more than friendship."

"Or maybe they're interested in the new girl because she has an honest, effervescent spirit that draws people in."

I don't know how to respond to that, but it feels good to hear it.

"I noticed you and Miller have had quite a few laughs tonight in between musical sets. I think he might fancy you, too."

"He's a great guy. We hit it off at Russ and Marlo's, and it's nice that neither of us is looking for more. It takes the pressure off."

"You really *are* looking to remain single?"

"Yes, definitely. I don't have time for the drama that goes along with dating, and with my writing schedule, I'll end up neglecting anyone who gets close to me, and then they'll resent me."

"Sounds like you're talking from experience."

"I worked a lot during my marriage, and that's never great for a relationship."

"I can see how that would cause stress, but the right partner will strive to help you be the best you can be in all aspects of your life and figure out ways to support that."

"I'm not sure people like that really exist."

"They do, baby girl. Marcus and I have always told our daughters, any partner worth their weight will be able to challenge them in the most difficult moments and support them at the same time. It's a difficult balance, but it's doable."

"I'll take your word for it, but I'm happy single. Friendships are what I've been missing. Take tonight, for example. I've never had this kind of get-together. I've gone to parties and had people over, but it was never relaxed like this."

"Why do you think that is?"

I take a moment to think about that. "Maybe it's because I don't have to act a certain way for a partner, and I'm *not* looking for a new one. I don't think I've ever been in this position before. I was twenty-three when Kenzie's dad and I divorced, and I was open to finding a new guy, so I was always looking for one. But now that I'm not, I can focus on the experience and being with friends. I never realized how much I missed by focusing on men. How lame is that?"

"It's not lame. It's normal. I gather you didn't have get-togethers when you were married?"

"Kenzie's dad and I never had them. We were so poor, and we had a new baby. And with my second husband, Tim, I probably enjoyed them at first, but they quickly became stressful. He changed during our marriage. He became all about appearances. I had to look just right and act a certain way. One of the greatest things that came out of my divorce was being able to dress for myself and act like myself again. No more trying to impress his colleagues or worrying about my hair all night. That shit wore me out, and quite frankly, dressing to impress is not in my bailiwick. I always felt like an imposter. After we divorced, my new motto became *Like me as I am or say goodbye*, and that will never change. There's a lot of freedom in being happy with yourself and not looking for someone else to try to make you happy."

"You're awfully young to have figured all that out."

"I'm kind of proud of myself. Imagine if it took me fifty years and another bad marriage."

The evening is a great success, and when people start leaving, I'm sad to see them go. I hug Maggie and Aspen. "Thanks for coming. Aspen, let me know if you ever want to go walking together in the morning."

As they leave with the other Oyster Run folks, a heavy hand lands on my shoulder. I don't have to look to know it's Declan. I sense his presence the same way I sensed him looking at me that first night at Russ and Marlo's.

"I've got to take off, Writer Girl."

"I'm really glad you came."

"Yeah, me too." His brows knit. "Looks like your boy toys are sticking around."

"They're not my boy toys."

"Hey, no judgment here. But from one friend to another, you should know that JT is not all that he talks himself up to be."

"What do you mean?"

"He put his mom in an assisted living facility when she didn't need to be there. He's a little self-centered."

Aspen's voice whispers through my mind. *I think he might fancy you, too.* I wonder if Declan is making things up to dissuade me from accepting a date with JT. "Why would he do that?"

"Because his brothers refused to help take care of her, and in his own words, why should he put his life on hold when they won't? There's a lot of unpleasant family history between the brothers, and it has nothing to do with their mother."

"If that's really true, then that's awful."

"Ask him," he says lightly. "He'll tell you. He doesn't have the good sense to hide it."

I glance at JT and realize how easy it is to misjudge people. "That's just one more reason I don't want to have anything to do with dating. You never know what someone's really like. What's the scoop on Mike?"

Declan shrugs. "He's a good cop, and from what I hear, a real stand-up guy. He's not from the area, so I don't know his family, but I talked with him for a while tonight, and I like him."

I was sure he'd find a way to undermine Mike, and I'm pleasantly surprised that he didn't, which tells me two things: Aspen was wrong, thank goodness, because he seems like he'll be a fun friend, and Declan Miller appears to be an honest man. As refreshing as that is, after what

I just learned about JT, I can't help but wonder if Declan's pulling the wool over my eyes, too.

"See you around, Writer Girl." He leans down and kisses my cheek.

His scruff tickles, and he smells like man and musk and . . . *Nope. Not going there.*

"See ya, Dimple Dude."

Chapter Ten

NICOLE

"Dani, Joe is going to be here any minute," I call down the hall for the second time. They don't have Lyft or Uber in Chatemup. They have Joe's Taxi Service, which is run by three men in their sixties, all named Joe.

"You know you have to be more direct if you want her to pay attention." Rachel hollers, "Get your ass out here, Dani."

Dani comes out of the bedroom dragging a suitcase. Her hair is piled on her head in a messy bun, and she's wearing the shirt she spilled coffee on at breakfast. "I can't find my green flip-flops or my Chatemup sweatshirt."

"I saw your flip-flops last night. Where were they?" I spin in a slow circle, scanning the floor, and see the tip of one of them sticking out from under the couch. "There they are." I grab them for her. "You put on your sweatshirt after everyone left last night. Remember?"

"And took it off while we were talking." Rachel walks over to the couch and fishes around behind the pillows. "Got it!"

"I love you guys!" Dani snags the sweatshirt as a honk sounds out front.

"I hate leaving. I feel like we just got here." Rachel pulls me into a hug. "Next year we have to plan two weeks together."

"I'm all for two weeks, or more, as long as I don't have a book to write, because now we know what happens to my writing schedule when we're together." I haven't written a thing in days. "You can bring Lucy if your parents are too busy to watch her."

"Get over here, Nic." Dani hugs me tight. "I'm so glad we got to meet your neighbors. I feel better knowing they'll watch out for you."

"I'll be fine with or without them, but I'm glad I have them, too."

As we head outside, Rachel says, "I think you should reconsider going out with Mike. He's a cutie."

"I can't fake chemistry, and I'm going to be busy with a fictional cutie."

"My vote is taking Daddy Dimples to the mattress," Dani says. "You two have great chemistry."

"That man is already enough of a distraction."

"Exactly," Dani says as a wiry man steps out of the car.

His thin gray hair is tucked behind his ears and stops just above his shoulders, his beard is scraggly, and his smile is as warm and friendly as most everyone else's we've met here. "Howdy, ladies. I'm Joe."

"I'm Dani, and this is Rachel. We're the ones going to the airport."

"And I'm Nicole. Thanks for taking them."

"My pleasure." He opens the trunk, and as he puts their luggage in, he says, "Do you gals like audiobooks?"

"We love them," Rachel says.

"Good deal." He closes the trunk and opens the back doors. "I've got mystery, thriller, and romance."

"Romance," Rachel and Dani say in unison.

"It's sweet romance. I hope that's okay. My wife says I'm too old to drive safely while listening to people gruntin' and thumpin'."

We laugh.

"It's fine," Rachel says.

The girls and I share a group hug. "Text when you get there. I love you guys so much."

"We love you, too," they say.

"Thanks for helping me get acclimated. It wouldn't have been as fun without you."

"You wouldn't have left your cottage without us." Dani gives me one last hug. "You're going to nail this book."

"Yeah, she is," Rachel says.

"Okay, ladies, wrap it up," Joe says. "We need to rock and roll if we're going to make your flights."

They climb into the car and wave out the back window as they drive away. Their leaving is bittersweet. We'll text often, and I'll feel guilty when I can't chime in on our group texts because I'm writing. But at the end of the day, I know if I went a year without saying one word to them, they'd still open their arms without any questions, just like I'd do for them.

I turn back to my still unnamed cottage and take a deep breath. It's *go time*, and no part of me wants to write. I want to take today and do nothing but lie in the sun thinking about the week we just had together and decompress. But I can't afford to do that, so I head inside and sit at my desk. I pull out my notes from our brainstorming session on the beach and skim them. But remembering that morning just makes me want to go in search of my new friends. So I set the notebook aside and put my hands on the keyboard.

"Okay, Liam. Talk to me." I drum my fingers on the keys, trying to get my brain to cooperate. I feel like there's a tiny version of myself whistling in my head. I can see the little rebel kicking the sand as she walks along the shore, taunting me.

Kiss off, woman. I've got work to do.

Visual inspiration, that's what I need. I spend the next thirty minutes picking out pictures of my hero and heroine and finding a cute bistro and a small-town setting and set them up on my monitor so they fill the spaces beside my blank page. I type *Chapter One*, and off I go.

Liam Roberts didn't know how to relax. Not strong enough. I hold down the delete button.

Liam Roberts didn't survive his wife's death to be taken down by a lioness in heels and a business suit. "Weak." I delete it and lift my eyes, feeling the sun beckon me. Maybe Liam will come out to play if we're outside. I push to my feet and unplug my computer.

After setting up on the deck, I try several more opening lines, but I can't stop thinking about being on the beach. When did I get the attention span of a gnat? I'm wasting time, and it infuriates me. I try to figure out why I can't concentrate. At home I write in the same place every day—my office. But that hadn't helped in the weeks before I came here, either. I obviously need a new home base for writing.

What could be better than living out my dream and writing in a coffee shop?

I pack up my laptop and notebooks and consider walking into town, but if I hit my groove, I could be at the coffee shop late, so I drive into town.

The sight of Rise and Grind fills me with happiness, and I'm sure I made the right decision. Bypassing the tables outside with a view of the water, because I've seen what happens with my own water view, I head inside. There's no line. My friends must be wearing off on me, because I take that as a universal sign.

Matt smiles as I approach the counter. "I've been wondering when I'd see you again."

"If my muse likes it here, you'll be seeing a lot of me in the coming weeks."

He looks around. "Where is this muse of yours? I'll make sure she loves it here."

He's so fun, I wonder why he's single. "If I could find her, I probably wouldn't be here."

"Then let's see if we can lure her out of hiding with the perfect drink. What can I get you?"

"Something cold and sweet with an extra jolt of caffeine."

He grins, punching in something on the register. "One salted caramel nitro blast coming up."

"That sounds promising." I pay, and when he brings me the drink, I take a sip, and the sweet, icy goodness slides down my throat. "*Mm. I think I love you.*"

I sit in one of the comfy leather chairs by the side windows, pull out my laptop, and snap a picture for social media. I post it with the caption *Vacation is over and I'm excited to get back to Liam and Susie's sexy love story. I can't wait to see what they have in store for me. What are you reading this week?* I come up with different captions for each of my social pages, and when I'm finally ready to write, I have an epiphany. I'll skip the meet-cute and get right to the story. I can always write the beginning later and then tweak the following chapter as needed.

Now, where to start . . . ?

Chapter Eleven

DECLAN

"Your brother owns a damn auto shop." I loosen the lug nuts on my ex-wife's car in the parking lot of the Fit Club where she works out. "Why isn't he doing this for you?" Her brother Brent's shop is in a neighboring town, but it's only twenty minutes away.

"He takes too long to respond, and I have to be at work in an hour."

I jack up the car, irritated as hell. "Couldn't you have asked one of your muscle-head admirers to help you?" At fifty-two, Lindsay is still a looker, tall and blond with baby blues that get guys all twisted up inside, as proven by the two guys checking her out on their way into the gym.

"You know I hate asking people for help," she whines.

"Save it." I put the spare in place. There's no use reminding her that I'm a person, too. I know why she calls me. The other people in her life treat her like shit, and it frustrates the hell out of me and makes her feel awful. "I'm not your personal mechanic."

"I know you're not, and I appreciate your help. You know I do."

She's a smart woman, a nurse, and sweet as sugar, but that sweetness is as much a detriment as it is an asset, and I am not immune to it. The combination of her apologetic tone and pleading baby blues has me going easy on her. "This is your third flat tire in six weeks. What are you doing? Lining your tires with magnets?"

She plants a hand on her spandex-clad hip and smiles. "Do you really think I'd do that, Miller?"

We met when I was in the military, and I thought it'd be a one-night stand or a weekend fling, so I told her my name was Miller. The name stuck better than we did. I give her a look that says *I wouldn't put it past you* as I tighten the lug nuts. She rolls her eyes and thumbs something out on her phone. I lower the car and put the jack in her trunk. "Where the hell are you driving that you keep running over nails?"

"Nowhere unusual. Thanks for fixing it. I owe you one."

More like a million, but who's counting? "You hear from Neil?" Our oldest just broke up with his latest girlfriend.

"Yeah," she says sadly. "He told me about the breakup. I'm totally bummed. I really liked her."

"I told you not to get attached." She had a harder time with Neil's last two breakups than Neil did.

"You've always known what's best for me." She flutters her lashes—my cue to get out of there.

"Try not to run over any more nails." I reach for my truck door.

"Would you mind dropping the tire at Brent's so I'm not late for work? He can patch it for me."

Between a trip to see my father that morning that took too damn long and this, my morning is already fucked. I pick up the tire and toss it in the back of my truck.

Twenty minutes later I'm at the auto shop. I head into the bay where her brother is working and drop the tire. "This is Lindsay's. Make her a priority, will ya? She's your fucking sister."

"What crawled up your ass and died?"

Years of this bullshit.

I don't waste my breath answering and head back to my truck. I cut through town on my way to the marina, and I'm stopped at a red light when I see a familiar mass of auburn curls hunkered down over a laptop in Rise and Grind.

Suddenly my shitty morning looks a whole lot brighter.

I park and head inside, grab a coffee, and drop into the chair across from Nicole. She's wearing a tank top that says WRITE ON, cutoffs, and those worn leather boots that reach a few inches above her ankles, showing off legs that would look damn fine wrapped around my body. Why do I find everything about her so damn sexy?

Curious brown eyes flick up to greet me, and a smile appears on her beautiful face. "Hey there."

"What're we working on?" I sip my coffee.

"A divorced woman's guide to meeting all the wrong men."

Damn, I like her sass. "Oh yeah? How's that going for ya?"

"Great. I'm almost done. Want me to read it to you?"

"Absolutely."

"Step one. *Move to Chatemup.* Step two. *Have a vagina.*"

I laugh. "Sounds like you've got it all figured out."

"What can I say? I'm a fast learner." She reaches for her coffee, and her gaze slides from my face to my chest, lingering there as she takes a drink. Our eyes connect again as she sets the cup down, but her expression doesn't change, and man, I like that confidence. "What are you up to today?"

"Working mostly."

"You get paid to sidetrack writers? I need to get in on that gig."

"Play your cards right and maybe I'll hook you up with the boss. How's your writing coming along?"

"Not so great. I thought I'd dive into my story without showing the initial meeting and write that later, but I can't do it. I've been here for a few hours and still can't figure out the opening scene."

"Writer's block?"

"Big-time. I've tried everything, including having the heroine spill coffee on the hero."

"You've been thinking about me, huh, Writer Girl?"

"*No*," she says emphatically, but her smile tells me otherwise. "I was brainstorming with my friends and it came up."

"Uh-huh. Well, you can't start with that. That's our meet-cute. You need something unique to the characters. Tell me about your story."

Her brows knit. "I don't want to waste your time. You must have something better to do."

"Stop worrying about me, and spill the goods. I'm a creative guy. You need to take advantage of that."

"Most guys want women to take advantage of their bodies." She lowered her voice. "I guess that means you think you're blessed in the brains department and not so much in the . . ." She glances at my crotch and whispers, "Don't worry. I won't tell anyone."

I bark out a laugh. "Come on. Let's get started on this story before you get too sidetracked thinking about my body and spend all night bitching to the other musketeers about how you didn't get any words written. Tell me about the hero. Wait, let me guess. He's a hunky fish peddler with dark hair and dimples."

"Close." She sits up taller, and her eyes brighten. "He's a hunky accountant."

"*Hunky* and *accountant* don't go together."

"I know some very hot accountants, and besides, that's what makes him special. Beneath that suit and tie is a killer body."

I take a drink and set my cup down. "I'm surprised at you, Boots. You're fishing in the cliché ocean."

"It's a *romance*."

"Is that what you're into? Egotistical muscle heads?"

"No. What do you expect me to write about? Guys with beer guts who think it's funny to burp the alphabet?"

"Admit it. You're into perfect guys with six-pack abs and chiseled features."

"I'm not saying guys like that aren't head turners, but my ex was like that, so I want to stay far away from anyone similar. If I were writing a guy for myself, he'd be loyal, smart, and laid-back, with some cushion around the middle because he likes to eat, so he can appreciate where I'm coming from. A guy who is kind to everyone and likes to laugh, even during sex, and looks like hell in the morning so he can be down with my frizzy hair and puffy eyes."

For a woman who's not looking for a man, you've clearly given it a lot of thought. "A guy who thinks Daisy Dukes and boots qualify as dressing up and would rather hang out around a bonfire with friends than in a five-star restaurant?"

"Exactly," she says excitedly. "And I don't want to be anyone's second choice that they settle for because someone else blew them off."

"I hear you on that." I take another stab. "You want a guy who runs?"

"Not necessarily, although I like men who are physically active."

"And who cheers you on while you're writing until midnight because you're late for a deadline?"

"Yes, *please*," she says a little dreamily. "And while we're at it, let's throw in a back rub when I'm done for the night and maybe a hand massage, too."

"Because he knows you'll support his dreams and use those talented hands to ease *his* aches and pains?" I hold her gaze, that thrum of heat that seems to live between us flaring.

She looks at me for a beat before blurting out, "How'd we start talking about me? I'm not looking, and I'm definitely not my target audience."

"I'm just getting a sense of the writer to try to help with the characters." I take another drink as she does something on her laptop.

"Let's focus on the characters." She turns her laptop around and shows me a picture of a good-looking dark-haired guy and a gorgeous blonde. "He's a single dad to three kids, but I don't know if they're boys, girls, or a mix, and she's his late wife's sister's cutthroat attorney. His wife died, and her sister is trying to take the kids away from him."

"Why?"

"Because she's out for vengeance. Her sister was depressed, and she blames him for her death."

"Got it. Let's start with the basics. He's too fit to be a single dad."

She looks at me like I'm crazy. "Single dads can be fit."

"How old are his kids?"

"I don't know yet."

"How old is he?"

"Midthirties."

"Okay, then the kids are young. Two boys and a girl."

"Why?"

"Because it feels right. Just go with it. You've got my creative juices flowing."

"Okay, two boys and a girl it is." She puts down her laptop and picks up a notebook and pen, scribbling something down. "They're three, five, and seven, and he has a nanny, but she's not live-in."

"Good choice, because otherwise, he'd be banging her."

She glowers at me.

So damn cute. "Three young kids, bath times, bedtimes. He doesn't have a lot of time to work out. Plus, he's an accountant, and they're all about being methodical, so he's not the kind of guy who grabs a workout on the fly when he has an extra half hour."

"I like that."

"Told you I was good."

She taps the pen on the notebook. "I see your ego doesn't need stroking."

"My ego is fully intact, but if you're offering . . ."

A challenge rises in her eyes. "Thought you weren't looking for a hookup."

"Yeah, you're right. But there are benefits to getting you riled up."

"Do you want to do this or not?"

"Are you propositioning me again?" I feign being taken aback. She scowls.

"No? Okay, sorry. I thought I was going to have to put you in your place, because I'm not that kind of guy."

"*Focus*, Brawny Boy."

"Brawny Boy, Dimple Dude. Do you have names for all your brainstorming buddies?"

"Of course. Doesn't everyone? I have a string of men coming through here today to sit in that seat, so we'd better get to it."

I chuckle. "How do you feel about pizza?"

"I don't know. I like it. Why? I thought we were talking about the book."

"We are. They meet in a pizza parlor. His rug rats are running around, and the littlest one bumps into the attorney chick and gets sauce all over her white skirt. She's uptight, and he can tell she's about to snap, but then their eyes lock, and they have a moment."

Nicole's eyes narrow. "Oh, that's *good*. They don't know they're going to be pinned against each other yet."

"In more ways than one," I toss out, because she brings out a playful side of me I haven't seen in forever. She rewards me with an adorable smirk. "But you can't make it too easy for them. She has to give the kid a look."

"That's harsh toward a child, which might make her unlikable to readers." Nicole points her pen at me. "But she can give *him* a look."

"Yeah, like *get your kid under control, buddy*."

We hit our stride, and a few hours later we're still feeding off each other's ideas, fleshing out scenes, and knee-deep in the characters' storylines. Nicole's passion and enthusiasm for her characters are contagious. My adrenaline is pumping, and I'm just as stoked about the story as she is. I haven't felt like this since my military days. We're talking through a scene when my phone rings, and CHUCK HAAS flashes on the screen. Chuck manages my drivers. "'Scuse me for a sec, Nic. I've got to take this."

"Sure."

She looks over her notes as I put the phone to my ear. "What's up?"

"Will's got food poisoning or some shit. He's been throwing up for an hour. I'm going to take over and finish his route, but I've got two guys coming up from Camden for interviews. I've been talking to these guys for a month. It took us three weeks to coordinate. Any chance you can get to the office to take over?"

Damn. There goes my good time. "Nah, buddy. You've got the connect with the guys who are coming in. You stick around and handle the interviews. I'll head over and finish Will's route. Where's his truck?"

"At his place. You sure, Boss?"

"Yeah, no problem. Did we get the contract revisions from the Seafarer yet?"

"Not yet, but I'll hit you up if we get it today."

"Thanks, man." I end the call and look across the table. Nicole's eyes have glittered with excitement the entire time we've been talking, and it's been a great sight. One I hope to see again soon. "Sorry about that. I'm loving our little adventure, but I've got to cut it short and take off."

"No worries. I've already taken up half your day."

"Best half day I've had in a while. We should exchange numbers and do this again sometime."

"I'd love to. I never get this much brainstorming done. Thanks for hanging out and helping me."

We exchange phones, and as she inputs her number, I fill in my information. *Dimple Dude. Your new adventure buddy.* I add my phone number and hand her back her phone, taking mine. "I'll text you. Don't screw up those scenes when you write them."

"I'll try not to, but you know, I am new at this." Every word is loaded with sass.

With a nod, I head for the doors and glance at her contact information. She put *Writer Girl* as her name. I steal a glance over my shoulder. She's looking at her phone and must feel my eyes on her, because she looks up, and a big-ass grin lights up her eyes.

Hell if it doesn't light a spark inside me, too.

Chapter Twelve

NICOLE

"Come on, girls, keep up!" Aspen says early Wednesday morning as we power walk by the shops along the harbor. She's trucking along at a good clip, decked out in a pink exercise bra and black leggings.

Maggie mouths, *She's killing me!*

"I heard that." Aspen tosses me a wink.

They're just as entertaining as they were last night when I ran into them on my evening walk on the beach. We ended up getting a group text from Russ inviting us over for drinks and staying until nearly eleven o'clock. Aspen twisted Maggie's arm to get up early and walk with us.

Aspen waves to someone driving by in a blue sedan. "Here comes the Big Kahuna."

"Marcus?" I look around for his car.

"*Ha!* No, the hill." Aspen motions to the road we're about to turn onto, which rises at a steep incline toward the main drag. "I only call Marcus my Big Kahuna in bed."

"How many times do I have to tell you that I don't need to know those things about you?" Maggie pants out as we start walking up the hill.

"Can I help it if I married a sex god?" Aspen asks, barely breaking a sweat.

"You'd better nip this in the bud, Nic," Maggie warns. "Or by the end of the summer, every time you look at Marcus, you'll think about the two of them going at it."

"I'm used to that. I think about my characters going at it all the time. Besides, I'm glad Aspen and Marcus are so in love."

"So am I, sweetie," Aspen says. "Don't you girls get lonely? I'd be lonely without my husband."

"Never," Maggie declares.

"What about you, Nic?" Aspen asks. "You were married for a long time. Do you get lonely?"

"I was at first, but now I'm used to it, and the solitude is good for my writing." My words have been flowing better, but my focus is still off. By late afternoon thoughts slip through my fingers like sand.

"I'm glad you're making progress," Aspen says as we reach the top of the hill.

Sweat is pouring down Maggie's face, and she's breathing hard.

"That hill is a killer. Mind if we slow down?" I ask so she doesn't have to.

"Thank God. I'm about to die," Maggie pants out as we turn onto the main drag and slow our pace. "Aspen is out to kill me. I know it."

Aspen giggles. "I keep telling her she should walk with me more often and build up her cardio. If Evelyn can do an hour of Pilates three times a week, you can speed walk. How can you enjoy all the goodies life has to offer if you get out of breath walking up a hill?"

"I won't be able to enjoy anything if I have a heart attack before we get home," Maggie says.

I gaze into the windows of the shops as we pass. "Would you mind if we stop at the coffee shop to get muffins for Claude and Evelyn? I ran across the edge of his lawn yesterday and he snapped at me. I feel bad."

"He snaps at everyone," Aspen says.

"I know, but he was nice enough to send his landscaper out earlier this week to take care of my weeds, and I just want to give him a reason to smile."

"He's married to Evelyn. That should be reason enough to smile," Maggie says as we head inside and stand in line. While we wait, she convinces us to order iced lattes and have a leisurely walk home.

"Hello, ladies," Matt says as we step up to the counter. "You're looking *hot* this morning."

Maggie grabs a napkin and wipes her brow. "Aspen ran us through hell this morning."

"Well, let's see if we can ease that pain," he says. "What can I get for you?"

I ask if he knows Claude, which he does, and he shares that Claude usually orders blueberry scones. I order two and our iced lattes.

When he leaves us to make them, Aspen says, "Isn't he adorable?"

"If I were into younger guys, I'd take him for a ride," Maggie says.

Matt returns with our drinks and hands me the bag of scones. "Should I be jealous that you're delivering muffins to another man?"

"Very," Maggie says, and she laughs as we walk out the door.

"There are only a few weeks until Independence Day. Nic, do you have plans?" Aspen asks.

"Just writing, as usual."

"Every year Marcus and I go out for a special dinner and then we meet everyone down on the beach for the fireworks. I hope you'll join us after you're done writing."

"Actually, I wanted to invite Nic to dinner at my place first," Maggie says. "My girlfriends and my brother are coming into town, and I know you'll like them. Cherry and Sarah are a lot of fun, and Seth is one of the good guys."

"Seth is finally visiting?" Aspen asks. "I have yet to meet him, but I can vouch for Cherry and Sarah. They're wonderful."

"Yes. Can you believe it? My brother usually has big travel plans for the summer," Maggie explains. "If you don't meet him this summer, it could be years before he comes back."

"I'd love to come to dinner. Just let me know what to bring." I like having something to look forward to.

"You don't need to bring anything but your appetite," Maggie says.

My phone chimes. I pull it out of my armband and see Declan's name on the screen. I can't suppress my smile as I read the message. *Morning WG. Wishing you thousands of magical words today. Don't forget to take a breather and enjoy the sunshine.*

"Someone's bringing you early-morning smiles," Aspen says.

"It's just Declan. He helped me brainstorm last weekend, and it really helped." I was pleasantly surprised when he texted a few hours after our impromptu brainstorming session with another idea for a scene. We've been texting back and forth ever since. Most of the time we toss around ideas for the book, but Monday morning he texted, *Good morning, WG. I hope you nail your scenes today,* and yesterday morning he sent, *Have an amazing day, WG.* Last night he reached out again to see how my writing had gone, and we texted for an hour.

I thumb out, *I'm already enjoying the sunshine. I'm out walking with Aspen and Maggie. I hope you have a great day, too!*

"Has someone cracked the hot terminal bachelor's code?" Maggie asks.

"No. We're just friends." I put my phone in my armband as we walk. "But I have to admit, it feels good to get good-morning texts. I never realized how much I missed that."

"My last boyfriend texted me nearly every morning, and even though I only half paid attention to those messages, I definitely noticed when I *didn't* get them," Maggie says.

"Why did you two break it off?" Aspen asks.

"Because I took him for granted."

I look at her curiously.

"I always do," she admits. "That's why I've never gotten married. I know my faults. I love my work and having the flexibility to take off whenever I want. I lived with a guy for a few months, and let's just say I'm too alpha to live with a male. I like things done my way. If I never have to share a bathroom with another man, I'll die a happy woman."

"You never know who might come along," Aspen says as we head toward Old Wharf Road.

"It doesn't matter who comes along," Maggie insists. "I'll take them for granted."

"Then why did you ask me to give Mike your number last night?" I made it clear to JT on the night of the barbecue that I wasn't interested in getting involved with him and haven't heard from him since. But Mike texted last night while we were at Russ and Marlo's, and when I told my friends I wasn't interested in dating him, Maggie asked me to give him her number, and I did.

"Why do you think?" Maggie says. "He's hot, and he's got a great personality. I'll spend time with him, and I promise to end things before I take him for granted."

"Good, because I wouldn't want him to feel bad. Honestly, I think most couples take each other for granted on some level. Getting comfortable in a relationship is a double-edged sword, isn't it? Being able to take the other person's love for granted is part of what's nice about being in a relationship. You don't have to worry about always putting your best foot forward, but if you do that too much, you lose that spark."

"It can be a slippery slope," Aspen says. "Marcus and I are mindful of that type of thing."

"The last couple of years, Tim and I were skiing down that slope. I was lonelier in my marriage than I could ever be living alone." That harsh reality makes me appreciate my new friends even more. "Maggie, do you have any kids?"

"God no. I'd probably take them for granted, too."

"Kids take a *lot* of emotional energy, but I never realized how much until this summer. This is the first summer since I had Mackenzie that she hasn't been with me."

"Where is she?" Maggie asks.

"We had to take a year lease on the apartment near her school, so she stayed for the summer."

"What's it like without her around?" Aspen asks as the water comes into view.

"Strange. This is the first time I've been able to just be myself since I was eighteen. But it's kind of wonderful rediscovering myself. I will say this, being single at twenty-three was a whole different ball game. I definitely feel my age when I'm around people in their early twenties."

Maggie scoffs. "I felt this age when I was twenty-three."

"I had a toddler underfoot back then. She kept me young, and my mindset was different. I didn't *feel* older. I felt overburdened at times, but I didn't mind because I love my daughter, and at that age everything seemed possible."

"Well, I haven't been single since Marcus and I fell in love when I was twenty."

"Do you ever wonder what you missed out on?" Maggie asks. "Or wish you could go back and start over?"

Aspen shakes her head. "I never have, and I don't think I ever will."

"She's got the Big Kahuna," I tease. "I wouldn't go back even if I could. I love being this age. I'm so much smarter than I was in my twenties. I never felt like I was enough, even for myself. Aspen and I talked about that the other night. I was always looking for my next boyfriend. Now I have this sense of peace, of knowing I'm enough for me, and that's all that matters."

"That's empowering, isn't it?" Maggie asks. "I think I was born with that feeling."

Aspen looks thoughtfully at Maggie. "I still think you should leave that door open. Both of you should. You're too young not to find your own Marcuses."

"I don't know about that, Aspen. I don't feel like something is missing. I'm enjoying doing what I want for a change, and not feeling guilty if I'm ignoring the rest of the world while I write."

"Don't you miss sex?" Aspen asks.

"You mean with a person?" I laugh, and Maggie high-fives me. "Sometimes I miss being held and touched and *wanted* and those little moments that I didn't have with Tim, but I write about it every day. Secret glances, holding hands, desiring someone. But all that usually comes with drama, and while sex with a living, breathing male can be great, a drama-free life is better."

"I think I know how we can have both," Maggie exclaims.

"Marcus is already taken, sweetie." Aspen winks again.

"I don't need Marcus. My idea is better." Maggie's eyes light up. "We should open a single ladies' service station. Think about it. A guy shows up for a *lube job* and leaves an hour later. No fuss, no muss, no strings or emotional attachments."

I love how her brain works. "I think that's called Tinder."

"I was thinking Jiffy Dude," Maggie says, and we all crack up.

Two chapters and far too many hours later, I'm staring out my bay window, trying to rein in my brain, which for the past forty minutes has been on a tour of all things Chatemup. The beach is calling me, but a coffee sounds good, too, and I can't stop thinking about how sweet and fun Declan's texts have been and how much I enjoyed walking with Aspen and Maggie. I wonder what the marina is like this time of day. It might be inspiring to watch the boats coming in.

My stomach growls, and I realize I forgot to eat lunch. That's what I get for giving myself a ten-minute writing break to sit in the sun on the deck. Ten minutes turned to twenty, and it had taken another twenty to find my characters' voices again.

Ice cream might hit the spot.

But I really should start another chapter. I need to get my characters moving.

But the beach . . .

The hell with it. Why did I move here if not to enjoy it?

I push to my feet and head into the bathroom to freshen up. My cutoffs and tee are clean, but I didn't wash my hair when I showered this morning, and the frizz is off the charts. I try to tame it, scrunching and primping. If I'm going to leave my house, I should at least look presentable. But today it appears *presentable* is a little Carrot Top and a lot Don King.

It'll have to do. I really need a BEACH HAIR. DON'T CARE shirt.

I shove my feet into my boots and head out the door. I snap a selfie with the water in the background and upload it to social media with the caption, *This writer girl is playing hooky!* I'm halfway down the driveway when my phone rings, and DIMPLE DUDE appears on the screen.

"Hey, Dimple Dude."

"What're you up to, Writer Girl?"

His deep voice and uplifting tone are just what I needed. "Playing hooky."

"Perfect. Want to go on an adventure with an awesome fish peddler?"

I love that everything with him is an adventure. "Do I need to dress nicely?"

"Hell no. You know me. Tees and jeans twenty-four-seven."

Maybe that's why we get along so well. "Will I be fed on this adventure?"

"Absolutely."

"In that case, sure." I start heading back to the cottage. "I just need to grab my wallet and keys. Where should I meet you?"

"You don't need either. I'll swing by and pick you up. I'm right around the corner."

"Okay." Then I remember my wild hair. "*Wait.* How do you feel about Carrot Top?"

"I think he's sexy as hell. Why?"

Good answer. "Just curious." I see his truck coming down Old Wharf Road. "See you soon."

He pulls up beside me. "Boots," he says low and gravelly.

"Should I change out of them?"

He scoffs. "That was an appreciative remark. Like *damn, I love those boots.*"

"In that case, thank you very much."

"Now get your ass in the truck, Writer Girl. We've got places to be."

I climb in and put on my seat belt as we head out. "Where are we going?"

"On our next great adventure."

Chapter Thirteen

NICOLE

Our next great adventure was thirty minutes away at Siren's Reef, an out-of-the-way pub with a statue out front of a seductive mermaid kneeling on a boulder, her long hair draped over her breasts. A group of chatty twentysomethings in shorts and midriff tops and tight mini-dresses hurries toward the building. I imagine that's what Mackenzie and her friends are like when they're out, hopefully *not* going into pubs.

It seems like forever ago when I was that carefree and confident in my own skin. I'm confident now, but I'd give anything to have my pre-pregnancy body back. Especially now, as Declan puts his hand on my lower back.

"You're going to love this place." He guides me past the entrance, following the girls toward an enormous, crowded patio.

One of the girls looks over her shoulder, openly eyeing Declan from head to toe. I feel a pang of unwanted jealousy and quickly give myself a virtual slap to shut it down.

"My buddy Chuck's band is playing tonight," he says as we step onto the patio among swarms of people. "They're fantastic, and Chuck's a great guy. You'll love him."

"Miller!" a dark-haired man hollers from within the crowd to our right.

"Is that Chuck?"

"Yeah." Declan moves in his direction, keeping his hand on my back.

A curvy brunette steps into our path. "Hey, stranger."

"How's it going?" He leans in to kiss her cheek.

"Good. My music is coming along, and work is work, you know." She eyes me and smiles.

I feel so far out of my element, I can't even remember how to spell the word. It's one thing to go to a bar with my girlfriends, but as she and Declan chat briefly and we move through the crowd, I feel old and underdressed. I'm pretty sure Declan is several years older than me, but men age like fine wine, while I . . . *Oh shit.* I remember I'm rocking the Don King look and reach up to touch my hair but stop myself. I'm *not* going to be that girl.

I hold my head up as Declan says hello to more women and men, some older, some younger, all very friendly. He introduces me to a couple of them, including Chuck, a shameless flirt who calls Declan "Boss." It's easy to see how much his friends admire him.

"Someone's popular," I say as we near the bar.

"I've been coming here for a while." His hand lands on my back again, and he leans closer, speaking into my ear. "I don't even remember that first girl's name. Otherwise, I would've introduced you."

"You probably shouldn't admit to that."

"Why?" He looks perplexed.

"It's kind of rude not to remember her name. I mean, I get it, and you must've had a good time because she looked ready for more, but still."

"What?" His head jerks back. "She's a *kid*. She and half the other kids here went to school with my sons."

"*Oh.* I thought you meant you . . . *you know*, and couldn't remember her name."

"You've got to be kidding me."

"Why? She looked at you like she was hungry and you were a succulent steak."

He laughs. "Well, I am, obviously, but not for her."

"I'm not judging you."

"I'm forty-seven, Nic. I can't even imagine what guys my age have in common with girls that young. I mean, these are great kids, but . . ." He shakes his head. "You really think I'd do that?"

"I don't know, and it's none of my business. Why does it bother you what I think?"

His brows knit. "That's a good question. *C'mon.*"

He heads up to the bar and orders our drinks. Then we make our way to a table, and he sits in the chair closest to me instead of across the table, which is nice. We don't have to shout to be heard.

"What time does Chuck play?"

"Pretty soon." He lifts his glass in a toast. "Here's to a summer full of adventures." We clink glasses and drink.

"I love that you say adventures, like we're twelve."

"Life is what you make it, and you and I are destined to have some great adventures. How'd you do today? You didn't fuck up our fantastic ideas, did you?"

"Not beyond repair, I hope."

"You think they're salvageable?" He flashes those dimples. "I mean, for a person with better writing skills."

"Well, obviously." I laugh softly. "How was your day? Did you peddle a lot of fish?"

"Something like that." He takes another drink, eyes remaining on me. "I googled you."

"*Why* would you do that?"

"To see who I'm hanging out with. I take my adventuring very seriously. Turns out you're a pretty big deal."

"No, I'm not. I'm just a girl who writes love stories."

"Don't play humble with me. You've published thirty books, and several have hit bestseller lists."

"I got lucky. Good marketing." I shrug and look out at the crowd to avoid talking about myself.

"I might believe that if it were only one or two books, but I read some of your reviews. Your fans love your work."

"Like I said, I'm lucky."

He studies me for a minute. "Luck has nothing to do with it, Writer Girl, and I want to know your story."

"What do you mean, *my story*?"

"Who are you? How'd you get here?"

"This guy picked me up in his truck, and—"

He narrows his eyes.

"Oh, you didn't mean tonight?" I tease.

"Give me the goods, Boots."

"What do you want to know? How I ended up in Chatemup? My life story?"

"Your life story sounds good."

"There's not much to tell. I'm twice divorced with a daughter."

He crosses his arms, brows slanting. "You're a storyteller. You can do better than that. How old were you when you got married? What happened to bachelor number one?"

"I got pregnant at eighteen and married my high school sweetheart. We lasted five years."

"Were you in love?"

I don't know many men who would ask that question, and it makes Declan even more intriguing. "Yes, but it was first love. The kind that feels bigger than life, and once we had Mackenzie and bills to meet, things got stressful. We lost that spark and grew apart, as everyone predicted we would." He's listening so intently, I keep going. "I was single for a couple of years after that, raising Mackenzie and working, and then I met Tim, my second husband. He had two boys, and we were together ten years, married for nine."

"How long ago did you get divorced?"

"Almost three years. How about you?"

"Much longer than that. Do you get along with your ex?"

"When we have to," I say honestly. "What about you and your ex? Were you in love?"

"We loved each other but not in the way you described."

That's interesting. "Do you get along?"

"Yeah, most of the time. My ex is complicated. Why'd you split from Tim?"

I don't want to bitch about Tim, so I say, "It was time. What about you?"

"It's not easy to be married to a military guy who's away a lot. Things had been going south for a while, and I was kind of a mess after I got out of the military."

"A mess like PTSD, or injured?"

"I was never injured, but yeah, the things I saw messed with my head, and we weren't equipped to deal with it. We stayed together for the kids, and we made it until they were teenagers, but then she found comfort in someone else's arms, and that was it."

He says it casually, but I can see pain, or something like it, in his eyes. "I'm sorry. That must've hurt."

"It did, but I don't blame her. We had other crap going on, and like I said, I was a mess."

"I researched PTSD for a book, and from what I read, I don't think anyone other than therapists or physicians could ever be prepared for that. It's not something people just get over with time. Did you get help?"

"Eventually, when I got my stubborn head out of my ass, but the breakup was for the best. Now, back to you. You don't seem like a quitter. Did your ex cheat?"

"No." I take a drink, mulling over what he's been through.

"Did you?"

"*No.* I couldn't cheat. I can't even lie well."

He sits up, his expression serious. "Was he abusive?"

"I'm not a victim, Declan."

His brows knit. "You didn't answer the question."

"It's a hard one to answer."

"Too personal? I'm not going to judge you. I just want to understand what made you the person you are."

"It's not too personal. It's just that in most people's eyes the answer is no, there was no abuse."

"And in your eyes? Because that's all that matters."

"In my eyes, when you tell your future partner the first day you meet him that you can put up with a lot of things but dishonesty isn't one of them, and as the relationship progresses, he lies about everything under the sun, gaslights you, and finds ways to passive-aggressively make you the bad guy in every scenario, it feels a heck of a lot like abuse."

Declan's jaw clenches. "Sounds like you married a narcissistic asshole."

"I never use that word to specify what type of asshole he is, but Kenzie and my brothers do."

"How many brothers do you have?"

"Three. Jerry is forty-six and lives in New York, Tommy is forty-four and lives in Colorado, and Kent is forty-one. He lives in Ohio. I was the *oops* baby, born three years after our parents thought they were done having kids."

"No wonder you're so tough. I bet your brothers have a few choice words for your ex."

"You could say that. They've always been protective of me. Jerry told me not to marry him in the first place. I should've listened. But *should've, could've, would've* does me no good."

"Live and learn. How is Mackenzie doing? It must have been hard for her to go through two divorces."

I like that he asks about her. "It was. Her real father never spent much time with her when she was young, although it wasn't his fault. He's always had to work two jobs to make ends meet, and he does the best he can." We're surrounded by laughter and conversation, but Declan's focus is solely on me, which makes it easy to open up to him. "She was close to Tim and his boys, so it's been hard. She loves Tim, but she also dislikes him."

"That's a shame about her real father."

"I know, but he *is* a good man. He loves her and she knows that. What about your kids? How old are they?"

"Neil is twenty-six, and Eric is twenty-three. They don't know about Lindsay's indiscretion. The divorce was rough on them, but you know, that was a long time ago."

"Divorce sucks for everyone, and in all fairness, the end of my marriage wasn't all Tim's fault. I wasn't the best wife for the last few years."

"How so?"

"You don't pull any punches, do you?"

"Not usually. At least not with people I like."

"From what I've seen, you like everyone."

"Not everyone." He grins.

I wonder what could make such an affable guy dislike someone, but I'd imagine whoever his wife cheated with is probably on his shit list.

"So, tell me about what made you a big bad wifey."

"That woman was drowning in her marriage. I supported my ex through a career change. He went into real estate and got connected with some really wealthy people he wanted to impress, and that's not something I'm comfortable doing."

"You're impressive as hell. What are you talking about?"

"It wasn't about me or my career."

"I wasn't talking about your career. You're a special person, Boots. You stand out."

Okay, wow. I don't know what to do with that. "I appreciate that, but I didn't like going to his corporate functions or wining and dining his clients. He used to make up stories about his background to make himself sound more impressive, and he'd tell everyone who would listen how amazing I was and how perfect our marriage was."

"Most women would probably like being bragged about."

I sigh. "Maybe, but I'm grounded in reality. It just made him a big fake. In writing, they say *show don't tell*, and I think that translates into real life, too. If your marriage is good, you don't have to brag about it. Everyone will see it or feel it. But to answer your question about what made me a bad wife, he was living a lie in all facets of his life. Not just in public, but with me, too. I never knew what to believe, and I *might* have pulled the deadline card a few dozen times to get out of going places with him."

"With a guy like that, I can see why you would. You don't seem like the kind of woman who has a lot of patience for egotistical assholes. Did you two argue a lot?"

"We got along fine as long as I didn't confront him about his lies, but I've never been someone who rolls over and plays dead. Mackenzie says I'm like the *wrongdoing* police. I'd rather call people on their shit than pretend it doesn't stink."

"That's a good trait but a hard way to live."

"Sounds like you know something about that."

He shrugs and takes a drink. "So, why did you stay with him for so long?"

"Same as you. For the kids. They'd already been through one divorce, and I didn't want to put them through a second one."

"So you grinned and bore it?"

"Partially. Arguing with someone who re-creates reality to make himself look better and *believes* it was exhausting. After a few years of listening to him lie to his family and friends, and to me and the kids, something inside me changed, and I did what I never realized I could. I gave up arguing."

"Because you stopped caring, or were you just holding it in?"

His questions are so pointed, I get the feeling he's been there before, too. "I think I stopped caring long before we got divorced. I guess I kind of did grin and bear it, until I couldn't anymore."

"Do you still talk with his boys?"

"Nolan and Connor? Yes. As a matter of fact, I'm going to Nolan's wedding at the end of August. I'm looking forward to seeing them, but I am not looking forward to seeing Tim and his girlfriend."

"I'll go as your arm candy. Show the guy what he's missing."

"Yeah, right."

He cocks his head, brows lifting.

"You're not kidding?"

"Hell no. I love snuffing out narcissistic assholes."

"Really? You'd do that for me?"

"It'll be an adventure. I look great in a suit."

I laugh because . . . who does this? I love it! "You're really serious? My mother's going to be there."

"I'm dead serious, and she'll love me. What color is your dress?"

"Forest green. Why?"

"Just picturing you in it. The last weekend in August?"

"Yes, but it's in Boston."

"I love Boston. It's a date." He holds up his glass. "Here's to another great adventure."

Chapter Fourteen

NICOLE

I take a drink and sit back, watching the man who just made my whole night as the waiter approaches our table. He greets Declan enthusiastically, and Declan introduces us quickly, like he's anxious to get back to our conversation. We order dinner, and when the waiter walks away, I speak before Declan has a chance to. "Okay, now it's your turn."

"I'm not done interrogating you yet," he says.

"What more could you *possibly* want to know?"

"Everything. But I'll settle for how you got into writing. Did you always want to be a writer?"

"Yes, for as long as I can remember."

"Why? Hard childhood? Easier to live in fictional worlds?"

"No wonder you're so good at brainstorming. That head of yours is always looking for interesting avenues, isn't it?"

He answers with another noncommittal shrug.

"I'm afraid my backstory is not quite that interesting. I had a great childhood with parents who adored me. They had me late in life, and I think I was an easy kid. I kept myself busy trying to keep up with my brothers and reading. But as far as writing goes, I won a short story contest in first grade and loved writing it so much, I knew it was what I was meant to do."

"That's very cool. How'd you get started?"

"I got lucky."

"You know I don't believe luck has anything to do with what happens in our lives."

"I didn't realize that, but in this case, it really was luck. I used to make up stories for Kenzie, creating worlds with her favorite toys as characters. *Mr. Bear, Mrs. Mouse, Professor Pupster.*"

He grins. "That's cute."

"It was fun. When Kenzie was little, I submitted them to a children's magazine on a whim, and the editor reached out two weeks later. She eventually bought most of them for the magazine and asked if I'd consider writing for them. I was twenty-one and completely blown away, so of course I accepted the offer, and as Jay and I grew apart, I started writing love stories."

"Hoping for your own?"

"Something like that." He holds my gaze, and I see empathy and something that looks a lot like commiseration in his eyes. I'm starting to understand his rapid-fire questions. It's easier to ask than answer. "Anyway, the magazine editor had a friend who was a romance editor for the publisher I currently work with. She connected us, and with a ton of guidance and working hand in hand with a developmental editor who taught me more than I could ever thank her for, I learned to hone my craft, and the rest is history."

"Wow, Boots. You created your own fairy tale. That's damn impressive."

"Lucky," I whisper, and finish my drink. "Your turn."

"One more question. How'd you end up in Chatemup of all places?"

"You'll love this. I went to Cape Cod sixteen years ago for a long weekend with Dani and Rachel, and I fell madly in love with New England. People didn't dress to impress, and they weren't honking their horns and pushing everyone to go faster. I write about a lot of small towns, and over the years it became a dream of mine to live in a close-knit community, and I *really* wanted to be able to see the water every day. One day, about three months ago, I went for a run in the park, and I saw my ex and his girlfriend there. That was my wake-up call. He's out there living his life, and I was too uncomfortable there to live mine. That was when I realized I didn't want to spend one more summer stressed out every time I left my house. I went home and did an internet search for water-view cottages in New England. I couldn't afford most of them, but then I found my little cottage on the hill, and starting over where nobody knows me seemed perfect. I bought the place on a whim, and it was the best decision I've ever made."

"That might be your best story yet. How do you like our little town so far?"

"I love it. The people are great, and knowing I won't bump into my ex or anyone from my old life makes every day exciting. And I found a new adventure buddy who's also a pretty good brainstormer. So that's a plus."

"*Pretty good* brainstormer?" He arches a brow. "*Phenomenal* is more like it."

"Yup, that ego of yours is definitely intact."

He finishes his drink and grins like a Cheshire cat. "Admit it, your new adventure buddy is the best part of your new life."

Our gazes hold, and there's an inescapable hum of energy that's been building all evening, but as tempting as this man is, I don't lean into it. "You might want to rein in that ego of yours, Dimple Dude. The jury's still out."

◆ ◆ ◆

Hours later, our bellies are full, and we've shared relationship war stories, funny child-rearing memories, and snarky banter. Whatever insecurities I had about my age, my clothes, or my Don King / Carrot Top hair are long gone. Declan has a way of making it impossible to focus on anything other than our private little party. The band is fantastic, playing a mix of upbeat and slow songs, and the patio feels more like a nightclub than a pub, with lights crisscrossing overhead as we dance to yet another song.

When the song ends and a slow one begins, Declan twirls me, drawing me into his arms. "You've got moves, Writer Girl."

"I haven't heard that in a long time."

He cocks a grin. "Keep hanging with me and you'll hear all sorts of things you're not used to."

My writer's brain grabs hold of that comment and sprints down Steamy Lane. He tightens his hold on me, one big hand spread across my lower back, the other slides under my hair, coming to rest just below my neck, keeping our bodies flush as we sway to the beat. He's big and broad and feels so good, every move stokes a long-forgotten fire. I must be losing it. This isn't even a date, and I'm not looking to hook up. But my greedy body didn't get the memo, and it's throwing a freaking celebration. I try not to think about how good it feels to be in his arms and how incredibly sexy he smells, but that's like trying not to breathe.

He presses his cheek to mine, the scratch of his scruff as enticing as the rest of him. "Do you like boats?"

His question catches me off guard. "*Um*, yes."

"What do you say we head over to mine?"

His voice is husky and seductive. *Is that code for wanting to hook up? Do I want it to be?* I close my eyes to try to focus, but I can't escape the feel of him, and in the space of a few seconds, my body says *yes*, and my brain doesn't argue. Maybe I'm misinterpreting, and he isn't thinking about anything other than showing off his boat. He is a fish peddler after all, and we were both clear about not wanting to get involved. *Yes, that has to be it.* I open my mouth to respond with something witty, but his hand slides lower, his fingers grazing the top of my ass. *Aw, hell*, he feels too good, and I hear myself saying "Sure" far too breathily.

He draws back, those heart-stopping dimples in full force as he takes my hand and heads over to the table. He drops a wad of cash on it, and in the next breath we're dashing away from the patio, heading for his truck like two teenagers who are definitely *not* just going to look at a boat.

I climb into the truck, asking myself again if I'm ready for this, and the answer teeters like a seesaw. I'm so nervous as we drive back toward Chatemup, I'm sure he can feel it or hear it as I ramble. "My father's friend had a boat when I was growing up. Sometimes we stayed on it."

"Yeah? What kind?" He's as cool and calm as ever.

"I don't know. It had a cabin. Does yours have a cabin?"

"Yeah, a big one." His phone rings, and he glances at the screen, uttering a curse. "Sorry, Nic, but I have to take this." He puts the phone to his ear. "What's up?"

He listens, and the light in his eyes fades, his jaw tightening again. I hear a female voice but can't make out what she's saying.

"Did you check—" He grips the steering wheel tighter. "Yeah. A'right, I'll be there in twenty." He ends the call. "Sorry, Nic, but I need to take a rain check."

"That's okay." I don't know if I'm relieved or disappointed, but he doesn't offer an explanation, and he's quiet for the rest of the drive back to my place.

◆ ◆ ◆

I pace my deck, feeling like my skin is too tight, and finally shoot off a group text to Rachel and Dani. *Mayday, mayday. Anyone around?* My phone immediately chimes with their responses.

Rachel: *Yes!*

Dani: *Are you okay?*

Me: *Yes, just . . . Declan and I went to listen to his friend's band tonight, and we had a great time.*

Rachel: *Yay! I'm totally Team Dimples.* She added a face with four hearts around it.

Dani: *Me too!* An eggplant and a peach emoji pop up, followed by *???*

Me: *We're supposed to be just friends, but we were slow dancing and I . . . felt things.* I tack on a shocked emoji.

Dani: *I bet you did.* Three more eggplants appear.

Me: *I'm not talking about that, but yes.* I add a laughing emoji. *I felt emotions I shouldn't.*

Rachel: *Did he feel it, too?*

Me: *I don't know. It felt like he did. He asked me to go see his boat, which felt a lot like, let's go someplace to be alone, but then he got a call and blew me off for whoever it was. It left me feeling weird. Feeling bad.*

Dani: *Who was it?!*

I hate the way I feel as I type, *I don't know. I heard a girl's voice.*

Dani: *Bastard!*

Rachel: *WTH?* An angry-faced emoji pops up.

Me: *He didn't seem happy about it.*

Rachel: *??? A friend in trouble? Sister? Mother?*

Me: *I don't know and it doesn't matter. This is why I don't want to get involved with anyone. I hate feeling like this. We had a great night, and he's an amazing guy. He listens, and jokes around, and he's so easy to be with, but then my stupid emotions got involved, and now I'm sitting here feeling like shit, wondering why he blew me off.*

Me: *It isn't like Declan did anything wrong. We weren't on a date!*

Rachel: *So what? It still hurts to be blown off. I'm sorry.*

Dani: *Want me to fly down and help you hide his body?*

I stop pacing and stare out at the water with knots in my stomach.

Rachel: *Are you there?*

Me: *Yes. Sorry. I hate this, and the thing is, I like him. I was totally cool just being friends, so why did I have to feel something and ruin it?*

Dani: *You didn't ruin anything. You finally put yourself out there and you were let down. Tell him how you feel.*

Me: *No way. What if he didn't feel anything and I'm totally off base?*

Rachel: *What did he say when he dropped you off?*

Me: *That he had a great time and was sorry to cut it short.*

Rachel: *It doesn't sound like you're overreacting. Why don't you sleep on it and see how you feel in the morning?*

Dani: *If he turns out to be a shithead, I can always make a Declan voodoo doll.*

When we were teenagers, Dani made a voodoo doll of a boy who ditched their date. That weekend he hurt his ankle and was out for the rest of the basketball season.

Rachel and I send laughing emojis.

We text for a while longer, and by the time we're done, I'm in a better mood, but those knots are still there. Painful reminders of the drama I don't need.

Chapter Fifteen

NICOLE

I wake to the chime of a text and glance at the clock: *6:03. Ugh.* Robbed of my last twelve minutes of sleep, I grab my phone and see a text from Declan. *Morning WG. Ready for a great writing day? Your boyfriend at Rise and Grind said you like things sweet and spicy in the morning. It's waiting for you on your deck.* It's hard to stay irritated when he's so damn charming.

With the promise of coffee, I turn off my alarm and climb out of bed. After a quick pit stop, I pad downstairs and see a to-go cup on the table on my deck. I head outside, shivering against the cool air in my sleeping shorts and T-shirt, and reach for the cup. "Come to Mama, you sweet hot thing."

"Good morning to you, too."

I spin around and see Declan standing by the steps with his own to-go cup. "Geez, you scared me. I didn't know you were out here."

"I told you there was something sweet and spicy waiting for you."

He's so damn likable, it doesn't even sound cheesy coming from him. His gaze slides down my body, leaving a trail of heat in its wake. *Damn it.*

"Aren't you adorable in all your morning glory." He brings out the big guns, revealing the dimples.

"You have a thing for messy-haired women?"

"I like your wild hair, Nic."

Why does that make me feel so good? "Is that why you're here? To see it at its wildest?"

"I bet we could have gotten it even wilder."

Whoa. I guess I wasn't misreading him.

He closes the distance between us. "I'm here because I couldn't give you apology coffee without an apology."

"Thank you, but you don't need to apologize."

"Yes, I do. Can we talk?"

"Sure." I'm curious about what he has to say. I hope he doesn't make up a ridiculous excuse.

He takes off his zip-up sweatshirt and hands it to me. "Mind putting this on?"

"It's okay. I'm not that cold."

"Just put the damn thing on. I have a lot to say, and you're distracting."

His words hit with a jolt of pleasure. I set down my phone and coffee and put on his sweatshirt. It's soft, and warm, and smells like him.

He pulls out a chair for me, and we both sit down. "Listen, Nic, I had a great time last night, and I really am sorry for cutting out early."

"I had a great time, too. But like I said, you don't have to apologize."

"That's not the only reason I'm apologizing. We went out as friends, and . . ." He looks out at the water for a minute, and when he meets my gaze, he's smiling, but his eyes are troubled. "Hell, I'm just going to lay it out there. You took me by surprise, Boots. I was attracted to you the first time we met. I mean, you're gorgeous, and you were so cute and flustered when you spilled coffee on me, but there's something deep and magnetic between us. I don't know if it burns so hot because we're two creative minds coming together, or because we've both been burned and we understand each other, or what. But every time I think about you, I get this rush of happiness. I'm sorry if it seemed like I was interrogating you, but I want to know everything about you, and if I wasn't talking, I'd have kissed the hell out of you."

I swallow hard, relieved I'm not alone in my attraction but still curious about the call that tore him away last night.

He holds my gaze. "Did you feel any of that?"

I'm surprised I don't want to hide my feelings from him. "Yes, I did."

"Good, because otherwise I just made an ass of myself." He smiles, but it's as tethered as my emotions are. "If we'd gone to my boat last night, I would have tried to kiss you, and if you were into it, then we'd have done a whole lot more. But that phone call woke me up, Nic." He sounds less passionate, more serious. "You're an incredible person, and as much as I want to explore what this is between us, you deserve a guy who can give you his attention for more than a few hours or a night of fun. Not someone whose life is a hot mess, like mine. I'm spread so thin, half the time I don't know if I'm coming or going."

Despite my resolve to avoid getting tangled up in a relationship, I'm disappointed. As I climb out from under those confusing feelings, I know this is for the best, but there's no escaping the emptiness boring into me at the prospect of not hanging out with him or sharing texts or joking around.

"It's okay, Declan. I appreciate your honesty."

"Do you? Because I'm not just making this up to let you down easy. Shit like my ex's basement flooding last night happens all the time."

"Is that why you left? To help her?"

"Yes, and the night we met at Russ and Marlo's, I left because she had another issue. And when I leave here, I've got to handle a mess my old man got into, so my younger brother Ethan doesn't have to deal with it. It never ends, Nic. When shit hits the fan, I clean it up, and I've got my own business to run. Miller's Seafood. That's why I left when we were brainstorming the other day. Chuck manages my delivery team, and he called to tell me that one of my employees got sick. We're short-staffed, and Chuck had interviews lined up, so I took over the driver's shift. What I'm trying to say is I can't be counted on for much more than fun on the fly."

His explanation should make me run in the other direction, but it's hard to not be drawn in by the selfless man he's revealing. And that's precisely why I need to shut down these feelings.

"The thing is, I love hanging out with you, Nic, and if you're willing, I would like to continue getting together as friends. But I know that's a lot to ask."

"Actually, I'm okay with just being friends. I don't need extra drama. My daughter gives me enough of that, and even though you didn't do anything wrong by helping your ex last night, it still felt crummy to get blown off and not know why, so this is better. I would miss you if you just disappeared from my life. But is everything okay with your father?"

"It will be. It's nothing I can't handle. We lost my mom two and a half years ago, and my father never fully recovered from it."

"I'm sorry to hear that. I know how much it hurts to lose someone you love. My dad and I were really close, and I was devastated when we lost him."

"I'm sorry about your father. I was close to my mom, too, but my father lost the person who had been by his side since he was fourteen. They were each other's first and only loves, and they beat the odds like they were put on this earth for each other."

"That's rare. I'm glad they had that kind of love."

He looks down at his hands. "Me too, but my old man kind of went off the rails after we lost her."

"What do you mean? Is he a drinker?"

He nods. "Unfortunately, and a gambler."

"That's a lot to deal with. Did he do those things before your mom passed away?"

"He wasn't a heavy drinker, and it's not like he's a sloppy drunk now. But he has his moments, and it makes him unreliable. His gambling was always part of our lives, but not in a bad way. He'd take us to the horse races or the racetrack when we were kids, and we'd make a day of it. It was always a big deal, and I have great memories of those times. I don't know if my mom kept him in check or if losing her is what broke him, but ever since she died, he's been a little lost. And as far as I know, there's only one other time he's been like this."

"When was that?"

Grief rises in his eyes. "When my younger brother Neil died."

"Oh, *Declan*. I'm so sorry." My throat thickens as the name registers. "You named your son for him?"

"Yeah." He leans his forearms on his legs, worrying his hands. "I joined the military after high school, so I wasn't here when it happened. My brother got drunk the weekend of his high school graduation and hit another car head-on, killing himself and the other driver."

My stomach sinks, and I put my hand over his. "I'm so sorry." I noticed he'd had only one drink last night, and now I understand why.

He clears his throat and sits up straighter. "It was a long time ago. Anyway, I get why my old man is having a hard time, although it didn't last this long when we lost Neil."

"Is he getting any help?"

He shakes his head. "You know what they say about old dogs. It's more like bailing him out and filling in when needed so Ethan doesn't have to pick up the slack. He's worked with our father for twenty years in our family's custom cabinetry business, and he has his hands full trying to keep the business afloat and taking care of his wife and kids. He's a hell of a good father and husband, and he doesn't need our old man's issues fucking that up."

"You really do have a lot on your plate, and I don't want to add to that. So don't feel any pressure to keep up our friendship if it's too much, and if you ever need an ear, I'm a pretty good listener."

His brows knit. "Our friendship is the best thing that's happened to me in years."

"Me too." As I say it, I realize the tether that held us back has shifted, and it seems to be binding us together.

"You're not pissed or feeling put off?"

"No, and if I were, I'd tell you."

He exhales with relief. "I was up half the night trying to figure out how to handle this. I really like you, Nic, and the thought of you not being in my life was killing me."

"I got a little scare of that myself when you first started talking."

He pushes to his feet, and I stand with him. "Get over here." He hauls me into an embrace. "You're awesome. Thanks for understanding."

He's big and warm and comforting, and once again I find myself trying not to notice how good it feels to be in his arms.

He makes a frustrated sound between a growl and a groan and steps back, jaw tight. "Maybe we should hold off on hugging for a few days."

I laugh softly and start taking off his sweatshirt, but he stops me with a hand on mine. "Keep it."

"I'm not keeping your sweatshirt."

"Then I'll get it another time. That whole messy-hair, fresh-faced thing you have going on is dangerous enough. Seeing the rest of you might do me in."

I've never once thought of myself as dangerous. I revel in that compliment as he heads off the deck and says, "Maybe you can work this into a book."

"Oh yeah? How's that?"

He glances over his shoulder, flashing a devastating grin. "The handsome fish peddler who got away."

He is too charming for his own good. "You mean the one with the ego that wouldn't quit?"

He laughs, and I watch him disappear around the side of the house. He carries so much weight on those broad shoulders, it's a wonder he's still standing.

As he drives off, I hold up my coffee cup and take a selfie. I send it to the group chat with Rachel and Dani, and type, *Dimples brought me coffee and apologized.* I add a smiling emoji with hearts around it. *He said he's attracted to me, but his life is a hot mess, which we all know I don't need. We've decided to continue hanging out as friends.*

Dani: *I knew he was into you!*

Rachel: *Friends with or without benefits?*

Me: *Without. Anything more would just be confusing.*

Rachel sends a sad-faced emoji.

Dani: *I'll send you a box of batteries until you two come to your senses.*

Rachel sends three laughing emojis.

I sit at the table, feeling a wave of relief and a tiny stab of regret.

Chapter Sixteen

NICOLE

I wondered if things would be weird between me and Declan after our talk, but it's been a week since his coffee apology, and if anything, our friendship has become stronger. His daily texts continue to brighten my days. We've also been sharing our daily trials and our triumphs, which is new, and I love having him to bounce things off. When Mackenzie went radio silent for a few days, I wanted to call just to hear her voice and know she was okay, but I didn't want to seem overbearing. It was Declan who convinced me to make the call. *You're her mother and you're footing her bill. She should never be too busy to respond to you.* I felt better after hearing her voice, even if she hasn't found a job yet.

My workdays passed in a whirlwind of half-written chapters, brainstorming at the café—once with Aspen and twice with Declan—afternoon walks on the beach with Evelyn, Maggie, and/or Aspen when I couldn't concentrate enough to sit at my computer, and an overall feeling of loving my life even if my writer's brain refuses to cooperate.

It's five thirty Thursday afternoon, and I've hit my daily concentration limit. I'm saving my manuscript when my phone rings with a call from my brother Kent. "Hey, Kent. What's up?"

"I was just thinking about you. Still loving beach life?"

"More than I ever imagined."

"Are you getting out at all, or holing up in your writer's cave twenty-four-seven?"

I shove my feet into my boots, picturing his dark brows slanting over serious dark eyes. "Actually, I just finished writing and catching up on emails, and I'm rewarding myself for staying at my desk all day with a walk into town to pick up dinner." I check to make sure my credit card is in my phone case and head outside. "There's a local haunt called the Wicked Whale I've been dying to check out. They're supposed to have the best fried clams."

"If a daily reward is what it takes to get you away from your keyboard, I'm all for it."

"I'm away from my keyboard *too* much. It's becoming a problem. My brain thinks I should be on vacation."

"I'm with your brain, sis. You work too hard."

"Says the computer geek who's up at all hours to work on ideas." I walk down the hill, enjoying the view of the water. "It's beautiful here. Want to switch to a video call so you can see the water?"

"Go for it." Kent lives in a dismal town in Ohio, with no views to speak of.

His handsome face appears on the screen as my seven-year-old niece, Jasmine, pipes up. "I want to say hi to Aunt Nic!" He lifts her onto his lap, and she beams from behind her messy dark curls. "Hi, Aunt Nic. Guess what!"

"What?"

"We're going to make chocolate cake, and I get to lick the bowl."

"Don't give Daddy the bigger spoon. He's a pig," I warn, and she giggles. "Want to see my beach?"

She nods, her curls bouncing around her cherubic face. I cross the street and turn around so I can see them and they can see the beach behind me.

"I wanna go there," Jazzie pleads.

"You want me to ship you off to Aunt Nic for a month?" my brother asks.

"Yes! *Please?*" she exclaims.

"We'll have to see if I can find a box big enough to fit you in."

"*Dad,*" she complains. "Bye, Aunt Nic!" With a wave, she disappears from the screen.

"She'd better come with a nanny. I've got a book to write."

"How's it coming along?"

"Not great but not terrible. I'll get there, and then I'll make it shine during my read-through." I head down the road toward town. "Brainstorming with my friends helps."

"How are Dani and Rach?"

"They're great, but I meant my friends here." I tell him about the people I've been hanging out with.

"Sounds like you found the community you were hoping for."

"I definitely have. Everyone is really nice." I tell him about my morning runs and afternoon walks and about going to the bar with Declan. "He's funny. You'd like him."

"Is that *interest* I'm hearing?"

"Yes, but *no.* He's pulled in a hundred directions. We're just friends, and as I've told you, I'm way too happy to risk messing that up for any guy. Especially one who calls his own life a hot mess."

"If anyone understands that, it's me." Kent has been divorced since Jazzie was a year old, when his wife not only left him but left town with another guy and broke his heart. He swears he'll never marry again. "Which reminds me, I talked to Tommy this morning. He's seeing a younger woman now. She's twenty-eight."

"From what Dani says, that's the new trend. *Daddy* vibes or something." As I say it, it dawns on me that Declan is nine years older than me, and even though we didn't hook up, I have no doubt we would have if we hadn't been interrupted. I guess I have no room to talk. "He'd better not tell Jer." Jerry is our oldest brother, a know-it-all. When he was thirty, he married a twenty-three-year-old. They divorced a year later. Now he's married to a woman his own age, and they're proud parents of a lovely son and daughter, but he's still quick to rant about age gaps in relationships.

The umbrellas in front of the Rise and Grind come into view. "Look how cute my new town is." I turn the camera so he can see the shops, then turn it back.

"I wish I had the time to bring Jazz out to see your new place this summer, but I'm slammed."

"There's always next summer."

"Definitely. Maybe we can get Jer and Tommy to come, too."

"We'll need more space for a family reunion, and Mom will want to come." I spoke to my mother yesterday, and she told me she had a new friend named Janice whom she met at the grocery store of all places. She seems to really like her. "Have you talked with her since I left?"

"Yeah, a few days ago. She seems fine. She was having dinner with a new friend."

"Good. I feel guilty for leaving her alone this summer."

"She's a big girl, Nic. Don't waste your energy on guilt. I'm glad you're doing well. Are you being safe?"

"Of course."

"Still got that Taser I gave you?"

Always the protector. "I don't need it here. I don't even lock my doors."

"Tell me you're kidding."

"*Dad*, can we make the cake now?" Jazzie asks from off camera.

"Go," I say. "It was good talking to you. Love you."

After we end the call, I head down a side street to the Wicked Whale, which looks like a dive, with picnic tables out front and a walk-up counter for ordering. The line is a dozen or more people deep, and after waiting forever to order, I'm told it'll be another half hour to forty-five minutes before my meal is ready. Aspen and Marcus swear this place is worth the wait, and I hope they're right. Even if the food isn't great, I love being out and experiencing something new.

Or, as Declan would say, I'm on an adventure.

The picnic tables are all occupied, so I stand. I catch sight of a guy who looks just like the hero in the last book I wrote. I turn away, stifling a laugh as I text Rachel and Dani. *I'm picking up dinner and I think I see Alex Applegate!*

Rachel: *I'm on my way!* She sends a drooling emoji.

Dani: *Get a pic!*

Me: *I'm not taking a pic like a creeper, but trust me. Six feet of clean-cut hotness, midforties, dark blue polo, khaki shorts, and loafers!*

Dani: *LOAFERS? It's him!*

Rachel: *Red alert. Billionaire on board.*

I laugh and steal another glance, catching him watching me. He walks over. I feel like a kid caught with my hand in a candy jar and pocket my phone, futilely trying to act like I wasn't gossiping about him.

"That smile says you're up to no good."

"Does it?" He's even more handsome up close. His hair is the color of walnuts, with a few strands of silver. His eyes are green, and highly amused, and he has a killer smile. "I was just thinking that you look like someone I know."

"Do I?"

"Well, not really someone I know, but someone I created."

"Now you've piqued my interest. *Created?*"

"I dabble in writing, and he was a hero in a story I wrote. It's silly. He's a businessman who's also into extreme sports."

"You're not that far off. I'm a mechanical engineer, and I'm into mountain biking, mountain climbing, and I've done several triathlons."

Holy crap. A mechanical engineer who is into extreme sports? That was another hero I created a few years ago. "That's an interesting combination."

"You can dress up a thrill seeker, but you can never tame one. With those legs, you must be into some kind of sports."

You noticed my legs? "Not really. I run, but that's about it."

"Where do you run?"

"Just through town in the morning. It's a good way to clear my head and start my day."

"Really? I sit out front at the Rise and Grind every morning for coffee."

"I go at six thirty. You're probably still sleeping."

"An early riser who dabbles in writing. I like it. What kind of stories do you write?"

"Romance." I ready myself to hear a cheesy comment.

"That's different. I know writers but none that write romance. Historical or contemporary?"

Pleasantly surprised not to have to battle the *cheese*, I say, "Contemporary."

"All about the here and now. Interesting." He studies me for a second. "Where do you get your inspiration?"

"Look around us. Inspiration is everywhere. Take that couple, for example." I nod toward a couple holding hands at a picnic table. "Are they new lovers entranced by the mere sight of each other, or childhood best friends reunited for the first time in a decade?" I motion to the table next to them, where a man is typing on his phone while two kids run circles around the table and a woman who is probably their mother tries to wrangle them. "Are they on the brink of divorce, or is she covering while he negotiates his next big deal?"

I lower my voice. "See the way she's eyeing the guy at the next table? My guess is she's the kids' single aunt, and the guy with the phone is their father who barely has time to breathe with two kids underfoot. Maybe he lost his wife in a car accident and feels like he can't keep his head above water, so his sister helps him out."

"You see all that, and all I see is a couple waiting for their dinner."

I shrug. "My brain is a crazy place."

"Intriguing is more like it. I'm Cory, by the way."

"Nicole. It's nice to meet you. Do you live here?"

"My family has a house about ten minutes from town, but I live in Connecticut. I just got back from a monthlong project in Japan."

As we talk, he tells me about his travels, the mountains he's climbed, and the races he's taken part in. He's not as easygoing or as handsome as Declan. I immediately kick myself in the ass for comparing them and force Dimple Dude out of my head to concentrate on the great guy before me whose life does not seem to be a hot mess.

We talk until his food is ready, and he waves as he drives away in his SUV. I feel a little high, and that feeling remains as I walk home and run into Maggie and Aspen crossing the street to Evelyn's house.

"Hey, baby doll." Aspen hugs me and looks down at my bag. "I see you finally got to the Wicked Whale."

"I did, and I met the most interesting man while I was waiting for my food."

Maggie hooks arms with me. "Then you must come have a frozen margarita with us at Evelyn's and tell us all about him. She's got a pitcher waiting."

A few minutes later I'm sitting on Evelyn's deck, margarita in hand, with three sets of eager eyes on me as I tell them about the hero lookalike I've just met.

"Cory? I don't know of a Cory. Are you sure that's his name?" Evelyn asks.

"That's what he said." I pop a fried clam into my mouth.

"It's not ringing a bell for me, either," Aspen says. "I'll have to ask Marcus if he knows of him. But he obviously caught our girl's eye."

"Of course he did," Maggie says. "It sounds like he's smart and has a good sense of humor."

Not as good as Declan's. Ugh. Shut up about him. I take a gulp of icy margarita, hoping to freeze thoughts of Declan away.

"Did you get Cory's number?" Evelyn asks, stealing a clam.

"No, and he didn't ask for mine. I'm not really looking anyway, so it doesn't matter."

"Fate will take its course," Maggie says.

"The way Lady Fate keeps dropping random guys in my path, I'm pretty sure *she's* had too many margaritas."

Aspen pats my hand. "The universe always knows what's best."

Then can someone please tell me why I can't stop thinking about my brawny, dangerously dimpled friend?

Chapter Seventeen

NICOLE

I'm pumped during my morning run, singing along to "Good as Gold" and ready for a fantastic writing day. Declan texted late last night, and I told him about meeting Cory. He seemed genuinely happy for me, which kind of bothered me, even though it shouldn't have. But as with all things, he made a joke, calling my *great guy* a novice for letting me get away without asking for my number, and we had a good laugh about it.

I sprint up the hill toward Rise and Grind, and as I cross the street, my heart nearly stops. Cory is sitting at a table in front of the coffee shop. This guy is either a stalker or a true-life hero who goes the extra mile to get his girl.

I'm sweaty, and I try to catch my breath as I slow to a walk and pull out my AirPods, eyeing him. "Did you just happen to get up early today?"

"I had a good incentive. I figured I'd tag along on your run and we could get to know each other better. If that's okay with you, of course." He pushes to his feet. He's wearing running shorts and sneakers and looks mighty rugged without his sharp casual wear.

I'm impressed that he doesn't expect me to interrupt my run to chat with him. "I don't run very fast, and you've got much longer legs than me. You might get bored at my pace."

"I have a feeling nothing could be boring with you." He motions to the sidewalk ahead of me. "Shall we?"

He just might be an extra-mile guy after all. *Okay, universe, do your thing.*

We run through town, and as we circle down by the water, we talk about my work and his, and he schools me in the cultural differences between the United States and the places he's traveled. We take a back road down to the marina, sharing opinions on books and movies. As we walk along the docks, he tries to goad me into debating politics. I'd rather eat tar.

"Sorry, but I can't have that kind of negativity in my head while I write."

"You're not writing at the moment," he goads lightheartedly.

"But I will be."

"Nic—"

"*No*, Cory. There will be absolutely no political discussions coming out of my mouth, so zip it."

We head over to the harbormaster's office to get water from the dispenser and stand out front while we drink it. I'm having such a good time, I don't even care that I should be writing.

"Okay, so let me get this straight." He tosses his paper cup into the trash. "You're not into scary movies, but you like suspense. You don't like flying, but you'll do it if there's no other option, and you *love* talking about politics."

"Almost nailed it." I throw away my cup.

He flashes a smile. "So, tell me, Nic. How do you feel about married men?"

It takes me a second to realize he's not kidding, and all at once I remember my brother's devastation after his wife cheated, and I recall the pain in Declan's eyes all these years later, when he told me about his wife straying, and I promptly lose my shit. "Are you fucking kidding me? You left your wife in bed at six thirty in the morning to meet a woman you shouldn't have been talking to in the first place? What did you think would happen? You'd charm my pants off, and I'd run around with you behind your wife's back?" I get in his face, poking his chest, not giving a damn about the two fishermen watching us. "Let me tell you something, buddy. It's low-life, egotistical assholes like you that give men a bad name."

He looks at the fishermen and holds up his hands in surrender. "Hey, I just wanted to be friends. Nobody said anything about cheating."

"Is that the way you're going to play this off? *Great.* Let's get your wife on the phone and ask her how she feels about you getting up extra early and waiting at the coffee shop hoping to see me this morning."

The blood drains from his face.

I lower my voice to a dead calm. "You know that sick feeling you have right now? That icy fear running through your veins? Remember it the next time you try to pick up a woman, you sick fuck. I can't believe I wasted my writing time on you."

I spin on my heel, and as I start running toward the road, one of the fishermen hollers, "You tell him, sweetheart!"

I make it home in record time, and I'm pacing my patio trying to cool down, when my phone chimes with a text.

Declan: *How does it feel to be the hot girl? Still dreaming of Mr. Perfect from last night?*

I start to text, but I'm too angry and I call him instead. He answers on the first ring.

"Hey, Boots."

"Mr. Perfect ended up being Mr. *Married.* The asshole."

"Wait," he says sharply. "I thought you didn't give him your number."

"I *didn't*, but he was waiting for me at the coffee shop when I went running. He was sitting there in running clothes, like he *didn't* just leave his wife in bed to try to pick me up. I just got back. I wasted an hour and a half with that no-good dirtbag before he asked how I felt about married men."

"He asked you that? What a douche."

"Yes! I guess I should feel lucky that he told me before I wasted any more time on him."

"I'd like to get my hands on that fucker. I hope you gave him hell."

I scoff and tell him exactly what I said to Cory. "You have the dirt on everyone around here. You could've warned me."

"Hey, I don't even know the guy. Maybe you should stop picking up every man you see."

"I'm *not* picking up guys. I swear, coming to Chatemup has made me some kind of hot mess magnet."

"Well, when you put it that way . . ."

The amusement in his voice makes me smile despite my anger. "I'm so mad. I'm sorry. You don't deserve to bear the brunt of my bad morning. I gotta get off."

"If you need a hand with that, I'm happy to help."

I laugh, which I'm sure was his intent. "Goodbye, Declan."

Chapter Eighteen

DECLAN

The line goes dead, and I stare at the phone. "Man, that woman is something else."

"Who's got you smiling like that?" Ethan asks as he carries a cabinet into his client's kitchen. Our father failed to tell Ethan he promised to have the cabinets installed yesterday, and since he is in Boston today, gambling no doubt, and their other employees were already booked with installations, Ethan called me to help out.

"My friend Nic. She just gave some married guy hell for trying to pick her up."

"Is that the author you told me about?"

"Yeah." I start setting up our tools. "She's a trip."

"She must be. I can't remember the last time you mentioned a woman. So? What's up between you two?"

"Nothing. We're friends."

"Uh-huh." Ethan is five years younger than me and the spitting image of our brother, Neil, with wavy hair a shade lighter than mine, our mother's hazel eyes, and our father's dimples. He crosses his arms and lowers his chin, looking at me the way our old man used to when we were kids and he knew I wasn't telling him the truth. "But you want there to be more?"

"It wouldn't matter if I did. She's twice divorced with a twenty-year-old daughter, who, from what I can tell, is a handful. She doesn't need me fucking up her life or letting her down."

"Dec, what are you talking about? You never let anyone down."

That's a load of bullshit, but there's no need to rehash old arguments. I head out to the truck, hoping he'll drop it.

When I return with another cabinet, he's leaning over the blueprints. He straightens, rolling his shoulders back, and I know by the set of his jaw that he's not done talking.

"Dec, you don't have to keep putting yourself out there and bailing Dad out. You can let him deal with the consequences if he doesn't want to get help."

"And *what*? Let some asshole bookie beat the shit out of our old man or take his truck? His house?" Same conversation, different day. "Or maybe you think I should let your family pay the price and watch your business go under. That's *not* happening, little brother."

Ethan's eyes narrow.

"What?" I bark.

His expression softens. "I appreciate everything you do for us."

"I *know* you do. I'm not complaining. Just stay off my back about Dad."

"It's not just Dad, Declan."

I glower at him. He knows Lindsay is not up for discussion. "Let's just get this shit done so I can get over to my office."

"Fine, but I need you to know I'm bidding on a big job over in Rockland. If I get it, I'll be able to hire more guys and get the company in a better financial position. Greg is doing great, and if we get this contract, I'll have him lead that team. If you have more buddies who need work, I may be able to help out."

Greg is an old military buddy of mine. He was living in Georgia and lost his job and the place he was renting. He was spiraling downhill fast when he called me. Normally I'd have hired him myself, but it was winter, and jobs thin out in the winter.

"That's great, but just concentrate on getting the business where it needs to be and keeping your head above water. You don't need to create jobs for my buddies." My phone chimes. I open a message from Nicole and find a picture of her holding up a sign that says *Sorry*, followed by another message bubble. *Sorry for breathing fire. My brother and my adventure buddy were both cheated on, and I guess my claws came out.*

"It's a shame you're so stubborn," Ethan says as he walks past. "That smile looks good on you."

It feels good, too, and it'll have to be enough.

I wipe the grin off my face. "Let it go."

"A'right, but you're no spring chicken. Your birthday is coming up, and you'll be a year closer to that downhill slide." He motions with his hand like it's sliding downhill.

"Are you trying to annoy the shit out of me today?"

"Nah." He flashes a shit-eating grin. "We both know I don't have to try."

Chapter Nineteen

NICOLE

"I'm *trying* to get a job, Mom, but nobody is hiring."

I pinch the bridge of my nose as I head into the bathroom to turn on the shower. "Kenzie, it's been a month. Half the summer is over and you can't find work anywhere? Retail? Fast food? You *need* to be earning money."

"I know. Are you in the bathroom?" She sounds annoyed.

"Yes. I'm getting ready to take a shower."

"Why are you showering at six at night?"

"If you must know, I tried a new schedule today and started writing early and went for a late run. Why does it matter? We need to talk about your lack of—"

"It's *not* lack of determination, Mom. I'm applying, but there are no jobs. Why can't you understand that? Look, if you don't want to buy me a dress for Nolan's wedding, I'll borrow one from somebody."

I close my eyes and count to ten. The last thing I want is for my daughter to show up in someone else's dress to her ex-stepbrother's wedding. "No, it's fine. Just put it on the credit card."

"Okay, can I get heels, too? Mine are all scuffed up."

"Yes, but when you swing by the university to buy your books for the fall, you should ask if they have any summer job openings."

"There aren't any. I looked, and I already got my books."

"You did? That's a plus."

"I'm trying, and I promise I'll keep looking for a job, but I've got to go. I just got back from yoga and need to shower before Macie gets here to go shopping. I'll send you pictures of the dress I choose. Love you!"

She hasn't gotten a job, but she never misses a yoga class. At least that money wasn't wasted.

I take a long hot shower, trying to drain the frustration from my body. My phone chimes as I'm drying off. Declan's name flashes on the screen. I grab it, feeling a little guilty for being relieved that the message is from him and not my daughter. He's become a bright light in my life. A trusted friend who is always around. Not physically, but he's always on my mind, and he texts so often, I know I'm on his, too.

Declan: *Hey, Boots. What are you up to?*

Me: *Just got out of the shower. Why?*

Declan: *Put some clothes on. I can't think straight knowing you're naked.*

As I search for a funny GIF to send him, another text pops up.

Declan: *A baggy sweat suit would be nice.*

I switch gears and send a GIF of a sexy girl in a minidress. *Sorry, this is my after-shower outfit.*

Declan: *With friends like you, who needs phone sex?* A heart-eyed and a flame emoji pop up.

"I do." I send an eye roll emoji.

Declan: *Feel like hanging out?*

"Always," I say as I type, *Sure. What're you thinking?* I head into my bedroom, and his reply rolls in as I pull on my shorts.

Declan: *Something chill. Rough afternoon.* Another message pops up. *Bonfire at your place?*

Me: *Sounds great. I have white zinfandel and beer.*

Declan: *Want me to pick up pizza and Snickers?*
Practically salivating, I type, *Yes! No anchovies.*

◆ ◆ ◆

Flames from the bonfire dance in the breeze as Declan and I kick back with our feet up on the edge of the firepit and scarf down pizza. He's wearing a dark green Henley that hugs his broad chest and brings out the green flecks in his eyes. He looks more delicious than the pizza as we talk about the first steamy scene for my book.

"All I'm saying is that you could have him do her in the woods and be done with it." He takes a bite of pizza.

"That does *not* sound romantic for a first time."

"What's not romantic about it?"

"*Do her in the woods?* It's winter. They'll freeze to death."

"Where is your sense of adventure? If the guy is not a total tool, he'll prepare ahead of time and make it so romantic, her clothes will melt off. Imagine this: He goes out earlier in the day and picks the perfect spot where they'll be out of sight from passersby and can see the moon through the trees, and because he knows his girl likes to keep things spicy, he picks a spot where if she's not careful, those passersby will hear her."

"Okay, I'm with you." He's good at this.

"He sets up blankets and pillows and prepares the bonfire so all he has to do is light it. But it's not just a regular fire. He adds scented fire starters, so when he lights it, it smells like cinnamon or pine or whatever she likes."

"*Wait.* Scented fire starters? Are they a thing? I've never heard of them."

He scoffs. "And you call yourself a romance writer?"

I grab two more slices of pizza, handing him one. "How do *you* know about them?"

"I was in the military. I know everything there is to know about wilderness survival." He takes a bite of pizza.

"The military doesn't teach about scented fire starters."

"You don't know that." He's not even trying to stifle his grin.

"Yes, I do. I've known plenty of military men. Let me guess, you've just described your go-to move with women. Do you throw them over your shoulder like a caveman and then try to woo them with scented fires before you pillage them in the woods?"

"*No*, but that's hot. I bet you'd like it, wouldn't you?"

"I'm not telling you what I like. You won't even tell me how you know about scented fire starters."

He leans closer, lowering his voice. "I'll tell you if you admit to thinking it would be hot to be carried off by the man of your dreams and ravaged in the woods."

"Not happening." I *chomp* on my pizza.

"Think about it, Nic. Your back is against a tree, and it's rough, and it hurts a little, but not enough to push his hard body away, because you secretly like a little pain with your pleasure. It's winter, and your skin is chilled, but when he kisses you, it's rough and possessive, and you're burning up from the inside out, desperate for more. But he doesn't just undress you. He tears off your clothes like he's been thinking of nothing but how you'll feel and how you'll *taste* for days."

Holy shit. Has he been reading my books?

"And then his hands and mouth are all over you, and you're wet and writhing against the tree, trying to get him naked, but he grabs your wrists and holds them over your head, refusing to strip until he's pleasured you so thoroughly, your legs give out."

I picture Declan doing those things to me, and I try to swallow, but my mouth has gone bone dry. I try to forget the sound of him saying those dirty things, but it's already taken root and playing on repeat. *Nonononono.*

He sits back, grinning coyly, as if he can read my thoughts. "Bootsy, your cheeks are rosy."

"Shut up. It's from the fire." I finish my wine and put the rest of my pizza back in the box.

"Those flames you're feeling aren't caused by the fire, darlin'. Admit it—you'd be into that."

I have never wished I could pull off a lie more than I do right now, and I know with great certainty it's not even worth trying. "Okay, *fine*. With the right guy, it could be hot." I refill my glass and take a gulp. "What were we talking about, anyway?"

"You getting hot and bothered in the woods."

I swat his arm and laugh. "We were not. We were talking about scented fire starters, so give it up. How do you know about them?"

"Oh." He shrugs. "My sister-in-law makes them."

"Seriously? You couldn't just tell me that?"

"And miss the fun of seeing you all riled up?" His expression turns wicked. "Not a chance."

And he thinks *I'm* dangerous? He's the apple to Eve's hunger.

I set down my glass and point at him. "Don't you ever do that to me again. It's been a long time since I've been with a guy, and apparently I'm running on a hair trigger."

He cocks a brow. "I could help you alleviate some of that pressure."

God, yes. Did he short-circuit my brain? There will be no alleviating. "What happened to just being friends?"

"We are. I was helping you with a scene. You're the one who got all hot and bothered."

"Ohmygod. We are *not* talking about this anymore. You said you had a rough day. That seems like a safer subject. Why was it rough?"

He lifts a brow. "Not for the reason I would've liked."

I stare at him, unamused.

He laughs. "Okay, okay. I just feel like a shitty dad today."

"Why? Did something happen?"

"I got a call from Eric." His expression turns serious. "He's a great kid. He's responsible and smart as a whip. Much smarter than me, or so I thought, and he's got a great job as a financial analyst. He works his ass off."

"Sounds like he learned from the best."

"That's the problem. He took on a second job working part-time at a gym so he can help his girlfriend of six months, Kate, pay for school."

"That's a lot of responsibility for him to take on so soon."

"Yeah. We had words about it today, and it did not go well. All I want is for my kids to have things easier than I did, but he's following in my footsteps in every way. I won't talk down my kids' mother, but she's not exactly self-sufficient, and I worry he's setting himself up to end up in my shoes."

"I hear you loud and clear on wanting better for your kids. At least he's working. He could be like Kenzie and let you foot the bill for his social life without ever giving it a second thought."

"The hell with that. I'd never allow it."

"It's not that easy. She's had two broken families, and that's my fault, so I feel guilty, and I want her to be happy. I should probably crack down on her, but I also feel like I shouldn't have to. She *knows* how hard I've worked her whole life. When I was her age, I was married with a child, and my life was all about pinching pennies and making the right decisions. I just don't get it. I keep waiting for her to come into her own. I know she'll be great at whatever she wants to do, but she'll never get a job if she doesn't gain some real work experience."

"You should've brought her here for the summer. I could have put her to work."

"Now, that would be something. The term *fish peddler* would send her running for the hills. Hey, is your other son single?"

"You're a matchmaker now?" He looks amused.

"Well, your boys like to pay, and my girl likes to spend. It seems like it could work."

He laughs. "Neil is a good man. He's an architect, and as stable as they come."

"See? Kenzie could learn something from him."

"She could learn something, all right. Neil has sabotaged every relationship he's ever had, and I'm pretty sure that's a direct result of my marriage to his mother."

"Uh-oh. I'm sorry to hear that. Have you talked to him about it?"

"You can't tell kids shit these days."

"I'm not sure parents ever could. So . . . we've *both* screwed up our kids?"

He holds up his bottle. "Here's to shitty parenting."

"No. I refuse to accept that. We love our kids, and we've tried to raise them right." I lift my glass. "Here's to doing the best we can with what we've got."

We clink bottle to glass and drink. Declan sits back, eyeing me with a contented expression. "This is pretty great, Writer Girl."

"What is?"

"Hanging with you. You make everything better. You've only lived here for, what? A month?"

"It'll be a month on Monday." I'm surprised he knew that.

"This has been the best month I've had in a long damn time."

"Me too," I say softly, thinking about how true it is.

"What are you doing this weekend?" he asks.

"Writing and *not* meeting married men."

"That's a step in the right direction. The Fourth is Tuesday. Want to grab dinner and watch the fireworks together?"

"I wish I could, but Maggie's brother and two of her friends are coming into town. I promised I'd have dinner with them. We're going down to the beach to watch the fireworks with everyone from Oyster Run afterward. Why don't you meet us there?"

"Maybe I'll do that."

"You should. It'll be fun."

We chat about the Fourth and a dozen other things.

"I have to ask you a *very* important question," he says.

"Okay." I take a bite of a Snickers.

"What do you think about Oreos?"

I gag, making us both laugh.

"How about Girl Scout cookies?"

"Don't get me started on Girl Scout cookies. They're second only to Snickers, and I would like to start a petition so they'll be sold door to door all year long."

"I'd sign that."

"I bet we could make an online petition and get thousands of signatures. It sucks that they only sell them once a year. Although they do sell them at Dollar General all year long, but they're always sold out. Do you even have Dollar General here? Are there Girl Scouts in Chatemup?"

"No Dollar General, and yes, we have a few Girl Scouts. What would you say if I told you I knew where we could get our hands on several boxes?"

"I'd say if you're lying to get me excited just so you can let me down in some cruel joke, I will slap those dimples silly."

He laughs. "I can't lie worth shit."

"Then let's go get them! I don't care if I have to pay twenty bucks a box."

"This is a covert operation. Money won't do you any good, and we can't go in guns blazing."

I'm getting excited. He's so fun! "Okay. Where are they?"

"I'll take you there. Do you own anything black?"

"Like boots?"

"Clothes, boots, a hat?"

"I moved here with one suitcase for the summer. I have combat boots, and I have your hoodie. *Wait!* I have black running pants, too."

"Go change. Then we'll swing by my place."

Twenty minutes later we park in front of his cottage. "Stay here." He climbs out of the truck and slams the door. The visor drops as he runs inside. There's a picture on the visor held in place with a rubber band. I move in for a closer look. It's taken from behind the branch of a tree, partially occluding the right side of a road. On the left are two young boys, maybe nine or ten years old, wearing flannel shirts and jeans. One boy is sitting on a suitcase, wearing a baseball cap. The other is standing behind him, wearing a backpack and a camouflage fishing hat, his pitch-black curls poking out from beneath it. They're holding fishing rods, and their left hands are outstretched, thumbs extended. I realize they're hitchhiking.

Declan bolts out the front door, and I quickly move back to my seat. He's dressed in all black and holding up two black knit hats. He gets into the truck, pushes the visor up, like it's a habit. "Put this on." As we put on the hats, he says, "Look at me."

His voice is full of hushed excitement, and it's contagious. He starts smearing something under my eyes. "What is that?"

"Camouflage."

"Are we robbing a bank?"

"Something like that." He smears it on my forehead and cheeks, and when he finishes, he does his own face.

I'm bursting with nervous excitement as he drives to a quiet neighborhood and parks by the curb. We get out of the truck, and he takes my hand, speaking in that adrenaline-inducing hushed tone. "Stay with me, and keep your voice down." He holds my hand tight as we jog into a backyard.

"Whose house is this?" I whisper.

He doesn't answer and runs into the next yard. There's a couple sitting on the deck. Declan waves. "How's it going?"

"Cookie run?" the man asks.

"You know it."

"Bring me a box, or I'll rat you out," the woman yells.

"Damn neighbors," Declan grumbles. "Stay low." We bend at the waist, and he tugs me into another yard and runs toward the back of the house. He flattens himself against it, and I do the same.

"Whose house is this?"

"Ethan's."

"Can't you just ask him for cookies?" I whisper.

"You don't know Ethan." We creep along the back of the house to the garage, and he holds a finger to his lips, then takes something long and metal out of his pocket and picks the lock.

"You're breaking and entering. That's a felony."

"We're not going to get caught."

"How often do you do this?" I whisper as we walk into the dark garage.

"As often as he buys them." He holds up his finger again.

I follow him on tippy-toes to the far side of the garage. He climbs up a ladder and pulls down a box from the top shelf. I barely register a two-by-four with a padded bar swinging down from the ceiling until it smacks Declan in the back, sending him flying off the ladder. I see it in slow motion as Declan yells, "Booby trap! Save yourself!" The box falls to the floor, and cookie boxes scatter as he lands on a pile of tarps.

I rush over, adrenaline coursing through my veins. "Are you okay?"

"Go, go, *go!*" he hollers.

"I can't leave you!"

He's tossing boxes of cookies at me. "It's a trap! Save the cookies!"

I grab as many boxes as I can and run for the door as the lights turn on and his brother storms outside holding a rifle. I stop on the lawn like a deer caught in headlights, my arms full of his cookie boxes. "I'm sorry. Don't shoot. I'm really not a thief!"

Ethan's arms fly up, and he yells, "Victory is mine!"

Declan sprints past him with an armful of cookie boxes, shouting, "Like hell it is!" He lowers his shoulder and barrels into me, tossing me over his shoulder like I'm a sack of potatoes, and sprints across the yard. I'm clinging to the boxes as he tosses one toward the neighbors on the deck, who are roaring with laughter, just like we are.

"I'll get you, you bastard!" Ethan hollers.

"I am the master!" Declan shouts as he books across another lawn.

When we reach the truck, he throws open the door and dumps me in, shoving me over so he'll fit. We're doubled over in hysterics as he starts the engine and floors it.

"Was that a gun?" I shout.

"A *water* gun!"

That only makes us laugh harder.

"You were awesome, Boots! How many boxes did we get?"

I try to count them, but I'm laughing too hard. Tears blur my vision, and I fall against his side, feeling like a kid again. "A lot!" I tear open a box and hand him a Thin Mint. He leans over and bites half of it right out of my hand.

"You eat the rest, Bootsy. You earned it."

A few minutes later we're at the beach, sitting in the back of his truck with several open boxes of cookies between us, chowing down as we watch the waves roll in. "Nothing is better than Samoas." I pop the rest of a cookie into my mouth.

He holds up a Thin Mint. "Those don't beat the sleek look and deliciousness of these, but they're a close second."

"We can agree to disagree, and I will be happy to do a taste test and reassess." I grab a Thin Mint. "You realize your brother will forever think of me as a thief."

"Or the coolest chick on the planet. His wife won't even get involved in our cookie wars."

I'm still reveling in *coolest chick on the planet.* "Why not?"

"I don't know. She just doesn't."

"Do you like her?"

"Annie? Yeah. She's a great mom, and she adores Ethan. They have two little girls: Mia, who's eight, and Ellie, who's six. They think their uncle Dec is the bomb, by the way."

"As well they should. I bet you teach them all sorts of bad things."

"Have you been talking to Annie?" He bumps me with his shoulder and grabs another cookie.

"How long has this cookie war gone on?"

"A long time." Declan finishes his cookie and gazes out at the water. "Neil and I started it when we were kids. I was probably around eleven, so he'd've been nine, and Ethan was six."

"I bet your parents had their hands full raising three mischievous boys."

"They did, but my mom was smart. When we'd fight, she'd say, *You boys work it out or don't, but I don't want to hear about it.*"

"My mom used to open the back door and tell my brothers to take it to the yard. As the oldest, did you automatically win every fight?"

"You'd think so, but no. Neil was a clever kid, and Ethan's fucking brilliant. We didn't have a lot of money, and Girl Scout cookies were like gold. We'd fight over them like our lives depended on them, so my mother started buying three boxes. One for each of us, and when they were gone, that was it. We wouldn't get more until the next year."

He grabs another cookie. "One year, right before we got our cookies, Neil broke my fishing rod. It was an accident, but I was pissed. So I stole his cookies. Neil, being the clever kid he was, faked being sick the next day and stayed home from school. While I was gone, he ransacked my room and found the cookies. He took his back and stole mine, so that night, after he was asleep, I snuck in and reclaimed them. Mine and his. You can see where this is going."

"All I can picture is young Dimple Dude stewing in a dark bedroom, plotting his next attack."

"You wouldn't be wrong."

"So you just kept it up, year after year?"

"Yeah. Ethan realized what we were doing, and the next year, the little bastard stole our stashes."

"Go, Ethan. Did he hold you up and threaten you with a water gun?"

"No. He snuck in while we were out after school and ate *all* our cookies."

"Smart boy."

Declan eats another cookie and shakes his head. "Not so smart. He was a spindly little guy and ended up sick to his stomach. Plus, we were pissed, and we gave him hell. Once the cookies are eaten, there was no more game."

"You mean you'd steal them and *not* eat them?"

"It sounds stupid, but we'd keep the game going for months. It became the three of us against each other, and it grew to booby traps and better hiding places. It kept us close, you know? Gave us something that was ours."

"That's not stupid. I couldn't do it. I love cookies too much not to eat them, but I love the idea of it." I reach for another cookie and stop short. "*Wait.* We shouldn't be eating these, right?"

"Yes, we should. The game has evolved into finders keepers." He hands me a Tagalong. "We stopped not eating them after Neil died. It just wasn't the same."

"But you kept playing the game?"

He shakes his head. "Not for a long time. It was Ethan who started it again after my son Neil was born. I was home from the military on break, and Lindsay had just bought Girl Scout cookies. I went to get one, and inside the empty box was a note that said, *Game on, sucker.* We've been doing it ever since. But we still haven't beat Neil's last, and best, hiding place."

"Where was that?"

"In the damn pantry." He grins. "Told you he was clever."

"You must miss him like crazy. I don't talk with my brothers often, but knowing I can gives me great comfort. I can't imagine not having that."

Sadness rises in his eyes. "Not a day passes when I don't think of him or hear him give me shit about something. Ethan looks just like him, so every time I see him, I also see Neil, or what I think he'd look like as an adult."

He pulls out his wallet and withdraws an old, creased picture of three young boys walking single file through thigh-high grass. "This is us, the year we started the cookie wars."

The boy in the front is carrying a net over his shoulder, his brown curls blowing with the breeze. Ethan is behind him with the same brown curls, caught midstride, like he's trying hard to keep up. He's a good foot shorter than his brothers. The grass comes nearly to his waist, and he's carrying a white bucket. Bringing up the rear is the tallest of the three, wearing cargo pants and a camouflage fishing hat, pitch-black curls poking out from beneath it. He's carrying a fishing rod that rests on his shoulder, and he's the only one looking at the camera. I'd know those dark eyes and deep dimples anywhere.

"Neil and I sat in our treehouse planning that fishing expedition all morning," Declan says thoughtfully.

"Earlier, when we stopped by your house and you went inside, I saw the picture on your visor. Is it you and Neil?"

He nods. "We were eight and ten, running away to start a fishing business. That was always the plan."

"What about Ethan?"

"He's always wanted to work with our father in his custom cabinetry business. I wanted to join the military and get the bad guys, and the plan was after one tour, I'd get out and Neil and I were going to open our own company. *Miller Bros Seafood*." He laughs almost silently and runs his finger over the image of the boy leading them through the grass. "He was my best friend."

The emotion in his voice draws tears. I move the cookie boxes and scoot closer, resting my head on his shoulder. "I'm so sorry." He puts his arm around me, keeping me close. It's easy and natural, and I wish I could climb onto his lap and kiss away his heartache.

"He's not gone." He pats his hand over his heart. "He's always right here. He'd like you, Boots."

He aims those dimples at me, and all I can think about is how easy it would be to fall for this man who loves so hard it oozes from his pores.

Chapter Twenty

NICOLE

Classic rock is a nice backdrop to my evening at Maggie's on the Fourth. Her kitchen is separated from the living room by a large wooden high-top table, where we've just finished eating shrimp scampi that she and her friend Cherry made. Cherry is our age and, like Aspen, believes in the power of the universe above all else. Maggie's brother, Seth, reminds me of a robust beer—big and burly, with a hearty laugh.

"That was delicious." I set my festive red-white-and-blue napkin beside my plate. "It's a shame your other friend couldn't make it. I was looking forward to meeting her."

"She met some guy on an online dating app and wanted to spend the Fourth with him," Maggie says.

"She's on my shit list," Cherry says.

"Why?" I ask.

"Because guys come and go, and we always spend the Fourth together," Cherry explains.

"Sisters before misters," Maggie says as she gets up to clear the table, and we all follow suit.

"That's a shame." I start loading the dishwasher as they finish clearing the table and putting away the leftovers. I love that everyone pitches in.

"That woman is always on the prowl." Seth hands me a plate. "Last year she was in love with a guy from Greece who she met on social media."

"Online dating scares me," I admit as I rinse another dish. "You never know if the person is real or not. What happened to that guy?"

"After leading her on for several months, he ghosted her," Maggie answers.

"No surprise there," Cherry says.

We finish the dishes, and Cherry brings out a box of tarot cards. "Who's ready for a reading?"

"You read tarot cards?" I'm intrigued.

"They're cheater cards. They come with a book that explains what they mean," Seth says as he guides me back to the table, and we all sit down. He sits beside me, across from Maggie and Cherry. "I'm going to do the readings tonight, and like it or not, you're playing along."

"Then I guess I'm in."

"Are you a manifester like Cherry?" Seth asks as Maggie shuffles the deck.

"Not really, but I have a friend who manifests everything."

"Smart woman," Cherry says. "How do you think Maggie got this cottage? I manifested it for her, because she refuses to do anything someone else's way."

"She did." Maggie points to a framed list on the wall. "That's the original list of what I wanted."

"Manifesting works," Cherry says. "We should start a list for you, Nic, and manifest your perfect man."

Seth nudges me with his leg, giving me an amused look. He's a good-looking guy, bearded with brown hair flecked with gray, and he's been flirting with me on and off all evening.

"I'm not looking for a man, and if I were, I don't think I'd make a list. I'm more about chemistry. If a guy has a good sense of humor and he's kind and loyal, those are the things that I find attractive." *And dimples, spontaneity, a love of Girl Scout cookies and Snickers . . .*

I remind myself that Declan needs to stay in the friend zone.

"How about ambition?" Cherry asks.

"I guess, but not really. I mean I wouldn't want a guy who sat on his butt all day, but I don't really care what he does for a living as long as it's legal and he's happy with it."

"But you don't want a couch potato, so ambition *is* important. You should put that on your list," Cherry says.

"How about we just do the cards?" Seth holds out his hand, and Maggie hands him the deck.

"I need a gummy for this." Cherry pulls a plastic bag out of her pocket and pops a gummy bear into her mouth. "These two don't like them, but how about you, Nic? Do you partake?" She holds the bag out.

"I *love* gummy bears."

As I reach for one, Seth says, "They're marijuana gummies. It's legal here."

"*Oh*. In that case, I'll pass. Thanks, but it's not my thing."

"More for me," Cherry says.

"Who wants to go first?" Maggie asks.

"How about our beautiful newbie?" Seth's blue eyes land on me. "It'll be nice to see what's brewing for her."

"Hopefully we'll find out that I have amazing chapters just waiting to be written. How does this work?"

"All you have to do is think of a question you'd like answered or a life problem you're trying to resolve, and then the cards will hopefully give you answers," Cherry says. "But don't tell us what the question or problem is. We keep that private."

I mentally tick off the questions I'd like answers to. *Why doesn't my writing hold my attention like it used to? Will Mackenzie learn to stand on her own two feet soon? And for the love of God, why do I feel so connected to Declan when his life is a hot mess?* I am so drawn to that man. He makes everything fun, and he can get me to do just about anything. We went to karaoke with Chuck Saturday night, and Declan convinced me to get up onstage and sing with him. It's one thing to sing in the car with my girlfriends, but I have *always* flat-out refused to do karaoke because I can't sing worth beans. But that didn't stop me from belting out a song onstage with Declan, and I didn't feel the least bit self-conscious.

Seth leans closer and whispers, "I'm all ears if you want to share."

"Trust me, you don't want to know." I decide not to choose a question but to throw them all out to the universe and see what happens.

Seth has me choose four cards. "Place them facedown in front of you. They represent something positive, negative, a result, and advice."

My nerves ping as I place my cards on the table. "Why am I nervous?"

"I get nervous, too." Maggie lifts her wineglass. "That's what the wine is for."

"Every card can have a positive or negative meaning depending on your question, and if the card is upside down, it's got a different meaning than when it's upright," Cherry explains. "Turn over your first card."

"*Great*," I say sarcastically as I turn it over. "The Chariot. Is that good?"

"Let the master read your fate." Seth thumbs through the book that explains what each card means and reads in a deep, dramatic voice. "The Chariot points to a triumphant feeling of freedom and represents a journey, ambition, overcoming obstacles, confidence, and willpower."

I exhale with relief. "That's what my cottage and this summer are all about. Maybe there is something to these cards. Do you mind if I take a picture of each card and its meaning?"

"Not at all," Cherry says. "I always write it down so I can digest it over time. I have all my readings from the past thirty years."

"That's amazing." As I take the pictures, I think about how I would like to be doing this with them thirty years from now.

"Remember, it's not about how you feel right now," Cherry says. "Think about how the card pertains to the question you wanted answered."

I think about my writing and remember that writing a book is always a journey, and there are a million obstacles to overcome. The fact that writing has been like pulling teeth over the last few months is just another obstacle. It's a good reminder, and I allow myself the grace to accept that, which takes my frustration down a notch. As for Mackenzie, she's on her own journey into adulthood and probably experiencing that sense of freedom that most college kids get. Granted she's been at college for a long time, but maybe her journey is just going to take a little longer than others'. There's only one way in which the card relates to Declan, and that's when I'm with him, I feel even freer than when I'm alone.

"Is the card helpful?" Maggie asks.

"Yes, I think it is."

"Are we ready for the negative?" Seth asks.

I inhale deeply. "As ready as I'll ever be." I turn over the next card. "The Four of Cups, but it's upside down. Should I turn it over?"

"No," Cherry says. "Never mess with the universe."

"Don't worry, I've never seen the cards lead anyone to hell." Seth thumbs through the book. "This is a long one, so I'm going to summarize. It's actually better that it's reversed." In that deep, dramatic voice, he says, "You've left regrets and a stale life behind, but be careful not to allow negative energy to interfere and prevent greater things from happening." His lips tip up. "It also speaks of passion and taking action." He winks.

"I'll take that wink." Cherry wiggles her shoulders. "I keep telling you, Seth, I might be like a sister to you out here, but I won't be in the bedroom."

"I don't want to know this about you," Maggie says.

I think about the reading, negative energy preventing greater things from happening, and wonder if I should try to talk to Mackenzie about her boyfriend again. My mind returns to Declan, and I wonder if the card refers to the complications in his life, too.

The next card is the Nine of Swords, meaning I'm being kept up at night due to worrying over a situation. Damn right I am, for obvious reasons with writing and Mackenzie. And I'm burning through batteries, thanks to Declan, so yeah, I guess I am kept up at night over him, too.

The last card is the advice card. "The Three of Pentacles," Seth says like he's a wizard about to cast a spell. "You should give someone you trust a chance to take some of the weight you're carrying off your shoulders."

I have no idea how that relates to my questions, because I have no one to hand off my stress to. "That one's not too helpful."

"It means you don't have to do everything yourself." Seth waggles his brows. "A single woman like you must get lonely up there in that cottage."

"How can I get lonely when I take my fictional boyfriends to bed with me?" I sip my wine. "And they don't talk back."

"I only speak with my hands," he retorts.

"No wonder you're lonely," I tease. "You have other body parts for a reason. Maggie, you should give your baby brother a lesson in the birds and the bees."

They laugh, and our banter continues through their readings.

When we finally make it down to the beach, we're all a little tipsy. Seth sticks by my side as we mingle with my Oyster Run friends. I notice a few curious glances. Russ asks Seth a million questions until Marlo drags him away. Claude takes one look at Seth and grumbles, "Who's the bearded guy?" Evelyn chides him for being rude, but Seth just smiles and offers his hand. "Just a token brother, here for a visit."

We chat with them for a while, and even though I'm having a great time, I wish Declan were there.

As the night progresses, more people come to watch the fireworks, and eventually Seth and I claim a spot in the sand with Maggie, Cherry, and our other friends. Seth asks about my writing, and he tells me about the brewery where he works.

"Next year we should have a community party for the Fourth," Aspen says. "We can make it potluck, and everyone can bring a dish."

Seth leans back in the sand with one hand behind me and says, "Count me in."

"If I'd known all it would take to get my brother to visit me was a pretty neighbor, I'd have found one sooner," Maggie teases.

They're discussing the idea of a potluck celebration when I see Declan coming off the path. His eyes find mine, and those killer dimples appear. My pulse quickens, and I pop to my feet to greet him.

"How's it going, Bootsy?" Declan leans in and kisses my cheek. "Sorry I'm so late. I had to take care of something for my old man."

Seth stands, stepping close to me, and offers his hand to Declan. "Hi, I'm Maggie's brother, Seth."

"Declan, nice to meet you."

As Declan shakes his hand, his gaze moves to the sliver of space Seth left between us. His brows knit, confusion and something darker rising in his eyes. I get a chill, as if the temperature suddenly dropped, but when he speaks to Seth, his tone is friendly. "You here for the night?"

"Supposed to be." Seth looks at me. "But I'm thinking I might stay for a few days."

The muscles in Declan's jaw bunch.

"Miller!" Aspen pushes to her feet. "Come here, sweetie. Give me a hug." As he does, she says, "Sit down and join us."

He looks right at me, and tension snaps in the air between us. "I can't. I just wanted to stop by and say happy Fourth to everyone."

"Happy Fourth," everyone says at once.

"Thanks. Enjoy yourselves." He glances at me. "We'll catch up another time."

"Okay." I hope I don't sound as disappointed as I feel, and I don't like how weird he's acting.

He looks at Seth. "Nice to meet you."

"You too, man. Drive safe."

We sit down, and Seth puts his arm behind me again, asking quietly, "Are you two seeing each other or something?"

I watch Declan walking away and face the truth, which feels like a jagged little pill. "No. We're just friends."

The fireworks display is fantastic, and I text pictures of the finale to Mackenzie, wishing her a happy Fourth. She sends a selfie of her and her friends and assures me she won't get in the car with anyone who's drinking. Rachel, Dani, and I exchange happy Fourth texts, and I consider sending one to Declan but decide not to. I need to stay on the right side of the friend zone and get my head on straight.

Everyone stays after the fireworks to chat, and by the time we head back to our cottages, it's after eleven. "Maggie, I had a great time tonight," I say as we walk up the hill. "Thanks for inviting me to join you."

"So did we," she says.

"I know you think the tarot cards are a little silly," Cherry says. "But if you're open to it, just thinking about them might bring you answers."

"I don't think they're silly. It was fun, and I have the pictures so I can revisit them."

"You should really be manifesting, too," Cherry says as we reach Maggie's driveway. "The universe is a powerful thing, and you should use it to your benefit."

"Okay, Cher. You can stop pushing your universal crap on her now," Maggie says.

"It's okay. I'll think about it, Cherry," I promise. "Next summer I'll have to make sure Rachel and Dani are here when you visit. Dani is all about using the energy of the universe to guide her." I look between Cherry and Seth. "It was nice meeting you guys."

"Come here and give me a hug." Cherry waves me into her open arms. "You're just as cool as Maggie said you were. Keep kicking her ass and making her walk with you."

"I plan to." I smile at Maggie. "Thanks again for a great night."

"I'll walk you home," Seth offers.

"It's just a few hundred feet up the hill."

"In the dark," he points out.

I follow his gaze to my cottage and realize I forgot to leave a light on.

As Maggie and Cherry head inside, Seth and I make our way up the hill, and my nerves prickle. What if he wants to kiss me good night? Do I want him to? I haven't kissed a man in almost three years. What if I've forgotten how?

He puts his hand on my back, and I have the strangest feeling that I'm cheating on my friendship with Declan. As if that spot on my back is *his*. Why am I even thinking of him? He made it clear he only wants to be friends, which is for the best, and he didn't even stick around tonight, so I shouldn't be thinking of him at all.

As we walk along the side of my cottage, I struggle to push thoughts of Declan away, and when we reach the door, I'm even more nervous. "Thanks for walking me home. I should really have a motion light installed."

"With a smile like that, you could light up a cave." He puts his hands on my hips and gets that look on his face that guys get right before they kiss you.

I know I have seconds to decide if I want to kiss him. *What could it hurt? I enjoyed our time together, and it's only a kiss. It'll be good practice.*

"If I stick around, maybe we can hang out tomorrow."

"I'm on a deadline. I have to write during the day, but I might be free in the evening." As I say it, my mind tiptoes back to Declan, and I wonder what he's doing tomorrow.

"Busy woman."

He pulls me closer, and his mouth covers mine softly for only a second before he deepens the kiss. His tongue invades my mouth, his whiskers abrade my skin, and he kisses the hell out of me. I know by the sensual way he moves against me that this guy could probably fuck me senseless, but I don't want to sleep with him. A devil on my shoulder says he'd be good practice to break my dry spell, but then Declan's face appears in my mind, and no part of me wants this man I've only just met to be the person I trust with that part of myself.

Hell, he isn't even the one I want to be kissing.

I pull away, wanting to take the kiss back, but he keeps me close. "Come on, baby. You know you want me."

Are you shitting me? Is every guy in this town a hot mess? I put my hand on his chest, gently pushing him away. "You seem like a fun guy, but we're not going there."

He tightens his grip, rocking his hips. His erection presses against my stomach. "You're going to send me away like this?"

It takes everything I have not to roll my eyes. I can't believe Maggie called him one of the good guys. "Lucky for you, nobody has ever died from blue balls." I push away, but he tugs me back. I don't feel threatened. He reminds me of a teenager who thinks if he asks fifteen different ways, he'll get a pity fuck. Maggie's brother or not, I've hit my limit, and *nice* goes out the window. I push out of his grip. "This is *not* happening. You need to leave."

He holds his hands up. "Sorry. I thought we were having a good time."

"That good time ended with the kiss. Good night, Seth." I wait until he leaves before going inside and tearing open a box of Girl Scout cookies.

I'm so annoyed, I want to punch someone.

The trouble is, Seth isn't the only guy I want to use as a punching bag.

Chapter Twenty-One

NICOLE

The next morning not only am I still annoyed, but I slept like crap. I'm so exhausted, I couldn't even muster joking with Claude when I accidentally stepped on his lawn. I'll be sure to bring him a treat later. I have no business running, but if I don't clear my head, I'll kill someone.

I'm jogging—*dragging*—my ass up a hill at a snail's pace when a text rolls in.

Declan: *I'm not interrupting morning fireworks, am I?*

I can admit there was some chemistry between me and Seth last night, but not the inescapable kind Declan and I have. His comment pisses me off, so I call instead of texting.

"How's it going, WG?"

He sounds as casual as ever, and as much as his voice is a balm to my annoyance, I won't allow it to do the job. "Oh, it's *going*. Did you watch the fireworks?"

"I saw enough fireworks on the beach," he says tightly. "Seth seemed nice."

I slow to a walk. "He was, until he kissed the hell out of me and tried to get me to sleep with him."

"Can you blame the guy?"

"For a kiss? No." I'll probably go straight to hell for saying what I do next, but I'm frustrated. "He can kiss, too. He's like a freaking porn-star kisser."

Declan is quiet for a beat. "Porn stars don't usually kiss."

"Whatever. That's what he is in my head. It's like he's practiced a zillion times and can take any woman to her knees."

"Sounds like you enjoyed it."

"The kiss? Sure, at first." I'm walking past the library, and as I look up at the gorgeous stone building, all I can think about is how I had wished I was kissing Declan and that strange feeling I had. I debate not telling him, but it claws its way up my throat. "But then I had the weirdest feeling, and I know this is going to sound crazy, but I felt like I was cheating on our friendship, and all I wanted was to take that kiss back."

There's another moment of silence, and I'm sure he thinks I'm crossing some sort of line. I try to think of a way to make light of it, but before I can get a word out, he speaks.

"I get that. We're attracted to each other, and there's no denying that there's something special between us, even if we're not acting on it. But we both know where we stand, so don't let our friendship hold you back. You can kiss anyone you'd like, Nic."

What if I want to kiss you is on the tip of my tongue, but it's trapped by the raw ache of the truth. "I know I can. I was just letting you know how I felt at that moment. I got over it the minute he became too aggressive."

"What do you mean by that?" he asks sharply.

"He just kept trying to get me to sleep with him."

"And you didn't want to?"

"Of course not," I snap. "I just met the guy."

"Lots of people hook up after knowing each other five minutes."

"Yes, but *I* don't. That was my first kiss in three years. I wasn't into doing more, and it took a while for him to get the message."

"Did that guy try to force himself on you?"

"He was pushy, but I set him straight, and I'm fine. It was nothing a sleeve of Girl Scout cookies couldn't fix."

"Funny, I ate an entire box of them last night."

That gives me pause. I want to ask if he wishes he was the one kissing me last night, too. But he's already given me that answer, hasn't he? It takes a second for the reality of our conversation to hit me, and I stop in my tracks. How the hell did I get here? Where are these feelings coming from? I'm too attached and too attracted to Declan. I need some space to try to put him firmly back into the friend zone before I do or say something I shouldn't. "Listen, I'm in the middle of my run, so I'm going to get off the phone."

"A'right. You want to hang out later?"

I want to, but as I always tell Mackenzie, *want* and *need* are two very different things, and right now I *need* to figure out why I feel like he's already become the blood in my veins. "I can't. I have to get some writing done."

"In that case, get your ass in gear, Bootsy. I want five thousand words on the page before your head hits the pillow tonight, or there will be harsh consequences."

"Such as?"

"Such as I'd better get off the phone before I say something inappropriate about putting you over my knee and you stop speaking to me."

If that isn't a reason to fail my word-count goal, I don't know what is.

Chapter Twenty-Two

NICOLE

I'm still thinking about our conversation three days later when I get a text from Rachel. *Remind me why we have kids again.*

Me: *To spend all our money? To give us gray hair? To remind us that we were young and annoying once, too?*

Rachel: *I was never annoying.*

I send an eye roll emoji.

Me: *What's up with Lucy?*

Rachel: *She likes a boy.*

Me: *And . . . ?*

Rachel: *I'm not ready for that.*

Me: *If it makes you feel any better, I like a boy and I'm not ready for it either.*

Rachel: *Seth?* She adds a heart-eyed emoji.

I send a detailed text about the porn-star kisser, who we dub PSK.

Rachel: *What is wrong with men?! Have you told Maggie?*

Me: *I didn't have to. I told Declan the next morning, and apparently he went straight to Maggie's and paid Seth a visit while I was out running. Maggie called me afterward. She was pissed at Seth, but thankfully, it didn't mess up our friendship.*

I gave Declan hell for going behind my back when I'd already handled the situation, but nobody has stuck up for me like that since I was a kid, and I secretly appreciated it.

Rachel: *Bold move by Declan. I'm glad he's watching out for you. So who is the mystery crush?*

I reply with my favorite deadpan-boy GIF.

Rachel sends a celebration emoji and a flame emoji, followed by *#TeamDimples.*

Me: *This isn't good. I reiterate the part of my conversation with Declan when he said I could kiss anyone I want to. I've never been in this position before. Please tell me how to be friends without wanting more when I'm totally into him despite his red flags. He keeps asking me to hang out, and I really want to, but you know I'm not good at holding in my feelings.*

Rachel: *You're not a woman who can't control herself. You've totally got this. Just hang out with him and keep your lips to yourself. Or sleep with him and get him out of your system.*

I send a shocked emoji and a facepalm emoji.

Rachel: *I'm buying Lucy a chastity belt. Maybe you should try that.*

I send three laughing emojis.

A minute later, I text, *Send me the website link.*

I'm sitting at my desk later that evening, posting on social media, when my door flies open, and Declan strides in, strikingly handsome in jeans and a white linen shirt. His beard is freshly trimmed, and the glint of happiness in his eyes causes hummingbirds to take flight in my chest. *God*, I've missed him. I don't even know how that's possible since we've texted and spoken on the phone several times since the Fourth.

"Get up, Bootsy. I'm taking you to dinner."

"Didn't I say I had stuff to do?" I check my phone and see my last text to him went through.

"Yes. I'm not buying that bullshit you're selling." He takes my hand, lifting me to my feet. "You've been locked in here for three days straight. You're liable to turn into a pumpkin or something. Get your boots on, and let's go."

I look down at my boho top and cutoffs. "Should I change?"

"You look gorgeous." He grabs my boots from by the door. "Come on."

As I shove my feet into my boots, he snags the sweatshirt he lent me off the back of my chair. He takes my hand and heads for the door. I grab my bag on the way out, hurrying to keep up with him. "Where are we going?"

"We're taking my boat over to Lightman's Island."

He opens the passenger door to his truck and helps me in. That's new. "What's on Lightman's Island?"

"Only the best seafood restaurant in a two-hundred-mile radius."

"If it's that good, I'll be underdressed."

"You look perfect, and you'll be the hottest woman there."

He closes my door before I can process the compliment. I watch him strut around to the driver's side, and as he settles in behind the wheel, he seems different. Like something is lighting him up from the inside out. "Are we celebrating something?"

"No." He glances over as he drives down to the main road, a smile playing on his lips. "Do you have something to celebrate?"

"No. I was just curious. You seem pumped about something."

"It's been three days since I've gotten to hang out with my adventure buddy. So, yeah, I'm in a great mood. I guess that is a celebration of sorts. Tell me about the chapters I've missed. Did our couple get down and dirty?"

Those hummingbirds are fluttering away as we talk about my book. He's as excited as I am, and I feel a new gust of life breathed into me, too. Until this very moment, I hadn't realized just how much effort it had taken to stay away from him.

◆ ◆ ◆

At the marina, he leads me down to a beautiful boat with Go Time painted on the side near the back. "This is yours?" I ask as he unties the ropes that secure it to the dock.

"Yup." He helps me onto the boat and stows my bag in a compartment.

"I can't believe we're taking a boat to dinner."

"Believe it, Bootsy." He hands me his sweatshirt. "Put this on. It'll get chilly once we get going."

While I put on the sweatshirt, he puts on sunglasses and starts the engine. I can't figure out what's gotten into him, but he seems determined. Like he's on some sort of mission. He backs out of the slip and pilots the boat out of the harbor. Declan always seems very much in control, but there's something about seeing him behind that wheel, with his hair curling in the wind and that white linen shirt rustling against his bronze skin, that takes him to a whole new level.

I turn away, trying not to get carried away. This isn't a date, even if it feels extraordinary to be jetting off on his boat to the best restaurant around. The wind hits my cheeks, bringing a long-forgotten memory with it. "I haven't been on a boat since I was a kid, when my dad took us fishing on one of those big boats with about a dozen other families."

"Did you enjoy it?"

"I loved it. My brothers and I had a competition to see who could catch the biggest fish."

"Did you win?"

"No. Tommy did, but I caught the second biggest."

"Attagirl. Do you like fishing?"

"Yeah. I've only gone a few times, but I loved the anticipation and that feeling when a fish takes its first nibble. Thanks to my brothers, I'm not afraid to take a hook out, and I don't get grossed out by the sight of fish guts."

"You are definitely the coolest chick around."

"And you clearly don't know enough women," I tease.

He increases the boat's speed as we leave the harbor, and even with the windshield, my hair whips across my face. I turn directly into the wind and try to gather my hair in my hands, but I don't have an elastic band to hold it back, and pieces keep coming loose. "I should've thought about this. I'm going to be a mess by the time we get there."

"Stop worrying. You've got great hair, and as far as I'm concerned, the wilder it is, the better. Have you ever piloted a boat?"

"No."

"It's about time you learned." He pulls me in front of him, and I put my hands on the steering wheel.

His body warms my back, and a flush of awareness washes over me.

"This is the GPS." He points to the electronic console. "See this icon? That's us, and this path is called a track. Just follow that track and it'll take us right to the marina on the island."

"Just like a car."

"Sure, we'll go with that. You'll need these." He steps beside me, and cooler air sweeps over my back as he puts his sunglasses on me.

"Thanks."

With a wink, he leaves my side and goes around to the front of the boat, where he proceeds to take a picture of me. "You look good piloting my boat."

I'm sure I look like I've been stuck in a wind tunnel, and the fact that he doesn't care makes me feel like a million bucks.

Chapter Twenty-Three

NICOLE

Lightman's Island is buffered from the sea by massive boulders and cliffs. Unlike Chatemup, there is only one dock on this side of the island and a peppering of cedar-sided homes interspersed with a few pines. A smattering of wildflowers adds color to the rocky landscape. A man is painting at an easel just beyond the shoreline, and in the distance, children are kicking a ball in the grass.

"Wow. This place is gorgeous."

"Some say it's the most romantic spot off the coast of New England." He puts a hand on my back as we come off the dock.

"Hey, Declan," the artist calls over.

"How's it going, Mack? Creating another masterpiece?"

"We can only hope," the guy says.

"I take it you've been here before?" I ask as we walk along a narrow dirt road snaking up a hill.

"A few times. This place has been seducing artists, birders, hikers, and dreamers for centuries."

"I can see the allure. Which one are you? A secret artist, birder, hiker, or dreamer?"

"If those are my only choices, I guess I'm a dreamer."

I think about what he said about the island and wonder if I picked up on the wrong part of his comment. "Is this where you bring women you want to seduce?"

"You tell me. Is it working?"

I'm sure he's teasing, so I don't respond, but I can't deny the part of me that's wishing he wasn't. When we reach the crest of the hill, the dirt road winds through a quaint village of homes and shops. A few people are milling about, but not as many as I'd expect on a beautiful island with the best seafood restaurant in a two-hundred-mile radius. I glance to the left and see rooftops between the trees. "Okay, Casanova, where are all the people?"

"Probably eating dinner or down by the gazebo on the other side of the island, listening to music. There are only about a hundred people who live here. They get a pretty good influx of tourists during the summer, but mostly day-trippers." He takes my hand, leaving the dirt road to walk across the grass. We come to a gentle slope, and about midway down is a cedar-sided mini-mansion among a few smaller homes. "That's the only hotel on the island. It only has twenty-two rooms."

"So the residents keep the overnight tourism down by design?"

"That's right. It's smart, if you ask me." We head back to the road. "The island is only two miles long and just shy of a mile wide. They don't even allow cars here."

"Now I really see the appeal. This is a perfect retreat, unless the people here suck."

"Ain't that the truth," he says with a laugh. "But the people here are pretty cool."

We make our way down another dirt road. This one is lined by white flowers spilling over a knee-high stone wall and leads to a handful of cedar-sided homes by the water. I realize Declan is still holding my hand. It's nice, exploring this new place with him. A young couple riding bicycles comes around a bend and heads up the hill. They wave as they near us, legs pumping.

"Hey, Declan," the man says as they pedal past us.

I guess he doesn't know him from the military.

"How's it going?" Declan answers.

"You know people everywhere you go." I'm getting curious about how much time he spends here.

"Gotta love small towns."

When we reach the bottom of the hill, we follow signs for Wild Rose Restaurant down another lane, and he leads me through a beautiful trellis covered with flowering vines. We walk along a pebbled path lined with enormous pink, white, and red rosebushes and a plethora of other gorgeous flowers, to a white clapboard house with a front-gable roof. Beside the door is a wooden sign that reads, WILD ROSE, COME FOR THE FOOD, STAY FOR THE COMPANY.

"This building has been in the Frank family since the early 1900s," Declan explains. "It's named for sea captain Sebastian Frank's wife, Rose, who, legend has it, ran a brothel here."

"Maybe it should be called the Naughty Rose." I point to the sign. "With that slogan, it might still be a brothel."

"It's not. I asked."

I laugh. "Seriously?"

"Do I look like I have to pay for sex? Let's go. I hope you're hungry. The food is incredible."

"I'm always hungry," I say as we head inside.

We're greeted by the din of conversation. The place is packed, and it smells heavenly.

"Declan," the petite middle-aged hostess says with surprise. "It's nice to see you."

"Hi, Julie. This is my friend Nic. I forgot to make a reservation. I don't suppose you've got a free table?"

"For you, I'll find one."

"No, don't do that," he says. "How about the raw bar? Is that open?"

"Yes, but you don't want to eat there." Her brow furrows. "It's noisy and not very private."

I wonder if she thinks we're on a date.

"We don't mind a little noise, right, Nic?"

"Not at all."

"Okay, well, you know the way," she says.

"Sure do. Thanks." Declan guides me through the crowded restaurant with his hand on my back. "Do you eat raw shellfish? Oysters? Clams?"

"I love it all."

"Perfect."

We make our way out another door to a deck overlooking the water. Large hurricane lamps sitting on tabletops and string lights wrapped around a pergola overhead give a splash of nautical elegance. As we walk past the other casually dressed diners, an elderly man wearing a baseball cap lifts his chin at Declan.

Declan claps his hand on the man's shoulder. "Hey, Stu, good to see you." He continues walking to the bar, where we sit on the only two vacant stools.

"*Miller*," a clean-cut, dark-haired guy behind the bar says as he serves clams to a couple sitting to my right.

"Hey, Foley," Declan says.

Foley finishes serving and comes over to us. He's got tattoos on both arms and sharp dark eyes that give him an edge. He nods at me. "How's it going?"

"Pretty well," I say. "How's it going for you?"

"I'm alive and kicking, so it's a damn good day."

"Foley, this is my friend Nic. Nic, this is Rich Foley, an old army buddy of mine."

Foley hands us drink and dinner menus. "Why don't you look these over, and I'll be back in a minute."

I scan the drink menu. "Every drink is named for a flower."

"I know. Do you like vodka?"

"With something sweet in it."

"Go for Petunia's Poison."

I find the drink on the menu. It's made with sweet pineapple juice, blue curaçao, and grenadine. "That sounds good. I'll try it." I set down the drink menu and scan the dinner menu. Declan's not looking at his. "Do you know what you're going to get for dinner? There's so much to choose from."

"Yeah. Is there anything besides anchovies that you don't eat?"

"You remembered."

"I remember every word you've ever said."

He can't know how much that means to me after being with a man who would forget what I said two seconds after it left my lips. "I guess I'd better be careful what I say, and to answer your question, I eat just about everything."

"Then why don't I order for us, and we can share?"

"That sounds great." I set down the menu as a cute brunette waitress comes over.

"Declan Miller is in the house," she cheers loudly, and a handful of people *whoop* and call out his name.

"Jesus, Bailey, really?" Declan says. "Nic, this is Bailey, the local troublemaker. Bailey, this is my friend Nic."

"Nice to meet you, Nic." She eyes me appreciatively. "You've got great hair, and I *love* those boots. What are you drinking tonight?"

Declan says, "She'll have Petunia's Poison, and I'll have a draft, but back off. She's straight."

Bailey arches a brow. "If you ever get curious . . ."

I smile, but Declan says, "You're ridiculous. Get outta here and get our drinks."

"It's good to keep him on his toes," Bailey says before walking away.

"Sorry about that," he says.

"She obviously likes to get under your skin. You must come here a lot to know this many people."

"They buy fish from my company. No big deal."

Downplaying things seems to be a running theme in his life. "Just how big is this company of yours?"

"A few guys and a few boats."

"Why do I get the feeling there's a lot more to it than that?"

Foley appears with a plate of raw oysters and sets them in front of us. "On the house."

"You don't have to do that," Declan says.

Foley hikes a thumb at Declan, addressing me. "The guy saved my life and thinks a few oysters is too much." He shakes his head and goes to help another customer.

"Was he talking about in the military?"

"No."

I wait for him to say more, but he doesn't. "How did you save his life?"

"After he got out, he was having a hard time, so I gave him a hand."

I'm usually okay with his cryptic answers, but after the reception he's received, I want to know more. "What does that mean, exactly? Or is it too personal?"

"It's personal, but he won't mind if I tell you. He uses his experience to help others, and he speaks openly about it. A few years ago, he called me because he was contemplating suicide, which is a lot more common among veterans than you probably think. I got him help and flew out to see him and stayed for a couple of weeks to make sure he had the support he needed. His family wasn't doing shit for him, so I packed his stuff, brought him back with me, and connected him with a therapist so he didn't lose the ground he'd gained. He worked for my company and stayed at my place for a few weeks, and once he was solid, I got him the interview here."

I'm in awe of this man who makes time to take care of everyone else. Including me, I realize. He warned me away because he thinks I deserve someone who can give me more time and attention than he can. But while he's playing white knight, who's taking care of him?

"Not everyone is willing to go above and beyond to help people. You're an incredible person, Declan."

"I did what any friend would do. He just needed a hand to get on the right path, but he's the one who did the hard work. He had to fight tooth and nail to get back on his feet." He looks at Foley with as much awe as I feel toward him. "He's the incredible one."

"Then you're both pretty special. Have you helped other veterans?"

A humble smile appears. "Yeah. I kept in touch with my military buddies, and once I got my shit together, I realized I could help others. Services are available, but you've got to fight for every ounce of support, and when they're at the end of their rope, they don't have the bandwidth to do it, so I step in when I can." He rolls his shoulders back and eyes the oysters. "If we keep yapping, these will be warm by the time we eat them."

"Swift diversion, Dimple Dude." I pick up the little fork that came with the oysters and stab one.

"Oh *no*." Declan sounds pained as he takes the fork from my hand.

"What's wrong?"

"Please tell me you weren't going to eat that oyster with a fork."

"Okay, I won't tell you. Can I have my fork back, please?"

"No way. Sorry, Dorothy, but you're not in Kansas anymore. If you're going to hang with a fish peddler, you've got to eat oysters properly. From shell to mouth." He loosens the oyster with the fork.

"It'll drip."

He leans closer with a devilish glint in his eyes. "Are you trying to tell me you don't know how to use that sexy mouth of yours without making a mess?"

"I never said *that*," I say, trying to ignore the way his seductive tone snags the attention of my very lonely lady parts.

He holds my gaze, the air between us simmering. "I hope not, because that would be a hell of a shame." He picks up the shell and tips it to his lips. The oyster slides onto his tongue, and he winks as he curls the tip up, closes his mouth, and swallows.

That just might be the sexiest thing I've ever seen.

His tongue glides along his lower lip, then retraces its path.

Okay, I was wrong. *That* was even sexier. I squeeze my thighs together and wonder what the hell he's trying to do to me.

"Your turn, Bootsy."

Yes, thank you. I'd like a turn to lick those lips.

He raises his brows.

Did I say that out loud?

He holds up the fork he was handing me, snapping my brain into submission.

"I'm watching you, Writer Girl. Don't even try to pick up that oyster with your fork."

I don't know if he's flirting or if my mind is playing tricks on me, but I make a split-second decision to throw caution to the wind and give him a little sexiness right back. "I won't." I loosen the oyster and set the fork down. "I just didn't want to embarrass you by slurping it down, but since you're into it . . ." I'm mildly aware of Foley watching us, but I can't back out now. I pick up the shell, slide the oyster into my mouth, and try to curl my tongue like he did, but it sends a dribble of salty liquid over my lower lip. Refusing to be one-upped, I try to play it cool and continue holding his gaze as I swallow the oyster and slide my tongue along my lip, soaking up the drip, hoping I look sexy and not like a dog licking its drool.

His eyes narrow, and I feel a droplet sliding down my chin. Gathering all my courage, I pretend I'm a heroine from one of my books, wipe it with my index finger, and suck it off.

"*Damn*, woman," he says huskily. "You are trouble waiting to happen."

Foley sets another plate of oysters in front of us. "I'm just going to keep these coming *all* night long."

We both laugh, and with Declan's eyes locked on mine, he says, "Please do."

Thankfully, Bailey brings our drinks, and I practically guzzle the tasty purple concoction.

Our playfulness continues through dinner, which is a delicious array of seafood and steamed vegetables. We watch the sunset, and as always with Declan, conversation is easy and fun. We speak in hushed voices, ad-libbing conversations between other diners as we wait to pay the bill, and my cheeks hurt from laughing.

Declan nods to a pair of twentysomethings at the other end of the bar. "What do you think he's saying?"

I watch them for a minute and speak in a deep voice. "What do you say we get out of here and go someplace a little quieter?"

In a hilarious high-pitched voice, Declan says, "You're very handsome, but I don't want to seem easy."

"Well, I don't want to seem *hard*," I say gruffly. "But some things just can't be avoided."

Declan laughs and uses his female voice again. "You are a naughty boy. I don't know if I can be with someone like you. I'm a good girl."

I lower my voice. "Why don't you let me show you how *good* naughty can be?"

We go on until we leave the restaurant, and we're still laughing as we make our way back toward the boat. "You're good at that, Bootsy."

"You made it easy. Everything's fun and easy with you."

"Is this where I say you make everything hard?"

"Would you *stop?*" I swat him and trip over a rock. Declan catches me around the waist, hauling me against him. Our eyes connect, and the heat that's been simmering between us ignites. I can't breathe for the way he's looking at me. He holds me tighter, and *my God*, I want this man. I want him to crush his mouth to mine and kiss me so deeply my knees give out. But my nerves get the better of me, and I ramble. "This is like a scene from a book. Girl trips, guy catches her, and sparks fly."

His lips quirk. "Sparks, huh?"

"I know. I'm fishing in the cliché ocean again."

His brows knit. "Well, I'd hate to be a cliché."

He releases me, and it takes a second for me to think past the blood rushing through my ears and process my disappointment.

When we start walking again, he puts his hand on my lower back. "Better be careful, WG. I wouldn't want our next adventure to be to the hospital."

"First day with my new feet," I say stupidly.

As we make our way to the dock and onto the boat, there's an awkwardness between us that has never been there before, and I hate it. I mentally replay those moments a hundred times, wishing I hadn't said a word and had just let nature take its course.

Declan doesn't say much as he pilots the boat away from the island, and I wonder what he's thinking. Maybe that fiery chemistry was all in my head. I cringe inwardly and wrap my arms around my middle.

"Cold?" he asks.

It's colder now that the sun has gone down, but I'm too nervous to feel it. I shake my head, but he pulls me closer and puts his arm around me, as if he knows I need it. I want to clear the air, but I don't know what to say, so I'm left feeling uncomfortable after what has been, up until my rambling, one of the best nights of my life.

Chapter Twenty-Four

NICOLE

As Chatemup comes into view, that awful feeling is still eating away at me. Declan hasn't said anything to feed that insecurity, but the tension between us is palpable.

"Fuck it." He powers down the boat and cuts the engine.

"What's wrong?"

He drops the anchor, and when he looks at me, there's no mistaking the fire in his eyes, but I can't tell if it's anger or attraction.

"Why did we stop?"

"Because I've got something to say, and it's driving me up the fucking wall. I can't stop thinking about that asshole kissing you the other night. That should've been *me*, and back there on the island, I wanted to kiss you so damn bad, but you said that shit about it being cliché, and . . . *fuck that*, Nic." He takes my face in his rough hands, brushing a thumb over my cheek, making it hard to breathe again. "I know what I said about you deserving someone who can give you more, and you *do* deserve that, but I can't stop wanting to get you naked."

A smile tugs at my lips, and my cheeks burn. "You can't?"

"Not even for a damn second. I've had more fantasies about you than I had in all my teenage years put together."

A nervous laugh tumbles out. "So . . . I *shouldn't* have called us cliché?"

"I don't give a damn what you call us. If we're cliché, then we're going to be the best cliché scene ever written."

He pushes his hands into my hair, fisting them as his mouth claims mine, greedily devouring me, unleashing a flood of desire that's been building for weeks. I cling to his shoulders, going up on my toes, wanting so much more. He takes the kiss deeper, tightening his grasp on my hair, sending a sting of pain and pleasure through my core. His other hand drops to my back and slides lower. He grabs my ass, grinding against me as we kiss, and holy hell does he feel good. I hear myself moan just as a growl escapes his lungs. The visceral sound makes me go a little wild. I claw at his shoulders, practically climbing him. His kisses consume me, drawing *want* and *need* with an intensity I didn't even know existed. Electric currents pulse through my veins, and I writhe against his hard body. Lust coils hot and tight low in my belly, and he's right there with me, grinding and moaning.

"*Fuuck*," he growls against my lips, and draws back. "Look at you, so damn beautiful with all those wild curls."

I try to pull his mouth back to mine, but his grip on my hair is too tight, keeping inches between us, and his eyes drill into me.

"Tell me that kiss was better than that other asshole."

"I don't remember kissing any other asshole, so shut up and give me your mouth."

Those dimples appear. "Good answer." Then his mouth is on mine, his scruff tickling my cheeks. I have a fleeting thought about protecting our friendship, but it's smothered by desire as we devour each other with feverish kisses. "Kissing you is like a drug," he growls, and cradles my jaw, brushing his thumb over my lower lip. "I want to do very dirty things to this mouth."

His words hit with a jolt of shock and pleasure. It's like he crawled into my head, digging up all my secret wants. I've been writing dirty talkers with unrelenting desire forever, but I've never had one of my own. He takes me in a merciless kiss, tongues tangling, teeth gnashing, and my knees go weak. His hand roams up my back, keeping our bodies flush, then down to my ass, clutching hard, hips grinding as he backs me up against the console. His teeth graze along my jaw, and he bites and sucks a path down my neck. My head falls back, and I close my eyes, reveling in the feel of his hot mouth, the way he takes what he wants. His every touch elicits shivers of heat, and all I can think is *More, more, more.* I grab his head, dragging his mouth back to mine, our passion igniting anew as we feast on each other. He leans back, putting space between our bodies, but doesn't stop kissing me as he unzips his hoodie I'm wearing and pushes it off me. I fist my hands in his shirt.

"I'm not going anywhere, darlin'," he says between ravenous kisses. "I just want to feel you." He reclaims my mouth, snaking a hand under my shirt, and I try to remember what bra I wore. Is it lace or cotton? Sexy or practical? He must feel me tense up, because he draws back and gazes into my eyes. "Want me to stop?"

"*No,*" I say quickly. "I just . . . I wasn't prepared for this, so don't expect Victoria's Secret."

He grins. "The only woman whose secret I want is the gorgeous woman standing in front of me."

"Oh yeah?" I whisper, grinning like a fool.

"Hell yeah, Bootsy. I want *all* your secrets, and I want to create dark and dirty secrets of our own." His lips graze mine as his fingers trail up my stomach and over my bra. He holds my gaze as he teases my nipple to a taut peak, making me ache with desire. I close my eyes against it, and he growls, "Eyes open, darlin'." When I open them, his eyes are volcanic. "I want to see what my touch does to you."

His words spur bashfulness, but it lasts only a second before bold confidence takes over. I've gone far too long holding back, not asking or taking what I want, and being okay with the men I was with getting off and leaving me hanging. I'm *done* with that. If I'm sharing my body,

I'm damn well going to get what I want, too, and Declan makes it easy. He makes me want to *play*. "Aren't you a greedy boy?"

He runs his fingertips along the swell of my breast. "When it comes to you, you have no idea how greedy."

His desires electrify me. He dips his head and kisses my neck, while his other hand slips under my shirt and caresses my breasts. My breathing hitches, and he takes me in another deep, penetrating kiss that has me moaning for more.

He tears his mouth away. "I'm going to put my mouth on you, Bootsy, so if you don't want that, now's your chance to tell me."

My breath rushes from my lungs, and I look around, feeling exposed. We're alone in the darkness, too far from shore to be seen, so I meet his hungry gaze and let Bold Girl come out to play. "I've had a few fantasies of my own. Let's see if you live up to them." I push up his shirt. "Take this off so I can feel your skin while your mouth is busy."

He reaches over his back and tugs off his shirt, tossing it aside. He doesn't have six-pack abs or those muscles that make girls go stupid. But he doesn't need them. Declan is one thick-bodied, fine beast of a man, and I want him like I've never wanted anyone before. I run my fingers through the dusting of dark hair on his chest and over his nipples. I press a kiss over his heart and slick my tongue over his nipple. He inhales through gritted teeth.

"*Oopsie.* Was I supposed to give you a chance to back out, too?"

His eyes narrow. "You little minx." He plants his hands on the console on either side of me, boxing me in with his big body. "For the record." He takes off my shirt and presses a kiss between my breasts as he unhooks my bra. "You can put your mouth on me anytime you'd like." He takes off my bra and drops it to the floor. "I'm hoping you'll grant me the same access."

My heart is racing. I should probably worry that my breasts aren't perky and my stomach is far from flat, but as his gaze takes a slow stroll down my chest, glowing with appreciation, those worries are far away.

"Mm-mm."

How can one sound make my entire body hum?

"Gorgeous, gorgeous Nicole." His hands skim up my ribs and brush the sides of my breasts. "What am I going to do with you?"

"A lot, I hope."

He growls again and seals his mouth over my neck, sucking and murmuring, "So beautiful . . . so fucking sexy." His words are as thrilling as his touch. I run my hands along his shoulders and into his hair as he cups my breasts and slides his tongue around and over one nipple, again and again, until my breathing becomes ragged. "You're perfect." He lavishes my other breast with the same toe-curling attention and sucks my nipple to the roof of his mouth. I fist my hands in his hair, inhaling sharply as prickling heat chases down my core. He does it again, harder this time, and I feel it between my legs. I dig my fingernails into his shoulders, and *"God"* comes out like a plea. He continues the exquisite torture, taunting and teasing until I'm dizzy with desire, rocking my hips. *"Declan, please."*

"I like you needy." He grazes my nipple with his teeth.

I gasp and pull his head up by his hair. Gone are worries of cotton or silk, replaced with raw desire. "You're driving me *crazy*."

"That's kind of the point." He nips at my lower lip.

"Point *made*. You're good at this, okay? Put your ego away, or I'm going to do the same to you."

"Now, *that* sounds promising."

I try to scowl, but I feel so good with him, it's hard to pull it off.

"Baby, this particular part of my ego hasn't been stroked in a very long time. If you think I'm going to rush when I finally have you in my arms, you're sorely mistaken." He looks around. "But we're going to need more room for what I have in mind."

He lowers his lips to mine and lifts me into his arms. I squeak in surprise as he carries me down to the cabin and tear my mouth away to say, "Impressive."

His eyes turn wicked. "You ain't seen nothing yet." He tugs off my boots and socks, still holding me up with one arm under my ass, and lays me on the bed. Those dark eyes never leave mine as he takes off his own shoes and socks and comes down over me. "Now, where were we?"

"You were about to stop teasing and start satisfying."

He reclaims my mouth, exquisitely rough and fiercely possessive. His arousal rocks eager and enticing against my center as his tongue delves deeper, so deliciously dominant I bow beneath him, grabbing his arms, his shoulders, wanting every inch of him. How could I have gone my whole life without ever being kissed like this? This man is a *master* at it, and I want *all* his kisses.

His fingers tangle into my hair, and he angles my mouth beneath his, taking the kiss impossibly deeper, stealing my ability to think about anything other than the pleasure consuming me. Moans spill from my lungs, and he tears his mouth away, leaving me bereft and breathless. But not for long. He tastes his way down my body, slowing to nip and tease my breasts. Every hot touch of his lips and taunting graze of his teeth steals a sharp inhalation. He bathes my stomach in open-mouthed kisses and long, tantalizing sucks that make my sex clench with anticipation. His teeth scrape my hip, and I squirm and claw at the blanket.

"Your body is insane." He trails feathery kisses from my hip to my belly button and circles it with his tongue. His fingers curl around the waist of my shorts, and I feel his eyes on me.

I meet his approval-seeking gaze. "Don't even *think* about stopping."

He touches his forehead to my stomach, his shoulders rocking with his chuckles. My stomach jiggles, and I have a flash of insecurity, but when he looks up, his hungry eyes make my heart skip. His expression turns devilish, and anticipation rushes through me as he lowers his teeth and tugs open the button on my shorts. *So damn hot.* He grabs hold of my shorts and panties and drags them lower, kissing the skin as he bares it. When he reaches my C-section scar, I hold my breath, knowing my stomach bulges above it. His eyes find mine, and they're brimming with so much emotion, I feel it stacking up inside me, too.

"That's one hell of a sexy scar." He presses tender kisses along the length of it, and I soak in each and every one.

He slides my shorts and panties lower, exposing my sex. I close my eyes, glad I shaved this morning and even more grateful that I thought to slip into the ladies' room before we left the restaurant and freshen up. He kisses just above my sex, and all around it. He continues dragging my clothes lower, kissing down one leg as he takes them off and up the other. My heart feels like it's going to beat right out of my chest.

He runs his big, rough hands up my hips as he kisses my inner thighs. I revel in the feel of his mouth on me, the way he takes his time, like he treasures every touch. He lifts my knees and presses his lips firmly to each inner thigh. "Jesus, Nic. You're so beautiful." He presses my legs to the mattress, holding me open to him. I've never felt so vulnerable or exposed, but with Declan, I feel safe and adored. His thumb slides along my wetness and presses on my clit. I gasp as pleasure shoots through me, my fingers curling into the blanket.

"I've been dying to taste you all night." His breath warms my center, and he drags his tongue along my sex in one slow glide, applying pressure with his thumb as he moves it in a circular motion, and a whimper escapes. He does it again and again, falling into a quickening rhythm that has me moaning and rocking my hips. Then his mouth is on my sex, devouring me, his tongue invading and licking, teeth driving me wild. When that talented mouth finds my clit and he pushes two fingers inside me, I bow off the mattress, a needy sound falling from my lips. He finds that magical spot inside me like a heat-seeking missile, turning me into a moaning, writhing mass of sensations that bowl me over. An orgasm builds like a mounting wave. I dig my heels into the mattress, unable to think, barely able to breathe. He takes my clit between his teeth and does something incredible with his fingers and tongue, and I *detonate*.

"*Declan*—" flies from my lungs as pleasure explodes inside me, spreading like wildfire through my chest, radiating all the way to my fingers and toes. He quickens his efforts, propelling me to new heights, and a stream of indiscernible sounds falls from my lips as I hit the peak and cry out his name again. My entire body quivers and quakes like never before. When I finally come down from my high, I collapse to the mattress, panting, trying to make sense of the dizzying world around me as he kisses his way up my body, slowing to cherish every oversensitive speck of skin.

By the time he reaches my lips, I'm trembling with need all over again. My eyes flutter open, and I've never seen such raw emotion looking back at me. He looks as drunk on me as I feel on him. I tuck that unforgettable look deep inside me and stroke his cheek. "I think I found your other hidden talent."

He laughs, and his head dips beside mine. "You're a trip, Boots." He presses a kiss to my shoulder and gazes down at me again. "You're in control, darlin'. Are we stopping here?"

"*Um.* That depends," I say with as straight a face as I can manage. "Do you have a death wish?"

He smothers our laughter with an excruciatingly passionate kiss that sends my body reeling again, then yanks his mouth away with a curse.

"What?"

"I didn't expect that we'd end up like this, and I don't have protection."

"I do!" I say it so cheerily, his brows slant.

"You carry condoms?"

"*No.* I mean, not usually, but Dani put them in my bag the first day we got to Chatemup. I didn't want them, but you met her. It's easier not to argue."

"Remind me to send her a thank-you card."

With a quick kiss, he climbs off the bed and dashes up the stairs, returning a minute later with my bag. I find the box and tear it open, holding up a condom like a prize.

"That's a start." He cocks a grin as he takes off his jeans.

I shove my hand back in and pull out the box. That's when I remember what size we bought, and my eyes drop to the formidable bulge behind his black boxer briefs. The guy is blessed in that department, but I can't resist walking on my knees over to the edge of the bed, hooking my finger in his waistband, and whispering, "Are these going to be too big? It's nothing to be embarrassed about. We can wait."

"Shit, Bootsy." He strips off his boxer briefs, and his impressive erection bobs against him. "What did you do, size me up at the coffee shop that first day?"

"No, but *damn*." I palm his cock, giving it a tight stroke. "I guess I got lucky, assuming you know how to use this thing."

"Never had any complaints."

That comment takes my head someplace I don't want to go, but seeing as I'm practically salivating on his cock, I force myself. "Do I need to worry about diseases?"

"No, Boots. You?"

I shake my head and run my tongue around the head of his cock. He groans, and his jaw clenches, so I do it again.

"*Nic*," he warns.

"Keep your warnings to yourself." I lick his length, getting it nice and wet, and his eyes bore into me as I lower my mouth, taking him in deep. I keep my eyes trained on his as I stroke and suck and tease. His muscles tense, and his hands dive into my hair, but he lets me set the pace. "*Fuuck*," he grits out, hands fisting. "I knew your mouth was made for me."

I smile around his shaft, stroking faster.

"Nic. *Fuck*. Nic, *stop*."

I still, blinking up at him.

"You've got to stop, baby. It's been a long time, and as much as I would *love* to see this through, I really want to be buried deep inside you when we come."

When we *come* plays in my mind as I release him. There's something warm and wonderful in knowing he's thinking of my pleasure, too, even as I offer him his on a silver platter.

He groans and grabs the base of his cock, squeezing tight. "Christ, you're good at that."

His praise bolsters my confidence even more. "Just returning the favor."

"I'll have to do favors for you more often. Now get up there like the sexy vixen you are."

I crawl up the bed, and he swats my ass. I glare at him as I turn onto my back.

"Next time that'll be my teeth."

"Promises, promises," I say as he comes down over me.

"Jesus, Nic. Now we've got more fantasies to live out. You make it impossible to resist you."

He buries his hands in my hair, devouring me again. The head of his cock is nestled against my entrance, and his chest hair tickles my skin. I rock beneath him, craving him inside me. He tears his mouth away again and says, "I need a fucking twelve-step program to stop kissing you."

I laugh as he snags a condom and goes up on his knees. He tears open the wrapper with his teeth and gives his cock a few strokes. *Okay, wow. That's hot.* I can't take my eyes off his hand.

"You like that?"

"Uh-huh." I bite my lower lip and force my eyes to his. I was married all those years, and never once did either of my husbands touch themselves in front of me. He strokes himself, and I lick my lips, wanting him in my mouth again. I have never been into blow jobs, but then again, I've never felt this type of connection with a man. "I can't wait."

I sit up and take him in my mouth. This time he threads his fingers into my hair, pumping his hips in time to my motions.

"God . . . Nic . . . So fucking good." He's breathing hard, his legs flexing.

I grab his ass with one hand, quickening my efforts. He thrusts faster. "Nic . . . *fuck* . . . *Nic.*" His warning is clear, but I dig my nails into his ass cheek with one hand and tug his balls with the other. "*Nic*—" flies from his lungs as his release spills down my throat. I take great pleasure in the string of curses he utters as his body pumps and jerks with aftershocks. When he withdraws from my mouth, he gathers me in his arms and lowers us to our sides on the mattress.

"What are you doing to me, Nic?"

"Whatever I want," I say playfully.

He nuzzles against my neck. "I'm gonna need a few minutes to recover." His hand slides down to my bottom and over my hip, settling between my legs. He moans against my skin. "You're so wet for me."

"I've never enjoyed doing that before. It's never turned me on like this."

"Because you weren't with me. I knew we'd be explosive together."

He kisses me slowly and sensually as he rolls me onto my back and works his magic again, lowering his mouth to my breast as his fingers send the world spinning away.

This time when he goes up on his knees to put on the condom, I stay on my back, watching this beautiful man protect us both. I'm not nervous or anxious as I reach for him and we align our bodies. It's as if I've been waiting for this, waiting for *him*, while running from everyone else. Our eyes lock as our bodies come together, and we both exhale, going still for that final moment when he's buried to the hilt. I'm acutely aware of his heart thundering against mine, his weight bearing down on me, and his thick length stretching and filling me. But it's the emotions in his eyes as he cradles my head in his hands and whispers "*Jesus*" that rock me to my core.

He slants his mouth over mine as we begin to move, falling into a cadence all our own. His kisses are deep and hypnotizing. My thoughts fragment as I lose myself in the rhythm of *us*. Our passion escalates with every thrust, every slide of our tongues, and we both go feral, groping, clawing, *biting*. Our skin grows slick from our efforts, our moans and his growls cutting through the air. I hook my heels around the backs of his legs, and he pushes his hands under my ass, lifting and angling so he can take me deeper. My limbs prickle and burn with a mounting orgasm, and he's right there with me, pounding harder, his muscles cording tight.

"*Nic—*"

The urgency in his voice matches the insistence of my climax barreling into me as we surrender to the power of our passion, crying out each other's names, lost in a kaleidoscope of pleasure.

Chapter Twenty-Five

DECLAN

Morning trickles in with a subtle tug, like the first nibble on a fishing line. Only that fishing line is my dick, and it's reacting to the feel of the beautiful naked woman who's been invading my fantasies for a month and is currently wrapped around me like an octopus. Her wild hair is tangled over my chest, her gorgeous legs intertwined with mine, and her enticing scent lingers in the cabin. I soak in the feel of her, remembering her taste, the sinful sounds she made, and the feel of her lips around my cock.

My dick readies for a replay.

Settle down, buddy.

Last night turned out a hell of a lot different than I imagined. But *damn.* I can't remember ever having so much fun in bed or feeling so in sync with a woman. And holy fuck, being inside Nicole? Feeling her shatter around me? That was nothing short of mind-blowing.

I've never met a woman who could break my resolve not to get emotionally involved, but Nicole Ross snuck under my radar, and she's got a naughty side I want to explore. As much as I want to take my fill, she's already been let down by the men in her life. I don't want to be the next in line, but man, I *really* like her. I've got to figure out how to navigate this without screwing up our friendship. Current octopus situation excluded, she doesn't seem the clingy type. Hopefully she'll be okay with keeping it casual.

The real question is, can I?

She makes a sleepy sound, and her eyes open. A sweet smile starts to appear, but I see last night registering in the *oh shit* look rising in her eyes as she rolls off me and stares up at the ceiling. Amused by her reaction, I go up on my elbow. "Morning, Bootsy."

"So . . . I guess *that* really happened."

"Yup."

Her beautiful eyes dart to the left, to the right, anywhere to escape mine, I assume. "We're still anchored away from shore?"

"The boat fairy didn't show up last night to take us back to the marina. I'll dock his pay."

Our eyes connect, and that gorgeous smile that always reels me in slowly appears. "I thought the walk of shame was bad. I can't imagine what the swim of shame will be like. I can already hear the gossip about the writer and the fish peddler doing the nasty in his boat." She pulls the sheet over her face.

I should cut this thing between us short, get out of bed, shower, and head to land. That would be the right thing to do, but the right thing doesn't stand a chance against the hold this woman has over me. I lower the sheet to her waist, and when she tries to grab it, I cover her hand with mine and dip my head to kiss her lips. She doesn't try to turn away. She returns my efforts, giving me the green light I was hoping for.

"Why would you want to do the swim of shame when we can go for an encore?"

Her eyes spark with heat. So damn sexy. I move over her, and she spreads her legs, welcoming me as I pin one of her delicate wrists to the mattress beside her head. "You're here." I graze my teeth along her jaw, and she moans. "I'm here." I lift her other hand and pin it to the mattress, too. "And I'm ravenous for another taste of you." I nip at her earlobe and rub my cock against her clit, earning another sensual sound. I angle my hips, pressing my cock against her slickness, and drag my tongue along the shell of her ear. "Tell me what you want, Nicole."

"*You*," she says breathily, and it's the best fucking sound in the world.

Second only to the sexy sounds she makes over our next debaucherous hour.

◆　◆　◆

Two mind-numbing orgasms and one incredibly sexy shower later, I'm flying high as we drive into town from the marina. Nicole is sporting that sexually satisfied glow I'm sure everyone can spot from a mile away, and hell if I don't feel like pounding my chest like a silver-backed gorilla. I park across the street from Rise and Grind and hop out of the truck to open Nicole's door.

"Are we getting coffee?" she asks as she climbs out.

"I thought I'd be a gentleman and spring for breakfast."

"You don't have to do that. I have to get back and write."

"A'right, coffee it is." We head inside, and I see Matt glancing at us from behind the counter. I touch Nicole's back and lower my voice. "You're in luck. Your barista boyfriend is here."

"Shut up, and wipe that smug look off your face."

"I don't know what you're talking about. This is my normal face."

She arches a brow, and I chuckle.

We get our coffees to go and drive back to her place. As I walk her up to the door, a mix of sexual tension and that awkward unsurety of *what's next* thickens between us. We've made it this far without talking about what this is or what it means, and I'm hoping to avoid having that particular discussion.

She digs out her keys. "So . . . thanks for a great night."

The slightly bashful smile I spotted last night reappears, tugging at something deep inside me. Damn, this woman. She has no idea how she knots me up inside.

That's my cue to get out of there. "Yeah, it was fun. We should do it again sometime." I lean and kiss her cheek, because if I kiss those lips, I'm not getting back in my truck. "Good luck writing."

And like a chickenshit teenager—or a man whose life is too complicated to drag her into it—I head back to my truck.

Chapter Twenty-Six

NICOLE

"How's the book coming?" Rachel asks on Tuesday afternoon on a three-way video call with me and Dani. Rachel is at a park, waiting for a couple to show up to take their engagement photos, Dani is walking four dogs at a very fast clip, and I'm writing.

"Oh, it's *coming*, but I'm going to have to change the title to something sexier. I can't stop my characters from fooling around."

"Why would you want to?" Dani asks.

"Because that's *all* I'm writing. The hero came to pick up documents from her office, and I swear, I had it all mapped out. It was going to be a sexually tense scene that led to a steamier scene the following week, but do they listen? *No.* He struts into her office all alpha and cocky and locks the door behind him. Their clothes go flying and they christen her desk, her credenza, *and* her couch."

"Bold and naughty. I like it." Rachel waggles her brows.

"Sounds like Declan's python has taken over your mighty pen," Dani says. "Have you seen him since you two hooked up?"

"*No.* We text all the time, and he's just as charming and great as always. Nothing's really changed. Except everything *has*, you know? I have no idea what to make of it."

"It's only been two days," Dani says.

"Yes, but this is Nic, and she hates loose ends," Rachel points out, and she's right. "Maybe casual sex isn't right for you."

"Or maybe it's not right for him," Dani suggests. "Maybe he's not sure how to move forward."

"Are you kidding? This is Declan we're talking about. I told you how he got me all hot and bothered before we even came close to hooking up, when he was just describing a sexy scene. That's not a man who doesn't know what he's doing."

"Especially in the bedroom," Rachel adds.

"He definitely excels in that area. But help me out here. I know we're both busy, and I don't want to be that person who needs to define things—"

"But that's who you are," Rachel says.

"I *know*, and this is exactly what I was trying to avoid. The drama of not knowing what's what. This is one more reason I didn't want a relationship."

"*Didn't* is the operative word," Dani says as she tries to wrangle two rascally dogs into submission.

"I *don't* want one." I barely get the words out before realizing it might not be true with Declan. But going there would be setting myself up for heartache, especially with a guy who describes his own life as a hot mess. "I just need clarity. I think I can be cool with just hooking up if I know the parameters. When he said, *we should do it again sometime*, do you think he meant dinner, going out on his boat, or screwing ourselves silly?"

"Screwing yourselves silly," they say in unison.

"That's what I thought, and obviously I want that." I snag the last of the lemon bars Evelyn brought up yesterday and take a bite as I head out to the deck. Just the sight of the water takes my anxiety down a notch. Well, the lemon bar helps, too.

"But can you do it without knowing how you fit into his life or when you'll see him again?" Rachel asks.

"What if you see him out with another woman?" Dani asks.

My stomach twists. "That could mess with my head, but I like my life the way it is, and I like our relationship the way it is, without the stress of checking in and making plans."

"Apparently you don't love that, or you wouldn't be having this much trouble dealing with it after two days," Rachel says.

"No, really. I *do* like it . . . but I also don't," I admit.

"*Girl.*" Dani points at me. "You need to learn to embrace the summer hookup and enjoy the fun. It's only complicated because you make it complicated."

"I might need shock therapy for that, but I really don't want to give up my independence or risk my happiness. You know what? You're right. I'm making it complicated. I'm overthinking, like always. I'm going to put this out of my head and let nature take its course. I should get some writing done anyway. My stupid brain refuses to work after six p.m., and all this confusion doesn't help. It's like someone reset my workday clock. Remember the good old days, when I wrote until ten or eleven at night?"

"Those were *not* the good old days. You're living what will become your good old days, and I'm proud of you for cutting out early," Rachel says.

"It's not like I have a choice. My next book will be called *Betrayed by My Brain*."

"Like hell. It'll be called *Fucked by Fish Peddler*," Dani chimes in, and we all laugh.

"I love you guys. Wish me some *wholesome* words today."

When we end the call, I'm tempted to go down to the beach, close my eyes, and let the world fade away. But work calls . . .

◆ ◆ ◆

Several hours later, I'm trying to coerce myself into writing another chapter with promises of ice cream and bingeing a show afterward, when Declan comes through my patio doors.

"And to our left, ladies and gentlemen, we see Writer Girl in her natural surroundings."

Those dimples, that smile, and a hint of wickedness in his eyes send heat rushing up my chest. *Down, girl.* I push to my feet, trying to act cool. "Hey, what are you doing here?"

His arm circles my waist, and he hauls me against him. "I said we should do it again sometime. How's now?"

"That wasn't meant as an open door for a booty call," I say playfully.

He smirks. "Should I go back out and knock?"

God, this man . . .

He touches his forehead to mine. "Bootsy, are you trying to tell me you weren't thinking about getting naked with me for the last two days?"

His voice is pure seduction, and I melt against him, pushing my hands beneath the back of his shirt. His skin is warm, his body hard, and I really want to tear his clothes off. "I didn't say that."

"Good, because getting you naked has consumed my thoughts, which makes it very difficult when I'm trying to negotiate contracts."

"Funnily enough, I can't seem to write anything but sexy scenes lately. If I'm not careful, my book will slip into erotica."

"Erotica, huh?" His eyes narrow. "We should act out those scenes and make sure you've got the mechanics right."

He brushes his lips over mine and bites my lower lip, sending a sting of lust spiking through me. I decide Dani is right, and I embrace the idea of a fun summer hookup with this man whom I adore. I push out of his arms, and as I head for the stairs, I take off my shirt and toss it over my shoulder. "First one to the bedroom gets to decide which scene we act out."

"Fuck that." He scoops me up, and I squeal with laughter as he runs—*runs!*—up the stairs with me in his arms. "The quicker we're both in the bedroom, the faster I can get you naked."

Chapter Twenty-Seven

NICOLE

After writing an exceptional scene on Friday morning, I reward myself with a walk into town for a latte and muffin at the Rise and Grind, where I hope to write another couple of chapters. I've gotten in the habit of writing there a few hours each week, and I really enjoy it. I've met some interesting people, and the coffee is way better than mine.

I pack my laptop and notebook into my bag and shoulder it on my way out the door. It's such a beautiful day, I wonder why I ever spent so many years chained to my desk.

"Hey there, baby girl," Aspen says as she and Marcus come out of their development dressed for the beach. She's carrying towels, and Marcus has a bag over his shoulder and a beach chair in each hand.

"Hi."

"We've been wondering what you've been up to the last few days," Aspen says. "You're positively glowing. You must be writing your little heart out."

More like screwing my brains out. Declan came over two of the last three nights, and we've gotten creative in the kitchen, in the living room, and on my desk, which was a fantasy of mine. The desk was horribly uncomfortable, and the height was wrong for what we had envisioned. We laughed the whole time, which made the experience even better. Not only is sex with Declan intense and fun, but we lie together afterward, talking and watching old episodes of silly shows, like we've been friends with benefits forever. Dani was right. Letting go of the need for definition has made whatever this is between us even more enjoyable.

"You really are glowing," Marcus says, drawing me back to our conversation.

"Am I? It must be from the sun during my morning runs or my walks with Aspen and Maggie. What have you been up to the last few days?"

"We're enjoying every minute of this fine summer," Marcus says.

"Our girls are coming to visit with their families next weekend. They'd love to meet you if you can spare some time away from writing."

"I've been quitting early lately. Let me know what day works, and I'll come down."

"Wonderful! I'll talk to the girls and let you know," Aspen says.

"Are you heading into town to write?" Marcus asks. "Folks are talking about you becoming a regular at the Rise and Grind."

"I don't know why that's news, but I like writing there. I'd better get going. Have a great afternoon."

On my way into town, I say hello to a few other neighbors I've met over the last six weeks. One of them studies me with amusement as I walk past. I give my outfit a quick check to make sure I haven't lost a button on my top or left my zipper down on my shorts, but all seems fine, and I let it go.

The coffee shop is busy. I enjoy Matt's flirting as I get a latte and a cranberry-nut muffin, and when I head for my usual comfy chair by the windows, I see Declan at a table with a handsome young man with short dark hair and serious eyes. Declan glances over and flashes a grin that I swear tells the world we're sleeping together. But I know that's just me worrying about becoming part of the town gossip. I'm not sure anyone else would recognize the difference in his smile or the secret glimmer in his eyes that I've found inescapable ever since that first night on the boat.

"Hey, Bootsy." He waves me over and drinks me in from head to toe as I approach, sending the hummingbirds that have become constant companions when we're together into flight.

"Hi." I smile at the younger guy.

"Nic, this is my son Neil. Neil, this is my adventure buddy, Nic. She's a writer, and she just bought a summer house here."

His use of *adventure buddy* feels oddly special, and not quite special enough, but in the spirit of embracing this undefined thing we're doing, I push that thought aside. "It's nice to meet you, Neil. Are you here for the weekend?"

Familiar dimples appear on Neil's cheeks. "Yes, to celebrate my dad's birthday."

"Your dad's *birthday*?" I eye Declan. "Shouldn't your adventure buddy know about your special day?"

Declan shakes his head. "It's not a big deal."

"My dad hates celebrating his birthday," Neil says. "Which is why my brother and I refuse to let him avoid it. We're having a barbecue at Dad's tonight around seven. Why don't you come?"

I feel a little uneasy. Declan would have mentioned it if he wanted me there. I'm about to kindly decline when Declan says, "You should come. It would be nice to see you."

Goodbye, uneasy. Hello, fluttery delight. "Maybe I will."

Declan nods toward my bag. "You're not going to write steamy scenes in here, are you? If your barista boyfriend catches wind of them, he's liable to try to hack into your laptop."

"I'm writing a family scene, thank you very much, and I'm pretty sure my barista boyfriend is better at making coffee than hacking into computers. I'd better get to work. It's nice to meet you, Neil. Maybe I'll see you tonight."

"I hope so," they say in unison.

As I walk away, I hear Declan say, "Stop looking at her ass."

There's definitely something in the Chatemup water.

◆ ◆ ◆

My hair decides to go rogue for Declan's party, with springy curls sticking out all over. *Lucky me.* I don't even try to tame it. It's fitting to have hot mess hair during this hot mess summer. *And I'm very much enjoying my hot mess man.*

After putting on a little eyeliner and blush, it takes me forever to decide what to wear, which irritates me. I'm far too nervous about meeting Declan's family. I finally decide on a thin gray long-sleeve boatneck sweater with bell sleeves. I tuck a little of the front into my cutoffs, slip on dangling gold earrings, and head downstairs.

Grabbing the gift bag with the card I made for him and an assortment of candy bars—because what else do you buy a forty-eight-year-old fish peddler / white knight / adventure buddy—and leave before I chicken out.

I wasn't sure if I'd remember the way to Declan's cottage, but I do, and I arrive at seven thirty, just as I planned. I pocket my key fob and phone, grab the gift bag, and hope I appear fashionably late rather than rude. There's music coming from the backyard, and I take a moment to try to calm my nerves. I don't know what to expect, or what he's told his family and friends about me, if anything, but suddenly I wonder if *adventure buddy* is code for *friend with benefits*, which makes me even more nervous.

Okay, Nic, pull it together. You're going to your friend's barbecue to celebrate his birthday. Nobody cares that you're sleeping with him.

I follow a walkway around to the back, and I'm surprised to see only a handful of people. A bonfire crackles in a stone firepit, where a shaggy-haired muscular guy who looks to be in his early twenties is roasting marshmallows with two little girls wearing shorts and sweatshirts. I recognize Ethan, even without his water gun, manning the grill with Chuck, but I don't see Declan or Neil.

Speak of the devil, Neil walks out the back door, followed by a pretty blonde whose hair is braided over one shoulder. They're carrying dishes of food.

"Hey, Nic," Neil says as they set the dishes on the table. "I'm glad you made it."

I head over to them. "Thanks for inviting me. Did the birthday boy skip town?"

"He wishes. He's inside with my grandfather. They'll be right out." He motions to the blonde. "This is my aunt Annie. Annie, this is Dad's friend Nicole."

Annie looks to be about my age, with bright blue eyes and a friendly smile, and her name rings a bell. "Hi. Are you Ethan's wife?"

"Yes, and you must be the cookie thief."

"Oh my gosh." I laugh softly. "I'm so sorry about that."

"Don't be. It was the highlight of Ethan's week," Annie says.

"Dad told me about your epic ninja skills," Neil says.

"I don't know how epic they are. I stopped cold when Ethan came outside armed with a water gun. But Declan wasn't about to let his brother steal his victory, and he carried me off like a caveman."

"Dad definitely has a competitive streak," Neil says as Declan comes outside carrying a plate of rolls. "Don't you, Dad?"

"Damn right." Declan's eyes land on me, and that secret smile appears as he sets the plate on the table and joins us. He looks nice in a casual short-sleeve button-down, jeans, and leather flip-flops.

"It was nice meeting you, but we should go do something over there." Annie gives me a conspiratorial glance and tugs Neil away.

"Aren't you a sight for sore eyes." Declan leans in and kisses my cheek. "You look beautiful."

I soak in the compliment. "Thank you. You look pretty sharp yourself. I thought there were going to be more people here. Am I crashing your family's celebration?"

"You're not crashing anything. I'm glad you're here, but this is one reason I didn't invite you. I figured meeting my family might scare you off."

I kind of love that he didn't want to scare me off. "Was there another reason?"

"Yeah. Having a birthday party for an almost fifty-year-old is a little silly."

"No, it's *not*, and for the record, if you're around when it's my birthday, I want a big party with friends and cake and music and wine."

He laughs. "Balloons, too?"

"Absolutely."

"When's your birthday?"

"January, but I'll be back in Virginia by then, so you're off the hook." I don't want to think about returning to the place where my old life feels like a perpetual black cloud hanging over my head, or how much I'll miss Declan and my other friends when I go back, so I focus on the here and now and hold up the gift bag. "I made you a card."

"You *made* me a card? This I have to see." He looks in the bag and grins when he sees the candy. "Did you buy me chocolate hoping I'd share?"

"Who, *me*? I'd never do that."

"You're right. You can't lie worth shit." He opens the envelope and withdraws the card. I watch him read what I've written on the front.

ADVENTURE (NOUN): AN UNUSUAL AND EXCITING, POS-
SIBLY DANGEROUS, ACTIVITY

BUDDY (NOUN): A CLOSE FRIEND

His eyes flick briefly to mine before he opens and reads the inside.

*It's your special day, Dimple Dude! I hope this year
is full of memorable adventures and all your wishes
come true. Thanks for making my summer great. Your
boot-wearing adventure buddy, WG*

I drew colorful balloons around the words and wrote *Happy 48th!*
in a bright yellow balloon beside *WG*. "I know it's not much, but I
figured you might have a few naughty wishes I could help come true."

"This just might be the best gift I've ever been given." He puts the
card back in the bag and sets it on the table. "Thanks, Nic."

"Who is this gorgeous lady?" an older, slightly heavier version of
Declan with a mop of gray hair, a mustache to match, and those telltale
dimples asks as he comes out of the house and joins us.

"Dad, this is my friend Nic. Nic, this is my father, Rick."

I notice Declan's eyes going to the bottle of beer in his father's hand.
"It's nice to meet you, Rick."

"Not as nice as it is to meet you. You're here for me, right?" Rick
winks.

"*Dad*," Declan warns.

"I'm kidding." Rick's laughter is as deep and hearty as Declan's
usually is. "I hear you're an authoress."

"I've never been called that before, but yes, I write a little."

"Modest," he says. "I like that in a woman. I write, too."

Declan's brows slant in confusion.

"Declan didn't mention that. What do you write?"

"Limericks mostly. Maybe you've heard them. Here's one of my
favorites." Rick clears his throat. "There once was a man from Maldives,
whose wives had many pet peeves. He brought home a whip and said
don't give me any lip, or I'll tie you down with a master grip and go to
town until you drip."

"*Dad*," Declan snaps.

"What? It's pretty good, right, Nic?"

I stifle a laugh. "You're very talented, and just as charming as your son."

"This guy?" He cocks his head at Declan. "The one eyeing my beer?" He lifts the bottle. "See the label? Nonalcoholic."

Declan takes a second look. "I did notice, Dad. Thanks."

"Finally, a little appreciation," he says, but I can tell he means it lightly. "Good thing I've got a whiskey chaser waiting for me back home."

Declan utters a curse, and his father claps him on the shoulder. "You can't change me, son, but I sure am glad you love me." He glances at me. "My son is a great guy but a terrible host. What can I get you to drink?"

"Anything is fine, thanks."

"I bought some white zin for her. It's in the kitchen."

"You've got it."

As Rick saunters away, I step closer to Declan. "Thank you for buying me white zinfandel, and I kind of love your dad."

"Everyone does," he says with loving exasperation. "Come on, I'll introduce you to Eric and Ethan and his girls."

"Mia and Ellie, right?"

"Good memory."

Chuck and Ethan intercept us. They're carrying plates of hamburgers and hot dogs toward the table. "Hey, Nic." Chuck gives me a one-armed hug. "Word on the street says you're gaining quite a rep as Miller's new partner in crime."

"It's crazy how fast word spreads in this town." I wonder if he knows about our mattress wrestling, too.

"The Wanted poster in the post office probably doesn't help," Chuck says. "It makes you and Miller look like Bonnie and Clyde."

Ethan chuckles, and Declan narrows his eyes at him. "Tell me you *didn't*."

Holy cow. Would his brother really go that far?

"No can do, bro. I've got to up my game with your new adventure buddy around."

That curious look my neighbor gave me is starting to make sense.

"I told him not to do it," Annie says, taking the plates from Chuck and Ethan. She looks at me and says, "Miller men don't listen very well."

As she walks away with the plates, Ethan says, "All's fair in cookie wars. Nic, we haven't formally met. I'm Ethan, the handsome Miller brother."

"He's as proud of that as I am of being the well-endowed one," Declan chimes in. "I still think he got ripped off, but no one said life was fair."

"Hey, Dad," the muscular guy calls over his shoulder from the firepit. "Did you forget I took over that title from you?"

"Nic, meet my smartass son, Eric."

Rick puts an arm around Eric's shoulder and says, "We all know the real reigning champ doesn't have to brag." He raises his brows and grins.

"Thanks, Gramps," Neil says. "I was trying to keep a low profile, but . . ."

I lean closer to Declan. "I see the apples didn't fall far from the tree."

The girls run over, and the older of the two, Mia, says, "Aren't you going to introduce *us*, Uncle Declan?" Her honey hair brushes the shoulders of her pink sweatshirt, which has MERMAID PRINCESS across the front in gold letters.

"If I must," Declan teases. "Nic, these are Ethan and Annie's girls, Daisy and Petunia."

The girls giggle.

"Uncle *Dec*!" Ellie complains with a big grin. The white bow around her ponytail matches the white hearts on her blue sweatshirt.

"Oh, sorry." Declan touches their shoulders. "Blossom and Tulip."

They giggle again, and Mia plants a hand on her hip with all the attitude an eight-year-old can muster. "I'm Mia, and that's Ellie."

"It's nice to meet you both," I say.

Ellie tugs on Declan's arm. "Is she the friend you said was pretty?"

"I told you that in confidence, Chatty Cathy." Declan lifts her off her feet and over his head. She beams down at him, giggling.

When he sets her on her feet, she wraps her arms around his waist, hugging him as she says, "She *is* pretty."

"And she's got killer legs," Eric adds.

"Dude, watch yourself," Declan warns.

"What? She does," Eric says. "Do you work out, Nic?"

"I run a little," I say. "You're in great shape. You must work out a lot."

"I lift six days a week," he says proudly.

Ellie bounces on her toes. "Eric, can we play monkey?"

"Monkey! Monkey!" Mia chants.

Eric puts his arms up and flexes, eating up the attention as the girls squeal with delight and jump up, hanging from his arms like monkeys.

"Okay, that's enough." Declan grabs one girl under each arm. "Eric's going to make Uncle Dec look bad."

Dinner includes more of the same happy banter and good-natured ribbing. We have table-wide debates about the best desserts, movies, and sports. Mia gushes about wanting to play basketball when she's older, and Ellie thinks sports are stupid. Declan teases his nieces, but they give it right back to him. Annie and I talk about what it's like to parent girls, and Rick chimes in on how different it was to raise boys. I learn Eric's girlfriend couldn't get off work this weekend but that she's read a few of my books, and Eric admits to being a voracious reader of historical nonfiction.

As we eat, Chuck and I commiserate about the ups and downs of creating music and art, and Neil shares his excitement for his current architectural project. Rick and Ethan talk about their family business, and Declan joins every conversation and fills me in on inside jokes. He boasts about everyone, including his father and *me*—not my writing, but *me*, as a person—and his sincerity comes out in droves. I enjoy seeing him as a loving father, joking brother, loyal friend, and caring son and learning more about all of them as Declan and I sneak furtive glances and his hand rests on my leg under the table.

When Rick brings up his late son, Declan and Ethan join right in, telling stories that make their brother, Neil, feel very much alive. There's so much love and good energy around the table, it makes me miss my own family. I don't want dinner to end, but eventually it does, and Declan pulls me aside.

"I know my family is a lot to handle, and you've been a real sport. Are they driving you crazy yet?"

"Not at all. I like your family. They're as loud and opinionated as mine, and Chuck seems like he's been at your dinner table for years."

He looks across the lawn at Chuck coming out of the house carrying two guitars. "He has. He's worked with me for a decade, and he's become part of the family."

I like that he says *worked with* rather than *worked for*. "Like Rachel and Dani are to me. I love that."

"I'm really glad you're here, Nic, and I'll understand if you've had enough and want to take off. But if not, we're about to play some music. It'd be cool if you stuck around."

"Sure. Is Chuck's band coming?"

He cocks a grin. "Nope. We're kicking it old-school tonight. I better go help the guys."

As the guys set up musical equipment on the patio, Mia and Ellie run around chattering, and Annie sidles up to me. "They're a wild bunch, aren't they?"

"I'm used to it. I have three brothers. Are you from a big family?"

"No. I'm an only child, but I'm used to it now."

"How long have you and Ethan been together?"

"We met at a builders' expo twelve years ago. I was working as an interior designer and trying to drum up clientele, and he had a booth for their cabinetry business. We stayed up all night talking, and the rest is history."

"Sounds like it was meant to be."

"I like to think so." She looks lovingly at Ethan, talking with the guys. "I love that man and this wacky family. What about you? How did you meet Declan?"

"First I spilled coffee on him, and then we met again at a neighbor's bonfire, and after that he just seemed to be everywhere I was. But we're not a couple. I'm only here for the summer, and we're just having fun."

"Yeah, I know you're his adventure buddy, which makes me curious."

"About . . . ?"

"The real scoop," she says like we're old friends. "I love Declan. He's kind of like the white knight of the family, known for saving people. But you sure don't seem like a damsel in distress."

"Thanks. I'd like to think I've got my shit together most of the time."

"Are you *really* just adventure buddies? Because you guys are good together, and it's great to see him hanging out and having fun instead of just working and taking care of everyone else."

I like Annie. She's warm and friendly, and I can see myself becoming friends with her, but I'm not about to out us to his family. "We really are just friends. He makes me laugh and gets me out of my own head, so I guess you could say he saved me from having a lame summer."

"Testing, testing," Declan says into a microphone, interrupting us.

I'm surprised to see him and his father holding electric guitars. Eric is sitting behind a drum set, Neil is standing at a keyboard, and Chuck and Ethan are holding acoustic guitars. "They *all* play instruments?"

"Yeah. They have for years. I guess Declan didn't tell you?"

His family just jumped out of my realm and into a universe all their own. "I knew he played the acoustic guitar, but . . . *no*."

They start playing "I'm on Fire," and when Declan sings, the rough timbre of his voice gives me chills. Our eyes meet, and it feels like he's singing directly to me, but somehow it also feels like our togetherness is still our little secret. The girls are dancing, and as Annie joins them, I take out my phone and record Declan looking and sounding like he walked out of a dream.

They sing one song after another, and the girls, Annie, and I applaud like fangirls and dance. As the night rolls on, the guys take turns taking breaks, and when they do, they dance with me, Annie, and the girls.

There's something wonderful about a family with pretty significant underlying issues setting them aside for a night to celebrate one of their own. I'm happy for Declan and just as grateful to be included.

When they start playing "Secret Garden," Declan puts down the guitar and comes off the patio, crooking his finger toward me. I go to him, and he twirls me into his arms, singing as we dance. When he looks at me the way he is right now, it feels like nothing else exists but the two of us. I have to remind myself that this is just a moment in time. This man's real life is complicated, and mine is hundreds of miles away.

But tonight, and the evenings we've managed to steal away from it all, are beautifully carefree and exhilarating, and I hold on to each and every one of those memories, stockpiling them like a squirrel gathering nuts for the winter.

Chapter Twenty-Eight

DECLAN

It's after eleven when we start cleaning up. Neil and Eric are putting away the instruments, and Chuck is inside handling dishes and wrapping up leftovers. He'll leave with a pile of leftovers, as he always does. Annie left early to put the girls to bed and gave my father a ride home on her way. Nicole took off a little while ago. I felt prying eyes on us when I walked her to her car and restrained myself from kissing her the way I've been dying to all night.

Now I wish I'd kissed her senseless. Hell, I wished I'd left with her.

"How does it feel to be one step closer to fifty?" Ethan asks as we clear the tables.

"No different than I felt yesterday, or last week, or last year." That's a load of shit. I don't care about getting older, but I feel a hell of a lot different than I did even before the party. This was the best birthday I've had in years, and spending the evening with Nicole and my family did something to me. Nicole might have looked as rattled as a chicken in a fox den when she first arrived and realized how small the party was, but she rolled with it and fit right in. She got along as well and as easily with my family as she does with me, and she didn't make me feel pressured to treat her like we were a couple.

I had those urges all on my own, and I think I did a damn good job of holding them back.

I glance at the gift bag, thinking about the card she made and the chocolates she bought. I had forgotten how nice it was to be thought of, and I try to remember if Lindsay had ever made those efforts toward me. Maybe it's resentment, or maybe she's just fucking selfish, but I can't recall anything more than a generic card with her name signed on the bottom.

"It's been a hell of a long time since I've heard you call anyone your adventure buddy," Ethan says.

"No shit." Our brother, Neil, was the only other adventure buddy I've ever had, and Ethan and my father are probably the only people left who know that. "It just came out one day."

"She must be pretty special."

"Thanks for a great time, Boss," Chuck says as he comes out the back door. He holds up two plastic containers of food. "Cleaned up the leftovers and left you the cake."

"Thanks, man. I appreciate you coming over tonight."

"You know I wouldn't miss it."

"You taking off, Chuck?" Neil asks as he and Eric pick up the drums to carry them inside.

"Yeah, but I'll see you on the boat tomorrow," Chuck answers.

We planned a fishing trip like we do every year. I wish I had invited Nicole to join us, but two family events in a row doesn't exactly spell *casual.*

"Looking forward to it," Eric says.

Chuck turns back to me. "It was fun hanging out with Nic again. She's a hell of a woman."

"Yes, she is."

Neil and Eric exchange a glance, making no move to go inside.

"You said she's your adventure buddy. Does that mean I can ask her out, or . . . ?" Chuck asks.

The green-eyed monster digs its claws in, and my chest knots up. My boys are watching me, and I know Ethan's listening. Chuck deserves a woman as great as Nicole. He's reliable, gives one hundred percent to everything he does, and he doesn't have a million people leaning on him.

But I'm not a fucking martyr. "That depends. Do you value your life?"

"Told you he was into her," Eric says.

"Who calls the chick they're into their adventure buddy?" Neil asks.

Ethan locks eyes with me and says, "That's a coveted title. Anyone can be a girlfriend, but not many can achieve adventure-buddy status."

"I knew there was a reason you've been whistling lately." Chuck flashes a shit-eating grin.

"Seriously, Dad, does she know that's a coveted title?" Eric asks. "Because my girl would be pissed at being called an adventure buddy."

"We're not kids, Eric, and she's not my girl. We're just enjoying each other's company."

"Like fuck buddies?" Eric asks.

I glower at him.

"What?" Eric splays his hands. "That's what it sounds like."

I clench my teeth against the need to straighten that out, but I don't fucking know what we are, either, and I'm not about to tell them that. "You know what? You guys can clean this shit up. I'm outta here."

As I head out of the backyard, Eric calls after me, "Don't stay out past curfew."

"Use protection," Neil hollers.

I flick them the bird without turning around so they can't see my grin and head to my truck.

◆ ◆ ◆

Nicole's lights are still on when I get there. I probably should've texted, but she's always so cute when I show up unannounced. Her eyes light up, and she gets that nervous smile. Sometimes she rambles, which is beyond adorable. I tell myself we're not going to have sex tonight. I don't want her to think that's the reason I like being with her. I didn't come over intending to have sex earlier this week, but I have no control with her. It's like coming together unleashed something primal in me, but tonight it's going to be different.

I hear music and follow it around to her deck. She's sitting cross-legged on a lounge chair with her laptop, her curls framing her beautiful face and her fingers flying over the keyboard. The knots in my chest loosen. My days are spent putting out fires, and when I see Nicole, hell, when I get texts from her, it's like applying salve to a wound.

"So this is what a genius at work looks like."

She looks up, eyes shining in the moonlight. "Declan? What are you doing here?" She sets her laptop on the deck and stands in sexy sleeping shorts and a long-sleeved shirt, her nipples pressing against the thin cotton fabric.

How am I supposed to resist her? "The birthday boy isn't done celebrating."

"You can't leave when your boys came just to see you."

"They're adults. I'll see them tomorrow." I slide my arm around her, pulling her in close. "We're going fishing for the day."

"They're going to know you left for a booty call."

"I don't give a shit what they know." I dip my head to kiss her neck, inhaling the sweet scent of her bodywash. "It's my birthday, and I missed you."

She winds her arms around my neck. "You *just* saw me."

"I didn't see enough of you." I push my hands into the back of her shorts and palm her bare ass. "I'm really glad you came tonight."

"I haven't yet," she says saucily. "But I'm hoping you're going to change that."

Heat flares behind my zipper. "*Jesus*, Nic. I'm trying to be a gentle-man. I promised myself I wouldn't just *take* you tonight."

"Why would you do a silly thing like that?" she asks so innocently, it's dead sexy.

"I'm having a hard time remembering why."

She laughs softly.

"I didn't want you to think I'm only here for sex."

"You shared your Girl Scout cookies with me." She presses all her soft curves against me and whispers, "We're good."

"Mind if we stay out here?" We're too high up for anyone to see us, but I don't want to assume she's okay with it.

"I was hoping you'd want to."

"*God*, I like you." I lower my mouth to hers, intending to go slow, but the first touch of our lips is electric, and my resolve shatters. I devour her, and she goes up on her toes, rubbing herself against me and pushing her hands into my hair. I fucking love that. I can't get enough of her taste, her scent, her *fervor*. She stumbles backward with the force of our kisses, and her back hits the patio door. I slip a hand between us, into her shorts, and we both moan as my fingers push through her wetness. I play her clit like a fucking fiddle and slide two fingers inside her. She gasps into our kisses. "How can I miss touching you so much?"

I reclaim her mouth as she rides my fingers and bury my other hand in her hair. I tug her head back and seal my mouth over her neck, sucking hard. She cries out, rising on her toes again, and I slow my efforts, prolonging her pleasure.

"*Declan*," she pleads.

"Better keep your voice down, or you'll wake the neighbors." I kiss her again, our tongues tangling, as I drive her wild. I revel in the sounds she makes, the way she rides my fingers like her life depends on it. My cock aches to get in on the action, and I quicken my efforts. It doesn't take long before she's spiraling over the edge. Her pussy clenches tight and hot around my fingers, and I swallow her sexy sounds as her hips buck and her body trembles.

When she goes boneless in my arms, I withdraw from between her legs, and her eyes flutter open as I lick my fingers clean. "So damn sweet."

She bites her lower lip, then whispers, "Have you been reading my books?"

I grin. "No, but based on the scenes we acted out the other night, I'm going to start. Tell me what you want, baby. Want my mouth on you? Want me to bend you over the table and take you from behind? Or do you want to be on top and ride my cock?"

"Yes to all of that, but this is *your* birthday," she says seductively, and unbuttons my jeans. "Tell me what *you* want." She lowers my zipper and pushes her hand into my boxer briefs, fisting my cock as she licks her lips. "Do you want my mouth on you?"

"Hell yes, but I want my mouth on you at the same time, so shed those shorts, darlin'."

As she takes off her shorts, I kick off my flip-flops, toss my wallet on the deck beside the chair, and strip off my jeans and boxer briefs. I lie on the lounge chair, and when I reach for her, her cheeks pink up. "No pressure, darlin'. If you'd rather not—"

"No, I want to. I've written this into books, but I've never done it."

"You mean I get to pop your sixty-nine cherry?"

"Ohmygod." Her cheeks turn bright red. "I keep picturing the chair flipping over."

She's so damn cute. "Not a chance. Get over here." I pull her over. "Straddle my face backward."

"That's not a flattering position. I should be on the bottom."

I can't help but laugh. "There's a bigger chance of me choking you if you're on the bottom."

"Oh." Her brows slant. "Good point. That would be a fun nine-one-one call. *She has what stuck in her throat?"* We both crack up, and as she tries to get situated, with her knees beside my head, she says, "This is much more erotic in books."

"I'll give you erotic." I guide her onto my mouth.

"*Ohhh. Yes.*"

She takes me in her mouth, and my hips buck. My dick hits the back of her throat.

"Sorry," I grit out, but she doesn't miss a beat, stroking and sucking.

I devour her, and when I bring my fingers into play, her hand stills. I grab her hip with my other hand, bringing her farther down on my mouth, earning more sensual sounds, and use my teeth, tongue, and fingers to take her right up to the edge of release. "Don't stop," she demands, and rises onto her knees, riding my mouth and using my legs for leverage. Her fingernails dig into my thighs, and "*Declan—*" sails from her lungs as her orgasm ravages her, and she shatters, sweet as honey, on my tongue.

She collapses, trembling and panting, on hands and knees above me. "*Wow.* I didn't expect that to be so intense. Sorry I stopped."

I kiss her inner thigh. "You were perfect."

She wraps her hand around my cock.

"No, baby. I want you to ride me."

"But it's *your* birthday, and I'm getting all the presents."

"There's no better present than bringing you pleasure."

"Ah, yes, an ego stroke for you," she teases.

I give her ass a slap. "Get up here so I can see your beautiful face." I tug off my shirt as she climbs off the chair and grab a condom from my wallet. "Lose your shirt, darlin'. I want to see all of you."

"Bossy, bossy birthday boy."

I roll on the condom as she takes off her shirt, and her hair tumbles over her shoulders and breasts. She slides her arm across her belly, and I gently move it. "Don't you dare cover up. You look like a moonlight goddess, and I want to see every inch of your beautiful body."

"That charm should come with a warning sign," she says as I take her hand.

She straddles me, and I guide her onto my cock. When I'm buried deep inside her, our eyes lock, and I know she feels the same intense connection I do. It radiates between us, bright and hot and inescapable. I slide my hand to the nape of her neck as she lowers her face toward mine, and her curls fall onto my cheeks.

"Sorry." She reaches up to move them, but I catch her hand.

"Leave it."

"It'll bother you."

"It won't." I remember what she said about her husband's lies, and I want to clearly separate myself from that prick in her mind. "When I said I liked your wild hair, I meant it. I know what it feels like to be blindsided by lies, and I will never do that to you." I caress her cheek, and I press my lips to hers. "Be with me, Nic. Don't worry about anything other than feeling good. Feeling *us*."

I take her in a slow, sensual kiss until I feel her tension ease, and then I kiss her longer, deeper, *rougher*, until we both nearly lose our minds and our bodies take over. We kiss and thrust, grope and moan. She rises, grinding her hips.

"That's it, baby. Fuck me. Take what you want." I caress her breasts. "You feel amazing."

"So do you," she says breathily.

I take her nipples between my fingers and thumbs, and she arches back, her hair spilling over her shoulders, a few tendrils bouncing against the swell of her breasts. She's so beautiful and feels so good, she steals my breath. I move one hand between her legs, and she makes the sexiest sounds as we pump and grind until I'm barely hanging on to my sanity.

Her breaths come fast and hampered, and I quicken my fingers and squeeze her nipple. She cries out, squeezing me so tight she draws the come right out of me as I pull her mouth to mine, trapping our sounds of ecstasy as we give ourselves over to something bigger than both of us.

Chapter Twenty-Nine

NICOLE

"Forget the party for my birthday. I'll just take more of this." We're in my bedroom. I run my fingers along Declan's scruff, wishing I could stare at him all night instead of sleeping. I like the little creases around his eyes and the way his skin is slightly weathered. There's no hiding those well-earned laugh lines, which will forever remind me of our awkward-turned-hilarious sexy times.

He presses his lips to mine. "I'll make sure there are orgasms on tap for your birthday."

"It's a long drive to Virginia. I can't imagine you take much time off."

"There's always phone sex."

"You want to pop that cherry, too?" I laugh softly.

He grins. "You'd be popping mine, darlin'."

"What? It's hard to believe your ego hasn't been stroked over the phone."

"I'm more of a hands-on guy."

"You are good with your hands, and apparently you have many more secret talents than you led me to believe. The electric guitar?"

"I play a little."

"You rocked it. I didn't know you were such a Springsteen fan."

"Springsteen was my mom's favorite. My dad used to play for her when we were young." He runs his hand down my hip. "Like father, like son, I guess."

"Like father, like *sons*. Your whole family is talented. Now I know where you got your personality from, too. Your dad is quite the charmer."

"He's somethin'."

"You're a lot like him. Except when it comes to drinking, of course. I don't think I've seen you have more than one beer."

"I never do." Declan is quiet for a second. "But back in the day, I did my fair share of drinking."

"In the military?"

"After I got out, when things were bad with Lindsay, I spent too many nights at the bottom of a bottle."

"Self-medicating. A lot of people with PTSD do that. That had to be hard on both of you."

"It was just one of the many troubles we had."

"I know you said she slept with someone else, but was that before or after you got help?"

"After, but there was no going back. There's a lot of history there. Not with my drinking. That was short-lived, but with the demise of our marriage."

"Do you mind if I ask what made you finally get help?"

He rolls onto his back, scrubs a hand down his face, and tucks his hand behind his head. "I was blitzed out of my mind one night, trying to drink my demons away, and Ethan showed up. I thought he was my brother Neil. I thought, that was it. I must've drank so much I killed myself."

I go up on my elbow so I can see his troubled eyes. "That's really scary, Declan."

"You're telling me. I don't remember most of that night. But Ethan said I was a mess, in tears, apologizing to Neil for not being there when he needed me most."

My heart breaks for him. "You felt responsible for his death?"

"I thought if I'd stayed in Chatemup and started setting up the legwork for our business instead of going into the military, I'd have been there to keep him safe."

"You couldn't have known what would happen."

"I get that, but I was dealing with a lot at the time. The things I'd seen overseas were eating away at me, and I guess that night, that guilt was at the forefront of my mind. Anyway, that was the catalyst for me to get my shit together."

"Do you still feel that way about your brother?"

"I'll probably always feel some level of guilt about going away."

"I guess I understand that, but you shouldn't feel guilty. That's a shame. Do you ever worry that one beer might lead to twelve?"

"No. If I did, I wouldn't even have one. They say there's an addictive gene, and I guess I don't have it. When I decided to pull my shit together, I stopped drinking cold turkey and never had any issues. Even on my worst days I don't want to get drunk. Alcohol was only my crutch at that one time in my life. I'd been drunk before, you know, in my early twenties, when kids are stupid, but it was never an ongoing thing until I came home from the military and my life was imploding, my brother was gone, and I couldn't escape the tragedies I'd seen."

"I wish I could've been there to help you."

"No, you don't. It was ugly, and you wouldn't have liked me." He reaches up and caresses my cheek. "Just so you know, that one beer I have socially is usually nonalcoholic."

"I didn't notice that."

"Most people don't." He puts his arm around me, holding me closer. "Nobody but Ethan and the therapist know I thought he was

Neil that night, so I'd appreciate it if you didn't say anything to my family."

"I won't. Why did you tell me?"

"Because I like you, and you deserve to know the man you're sleeping with."

Every time he shares another piece of himself, I want to wrap it in a ribbon and tuck it away for safekeeping. I snuggle closer. "I like you, too."

"Can I ask you something?"

"Sure."

"Did you leave the party to come home and write?"

"No. I left so you could have time alone with your family. I usually don't write at night anymore. Up until a few months ago, I wrote from first thing in the morning until ten or eleven at night. But nowadays, when it hits five or six, my brain refuses to work."

"What happened tonight?"

"I took a shower after I came home, and I was thinking about you and your family playing all those instruments, and I realized the thing my hot accountant was missing was a hobby."

"So now he's in a band?"

"No. He carves things out of wood, mostly for his kids, but it was exactly what the story needed. And that inspiration was exactly what I needed. I was getting worried about why I couldn't concentrate for very long anymore."

"Did you work that late when you were married?"

"Not at first. The kids were young and needed me, but for the last few years of our marriage, I did. I had a lot of stories I wanted to write."

"Is that all it was, or were you avoiding your husband?"

"I definitely used writing to keep from going certain places with him, but I don't think I was . . ." I stop myself and really think about what he is asking, and the years in which my writing took over my life.

"I didn't think I was avoiding him, but I might have been. Remember how I said he used to brag about me?"

"Yeah."

"It wasn't really about me. He bragged about my writing like my career was his arm candy. If I hit a list or was featured by a retailer, he would brag about that and then add that I was a great wife. Like I wouldn't have been without those accomplishments. But he never wanted to celebrate my accomplishments. Not that I needed a celebration, but a 'good job' every now and then would have been nice."

"Let me get this straight. He bragged about you to others but never told you how great you were?"

"Yes, but I don't think he believed I was great. When I look back at the beginning of our marriage, I see the cracks so clearly. He needed someone to help raise his kids so he could focus on himself. I was too blind to see it back then. He paid more attention to me in those early days, but as time went on, I realized my writing gave him something to talk about that he thought made *him* look good."

"Nic, you *are* great, and not because of your writing. Your writing is icing on the cake. You're one of the most down-to-earth, adorable, funny, smart, sexy women I know. That man was a fool, and he didn't deserve you."

My heart swells. "Thank you for saying that."

"I'm not blowing smoke."

"I know. I've never heard you blow smoke, and I appreciate it. Since you figured out why I worked so many hours, any idea why I can't concentrate in the evenings?"

"You had nothing else vying for your attention, so burying yourself in writing wasn't just easy; it was preferable. Now you have a life you *want* to live."

"But it started before I got here."

"Was it around the time you started looking to buy a cottage?"

"Yes. How'd you know?"

"I just had a feeling." He plays with the ends of my hair. "You told me you took time to heal from your divorce, and I assume you buried yourself in work during that time."

"I wrote a ton of great books."

"I'm sure you did, but eventually you were ready to break out of your old life. It makes sense that once you started thinking about buying a cottage, that creative brain of yours had to find a cutoff time and stop creating in order to give you space and time to think about your new endeavors." He runs his hand down my back. "And now that you're here, you have friends right down the hill and the best adventure buddy on the planet, and you don't want to miss out on evening walks and great sex."

I laugh. "I think you're right. Especially about that last part."

"I think you should stop stressing over why and just go with it. It sounds like you've been on a hamster wheel for a long time, and you're ready for a change. The more you fight it, the harder it'll probably be to write."

"You might be right." I kiss him, feeling like a weight has been lifted from my shoulders. "How do you see all the hidden parts of me so clearly, when I don't even know they're there?"

"I don't know, Bootsy. It's never been like this for me before. But when I'm with you, you eclipse everything else, and you're all I see."

I lay my head on his chest and close my eyes. "Careful saying things like that, Dimples."

"Why? It's the truth."

"Because it makes you even more dangerous than me."

Chapter Thirty

NICOLE

"What is that?" I point to the royal-blue wristband on Maggie's wrist as she drives down to the marina. It's late afternoon, and we're meeting our friends to go out on Russ's boat for the evening. Evelyn and Claude begged out because it'll be a late night, and Declan texted earlier to say he had to work late and couldn't make it. I'm bummed, but I know how busy he is.

"It's an anti-nausea wristband."

"You get seasick?"

"Wicked sick." Maggie flashes a cheesy smile. "But don't worry. I won't puke on you. I did an online hypnotizing session specifically for motion sickness, some anti-nausea yoga, and tossed a prayer out to the universe for good measure."

"What, no shaman?" I tease. Maggie has become one of my favorite people. I adore her snarkiness and her outlandish ideas. I've been walking with her and Aspen two or three times each week. Or, as Maggie calls it, we've been torturing her. Our walks usually end with iced lattes and treats for Claude. Claude has become a favorite, too. I earn an occasional smile when he gripes at me now. A feat I'm quite proud of, since nobody thought I could eke a single one out of the guy.

"Mag, why are you going on the boat if you get so sick?"

"Because I like being on the water as much as you like writing. You've been writing your ass off this week, so you should understand. I bet you'd go nuts if you couldn't write."

"I probably would. The last week and a half have been a godsend. Words have flowed like blood from a vein, and it's all because of something Declan said." I embraced the seed he'd planted the night of his birthday party about enjoying life instead of stressing about why I can't focus after hours at my keyboard, and it gave me freedom I didn't realize I needed. My writing has taken off because of it, and my personal life has flourished, too, which I'm loving. If Russ isn't coordinating an evening with friends, like this outing on his boat, Declan is stealing me away for an adventure, and I'm still making time for myself. Maybe that Three of Pentacles card was right after all. I didn't think anyone could help me figure out why I couldn't focus, but Declan put things together in a way nobody else had.

"Let me guess. He said something like, 'Hey, Boots, wanna fuck?'" Maggie smirks.

She has no idea how accurate she is. Although that's not exactly what spurred the change in my writing, it definitely amped up my sex scenes. I want to tell her the truth about me and Declan, but he and I haven't discussed what this is between us, and even though we end the nights we see each other tangled up in the sheets and those steamy nights lead to incredibly fun, sexy mornings, why put a label on it and get people talking when I'm not staying in Chatemup past the summer?

"Not quite," I say lightly. "He pointed out that I was probably avoiding my marriage by working a million hours a day, and now that I have a life and friends that I enjoy, I was subconsciously rebelling against sitting in front of the computer until my eyes bled."

"*Wanna fuck* would've been more fun. But he's probably right about all that other stuff." She pulls into the marina and parks by the docks. "The water looks pretty calm, but maybe I should've consulted a shaman just in case."

"You don't have to go out on the boat. How are things with Mike, by the way? You haven't mentioned him on our morning walks."

"I had fun with him, but I told him last night I was done."

"Already? The poor guy. Why?"

"Because it was *time*, and trust me, he was fine with it. He's not into long-term relationships, either." She cranes her neck to look out my window. "Is that . . . ? Oh yeah, baby. That's my harbormaster, Jiffy Dude."

"*What?* You have a Jiffy Dude?"

"No, but I hope to. I suddenly feel much better. I'll meet you at the boat." She hurries out of the car and rushes toward the guy.

I grab my sweatshirt, and as I step out of the car, I see Declan's truck heading this way. I wave, elated to see him even if he's just stopping by while he's working. He parks next to Maggie's car. I walk over as he climbs out, looking like sex on legs in jeans and a dark T-shirt, fisting a sweatshirt in one hand. "I thought you couldn't come."

"Baby, with you, coming is never a problem." Those dimples appear. "I might have raced around at breakneck speed so I could finish work in time to see you."

Oh, my heart. "Really?"

"Yeah, Bootsy. But now we have a problem."

"Why?"

His gaze slides down my body. "Look at you in those sexy shorts and my favorite boots." He glances to our right, and I follow his gaze to Aspen and Marcus chatting with Russ and Marlo by Marcus's car. "How am I supposed to keep my hands off you all night?"

Why is that so exhilarating? My thoughts turn to the other night, when we went to a concert on a beach in the next town over with Ethan, Annie, and the girls. Declan and I kissed and held hands, and it was wonderful being so close to him. But it's different doing that around our friends. It'll make our relationship bigger, give it a label in their heads, and maybe even ours. But as much as I don't want to label us or start gossip, what I don't want even more is to pretend I'm not dying to be close to Declan.

"Do you *want* to keep your hands off me? I know we haven't talked about any of this, and I'll understand if you don't want our friends—"

My words are lost to the hard press of his lips. He pushes his hands into my hair, taking the kiss deeper, and my back hits the side of the truck. This isn't just a kiss. It's an act of raw, untethered *possession*.

Our lips part slowly, but he stays close, his eyes searching mine, his breath warming my lips. "I don't want to keep anything off you."

Trying to think through the haze of lust, I hear cheering coming from our friends. "I guess they don't want you to, either."

"Time to face the music." He gives me a quick kiss and drapes his arm around me as we head toward our friends. "Nic and I are an item," he calls out to them. "So deal with it."

"About time you two came clean," Marcus calls out. "Do you think we didn't notice your truck leaving Nic's house a little too early in the mornings for adventures outside the bedroom?"

Everyone laughs, and as we make our way down to Russ's boat, I swear Declan is strutting like a proud peacock.

An hour later we're surrounded by open water, the guys are swapping fishing stories, and I'm filling a plate with the delicious food Russ and Marlo brought as Aspen, Marlo, and Maggie sidle up to me. I can tell by the look in their eyes, it's interrogation time. I thought I was in the clear, but I'm not surprised. Dani and Rachel would have pounced the second Declan was out of earshot.

"Someone's been keeping secrets," Maggie says.

"I'm sorry I didn't tell you guys, but our friendship just sort of grew into more, and Declan and I hadn't talked about whatever this is between us until he showed up tonight. We still haven't really talked about it. We just decided not to pretend we aren't into each other."

"I'm happy for both of you. You're good together," Marlo says.

I want to gush about the things Declan says, how attentive and talented he is in bed, and how mornings when I'm in his arms, I just want to stay there all day. I want to tell them how fun our closeness makes our non-sexual adventures, too. But those aren't the kind of things you say when your relationship is temporary. "Thanks. We're having fun."

"I bet you are," Maggie says. "I knew something was up when he went after my brother."

"We weren't even together then. He was just being a protective friend."

"You might not have consummated your relationship yet, baby doll, but make no mistake, you and Miller had already formed a connection," Aspen says. "I felt it that first night at Russ and Marlo's. But you were both so determined to remain single, I worried the walls you built around your hearts would be too solid to let each other in."

"Honestly, I thought I had bolted that door shut. I don't know how Declan snuck in, but I'm glad he did." Our friendship makes our connection even stronger, which is another kind of dangerous. I have to keep reminding myself not to fall for him.

"You two workaholics are two peas in a pod," Marlo says. "I'm glad Miller is finally making time for himself. Between his father's issues and the way his ex still calls him for every little thing, I didn't think he'd ever get close to someone else. It sounds like you two were meant to be."

Every little thing is right. We had plans the other night, and Declan was late because his ex was at the grocery store and had forgotten her wallet. He swung by to pay for her groceries. That seemed ridiculous to me, but I wasn't about to tell a grown man what to do.

"Meant to be for the summer. I don't want to give you the wrong impression. We're not looking to run off and get married. I'm still going back to Virginia at the end of August. Our friendship is just on steroids." I glance at Declan just as he looks over and winks, causing those flutters in my chest again.

"*Wow*," Maggie says. "Even I felt that. I'm a little jealous."

I can't help but gush a little. "We do have amazing chemistry, and I love hanging out with him. We do things and go places I would never go on my own, and he makes me feel *alive*. The other night we went to an evening concert in another town and watched the sunset and danced, and last week we went night fishing and four-wheeling. I'd never done either of those things. Talk about exhilarating."

"Now I'm jealous," Marlo says. "Russ and I used to do fun stuff like four-wheeling, but then we got old."

"You're not old, sweetie," Aspen says. "You got busy raising a family and working. You can still do those things, and your husband is always putting together parties."

"That's true; he is."

"Marlo, if it makes you feel any better, my life has never been like this. I've been the responsible mom since I was eighteen. Now I finally get to play, and I highly recommend doing all the things you loved when you were younger."

"I think we will." She looks adoringly at Russ. "I know he'll be up for it."

"Nic, do you see Declan every night?" Aspen asks.

"No. We talk and text all the time, but we usually only see each other a few times each week. Although I have to admit, sometimes he surprises me. Like last night. I didn't think I'd see him because I was in a writing groove and working late, but he showed up with takeout around eight, intending to drop it off and leave me to my writing. But I'd just finished a big scene, and it was a perfect stopping point, so we ended up eating together and watching a movie."

"And then you had a lovefest for dessert, and he left early this morning," Maggie says knowingly. "I bet you'll miss that when you go back to Virginia."

"That *and* so much more. You guys and this place feel more like home than Virginia does."

"Then stay," Maggie encourages.

"I wish I could, but now that my father is gone, I can't leave my mom."

"Having taken care of my parents, I totally understand," Aspen says reassuringly.

"Your mom could move here, too," Marlo suggests. "I know some pretty great ladies she could hang out with."

"She would love you guys, but I don't think she'd want to leave the house that holds memories of my dad."

"That would be hard," Aspen agrees.

We talk a little longer before joining the guys. Declan reaches for my hand and pulls me to his side, whispering, "Did you give them all the dirty details?"

"Just enough to keep them guessing." I don't know if it's the romance of being out on the water at night, the freedom that came with coming out to our friends, or just the thought of how good it feels to be naked in his arms, but I'm dying to get back there.

"Let's fuel their fire." He presses his lips to mine, and I want to melt into him.

He keeps me close for the rest of the evening, as if he wants the same. Maggie is telling us about a trip she's hoping to take next spring, but my mind is on the man beside me, kissing my temple. His breath is warm on my cheek as he whispers, "I can't wait to get you alone." My temperature rises, and he nuzzles against my neck. "Think they'll mind if we disappear into the cabin?"

I put my hand on his leg and squeeze, my need growing stronger as he continues whispering all the dirty things he'd like to do to me. By the time we get back to the marina and say goodbye to our friends, I'm vibrating with desire.

Chapter Thirty-One

NICOLE

We barely make it into Declan's truck before his lips capture mine and our control snaps. His hands are everywhere. In my hair, groping my breasts, pushing beneath me to feel my ass, and he's so hard and tempting, I want to strip his jeans off right here and straddle him.

"*Fuck*," he growls against my lips. "I can't get enough of you."

"Home," I pant out. "*Drive.*"

"If I don't cool down, we won't make it home."

He rolls down the window, but the cool air doesn't help. He devours me at every stoplight, and as he drives, I tease the hell out of him, kissing his neck, stroking him through his jeans, earning sounds so potently male, I'm tempted to unzip his zipper and take him in my mouth while he's behind the wheel. He speeds into my driveway and kills the engine, reclaiming my mouth as urgent and rough as a man on fire.

"*Mom?*"

I freeze. It can't be—

"Mom!" Mackenzie peers into the truck, jaw agape.

"Kenzie?" I pull away from Declan, but his hand is tangled in my hair, and it takes a minute to disengage. "What are you doing here?" I scramble out of the truck and hug her.

She plants a hand on her hip, looking like her father with breasts, tall and lanky with straight, shiny brown hair. "I think I should be asking you that question." Her sea-blue eyes shift curiously to Declan. "Hi. I'm her *daughter*, Kenzie."

He's as unflappable as ever. "I'm Declan. I've heard a lot about you."

"Yeah? Well, I haven't heard anything about you," she says snarkily.

"Okay, that's enough." I give her a stern look.

"What? You don't even bother telling me you're seeing someone? I have to find out like this?"

"I don't need to report to you about all my friends."

"Do you make out with all your friends?" she asks.

Declan looks amused. "Only the lucky ones."

I stifle a smile and try to give him a look that says *you're not helping*. "What are you doing here, Kenzie? Is everything okay?"

"Everything's *fine*. I just flew up to surprise you."

My chest knots up. "How did you pay for the tickets? Did you get a job?"

"I charged it to your card. It was only like eight hundred dollars, and you'll be happy to know that I have interviews Thursday *and* Friday afternoon. That's why I'm only staying two nights."

Only eight hundred dollars? "Why didn't you tell me you were coming? We're going to see each other at the wedding in a few weeks. We could have saved that money."

She rolls her eyes. "If I had told you, it wouldn't have been a surprise. Is it so bad that I missed you and wanted to see you before I start school?"

I take a deep breath, her words sneaking beneath my irritation. "No, of course not. I'm glad you're here. I've missed you." My mind races to another issue. I'm going to lose writing time. I hate that every minute counts when I'm on a deadline, but it's my reality. I'll have to work longer hours after she leaves. I turn to Declan, longing for what she interrupted and for the evenings we'll lose together and, at the same time, thankful my daughter thought of me for once.

"Declan, I'm sorry, but—"

"I know, darlin'. No worries. I was just going to take off." He leans in and kisses my cheek. "Kenzie, I'm glad we had a chance to meet. Maybe I'll see you around."

"Sorry about interrupting your lip-lock," she says.

"Mackenzie."

"She's got your spunk, Nic. You're a lucky girl, Mackenzie. Use it wisely." He climbs into his truck.

As he drives away, we head up the walk, and Mackenzie says, "You've totally ruined the image I had of you."

"What does that mean?"

"I pictured you the way you are at home, hiding away in your office twenty-four-seven. But you're out here with a hot guy, living your best life."

"Mackenzie, I don't need to explain myself to you."

"Mom. I'm happy for you. You're too great to waste away in your office. You *should* be enjoying yourself."

I stop in my tracks. Our relationship has been strained in so many ways the last few years, I get choked up. A small part of me wonders if she thinks I'm great because I pay for everything, but I don't ask, because I don't really want to know the answer.

"Thanks." I hug her again. "I'm glad you're here. Where's your stuff?"

"I put it inside. You should really lock your doors." We head inside, and she struts through the living room. "This place is amazing. I took the bedroom on this floor. I hope that's okay. I love your furniture and that you're not writing in an office. You must love the view. Can we sit upstairs on your deck? The view is even better up there."

My whirlwind daughter is already halfway up the stairs.

We sit outside, and she catches me up on the latest with her boy-friend and friends. I watch with awe this young, confident woman who is so bright and capable, she could accomplish anything she put her mind to and wonder if I'll ever fully understand her. I think about my conversation with Declan about our kids and what Marlo and Evelyn had said about their children. Maybe all parents feel the same way. Maybe we're supposed to, or the world would never change.

I don't have the answers, but I know one thing. I don't have to understand Mackenzie in order to teach her to respect other people's money. I bide my time, waiting for the right moment to broach the difficult subject.

"What about you, Mom? Is Declan your boyfriend?"

"It's a little different at my age, honey. We have our own lives, and they're busy, so we're enjoying each other's company while I'm here."

"I get that." She traces a seam on her shorts. "Are you seeing other guys?"

"No, and this thing with Declan grew out of a friendship. I didn't come here looking for a guy."

"Do you think you'll ever get married again?"

"I don't know. *Ever* is a long time, but I'm not looking for that." When Mackenzie was a little girl, she'd think about something for days before talking about it. I have a feeling there's more behind her question. "Why do you ask?"

She shrugs one shoulder. "Most of my friends think marriage is outdated. That no two people can fulfill each other's every need forever."

"Maybe they're right. Who we are at twenty is different from who we are at thirty. But some couples beat the odds and evolve together. I have friends here who are still madly in love after decades of marriage. What do you believe?"

She lies back on the lounge chair. "I'm not sure. But I don't think I ever want to get married."

"Okay. That's your choice." Questions come at me from all angles. Does she feel that way because of my two failed marriages? Did something happen with Chad that she's not sharing? Does she ever want a family? But those are hard questions, and my daughter has never been one to sit through interrogations. I have to choose my discussions wisely, and I take the opening she's given me to bring up the most important thing on my mind. "I envy you, Kenz."

"Why?"

"You have your whole life ahead of you. You can take it by the horns and make it into whatever you want."

"As if it's that easy."

"Nothing is easy, but it's doable. You're old enough to start mapping out your future so you won't ever have to rely on anyone else."

"Mom." She closes her eyes.

"We need to talk about this, honey. I'm glad you're here, but eight hundred dollars is a lot of money. Do you realize I have to earn sixteen hundred in order for you to spend eight hundred?"

Her eyes open. "No."

"I do, because of taxes, and that puts a lot of pressure on me."

"Taxes take that much? That's a rip-off."

"Tell me about it. I would like you to be more careful with my money and ask before you charge anything on the credit card, okay?"

She nods. "Sorry. But it's not like you can't afford it."

"That's not the point. Spending adds up, and I have to work really hard to keep us going. I don't have a company funding my retirement, and your dad can't help with school expenses. It's all on me, honey, and I don't mind, but I need you to be more careful."

"Sorry. I didn't think about it like that. I'll be more careful."

"It's okay. Just learn from it."

"I'm also sorry I haven't been able to get a job, but I have been looking, and I really do have two interviews coming up."

"That's all I can ask for. Did you make sure the hours will work with your class schedule?"

"Yes." The word is laced with impatience. "Can we go to the beach tomorrow?"

"Sure. Do you want to go running with me in the morning first?"

"I'd rather lick dirt."

I grin. "How are you even my child?"

"I believe it was a broken condom."

I shake my head, and we both laugh. "I was thinking I'd introduce you to my friends and show you around the town tomorrow. When do you fly back?"

"Thursday morning. Can we see Declan again?"

"Why? So you can give him a hard time?"

"Someone has to watch out for you. The world has changed since you were last single. Is he on dating apps? Because if he is, he's probably got lots of women he's hooking up with, and you need to be careful that he doesn't give you crabs or something. He's a good-looking guy, so he'd get swiped a lot."

"Kenzie."

"I'm serious, Mom. Oh my God. Are *you* on dating apps? Is that how you met him?"

"No."

"Maybe you should be. A lot of people your age are on them. Guys would probably line up to take you to dinner and—"

"I'm *not* getting on dating apps."

"Why not? They're like buffets. You can check out the goods, taste a few, go back for seconds or thirds."

"Mackenzie, *stop*." We're both laughing. "Wait. Are *you* on dating apps?"

"I plead the Fifth."

She presses her lips together, but there's no hiding that smile. As we joke around, laughing until our stomachs hurt, I am grateful to have this time with my daughter, who drives me nuts as often as she melts my heart.

Chapter Thirty-Two

NICOLE

Before going for my run the next morning, I peek in on Mackenzie. She's fast asleep with her phone in her hand. I remember when that would have been her favorite teddy bear. Was she talking with her boyfriend half the night? Her girlfriends? Scrolling through social media? There's so much about her life that I'm not privy to, and I know that's how it's supposed to be so she can grow up and find her way. But I know my daughter well enough to realize there's a bigger reason for this visit. I just hope she'll share it with me when she's ready.

I close the door behind me and head out for my run.

It's another beautiful morning. Claude is hard at work trimming his bushes. He's dressed in a coral polo, and I'm hoping the bright shirt is reflective of his mood. I mute my music and stop to talk with him. "Good morning, Claude."

He doesn't look up from the bush he's trimming. "We'll see about that."

So much for a brighter mood. "Your bushes look nice."

"Good morning, Nic," Evelyn says as she comes out the front door in her bathrobe. "Is my husband trying to sweet-talk more treats out of you?"

"I don't sweet-talk," Claude grumbles.

"Not anymore, but once upon a time," Evelyn says fondly, and Claude mumbles something I can't make out.

"No Pilates this morning, Evelyn?" I ask.

"My instructor is on vacation this week, so I'm being lazy."

"Well, my daughter is here, and I'd love for you to meet her. Maybe we'll see you on the beach later."

"*Great*," Claude says sarcastically. "Just keep her off my lawn."

"Claude," Evelyn chides. "I'd love to meet her. I'll keep an eye out for you guys. Do you think she'd like lemon squares or chocolate drop cookies?"

"She'd love either, but you don't have to go to that much trouble."

"It's no trouble at all. I'd better get busy. Have a nice run."

I head down the road and crank up my music. "Sparks Fly" by Taylor Swift comes on, and my thoughts turn to Declan. I turn onto the street that leads to town, and as if I conjured him out of thin air, I see Declan up the hill, leaning against the tailgate of his truck in jeans and a dark T-shirt, coffee in hand. His hair looks windblown despite the lack of wind, a look I've come to adore. His legs are crossed at the ankles, and a heart-stopping grin spreads across his gorgeous face.

I pull out my AirPods. "Did you give up fish peddling for stalking?"

"I'll never give up fish peddling." His arm sweeps around my waist.

"I'm sweaty," I warn as he pulls me in and crushes his lips to mine, tasting like coffee and sunshine and unrelenting happiness.

"I like you sweaty." He squeezes my ass.

"In that case." I put my arms around him and kiss him again.

"You're too damn sexy. If I didn't have to get back to work, I'd take you to my place and finish what we started last night."

Heat curls through me. "Thanks for that thought. Now I'll be even hotter while I'm running. What's on your mind this morning that earned me a visit instead of a text?"

"I *might* have missed you a little last night. I wanted to call to say good night, but I didn't want to interrupt your time with Kenzie."

I feel a tug in my chest. "I missed you, too. We were up pretty late."

"She's a firecracker. Is everything okay? From the things you told me about her, she doesn't seem like the missing Mommy type."

"You've got that right. It's hard to tell where her head is."

"Are you okay?"

I love that he cares this much. "Yeah. You know how it is. The worry for our kids never turns off."

"The curse of parenthood. I know this visit will set you back in your writing, so I'll refrain from showing up out of the blue until you give me the okay."

"Don't you dare, you thoughtful beast." I have no idea who said those words, because it sure as heck wasn't the workaholic who came to Chatemup. I'm starting to wonder if I'll ever be that woman again, and I'm not sure I want to.

"I was hoping you'd say that." He brushes his lips over mine and kisses me. "I know you and I are just having fun, and you don't have a lot of time with Kenzie while she's here. But she's a big part of your life, and unless you'd rather I didn't, I'd like to get to know her. If you and she would be into it, I'd love to take you both on an adventure tonight."

I'm elated that he wants to get to know her, and he asked so carefully, it's endearing. "I don't know, Dimple Dude. That's a pretty big commitment. Are you sure you're ready for that?"

"She caught me sucking face with her mother, which is probably not much better than if she'd met me as your arm candy at the wedding."

"I almost forgot about that. I can't believe you remembered."

"I told you I remember everything you say. Listen, Nic, I'll understand if you think taking you and Kenzie to dinner will give her the wrong impression or if it makes you uncomfortable."

"I don't think it can get more uncomfortable than being caught making out in your truck. She asked if we could see you, so I think we're good."

"Smart girl. She knows a good thing when she sees it."

"You might want to reel in that ego when you see her. She said you might be hooking up with a lot of women, and I'd better make sure you don't give me crabs."

"*Crabs?* What the hell?"

I can't help but laugh. "Still want to take us on an adventure?"

"Hell yeah. But I'm going to set her straight, so be ready." He kisses me again. "Does six thirty work, or is that too early?"

"It's perfect. Where are we going?"

"You should know better than to ask. I gotta go." He gives me a quick kiss, groans, and pulls me back for a deeper one. "See you, Bootsy." He climbs into his truck.

"Hey, Declan."

He lifts his chin.

"For a guy who's stretched too thin, you seem to make an awful lot of time for me."

He starts the truck, a cocky grin curving his lips. "Don't analyze it, Writer Girl." He winks and drives off.

I put in my AirPods, and as I start running again, I analyze the hell out of it.

On my way back from my run, I stop at Claude and Evelyn's to drop off scones from the Rise and Grind. Claude answers with a furrowed brow. I hold up the bag, and a smile lights up his eyes.

"Cranberry-nut scones." I hand him the bag.

"Thank you, Nic. Maybe I'll save one for Evelyn this time."

I laugh. "Did she go out?"

Hot Mess Summer

He shakes his head and hikes a thumb over his shoulder toward the beach. "That girl of yours is out there with all the ladies."

"I haven't introduced Mackenzie to anyone yet. Are you sure it's her?"

"That's what she said her name was when she traipsed across my lawn."

"Oh, Claude, I am so sorry. I haven't seen her yet this morning. I'll say something to her."

"I took care of it. She's a sweet one, that girl of yours. She must get that from you."

My daughter is a lot of things, but I wouldn't exactly consider her sweet. "Are you sure you're talking about Mackenzie? Tall and thin, straight brown hair?"

"That's her. It takes a real special person to see past people's hard edges."

"Did she see past yours?" I ask carefully.

He nods. "Same way you do. You're doing something right with her."

I tuck that away for the million times I know I'll need reassurance in the future. "What did she do or say?"

"You won't get any gossip out of me. You can take that up with her."

He's never talked this much, and I like the man he is showing me, which makes me curious about why he doesn't act like this with everyone. "Claude, why do you work so hard to push people away?"

His eyes narrow.

My stomach knots up. "I'm sorry. I didn't mean to offend you."

"You've got to check yourself, young lady." He steps onto the porch and peers up the street, then in the other direction. "Voices carry around here."

"I'm really sorry. It's just that sometimes . . ."

The edges of his lips twitch into an almost-smile. "Sometimes I hear every word and I don't push you away?"

251

"Yes," I say softly.

"Have you met my wife?"

I wonder if he's having a senior moment and has forgotten who I am. "Yes. Claude, it's me, Nicole. I live up on the hill."

"I know who you are," he grumbles. "You asked me a question and I'm answering it. You've met my wife. She's sweet as sugar and bakes like she was born to do it. Cooks like Julia Child, too." He lowers his voice. "You know how social the beach family is. If I was a nice guy, I'd never get a minute alone with Evelyn. It'd be just like it used to be. Our house was crawling with neighbors and their children every minute of the day. We've been married fifty-one years, and I'm no spring chicken. I don't know how many years I've got left, but I know one thing for sure. I want to spend as much of them with my girl as I can."

I put my hand over my heart, choked up over his love for her. "You do it to have alone time with her? Why don't you just establish boundaries?"

He scoffs. "And be seen as a jerk? No, thank you. This is better. A few years ago I had the flu and my ears got stuffed up. It lasted even after I was feeling better. I couldn't hear myself talk, and I got frustrated and snapped during one of Russ's parties. We had a reprieve from everyone and their brother coming over after that." He holds up his index finger, and his eyes light up. "That was my *aha* moment. I realized if I was the grumpy old man, I'd get some time alone with my wife."

"You're not worried about what people think of you?"

"I don't give a rat's ass what anyone other than Evelyn thinks of me."

"But she worries about you, and she thinks you're rude to your friends."

"I *am* rude to them, and when she worries, I get even more atten-tion. You can call me selfish, and you'd probably be right, but that woman has owned my heart since the day we met, and I worked hard our whole lives so we could be together in our golden years. I'll be gone long before she will. The men in my family don't last past eighty-five or -six, but the women in hers last into their nineties. I know our friends will make up for lost time when she needs it most."

Tears burn my eyes. "Now, *that's* a love story."

He waggles a crooked finger at me. "If you breathe a word of this, I'll deny it to my dying days."

"I would never breach your trust, but why are you telling me, of all people?"

"Evelyn worries about you. You're too young not to believe true love exists. Now get outta here so I can eat my scones."

Overcome with emotion, I start to leave but hesitate and turn back as he's walking inside. "Claude?"

He glances over his shoulder.

"Thank you."

He waves his hand dismissively and shuts the door.

Chapter Thirty-Three

NICOLE

I follow the path to the beach, and it takes me a moment to realize the four women standing in a lunge position, holding their arms up like they're reaching for the sky are my friends, and the lithe self-assured young woman wearing peach yoga pants and a matching sports bra correcting their stances is my daughter. Aspen, Maggie, and Marlo are dressed for the beach, while Evelyn is wearing white capris, a yellow tank top, and a matching visor. I know how much Mackenzie enjoys yoga, and I wonder if she railroaded them into joining her.

"These legs aren't meant to hold up this body in this position," Maggie complains, leaning like the Tower of Pisa.

"It takes time. Trust your body," Mackenzie encourages as she repositions her. "You should have seen me when I first started. It was right before winter break, and I was totally stressed out over my classes. It takes time, but you'll get stronger, and I swear it saved my sanity."

"I could use a little sanity saving, but I'll stick with chocolate cake," Maggie says.

I take out my phone and snap a few pictures as I make my way over. Mackenzie adjusts Aspen's foot and gently realigns Evelyn's arms, explaining the adjustments as she makes them. I've never seen Mackenzie helping others. She is sweet with them. I'm proud of her. "Is this the Oyster Run yoga class?"

"Hi, Mom," Mackenzie says as she adjusts Marlo's stance.

"Hi, sweetheart. How did you wrangle my friends into this?"

"No wrangling necessary," Aspen says. "We brought our morning coffee to the beach and found Kenzie and Evelyn doing yoga, so we joined them."

"I knew she was your daughter the second I saw her," Evelyn says. "She has your smile."

"Want to join us?" Mackenzie asks.

"Sure. In a minute."

"Don't do it, Nic," Maggie warns. "It's a trick. She tells you you'll feel great, but trust me, this is *not* great."

"Hang in there, baby doll," Aspen says. "This is good for you."

"So is bourbon, but I'm not drinking that at the ass-crack of dawn," Maggie says.

As they debate the benefits of yoga, I sit down to take off my running shoes and send a picture of Mackenzie to my mother. *Look who came for a visit.* I also send one to Dani and Rachel. *Look who showed up on my doorstep last night. She caught me and Declan making out in his truck.* I add a shocked emoji. *She says she missed me, but I think there's more to it.*

My phone vibrates as I take off my sneakers.

Mom: *Why? What's wrong?*

I don't want to worry her, so I reply, *Nothing. She just missed me.* I tug off my socks as more texts roll in. I skip Rachel's and Dani's replies to read my mother's.

Mom: *Uh-huh. Let me know if something's happened. Okay?*

Me: *Okay.* I add a red heart emoji. With that settled, I move on to my friends' messages.

Rachel: *I bet Dimple Dude had fun with that.* She added an eggplant emoji. *You're probably right about Kenzie. Tread lightly and see if she opens up.*

Dani: *Did something happen with her bf? Is she pregnant?*

Me: *Really? You go right to pregnancy?!* I add a scowling emoji.

I look at my daughter showing the ladies how to do the triangle pose and pray Dani is way off base. I wouldn't trade Mackenzie for the world, but I don't want her to have to deal with the stresses that I did before she has her path figured out.

Mackenzie looks my way. "Come on, Mom. Or do I have to take your phone away?"

I put my phone in my armband, musing at her parroting what I've said to her time and time again since she was a teenager. She nailed my attitude, too, so I push to my feet and nail hers. "But, *Mom*, my phone is my life."

After a fun morning with my friends, we head into town for lunch and spend the rest of the day exploring Chatemup. If there's something important on Mackenzie's mind, she doesn't share it with me. She seems relaxed and happy to be here and to be with me. Maybe—*hopefully*—she's outgrowing the self-centered stage that came with her teenage years and has stuck around far too long.

Twenty minutes before Declan is supposed to pick us up for dinner, Mackenzie is in her room getting ready, and I'm at my computer checking email when a text rolls in.

Declan: *Hey, Bootsy, sorry, but I'm going to be about a half hour late.*

Me: *Okay. More fish need peddling?* I add a fish emoji.

Declan: *No. My ex's car won't start. I'm heading over to jump it now.*

My good mood deflates. *No worries. See you soon.*

"What's wrong?" Mackenzie asks as she comes into the living room carrying a hoodie. She looks cute in tan shorts and a blue top.

"Nothing. Declan's running a little late. His ex's car won't start, and he's going to jump it."

"*O-kay.*" She drags out the first syllable. "That's weird."

"It's not weird. Plenty of divorced couples help each other out." As true as that is, I'd never call Jay or Tim for help as often as Lindsay calls Declan.

"Is that why you're annoyed? Does she want him back or something?"

"I'm not annoyed." *I'm disappointed.* But Declan has been nothing but honest with me, and even though I have no idea how Lindsay feels about him, at this point, it doesn't matter. I'll be gone in a month, so it's not even worth bringing up.

"Well, you should be. We had plans with him, and he put you off for another woman." She sits on the arm of the couch.

"Stop being dramatic. It's not another woman. It's his ex-wife. It would be like your father helping me out. It's not a big deal."

"If you say so."

She takes out her phone, and I'm relieved when she focuses on that instead of me. I go back to reading emails, telling myself to let it go.

When Declan picks us up, he apologizes for being late, and his sincerity makes it easy to forgive him and move on. I'm relieved Mackenzie doesn't get snarky with him. I'm pretty sure she's let it go, too, because she's in a great mood. I offer to drive, since his truck is a single cab, but he insists we take it, and Mackenzie asks me to sit in the middle of the bench seat. I don't mind, but I feel like a kid sitting between them, which is amusing. Mackenzie tells Declan about our day, and she's so enthusiastic, I wonder who this new young lady is. She doesn't let him get a word in edgewise, and when she finally takes a breath, it's only to ask where we're going.

"On an adventure," Declan says.

"An *adventure?*" she asks skeptically, and looks at me. "What does that mean?"

"It means we're about to have fun." I'm excited to see what he has in store for us.

Mackenzie's brow furrows. "I thought we were going out to eat."

"She's definitely your daughter, worried about the food," Declan teases. "Do you like pizza, Kenzie?"

"Yes, but how is that an adventure?"

"You'll see."

We drive for a long time, and when Declan pulls up to Slice of Heaven pizza parlor, I have no idea where we are.

"You ladies stay here. I'll be right back." Declan hops out of the truck.

When he closes the door, his visor falls, drawing my attention to the picture of him and his brother Neil running away to start their fish business when they were kids. I've seen the picture a number of times, and it never fails to bring a pang of sadness. But tonight I gain something else from it. A painful reminder to enjoy every minute I'm given with my family and friends.

"Why do we have to wait outside?" Mackenzie asks.

"I guess we'll find out."

"This is weird, Mom. Is he always like this?"

"Yeah, pretty much. He makes everything fun."

"If you say so."

A little while later, with warm pizza boxes on my lap and a bag of drinks and napkins and such on Mackenzie's lap, we're driving up a steep incline through brush and long grasses, over unfamiliar rocky terrain. No wonder we needed to take his truck.

Mackenzie clutches the door handle as the truck rocks and lurches. "Are you sure this is safe?"

"Moderately," Declan says. "It'll even out at the crest of the hill."

Mackenzie gives me a pleading look, and I put my hand on hers. "It's okay, Kenz. There's nothing to be nervous about."

"Who *are* you?" she asks. "You never do anything like this."

"Are you kidding?" Declan says. "Your mom is the adventure queen."

"She is *not*. Her biggest adventure is answering the door when the groceries are delivered."

"Hang on tight," Declan warns, and a minute later the truck lurches over the crest of the hill. Mackenzie gasps as we jerk forward, then back, and the land beneath us finally levels out. Declan eyes us both. "You okay?"

"Yes," we answer, and I take in the long stretch of land before us, leading to a lighthouse.

The truck rocks as Declan navigates over more brush-covered pits and valleys. The land falls away on either side of us as we near the lighthouse, until we're driving on a narrow expanse, surrounded by water on three sides.

"Whoa," Mackenzie says, wide-eyed. "This is so cool."

"Welcome to your first adventure, Kenzie. This is Dogmire Cliffs." Declan smiles at me, and I'm even more drawn to him, knowing he made this effort for my daughter.

Mackenzie looks over her shoulder. "Are we allowed to be here? There's no road."

"It's not open to the public," Declan says.

"So, we're trespassing?" she says accusatorily. "Are we still in Chatemup?"

"Nope." He pulls up beside the lighthouse and cuts the engine. "Grab your sweatshirts, and let's go, ladies." He opens his door and steps out of the truck.

"*Where?*" Mackenzie asks.

"Kenz, why so many questions? Just go with it. Enjoy the adventure."

"*Just go with it,*" she says, mocking me, and throws open her door.

I hand Declan the pizza boxes and climb out his door.

"I hope I didn't make a mistake," he says quietly.

"She'll be fine." At least I hope she won't give us attitude all night.

We walk around the lighthouse to the door. "Mind holding these a minute?" He hands me the pizza boxes.

"Are we allowed to go in there?" Mackenzie asks.

"Depends on who you ask." Declan smirks as he takes a key out of his pocket and dangles it from his fingers. "I asked the right person." He opens the door and takes the pizza boxes from me and the bag from Mackenzie. "After you, ladies. We're going all the way up to the top."

Mackenzie peers up the spiral staircase. "*All* the way up?"

"If you get tired, take a knee." Declan motions for me to lead the way. "Your mom and I will meet you at the top."

She looks imploringly at me.

That look has always tugged at my heartstrings. "You'll be fine, honey."

"Can't we just eat here? Why do we have to go up? It's cold in there, and it smells funny."

"That's the smell of history," Declan says. "The lighthouse was built in 1802. It's one of the oldest lighthouses in New England."

"If I wanted a history lesson, I would have taken summer school," Mackenzie says flatly.

"Mackenzie Lynn." I glare at her disapprovingly.

"I can't believe *you* want to do this," she says.

"I'm sure there are a lot of things about me you're having trouble believing right now, but I'm excited to see what's up there. Can you just give it a try?"

"You know what?" Declan takes the bag from Mackenzie. "Life is short, and the pizza is getting cold." He fishes out a soda, places it on the step, and hands Mackenzie one of the pizza boxes. "If you want to eat down here, go for it. We'll be up top, but you're missing out." He nods toward the steps. "Let's go, Nic."

I don't like the way Mackenzie is acting, but I also don't want her to think I'm choosing Declan over her, so I try one last time. "Kenzie, when will you ever be able to do this again? Can't you just put a little faith in Declan? He's never led me astray."

She rolls her eyes. *"Fine."*

"Attagirl. You won't be disappointed." Declan takes the pizza boxes and carries the bag as we start our journey up the winding staircase.

"This thing needs an elevator," Mackenzie says when we're halfway up. When we finally reach the door at the top, she says, "That was a *lot* of steps. Paybacks are hell, Declan. Keep that in mind."

"I'm counting on it, spitfire." He flashes those dimples, and Mackenzie almost smiles. "Now get your whiny ass up here and you can be the first to see what we came for."

He hands me the pizza box and unlocks the final door as Mackenzie joins him on the landing.

"Prepare to be amazed, young adventurer." Declan throws open the door, and cool air rushes in. He sets the bag of drinks outside the door, and as Mackenzie steps onto the balcony, he takes the pizza boxes from me. "After you, darlin'."

"Sorry about her attitude," I say quietly.

"I raised two boys. I know how this works." He gives me a quick kiss, and we follow Mackenzie outside.

The lighthouse searches the inky water, bathing the land below us in light as it falls away in sharp jagged cliffs. Lights arch over the water in the distance like hundreds of eyes watching us, and the breeze carries a nautical mix of scents, chilling my cheeks and bringing the taste of the sea. But the mesmerizing look in my daughter's eyes blows all that away.

"Mom . . ." Her voice is full of wonder.

"I know. It's incredible."

"I'm sorry for not trusting you, Declan," Mackenzie says. "I take back all my complaints. This was worth the climb."

"That's okay. Trust is a tricky thing, but sometimes a leap of faith pays off." Declan puts a hand on my back. "See the lights arched over the water? That's the bridge to Chatemup, and the mass of lights just beyond is our little town."

"This is so cool," Mackenzie says.

"How about a picture?" Declan suggests.

"Good idea!" Mackenzie whips out her phone and starts taking pictures of the view.

Declan arches a brow in my direction. "I meant of you and your mom."

"Oh, *sorry*," Mackenzie says.

I put my arm around her, and Declan says, "Okay, ladies, say *Declan rocks*." We laugh and say it as he takes a picture.

"Want me to get one of you two?" Mackenzie offers.

"Yeah, thanks." Declan hands her his phone, and she takes a picture of us arm in arm.

As she hands him his phone, she says, "You should thank my mom. She makes you look good."

He laughs. "Don't I know it."

"Would you mind if we take one with all three of us?" Mackenzie asks tentatively.

"Want to show your friends the ogre who made you climb the lighthouse?" Declan teases.

"That *and* the guy I caught sucking face with my mom."

Declan takes a selfie of the three of us. We take dozens of other pictures of each other and the view, and eventually we sit on the balcony and eat our cold pizza.

"So, Declan, what are your intentions with my mother?" Mackenzie asks with a mischievous grin.

"Sorry, spitfire, but I don't say those things in mixed company," he retorts.

"You're a funny one," she says. "Are you seeing other women?"

"Mackenzie." I glower at her.

"What? I want to know, and you should, too."

"I'm seeing just one other at the moment," Declan says, and my stomach sinks. He bumps me with his shoulder. "This beautiful woman and her snarky daughter."

Relief washes through me, even though I didn't think he was seeing anyone else.

Mackenzie takes another bite, eyeing him. "What do you do for a living besides drag people out to the middle of nowhere to show them cool things?"

"Obviously that's my main gig, but I'm also a fish peddler."

"A *what*?" She takes a bite of pizza.

"I keep the restaurants around here stocked with fresh seafood."

"So, you're a fisherman?" She tilts her head.

"Not so much anymore. I'm more of a desk jockey. What are you studying in school?"

She tucks her hair behind her ear. "Communication."

"That opens a lot of doors," he says. "Do you know what you want to do when you graduate?"

She shakes her head and takes another bite.

"What area of communication interests you?" he asks.

"I like social media and anything dealing with people." She finishes her slice and takes a drink. "Two of my friends just got internships at a telecommunications company for the fall. If they like it, I might try for one the next time they have an opening."

This is the first I've heard about internships. "Why didn't you apply when they did?"

"The hours conflicted with my yoga classes."

No wonder she didn't tell me. "Honey, school should be your top priority, or when you graduate everyone else will have experience and you'll have a tough time getting a job."

"I *know*. But school is stressful, and yoga is the only thing that keeps me sane. That's important, too."

I breathe deeply, tabling the discussion for another time. "You're right. It's important to feel centered."

"I get that," Declan says. "My son works out to relieve stress."

"You have a son?" Mackenzie's eyes light up. "Is he single?"

I can't keep up with this daughter of mine. "I thought you were dating Chad."

"It's not like we're married. I met him on . . ." Her eyes widen. "Never mind."

Declan gives me a knowing look.

"I don't even want to know," I say.

"What? How did you and Declan meet?"

"Your mom was trying to pick up a barista, and—"

"I was *not*. He's lying, Kenz."

Declan mouths, *No, I'm not.*

"This sounds like a story I need to hear," Mackenzie says.

"I spilled coffee on him, okay? No big deal."

"She was flustered from flirting with the twenty-five-year-old barista," Declan adds.

I swat his leg. "That's not true!"

He cocks a grin. "Did she tell you about Porn-Star Kisser?"

"Ohmygod, *Declan*. My daughter does not need to hear that."

Mackenzie goes up on her knees, grinning for all she's worth. "Yes, I do. I *really* need to hear it. Tell me everything."

Declan spends the rest of the evening embellishing stories about the random men I met and making up new ones, just to make my daughter laugh. By the time we leave, they're thick as thieves. The drive home is fun and conversational, and when we get to my place, I'm sad to see our evening end.

"Thanks for sharing your time with your mom with me," Declan says to Mackenzie. "I'm really glad we had a chance to meet."

"Me too. Sorry I was bitchy at first."

"It wasn't the first time someone's bitched at me, and I'm sure it won't be the last," he says.

Mackenzie hugs him.

"Do well in school, spitfire, and if any guys bother you, you let me know. I'll come down there and whoop their asses."

"I'm not sure mad desk-jockey skills will help," she teases.

He smirks. "I can wield a stapler like nobody's business. I look forward to seeing you at the wedding."

"Oh, *yeah*. That should be awkward and fun," she says.

"I'll meet you inside, Kenz," I say, wanting a minute alone with Declan.

As she saunters away, she says, "Enjoy your smooches."

"I plan to," Declan calls after her, and draws me into his arms. "You've got your hands full with that one."

"Always have, always will." I put my arms around him.

"She adores you, Bootsy."

"She puts up with me. But that's parenthood. Thank you for making tonight special. I'm sure it's a night she'll never forget. I know I won't."

"Me either, darlin'. Are you going to be tied to your desk after you take her to the airport tomorrow morning?"

"Yes, for a few days. But I'd still like to see you if you have time."

"I was hoping you'd say that."

His lips come down coaxingly over mine in a long, slow kiss, unearthing the desire I've been trying to keep hidden from my daughter. As our lips part, I whisper, "Just one more?"

"I could kiss you forever." He takes me in an earth-shattering kiss that brings me up on my toes and leaves me wishing we had an hour alone. "If I don't leave, your daughter's going to find us naked in your driveway and be scarred for life."

I sigh, and he drops a tender kiss on my lips. When I turn to leave, he takes my hand. I glance over my shoulder, and the emotion in his eyes nearly takes me to my knees. He gives my hand a squeeze and loosens his grip, but he doesn't let go. Our fingers slide all the way to the tips as I walk away.

"See ya, Bootsy." He winks and climbs into his truck.

I watch his taillights descend the hill, and all I can think about is how much it's going to hurt when I leave to go back home.

Chapter Thirty-Four

NICOLE

"I really like Declan," Mackenzie says the next morning on the way to the airport.

"I'm glad. He likes you, too, and we have a good time together."

"Going on *adventures*?" she says teasingly as she thumbs out a text.

"Yes, and brainstorming for my books and just hanging out."

"I can tell how much he likes you, *darlin'*."

There's no hiding my smile. "I like when he calls me that."

"I like it, too. He sounds like a seventy-year-old cowboy."

I laugh. "Or a forty-eight-year-old fish peddler."

"I googled him last night."

"Mackenzie," I say sharply.

"What? You mean you haven't? That's dating 101. What if he was a perv or a serial killer?"

"I'm fairly certain he's neither of those things."

"But he could have been. I leave you alone for *one* summer, and you meet a bunch of random guys and invite them over without googling them? You really need to be more careful."

"Yes, *Mom*."

"Now I know why you worry about me so much."

"Then this was a good lesson."

"Whatever. Anyway, Declan's not just a desk jockey. His company is a big deal around here. He has a whole fleet of boats and dozens of fishermen who work for him."

"I know."

"He acts like he's just a regular guy."

"Because he *is* a regular guy. Success doesn't make a person better than anyone else."

"I know. I guess I'm used to Tim, and Declan's nothing like him."

I want to say *Thank God*, but I try not to talk smack about Tim around her. "That's true."

"But he's kind of like Dad."

"You think so? In what ways?"

She puts her phone under her leg, giving me her full attention. "Dad jokes around a lot, and he's fun, when he has time to be."

I think about Jay, but I don't really know him as an adult. We talk when necessary, like when Mackenzie was deciding where to go to college, but we haven't spent any real time together in years. "I guess that's true. When was the last time you saw your father?"

"Spring break when I was home, but we text a lot."

"Good. I'm glad." I pull into the airport parking lot and find a parking spot.

She grabs her bag from the trunk, and we head inside. "Are you all set for school? Do you need anything?" Her classes start in two weeks.

"I have everything I need."

As we make our way to her gate, she's unusually quiet. "Kenz, is there something bothering you?"

She looks at me for a long silent moment, her expression serious.

"You know you can tell me anything, honey."

She nods. "I know. I'm fine. I just missed you and wanted to see you before I start school."

I'm not buying it, but I know better than to back her into a corner. "I'm glad you came. I've missed you, too." I hug her. "I love you, honey, and I'm proud of you."

"Why? I can't even get a job."

"I know, but you could be out doing drugs or something else, and you're finding your way. We need to work on your expenditures and start thinking about an internship or part-time job in your field, but that doesn't mean I'm not proud of the young woman you're becoming."

She tucks her hair behind her ear, focusing on her bag. "Thanks, Mom. I love you."

"I love you, too. Text me when you land so I know you got there safely."

"I will."

I pull her into one last hug, wishing I could climb into her head and see whatever she's not telling me. "I hope you know that I will always love you no matter what."

"I know. I have to go."

As she hurries toward the gate, she turns and waves, and I blow her a kiss. I've seen her off to much more trying situations than this. Like every time she went to stay with Jay overnight, her first day of preschool, her first sleepover at a friend's house, and dozens of other times. So why does this feel so much harder?

I head back to my car and call the one person who might be able to give me answers. My mother answers on the second ring.

"Hi, honey. Did our girl get off okay?"

"Yes. I just dropped her off." I drive out of the parking lot and head back to Chatemup.

"How is she? Tell me everything. I can't wait to see her at Nolan's wedding."

I tell her about our morning with my friends and our time alone as I showed her around town, and then I tell her about last night with Declan.

"You introduced her to your friend? How interesting."

"Why?"

"You were so careful not to introduce her to the men you dated after you and Jay divorced, I guess I assumed you would keep Declan under wraps since you said it's just a summer fling."

My chest constricts. "I don't think I ever used the words *summer fling.*" That makes our time together sound meaningless, and it sure doesn't feel that way. "Kenzie was little back then. It would've been confusing for her. Besides, she caught me and Declan kissing the night she showed up, so it wasn't like I could hide it from her."

My mother laughs.

"It wasn't funny."

"Oh, honey. That brings back memories. Remember the time Mrs. Schofield caught you and Jay in the back of his parents' car?"

"How could I ever forget? I thought you and Dad were going to ground me for life." Instead of a punishment, I got a stern talking-to and had to give them my word never to do it again. I kept my word, and I'm pretty sure I got pregnant when we got carried away out at the falls one sunny afternoon.

"And have to deal with you complaining every day? *Ha!* Not a chance. We learned a few things by raising your brothers first. In any case, it sounds like you and Kenz had a nice visit."

"We did, but I can't shake the feeling that she's not telling me something."

"And that surprises you?"

"Yes. Why shouldn't it?"

"Oh, I don't know," she says with a teasing lilt in her voice. "Did you conveniently forget that you didn't tell me you were pregnant until you were four months along? I'm pretty sure you stopped telling me certain things when you were around thirteen, and that has never changed."

"I tell you everything." *Almost everything. Well, enough for a mom.* "Shit."

"Mm-hm," she says knowingly.

"Raising a young adult is hard. I miss when she was younger and told me all her secrets. It's strange watching my child grow up and face her own challenges."

"Yes, it is, and it never ends. I'm still watching you and your brothers and wishing I could fix things when they go wrong."

"I know you do, but you don't have to worry about me. I'm in a good place."

"I'll take you off my worry list and add a little more worry time to Kenzie."

"I didn't mean to worry you about her. I just feel a little disconnected to her sometimes. I thought we'd be so close when she grew up, like you and I are, but I must be doing something wrong."

"You could pull the reins a little tighter, but that's not the issue. You're just expecting too much too soon. Boys find their compassion for their mothers long before girls do. Kenzie loves you. She just needs about a decade to grow up and gain perspective."

"I wasn't like that with you at that age."

"Because you had a baby, and you needed me. Just give her time. She's still in the trial-and-error stage of finding herself, and you're her safety blanket. That's why she came to see you. Even if she didn't tell you what's bothering her, just being with you probably helped."

"I hope so." As I say it, I realize she might be right, because just knowing my mother is there helped me, too.

Chapter Thirty-Five

NICOLE

August traipsed through Chatemup armed with Sahara heat and Cupid's arrows. I can't believe it's the last Friday in August and my summer is coming to an end. I feel like just yesterday I was driving over the bridge to this unfamiliar town, hoping for the best. I've spent the last month writing like the wind, enjoying my friends, going on exciting adventures with Declan, and savoring every blistering night spent tangled up in the sheets, sometimes out at sea, with a man who has turned my heart into a pincushion for those Cupid's arrows.

I'm trying my best to ignore that last fact and focus on my phone call with my editor, but it's about as easy as forgetting my own name. "I only have a few more chapters to write, unless my characters decide to misbehave and make the book longer."

"That's fantastic. I know you were worried about meeting this deadline. I guess staying in Chatemup for the summer helped clear your head."

"I got lucky. Chatemup is nothing like I expected and far more than I could have ever hoped for. I'll be sad to leave." *Sad* is an understatement. I get stomachaches just thinking about going back to Virginia.

I want to see my mother, but the thought of living under the cloud of my old life makes me want to crawl out of my skin.

"When are you heading home?"

"I have that wedding this weekend, and my friends are throwing me a farewell party when I get back on Sunday night. I plan on leaving Monday morning." Declan and I are driving to Boston tomorrow afternoon for Nolan's wedding and staying overnight. I'm nervous about seeing Tim and his family and our old friends, but I'm looking forward to seeing Mackenzie and my mother. Mackenzie seems to be enjoying her classes, and other than a little boyfriend drama, she hasn't had any new crises. Russ insisted on throwing the party, which is fitting, since my summer started with a party at his and Marlo's cottage.

"Sounds like you have a busy weekend and a long drive ahead."

"I do, but my muse seems to be more creative when I allow myself a little playtime. Once I'm back in Virginia, I'll knock out the last few chapters, take a couple of weeks to read and revise, and you'll have the manuscript by October first, as promised." I'll need the distraction of working hard to keep my mind off missing Declan and my friends.

"I have complete faith in you, Nic. You have never missed a deadline, and I'm glad you're finally taking time for yourself. I was worried you'd burn out if you kept up that pace. Are you ready to talk about your interview and signing schedule?"

I'm ready for anything that will take my mind off the fact that tonight is, as Declan has reminded me several times, our last big adventure in Chatemup. The wedding is an adventure of sorts, but it's not like our adventures here. I don't think anything could be. While we've talked about tonight being our last adventure, we've avoided talking about my going back to Virginia and what it means for us. Not that it can mean anything at all. It's not like I can abandon my mother or he can move to Virginia. I wish I had a remote control for my life. Like in that awful movie *Click*, so I could hit pause and live forever during this one incredible summer or press rewind and experience our time together anew.

Time to put on my big-girl britches and act like a grown-up.

"Yes. What have you got?"

◆ ◆ ◆

Declan texts at a little after six. *Are you ready for this summer's last great adventure?*

"Nope. I want more time." I thumb out *Yes!* and take one last look in the mirror. I swear there's something in the water here, because my hair has grown like weeds, and it's wilder than ever. Declan asked me to wear jeans and sneakers, which piqued my curiosity, since even after seeing me wear cutoffs and boots all summer, he still makes comments about how sexy I look.

I head downstairs, and as I put on my sneakers, I see Declan on my deck, heading for the glass doors. His thick thighs are wrapped in worn denim, and a familiar dark T-shirt hugs his shoulders. He flashes those dimples, sending my heart aflutter, but he makes no move to open the door. Instead, he rakes those dark eyes down my body through the glass and bites his lower lip, brows slanting. I can almost hear his growl.

God, I'm going to miss him.

I open the door. "Take a picture. It'll last longer."

"Woman, your image has been seared into my mind since the first time I saw you."

"So, you've been drooling over me looking mortified for spilling coffee on you?"

"*Drooling?* Yeah, we'll go with that." He leans in and kisses me. "You ready for our big night?"

"Yes. I'm looking forward to it. Are you finally going to tell me where this adventure will take place?"

"Not a chance. I thought about bringing you flowers to commemorate our big night, but flowers are so ordinary, and you, my sweet writer girl, are quite extraordinary, so I leveled up."

"You didn't have to bring me anything, but I'm curious about this leveling up you mentioned."

"Don't move." He steps out of sight, returning a few seconds later with a massive bouquet of Snickers bars and boxes of Girl Scout cookies in a silver bucket with #1 ADVENTURE BUDDY painted in red across the front.

Laughter falls from my lips, but tears sting my eyes. It's perfectly *us*. "I love it. Thank you." I go up on my toes and kiss him. "Before you ask, of course I'll share it with you."

"Actually, there's a little something else in there that I was hoping you'd share."

The seductive glimmer in his eyes gives me tingles as he steps inside and lowers the bucket so I can see the center of the bouquet. There's a cloth bag tucked between the candy bars and boxes.

"You're spoiling me." I grab the bag and fish out the contents to reveal an edible bikini made out of candy. Thrills battle with *Holy shit, can I really wear this?* But one look at his wicked grin pushes my hesitation aside. "I don't wear bathing suits anymore, but I'll definitely make an exception for this." I dangle it from my fingers. "Is *this* our last great adventure, you dirty boy?"

"That's only part of it, and it's for later." He places it, and the bucket, on my desk, takes my hand, and laces our fingers together. "Let's go, Bootsy. Our adventure awaits."

In pure Declan-style, he gives away nothing as we drive to the outskirts of town and down narrow, winding roads that skirt the edge of a marsh. Eventually we follow an overgrown dirt road through a heavily wooded area and come to an old metal gate. He gets out and unlocks a padlock on a heavy chain that reminds me of the kind my brothers used to lock up their bikes when we were kids.

"Almost there," he says as he climbs behind the wheel.

I don't bother asking where, but I'm excited to find out. He drives slowly through overgrown grass, the ruts in the land the only evidence of a long-forgotten driveway. He navigates around low-hanging branches and one fallen tree, and we pull up in front of a dilapidated house that looks like it's being swallowed by the earth. Vines stretch like cobwebs across the front of the house and climb up moss-covered boards, snaking around slanted posts that look like they're barely holding up a small front porch. Tall trees loom over the roof, their gnarled branches reaching like arthritic fingers over the edges.

"Okay, I'm officially creeped out. Is this where you plan on leaving my body? Because Rachel, Maggie, and my mother all know I'm with you tonight."

"Damn, Bootsy, you foiled my plans," he says with a laugh. "Have a little faith in your adventure buddy."

He grabs a flashlight from under his seat and hooks it to his belt loop with a carabiner. We climb out of the truck, and the grass nearly reaches my knees. I'm glad for the jeans. "Are you sure it's safe here?"

"Well, there were two kids who came here and haven't been seen since, but that was decades ago."

"Seriously?" I reach for the truck door.

Declan laughs and tugs me into a kiss. "I'm kidding. Come on. I want to show you something." He takes my hand, leading me toward the house.

"Are we going *inside*?"

"That's the idea."

Gulp. "Whose house is this?"

"It belongs to the Rutger family, and it's been boarded up since I was a kid." We walk around the side, making our way through tangles of brush.

"There might be snakes in there."

"Snakes, raccoons, maybe a few ghosts. It's all part of the adventure." He picks up a big stick and bats at the brush. "This will scare snakes and raccoons, but we're going to have to negotiate with the ghosts. You don't have any sage on you, do you?"

I cling to his hand. "I'm really fighting the urge to sound like Kenzie and suggest we get out of here."

"Don't let me down now, Bootsy. I saved the best for last."

"I can't believe I'm doing this." We make our way around to the back, where a massive tree with sweeping, pendulous branches that weep from crest to ground, like Quasimodo, spans nearly the entire width of the house.

Declan pushes leafy branches aside and pulls me beneath the umbrella of what turns out to be the most interesting and gorgeous tree I've ever seen. Massive, intrusive roots crawl along the surface of the ground around the thick trunk like claws coming up from the earth. Branches sprout from the massive trunk just above the roots, low and wide, and more grow along the length of the trunk, twisting and curling as wild and free as my hair.

"Wow, Declan. This tree looks like it belongs in the South."

"Isn't it gorgeous? It's an English weeping beech, and tonight, it's our ladder."

I'm sure I heard him wrong. "Our *what*?"

He points to a second-story window frame that has no window. "That's how we're getting in."

"Breaking and entering wasn't on my to-do list."

"We won't get caught. The police are afraid to come out here because of the ghosts."

My eyes widen, and a low laugh tumbles from his lips.

"Seriously. Nobody has been up here in years, Nic. When I was a kid, only the bravest of the brave came here. There are all sorts of rumors about the place being haunted, and I'm not going to lie. There were times Neil and I hauled ass out of here because of something we heard or felt."

"And you want *me* to go in there?"

"You have to, or you'll never forgive yourself. This is the best adventure of our summer, and what's inside is the kind of mind-blowing shit you can't make up."

"I don't need to be scared to be happy."

He pulls me closer. "I'm not bringing you in there because of the ghosts. Millicent Rutger was the last person to live here. She was known for being eccentric and telling tall tales of horrific stories about her ancestors and the atrocities they carried out in this house. That is why everyone thinks the place is haunted. But there was another side to Millicent, and that's what I want to show you."

"Great. Now I'm really afraid to go in there."

"I probably shouldn't have told you all that, but you're a writer, and I know backstory is important. I wanted you to know who she was before we went in." He takes both my hands and gazes deeply into my eyes. "Will you do this for me?"

He's never asked me for anything. I can hear how important this is to him, so I ignore my fears and agree.

"Thank you." He wraps me in his arms and kisses the top of my head. "A'right, Bootsy. It's time to show me what you're made of." He hoists himself onto a low branch. "You're going to follow me up."

"I haven't climbed a tree since I was a kid."

"You can thank me later for keeping you young."

I follow him up the tree, balancing on branches and clinging to the wide trunk. He jumps up, grabs the thick branch that leads to the window, and pulls himself up. It's pretty damn impressive.

"I don't think I can do that."

"Don't worry. I've got you." He crouches and holds out his hand. "Take my hand, and I'll pull you up."

"You can't pull me all the way up there. I'm too heavy."

"Darlin', I've caught fish heavier than you."

"While balancing on a branch?"

"Give me your hand before I change my mind."

I reach up, and he snags my hand, pushing to his feet and taking me with him. I gasp as my toes hit the side of the branch, but he catches me around my waist, crushing me to him, and uses the trunk for balance. My heart is hammering, and as I process what he's just done, I feel his heart slamming out the same rapid beat.

He kisses my head. "Take a deep breath. Get your bearings."

"How did you do that?" I look at him, dumbfounded. "Do you dye your beard gray? Are you really thirty-five?"

He grins. "I wish I were, but only so you and I could have an extra decade of adventures together."

I'm struck speechless.

He must realize what he said, because his brows slant, and he adds, "I mean summer adventures."

"I know." I need to get onto an easier subject. "When's the last time you climbed this tree?"

"Thirty-one years ago. Listen, I'm going to run across the branch, but I don't want you to do that. It's too dangerous. I want you to crawl, and I'll help you into the window. Got it?"

"Don't worry. There's no way I'm running across this gnarly balance beam." It's a thick branch. I could probably walk across it if I had a rope over my head to hold on to, but still.

"Okay." He kisses me, and then he darts across the branch like Spider-Man and leaps through the window frame, landing with a *thud*.

Who *is* this man?

He appears in the window. "A'right, Nic. Take your time, and crawl to me."

"Now you sound like a Dom." I lower myself onto my hands and knees and start crawling across the branch.

"On your knees, you sexy little . . ." He winces. "I can't do it. I'm too old-fashioned. I can't call you a sexy little slut."

"*Good.* I don't want to be called that."

"But now that you've opened that door, I'm not sure I can stop, and there are things I can definitely say." His voice goes low and rough. "Take it deeper, baby. Suck it like you never want to stop. That's a good girl."

"*Declan!*" I cling to the branch. "I need to concentrate, not think about sucking your . . ."

"Cock?" he says with amusement.

I laugh. "If you don't stop, I'm going to fall off this thing."

"That's probably not a good idea."

I shoot him a death stare and hurry across the branch.

He leans farther out the window with both hands outstretched. "Now take my hands, and stand up like a good girl."

"I've created a monster." I take his hands and push to my feet.

"I'll give you a monster." He pulls me through the window. "*If* you're a good girl."

I can't help but smile at his playfulness, but when I look around, chills claw up my spine. The walls are peeling and filthy. Springs stick out like bones from a torn mattress curled in on itself in the corner. Empty beer cans, soda bottles, trash, and animal feces litter the floor, all covered with a layer of dust so thick it looks like carpet. "I'm not going to be *anything* in this place."

"Don't think too hard or you'll freak yourself out." He unhooks the flashlight and takes my hand. "Watch your step."

"This is disgusting."

"I know, sorry." He leads me into the hall. "Stay here."

Panic flares inside me. "Where are you going?"

He points to the other side of the hall. "To pull down the attic stairs." They creak eerily as he pulls them down and then *thunk* to a stop. He waves me over. "I'm going up first in case there are animals up there."

I nod, too nervous to speak, as it's getting dark out, and this place reminds me of every horror movie I've ever seen.

He turns on the flashlight and climbs the rickety steps, peering into the attic. *"Holy shit!"* He jumps down, startling me into a scream so loud it echoes off the walls. "Gotcha!"

"What? You ass!" I smack his chest. "I hate you! Ohmygod. I almost had a heart attack!"

He pulls me into his arms. "I'm sorry. I couldn't resist."

"You're an evil bastard."

"I deserve that." He hugs me tighter before letting me go.

"I just lost years off my life. Don't *ever* do that to me again."

"Ever?" He looks pleadingly at me.

I glare at him.

"Okay." He holds his hands up. "Come on. There's nothing up there."

"Then why are we going up?"

"Because that's where the real adventure lies." He waves to the stairs, and I see the flashlight on the edge of the attic floor. "After you, gorgeous." As I climb the stairs, he says, "I'm going to miss seeing that ass."

"Is that why you wanted me to go first?" I love that he's so crazy about my looks. I know he likes me for who I am, but it sure feels good to be liked for my frizzy mop and mom-bod, too.

"I'm no fool."

He follows me up to the unfinished attic, which is littered with wooden crates, old toys, a few pieces of furniture, and wooden chairs. Horizontal boards form the peaked roof, and rafter ties run across the room at eye level. There are stains on the boards and a hole in the far end of the roof.

"This is a cool attic, but exactly what did you want me to see?"

He puts a hand on my back, guiding me to the side of the room. "Look closely at the boards."

I shine the light on them, and then I see it. They're covered with writing. I shine the light from the knee wall all the way up to the peak, and every one of them is written on. I read a few lines.

We lie naked in each other's arms beside the creek, listening to the water trickle and the sounds of our hearts beating in the air around us. In the dim light of dawn, I recall my lover's face when he stood up to the father who was supposed to protect me from the hideousness of life but had chosen to ruin me. I can still see my lover's eyes, which look at me so lovingly, filled with hate, his sharp features tight with ire, rage rising off his sturdy frame like smoke, as he challenged my father to give chase when we left. For I know he relished the thought of putting down the animal who had ravaged me.

"Who was it that wrote this?" I'm mesmerized, not just by the words but by the medium on which they're written.

"Millicent Rutger."

I walk along the boards, stopping to read between the rafters. *It's unfathomable to think some women will never feel the burn of lust or the heat of anger. Ladies. That's what society calls them. I call them poor, lost souls.* "She's the same woman who told horror stories?"

"Wicked ones."

"But why here? Why in the attic?"

"If you believe the rumors, her father kept her up here."

I run my fingers over a board as I read. *I hear my lover in the woods as I hang laundry on the line and await the day he will save me.* "Is this all one big story?"

"As far as I can tell, it's a few love stories that read like a saga and take place over several years."

"This is incredible." I read more as I walk from one side to the other. "You were right. You saved the best for last. In today's day and age, when everyone wants to earn a buck off someone else, it's surprising no family members have tried to publish it."

"I don't think there are any left, and if you read all of it, I'm not sure you'd think it should be published. Nobody knows if the horrific stories are real or not. This could be fiction or her memoir."

"Whatever it is, it's incredibly compelling, but I'd never want to publish it, regardless of whether it's fact or fiction. This is her private diary. I probably shouldn't be reading it, but I'd like to read all of it. Do you think I can take pictures, or will that rattle her ghost?"

"You can do anything you want, darlin'. That's why I brought you here. I'll hold the flashlight."

With Declan on flashlight duty, we find what we believe to be the beginning of all the stories and work our way around the room taking pictures. When we finally finish, I scan several to make sure I can read them.

"When I was a kid, people hung out here because of the stories about hauntings, but I was always drawn to the writing."

"Really?" I take a picture of him.

He draws me into his arms as I pocket my phone and gazes deeply into my eyes. "Yes, and I think I just figured out why."

"Why?"

"So I could bring you here."

"You say the sweetest things. Does that mean you haven't taken other adventure buddies here?"

"I was wondering if you'd get around to asking that. I've only had one other adventure buddy, and he's been here many times."

"Only one? I thought maybe this was your *thing*." Now I feel even more special.

"My thing?" He smiles.

"You know, like what you do with women."

He scoffs. "Hardly. My brother Neil was my first and only adventure buddy. Then I met you, and like I said, I knew that day in the coffee shop that there was something special about you, only I didn't think I'd ever see you again. With my life the way it is, I figured that was for the best. Then I saw you at Russ's, and I felt it again, only stronger. You have this energy that draws me in, Nic, and for the first time since I lost Neil, I wanted to think outside the box and experience the good parts of life again, and I wanted to do it with *you*."

Knowing he's shared such a special part of himself with me makes my emotions whirl, and I get teary. "I'm glad you did. This has been the best summer of my life."

"Mine too, Bootsy. Any second thoughts about me going to the wedding with you tomorrow?"

I shake my head. "I'm glad you're going. It'll make it a thousand times better."

"Good. I'm looking forward to getting out of here with you for a night and seeing spitfire again." He touches his forehead to mine, holding me tighter. "I don't want to think about you leaving and not hearing your laugh every day or seeing your beautiful face."

A lump lodges in my throat. "I've been trying not to think about it, too. This has become my happy place."

"You have a thing for haunted attics?"

I smile. "Only when they're in Chatemup."

"And by that you mean, only when *I'm* in them. I'll take that as a compliment," he says smoothly.

"You're a big part of the appeal, and being in your arms has definitely become my favorite place. But even if we weren't together, I'd still feel more at home here than I do in Virginia."

"*Stay.* Don't go back. We'll have endless adventures."

"As much as I want to, you know I can't do that to my mother any more than you could abandon your father."

"There are days . . ." His phone rings, and he takes it out of his pocket, glancing at the screen. "*Shit.* I've got to take this." He hands me the flashlight and puts the phone to his ear. "What's up?"

I take a closer look at the writing on the boards.

"Is he okay?" Declan's jaw clenches. "*Yeah*. Thanks for letting me know. I'll be there in thirty." He pockets his phone. "Nic, we've got to get out of here."

"What's wrong?"

"My old man got into a scuffle at a bar with a guy he owes money to, and he's at the hospital. I'll drop you at home."

I follow him down the attic stairs. "Don't waste time taking me home. I'll go with you."

"You don't have to do that."

"Declan, it's your *dad*. I don't mind, and maybe I can help."

Chapter Thirty-Six

DECLAN

My muscles cord tight as we make our way through the emergency room to see my father. I hate the idea of Nicole witnessing this aspect of my life, but I know how much she likes him, and the truth is, I don't want to miss a minute of the time I have left with her.

I hear my father laughing. He can't be too bad off. I pull the curtain and officially enter hell. My father is lying on the bed talking with Lindsay. He's got a knot on his head covered with a bandage, and his jaw is black and blue.

"Hey, Miller." Lindsay flashes a smile. She's dressed in scrubs, and her hair is pinned up in a high ponytail, which makes her look younger than me. "Looks like Daddy's been a bad boy again."

Christ. Can we please act our age? "*Lindsay,*" I say curtly, and put my hand on Nicole's back. "This is Nic. Nic, this is my ex-wife, Lindsay."

Tension rises beneath my hand, but Nicole manages a pleasant enough smile for a kitten being thrown into a viper's cage. "Hi, Lindsay. It's nice to meet you."

"So you're the one people are talking about," Lindsay says sweetly.

"*Lindsay,*" I warn. She knows how to stir shit up, and I'm not in the mood.

"What? You know how this town is. Everyone feels the need to tell me about you two." She glances at Nicole. "Like it's any of my business who he's hanging out with." She laughs in a forced-but-trying-to-seem-casual way. "It's a pleasure to meet you, Nic." She covers my father's hand with her own. "Now you, Daddy dearest, need to take it easy and stay out of bar fights, you hear?"

"Yeah, yeah." My father peers around her. "Hiya, Nic. It's good to see you again."

"You too. I wish it was under better circumstances."

"Let's get this show on the road." I look at Lindsay. "What do I need to know?"

"Not much. He took a hit to his jaw that sent him reeling, and he hit his head on a table as he went down. He got six stitches in his forehead. No signs of concussion. He needs to keep his wound dry and clean and get some rest. He's just been discharged, so you're good to go."

"How did he get to the hospital?" Nicole asks. "Do you know if the other guy is pressing charges?"

Damn. I should've asked those things.

"One of the guys from the bar dropped him off," Lindsay answers. "And nobody presses charges in Chatemup."

When she leaves, I help my father up. He pushes to his feet, a little unsteady, and I notice his knuckles are black and blue. "Jesus, Dad. You're too old to be getting into fights."

"You should see the other guy." He winks at Nicole.

"This isn't funny. You could've been hurt a lot worse than this." *And you fucked up another night for me.*

Nicole points to the table on the other side of the bed. "Are those your discharge papers?"

"I think so," he says.

"I'll grab them. Did you have anything else with you when you arrived?"

"Nah," my father says. "I left my dignity back in the bar."

I bite my tongue.

My father is still three sheets to the wind, and he's chatty on the way back to his place. I try talking with him about why he was at the bar, but he gives me the same bullshit answers as always. Once he's settled, I make arrangements to pick him up first thing tomorrow morning to take him to get his car, and by the time we head back to Nicole's place, it's late, I'm in a foul mood, and she's wound tighter than a top.

"I'm sorry our night was ruined."

"Nothing could ruin what you did for me tonight. You must have put a lot of thought into taking me to that house."

"I did, and I'm glad you enjoyed it."

"Declan, your father is such a wonderful man, and I know how much you love him despite his faults, but he could have really been hurt tonight."

"You think I don't know that?" I tighten my hold on the steering wheel.

She shakes her head. "I know you do, and I can only imagine how hard he'd fight you on this, but don't you think you should *try* getting him some help?"

"Been there, done that." My gut roils. I don't have the patience for this conversation right now. "He has to want it."

"Yes, he does, so maybe you need to stop being his lifeboat. Sometimes people need to sink before they can see the damage they're doing and find the need to swim."

"And just fucking watch him drown? After he took in Lindsay when I got her pregnant? Gave her a home above our garage and watched out for her and my family when I was away?" I turn onto her road. "That's not happening, Nic."

"So you'd rather pick up the pieces every time he can't pay a debt, or gets into a fight, or can't go to work, all because he helped you when you were barely more than a kid? You realize you're enabling him, don't you?"

I drive up the hill to her place, gritting my teeth. "I'm not fucking *enabling* him. I'm just doing what's best."

"For *who*?" Her voice escalates. "You look like you're ready to tear someone apart, and your father—"

"You want to talk about enabling? You really want to go there, Nic? Let's talk about your daughter." I throw the truck into park, knowing I'm being a dick and too fucking irritated to stop. "How's her summer job working out? Is she going to pay you back for that airfare?"

Her mouth snaps shut, hurt and anger rising in her eyes.

"That's what I thought."

"At least I tightened the reins on her spending," she fumes.

"Did you? You think that little talk will help?" I need to get the hell out of there. "Look, it's been a shit night, and I have to go over to the bar and get the lowdown to make sure my father didn't screw anyone else over, so I know what's coming."

"Good luck with that." She climbs out of the truck and slams the door, stalking away without so much as a glance in my direction.

Fuck. Fuckfuckfuck.

I don't know who I hate more right now—myself or my father.

Chapter Thirty-Seven

DECLAN

I've seen some awful shit in my life, but nothing wrecked me like seeing the hurt in Nicole's eyes when I spewed venom at her last night. What a fucking mess.

I look at my father as we head over to the bar to get his car. He looks so tired and has aged so much since my mother died, I'm starting to forget the way his eyes used to shine with excitement at every little thing. I knew he'd lost his best friend and the love of his life, but I'm not sure I ever fully understood how deep that type of loss could cut until last night. There's no comparison between losing someone to death and losing someone because you were an asshole, but there's also no comparison between loving someone and being *in love* with them. I knew I was falling hard for Nicole, but I didn't realize how hard until she stormed away and I was swept into a new world of pain that I still don't know what the hell to do with.

My heart breaks for my father, but that doesn't stop the resentment from eating away at me for his inability to hold his shit together, and I hate that. How can I feel so much resentment, and just as much love, toward the man who taught me right from wrong and supported my every endeavor?

"Dad, we have to talk."

"I know. I'm sorry I screwed up your night with Nic. I drank a little too much and let some twit get my goat. I won't let it happen again."

Like a fucking broken record. "How many times have you told me that?"

"Probably more than you'd like, but I'm doing the best I can, and I'm sorry if that's not good enough for you."

"Why is it good enough for *you*?" I bark as I pull into the parking lot and park next to his car. "And he wasn't some twit. It was Douglas, and he said you owe him four thousand dollars for some card game you played in last month. What the hell, Dad?"

"Douglas *is* a twit, and he knows I'm good for the money."

"That's the problem. You're *not* good for it. Do you have any idea how hard Ethan has to work to keep up with the shit you promise customers to make up for your debts?"

His jaw clenches, and he grabs the door handle.

All the anger I've been holding back comes raging out. "Where's your self-respect? Aren't you embarrassed that you got into a fight with a man you've known since I was a kid? In front of people you work with? People Ethan and I do business with? Or that Nic saw you that way?" I don't mention my ex, because she's seen him in far worse condition.

"I don't give a damn who saw me." He throws open his door.

"Dad, you're *not* this guy."

"Wake the hell up, son," he says angrily as he climbs out of my truck. "This is exactly who I am."

Chapter Thirty-Eight

NICOLE

"I can't believe he hasn't reached out to at least let you know he's not going to the wedding," Dani says on a three-way call with me and Rachel.

"Maybe it's for the best." I'm pacing my deck, wishing I could skip Nolan's wedding and eat a gallon of ice cream to drown the ache of hating how Declan and I left things last night. But like a responsible adult, I ate three Snickers bars last night, two more this morning, and I'm suppressing my feelings and carrying on. I'm dressed and ready for the wedding, and my overnight bag is already in my car.

"You sound strange. It must be that stiff upper lip," Dani says.

"I'm *fine*. I should thank him. He's right. I have enabled Mackenzie to some extent, and last night made me take a good long look in the mirror and see that." My talk with Aspen this morning also helped me see it more clearly. Instead of going for a walk through town, we headed down the beach and found a quiet spot to sit and talk. It was nice getting advice from someone other than my mother who has gone through the ups and downs of raising young adults.

"You don't have to pretend like it doesn't hurt, Nic," Rachel says. "We know you fell for him."

"You're only human," Dani adds. "*Come on.* Those dimples? That charm? You never stood a chance."

"It does hurt, but we were just having fun, and sure, I developed feelings for him, but it's not like I can't live without him. I know I can." I missed sleeping in his arms last night and getting a text from him this morning. When I think of my life without Declan in it, it's vanilla, and I want mint chocolate chip. But I can't afford to wallow. "Like I said, it's for the best. He's got a lot of stuff going on, and this is exactly why I didn't want to get involved with anyone."

"But you *did* get involved," Rachel says. "Do you want me to buy a plane ticket and meet you in Boston for the wedding?"

"No. I'll be fine, and as much as I'd love to stand here and chat about how much it sucks that my adventure buddy blew me off, I have a wedding to get to and a house to pack up when I get back, so I'd better go."

"Try to have fun with Mackenzie and your mom tonight," Rachel says.

"Tell Tim he's an asshat for me," Dani says.

When we end the call, heartache sneaks back up to the surface. I turn to go inside and see Declan coming up the walk dressed in a dark suit with a forest-green tie that matches my dress. He remembered. Happiness blooms inside me, and I remind myself that we are not all well and good. But holy smokes, he looks like he walked off the pages of a magazine.

As he climbs the deck steps, a tentative smile brings out his dimples. "Damn, Bootsy, you sure do clean up nice."

"Thanks. So do you. I didn't think you'd show up."

"I wasn't sure you'd want me to, but I made you a promise, and I always keep my promises." He puts his hands out to his sides, palms up, and gives me a panty-melting grin. "Even if you never want to see me again after tonight, you might as well rub all this arm candy in your ex's face."

I laugh softly as he closes the distance between us, bringing the scent of man and musk and that deep-seated connection I've come to treasure.

"I'm sorry, Nic. I was overwhelmed last night, and I never should have spoken to you the way I did."

"I probably shouldn't have butted into your business."

"You had every right to say something. You had just witnessed a part of my life I try to keep separate from everyone and everything else. My worlds collided, and that was a lot harder than I expected, but I *want* you in my business. You've changed my world, darlin'. Hell, you've changed me. I want to be able to talk honestly with you about our lives, and I had no right to be an ass, and I'm truly sorry. There is no excuse for the way I spoke to you or the harsh way I said what I did. I should never have thrown that in your face in the heat of anger."

His voice drips with sincerity. "I understand."

"I appreciate that, but it's still inexcusable. If you have five minutes, I'd like to tell you what was going through my head."

"Okay."

"I've been told I enable my father plenty of times by Ethan and Annie and, to a lesser degree, by my own kids. It usually only bugs me for a minute or two, but when *you* said it, it hit differently. I felt completely exposed. I hated you seeing my father like that and seeing my role in it, or my weakness."

"Declan, I get it. Life is messy."

"Please let me finish. I've been carrying this secret for a long time, and I want you to know. My father has his faults, and God knows I do, too, but the truth is, I've been afraid to let him hit rock bottom. Losing Neil did me in, and I told you that I was close to my mother. But I never told you how close. She was my secret keeper. When things got to be too much, she was the one I turned to. She would tough-love me and straighten my ass out. She wasn't able to do that when I got out of the military, but she was the only one who saw *all* the reasons I was so messed up. While everyone else was telling me to put what I'd experienced in the military behind me and move on, she was trying to get me to talk about Neil, which I couldn't do. She knew before I did that being home to stay, without the brother I'd made all sorts of future plans with, was too much for me to bear. She knew before I did that it was easier for me to distance myself from the reality of Neil being gone when I was away. Once I was back in our old stomping grounds, she saw that I was grieving for what was really the first time on top of the PTSD I had from the military. I never told her about the night I thought Ethan was Neil, but we talked about everything else, including the fact that I thought I'd made a mistake marrying Lindsay, but I'd taken a vow and I was going to stick to it. Needless to say, when she died, it hit me hard." He takes a deep breath. "The truth is, Nic, I guess I'm weaker and more selfish than I thought, because I couldn't chance my father's rock bottom being so bad that I might lose him, too."

How much grief could one man carry before the weight of it crushed him? *"Declan."*

"I don't want you to feel sorry for me. I just wanted you to know the truth. I was up all night fighting the urge to come over here, but I didn't have anything to offer but an apology. I changed that today. I met with Ethan and Annie, and we called my boys and got in touch with a rehab center. We're preparing to hold an intervention. I can't promise it'll go well. Hell, I can't promise anything. But when you walked away last night, I felt like my heart was being ripped from my chest."

My throat constricts. "Me too," I admit softly.

"I'm not letting you get away that easily, WG. I know you're leaving, and I don't know if any of this will make sense or if it's even fair for me to ask, but if you can find it in your heart to forgive me, I promise to do my best not to lash out like that again. You're everything, Nic. Your laugh, your smile, that wild hair. I've never met anyone like you, and this thing between us is unstoppable. We're not just you and me anymore. We're *us*, and I don't want to lose how far we've come just because I was an idiot or because you're moving away. If you're willing, I'd like to try to continue seeing each other long distance. I can come to Virginia, or you can come here. I mean, if you want to. If you're into it."

I don't even hesitate. "I'm into it. I'm into *you*, Declan."

He exhales loudly, relief shining in his eyes. "Thank God, because I don't want to spend another day without hearing your voice. Today sucked."

"For me, too, but you're stretched to the limit. We both know you're not going to be able to find time to come see me. It's a pipe dream."

"Never underestimate a fish peddler. I made time to see you all summer, didn't I?"

"Yes, but—"

"Please trust me, Nic. I might be going gray, but I know how to move heaven and earth for the people I care about."

"That you do."

"I may be kicking myself in the ass in a minute for saying this, but let's take a second to be sure we're doing this with our eyes open. Just because I've seen the light doesn't mean my father will. That situation might get even messier, and I know you didn't want drama in your life."

"I don't like drama, but you're trying to do the right thing, and that makes all the difference in the world. And you were right about me enabling Mackenzie."

"Yeah, I know I was." He smiles. "But like I said, I could've found a better way to say it."

I shake my head, but it's that honesty that has drawn me to him since we first met. "You're lucky you're cute."

"No. I'm lucky you've seen the best parts of me and are willing to try not to let the worst parts scare you off. We're going to fight, Nic. That's what passionate people do. But I'll try not to be a dick. I saw how much I hurt you last night, and I never want to cause you pain like that again."

"I hate fighting and all the feelings that come along with it. But what I hate most is the hurtful way you spoke to me, so thank you for recognizing that." I grab the lapels of his suit and tug his face closer to mine. "Now can you stop being a responsible grown-up who says and does all the right things and kiss the hell out of me before I go into withdrawals?"

His smiling lips cover mine in an intoxicating kiss. He pushes his hands into my hair as mine move to the back of his neck, and we lose ourselves in each other. When we finally come up for air, he slides his lips to my cheek, pressing a kiss there.

"I had something made for you that I was going to give you last night after our adventure, but you know what they say about the best-laid plans." He pulls a long black jewelry box out of his jacket pocket.

My pulse quickens. "Declan . . . ? You didn't have to get me anything else."

"Well, I'm a little selfish. I wanted you to have a reason to think of me while we're apart."

"As if I wouldn't think about you all the time anyway? Do you really think you've made that insignificant of an impact on my life?" That would make me sad, if I didn't know him well enough to realize he knows the truth.

"No, darlin'. A connection like ours is once in a lifetime. But I'm not taking any chances."

He opens the box, and my breath catches at a stunning necklace of baguette and circular diamonds with a few gold flowers in between. "Declan, I've never seen anything so unique and beautiful."

"I was hoping you'd like it. It's Morse code." He takes it out of the box and puts it on me.

"Morse code?" I reach up and touch it. Everything he does is so special. "What does it say?"

"Oh, no, you don't. It's an adventure. You'll have to decipher it."

My heart fills up at the thought he must have put into this gift. "Of course I do. I can't believe you had it made for me. When did you have time?"

"I ordered it about a month ago. Right after we came out to our friends. I figured if you were okay with that, there was a good chance you'd want to hang out with me next summer."

"You're too much." I put my arms around him. "And I like you that way."

We kiss, and he holds me tight as his lips slide to my cheek and he presses a kiss there, whispering, "When you introduce me to your ex-husband, feel free to call me your boy toy instead of your adventure buddy."

I laugh and lean back so I can see that twinkle in his eyes. "Why don't we go all out and I'll just call you my lover?"

"Your lover boy?" He grabs my butt. "Will you crawl across the dance floor like Jennifer Grey in *Dirty Dancing*? Because that was hot."

"What is it with you and crawling?" I push from his arms, swaying my hips as I walk toward the patio door and crook my finger, mimicking that scene from the movie. "*Come here, lover boy,*" I say in my huskiest voice, and he darts toward me. I squeal as he tugs me into his arms, and we stumble into the living room, falling onto the couch in a tangle of messy kisses and joyous laughter.

Chapter Thirty-Nine

DECLAN

The ceremony was long, drawn-out, and overdone, and Nicole's ex's speech was about as fake and pompous as they come. Nicole is so down-to-earth, I can't imagine her spending an hour with Tim, much less giving him so many years of her life. I also wonder how Mackenzie managed to hold her tongue around the asshole for so many years. The reception is in full swing, and Nicole has done an impressive job of mingling with people she knows from Virginia, but she's still so damn tense, I want to take her up to our room and make love to her until she's too spent to think about anything else. At least her mother, Marion, has a good sense of humor about the whole situation, and Mackenzie is enjoying herself, dancing with Tim's younger son, Connor. I haven't had the pleasure of meeting his dickhead father, or the bride and groom yet, but Connor seems like a cool kid.

"Marion, you must be excited about Nic coming home and getting back to your dinners and movie nights." Her mother is feisty, with curly auburn hair she wears just above her shoulders.

"It hasn't been the same without her, but look how happy she is. This time away has been good for her." Marion glances at Mackenzie on the dance floor. "And as much as I dislike being around you-know-who tonight, seeing the boys is good for Kenzie. Look at her out there. She misses Connor and Nolan. Despite how tough those years with Tim were, I think having brothers helped her a lot."

"I guess," Nicole says. She's beautiful in a forest-green wrap dress that ties above her right hip, those wild curls I adore tumbling over her shoulders, and the necklace I gave her sparkling against her silky skin. But her knee is bouncing like a jackhammer under the table.

"What was it like raising Nic with three older brothers?"

"Nothing like I thought it would be." She looks lovingly at Nic. "Nic's brothers are several years older than her, and she was determined not to be left behind. I had to beg the swim coach to put her on the swim team when she was only four, which was unheard of, but her brothers were on it, and she'd be damned if she'd sit on the sidelines, and she learned to ride a two-wheeler at five, well before her brother Kent did."

I put my hand on her leg. "You were a tough little one, huh, Bootsy?"

She smiles, but her leg is still drilling a hole in the floor.

"I bought her dresses and ribbons for her hair," Marion says. "But all she wanted to wear was her brothers' hand-me-downs. Only *once* did I convince her to wear a dress to school. She was in first grade, and she insisted on wearing shorts under it."

"I remember that," Nic says.

"I got a call around lunchtime that I needed to bring a shirt to school for Nic, because she took off her dress and refused to put it back on."

"You were a little exhibitionist?" I chuckle.

"*No*," Nicole insists. "I got in a fight with a boy. I was playing dodgeball, and he said I threw like a girl. I had to show him just how tough girls could be, and I took off my dress first because I was afraid my mom would be upset if I got it dirty."

"She proceeded to give the kid a shiner," Marion says.

"That's my girl." I put my arm around Nicole. "I knew when I met her, she'd be up for adventures."

"I'm glad to hear that." Marion nods approvingly. "Too many people have underestimated her over the years." She tosses a snide look in Tim's direction, and then her face brightens. "*Oh*, there's my friend Janice. I need to talk with her. Would you excuse me?"

"Sure, Mom. Have fun." As her mother walks away, Nicole says, "She likes you. She's never that chatty unless she likes someone."

"That's good, because I think she's almost as great as her daughter. But if you bounce your leg any harder, you're going to start an earthquake. Time to trip the light fantastic, beautiful." I rise to my feet, taking her hand and bringing her up with me.

Her eyes light up. "Trip the light fantastic?"

"I haven't been able to take my eyes off you all night. I'll say anything to get you in my arms." As I lean in for a kiss, I see Tim approaching. *Great.* I'm pretty sure Nicole has been avoiding him.

He holds his chin up with an air of entitlement, flashing painfully white teeth. His short hair is perfectly combed, his face clean-shaven, and his tuxedo perfectly pressed. My mother used to say my father's scruff and wrinkled clothes were signs of a well-loved, hardworking man who had better things to do than worry about nonsense. Tim clearly enjoys nonsense.

"Nicole, it's so good to see you." He leans in to kiss her cheek, and I feel her tense up, which makes me want to grab him by the throat and haul his ass away.

Nicole feigns a smile, and I know exactly why she doesn't return his platitude. My girl hates lies too much to lower herself to lying just to make this egotistical ass feel good.

"Tim, this is my friend Declan. Declan, this is my ex-husband Tim."

I refuse to tell the fucker it's nice to meet him. "Hi, Tim. I've heard a lot about you." I offer my hand.

He gives me a once-over before shaking it. "Mackenzie said there was a new man in Nicole's life. She seems to have taken a liking to you."

"Kenzie's a great girl." I toss in a little extra just for fun. "It's nice to know she has good taste, too."

His brows knit.

This guy wouldn't know a joke if it slapped him in the face.

"Nolan is glad you made it," he says to Nicole.

"Connor seemed happy to see her, too, as did so many other lovely people in this room, including your parents," I point out.

"Yes, of course." He lifts his chin to Nicole. "Quite frankly, I'm surprised you left your keyboard long enough to attend." He eyes me. "I'm sure you know Nicole is a bit of a workaholic."

Nicole's eyes narrow, and I want to throttle the guy.

"A workaholic?" I laugh. "I can't say I do. Nic is dedicated to her craft, and it shows. Her fans rave about her, but she goes running every morning, and between hanging out with friends and our many adventures and the nights we spend on my boat, she doesn't have time to be a workaholic."

"Really?" He looks perplexed. "The woman I was married to never left her desk chair."

I lean closer to him and lower my voice. "And that was a problem for you? I like when she's in her chair. It's ergonomic, and you can do a *lot* with ergonomic, if you catch my drift." I toss him a wink and slide my arm around Nicole's waist. "Isn't that right, darlin'?" I kiss her temple, and she stifles a laugh.

Mackenzie and Connor are making their way over to us with Nolan and his bride, Amelia. I notice a silent message passing between Kenzie and the two young men before they reach us.

Connor, a younger version of his father minus the asshole attitude, sidles up to his old man, and says, "Nic, you don't mind if I steal my dad, do you? A friend is looking for him across the room."

"Not at all," Nicole says, and Connor whisks his father away.

I feel the tension draining from her body.

"Rescue mission complete," Mackenzie says, high-fiving Nolan and Amelia.

"Coolest kids *ever*," I say.

"You can say that again." Nicole looks lovingly at Mackenzie and Nolan and smiles affectionately at Amelia.

"I know my father isn't easy to be around," Nolan says. "But, Nic, you're a second mother to me, and it means the world to me and Amelia that you're here."

"I wouldn't have missed it for anything." Her eyes find mine, and the emotions in them double down, nearly bowling me over. "Besides, lover boy over here knew just how to handle your father. Nolan, Amelia, this is Declan."

"It's nice to meet you both. The wedding was beautiful. Congratulations."

"Thank you," Amelia says.

"Kenzie told us about the adventure you took her on," Nolan says. "It sounded awesome."

"*Wait!* Hold on." Mackenzie holds her hands up. "I just realized what Mom said. Lover boy? That's a lot different than just enjoying your time together."

"Kenzie, don't start," Nicole warns.

I pull her closer. "Your mother's no dummy, Kenz. Did you really think she wouldn't claim me before she left town?"

"I did *not* claim you," Nicole says.

"You totally did," Mackenzie says. "I can see it in your face. The woman who said she was done with men now has an adventurous lover boy."

I can't help but smirk.

Mackenzie wrinkles her nose. "I didn't mean it like that."

"Well, for your mom's sake, I hope he is," Amelia says with a laugh.

Nicole looks at me. "Look what you started."

"At least with me, you don't need a rescue mission."

We have fun chatting with Mackenzie and the others, and eventually we make our way to the dance floor. As Eric Clapton's "Wonderful Tonight" plays, I *finally* get my incredible woman in my arms. "Are you glad you came?"

"In some ways, yes. I'm glad I'm here for Nolan and Amelia. It's nice to see him in love, untainted by the bad marriages of his parents, and I'm glad to see my mom and Kenzie. But being around all these people from my old life makes me want to climb out of my skin. I'm really glad you're here with me."

"I'll always have your back." I lower my lips to hers in a tender kiss.

As the night wears on, we spend most of the time on the dance floor. When Nicole is in my arms, she's far less stressed, and I take full advantage, telling her all the dirty things I want to do to her when we leave.

"Keep talking like that and I'm going to have to change my panties."

"Then let's get out of here now and get rid of that pesky garment."

She takes my hand and practically runs to the table for a quick round of goodbyes and congratulations. Marion is leaving on an early flight in the morning, and as we say goodbye and I tell her how glad I am to have met her, I'm pretty sure she sees right through the headache excuse Nicole is giving her, because when she hugs me, she says, "Whatever you're doing, don't ever stop."

Chapter Forty

NICOLE

As soon as we step into the empty elevator and the doors close, Declan takes me in a soul-searing kiss, and all the discomfort and stress of the evening fall away. My back hits the wall, and I give myself over to the emotions that have been trapped beneath stress for hours. A growl rumbles up his throat as he palms my ass beneath my dress. "I love when you wear thongs."

"Show me how much," I pant out.

He wastes no time, kissing me hungrily and moving his hand between us. His thick fingers push inside me, and I moan into his mouth as his thumb finds my clit, working it masterfully, until I'm trembling all over. I rise up onto my toes, an orgasm mounting inside me. The elevator chimes at each floor, but I'm too gone, too head over heels for this man, to care if it stops as I tear my mouth away, clinging to him. *"Faster . . . Oh God, don't stop."*

"That's it, baby. Come for me." He bites my neck, and I cry out as scintillating pain and pleasure envelop me. He sucks on my neck, heightening the sensations as I writhe, moaning and whimpering with sheer ecstasy.

As I finally start to come down from the peak, he says, "I want to take you right here."

My head screams, *Yes*, but thankfully, I'm still too lost to speak. My legs give out, and I collapse against him. He withdraws his fingers and cups my sex. I clench needily against his hot palm. "I want *you*."

His eyes bore into me, a slow grin curving his lips as the elevator doors open on our floor. We barely make it into the hotel room before our clothes and shoes go flying, and we tumble to the bed, kissing like we'll never get another chance. We're desperate for a deeper connection. He grabs a condom and quickly sheaths himself. I can barely breathe for the anticipation stacking up inside me as he comes down over me. His powerful thighs press against mine, his thick cock nestles against my entrance, and he reclaims my mouth. I love the way he kisses me, impossibly deep and painfully slow, forcing me to endure the need pounding inside me. I lift my hips, pressing down on the backs of his, and he thrusts into me. I gasp at the delicious intrusion. He stills and gazes down at me. His eyes are dark as night, his expression so intense, it feels like he can see all the way into my soul. Would it scare him to know how hard I'm falling? To know that when I leave for Virginia, I'll leave a big part of my heart behind?

"Feel that passion, baby? That's the power of us."

I nod, afraid if I try to speak, my heart will pour out. I lean up as he lowers his mouth to mine, kissing me with the force of a summer storm, causing a tsunami of emotions. We rock and grind, our heated flesh melding together, the sounds of our lovemaking rising like a sinful symphony. He thrusts harder, faster, my fingernails digging into his skin. When he pushes his hands beneath my back, curling his fingers over my shoulders, he grits out, "Can't get enough of you." He tugs me down hard onto his cock with his every inward thrust, setting off an explosion of sensations. I cry out, and he's right there with me, consumed by his own powerful release, gritting out, "*Nic. Nic. Jesus, Nic.*"

We cling to each other in the aftermath, hearts hammering, breathing hampered, our bodies slick from our efforts. As the room slowly comes back into focus, he presses his lips to mine. "How can that get better every time?"

"I don't know," I pant out. "But I'm not complaining."

He laughs and cups my face, caressing my cheek with the pad of his thumb. "You've changed my life, darlin'. I've lost too many people I loved to believe in universal powers or any of that otherworldly stuff Aspen preaches, but I have to wonder how many stars had to align to bring us together."

Chapter Forty-One

NICOLE

My heart races as I search the Morse code alphabet on my phone and scribble another potential letter on the pad. I'm sitting on the bed in our hotel room, trying to decipher the necklace Declan gave me. This is the first chance I've had to do it. I thought it was going to be easy and I could figure it out while he was busy getting ready to leave, but it's next to impossible to match the symbols to the diamonds. There are no spaces between Morse-coded letters on the necklace, only gold flowers between each word. The beautiful diamonds blend together in a torturous guessing game.

Declan is brushing his teeth, and I hear the water turn off. *Damn it.* I'm dying to know what this says. The bathroom door opens, and he struts out wearing only his jeans, flashing those dimples. My greedy, Declan-addicted body throws a party like we didn't just make love an hour ago and hadn't stayed up half the night satisfying our naughty addiction.

"How's it coming, WG?"

"Not great. There are no spaces between letters. Have you tried to decipher it? It's impossible."

"Nothing is impossible." He leans down and kisses me, smelling fresh and enticing. "You're too damn cute when you're riled up."

I stand, showing him the necklace. "*Look.* There are no spaces."

He just grins, which is playfully infuriating.

"*Declan.* Am I missing something? Look at this." I show him the Morse code alphabet on my phone. "An *E* is one dot, an *I* is two, *S* is three, and a dash is *T*. But a dot and a dash is *A*, and a dash and a dot is *N*. I'm going to lose my freaking mind. Can't you just tell me what it says?"

"Where's the adventure in that?"

"I'll give you an adventure." I set the necklace and my phone on the dresser and push him down to the bed. He lands on his back and laughs as I straddle his hips and pin his hands to the mattress. I lean over him, and my hair curtains our smiling faces. "You're not leaving this room until you tell me what it says."

He rocks his hips, grinding against me. "And you think that is some sort of punishment? Being held captive by a sexy woman I happen to adore?"

God, I love this man.

I kiss him possessively, demandingly, and when he growls with desire, I tear my mouth away. "Are you going to tell me?"

He licks his lips. "Not a chance."

"How about a hint?" I dip my head and nip at his neck. "Just tell me *how* to decode it."

"I can't quite remember."

I narrow my eyes, and heat simmers in his. I begin kissing his chest and drag my tongue over his nipple, earning a moan. "Hint?"

"It's still out of reach."

"Bastard." I bite his nipple, just hard enough that his hips bolt off the mattress, and he hisses through clenched teeth. I brush my lips over his, grinding my ass against his erection. "If you tell me, I'll relieve that pressure behind your zipper."

"Fuck."

I whisper in his ear, "That can be negotiated."

He grabs my ass, his hips gyrating.

"I can use my mouth first." I nip at his earlobe, earning another heat-inducing sound. "Don't you want me on my knees, my mouth on your cock?" I lick the shell of his ear. "Licking and sucking until you come?"

"Hell *yes*." His hands spear into my hair, and he tugs my mouth to his, devouring me. My thoughts fracture, and he rolls me beneath him without breaking our kiss and shifts his hips to the side, pushing his hand into my underwear and shorts. "So wet and ready. I need to be inside you, Nic."

I squeeze my legs together. "What does the necklace say?"

He grins, working my clit so perfectly, I fist my hands in the sheets. He grinds his erection into my leg, his eyes boring into me as his talented hand takes me up, up, *up*, until I'm barely breathing, begging for more. But he doesn't relent. He continues the torture. His mouth captures mine in another toe-curling kiss, and now he's the one tearing his mouth away, gazing down at me, eyes blazing as his hand stills.

The air rushes from my lungs. "Declan, *please*. Don't stop."

"I'll make you come, baby. When I'm inside you."

"Then *get* inside me." I shimmy out of my shorts and underwear.

He strips and sheaths his length in record time. He comes down over me, pinning my wrists to the blanket as he thrusts into me, burying himself to the hilt. "Fucking hell, Nic. You *own* me."

"Apparently not, since you won't tell me what the necklace says."

"I believe I promised to make you come."

"That's inappropriate for a necklace."

He laughs. "Damn. Guess I have to return it." He lowers his lips to mine, making love to me so exquisitely, he obliterates my ability to speak, much less think.

When we finally come down from our high, spent and sated, he kisses me tenderly and says, "You are my greatest adventure."

"I want to wrap up those words and bundle them with a ribbon so I can revisit them while we're apart."

He brushes a kiss over my cheek. "You won't have to, darlin'. That's what the necklace says."

Chapter Forty-Two

Nicole

I'm still on cloud nine as we pack. Mackenzie texted a little while ago to say she decided to ride to the airport with Connor instead of having us drive her, and she would stop by our room to say goodbye before she leaves. I gather my toiletries and catch a glimpse of myself in the mirror. Between my sun-kissed skin and the happiness radiating from my entire being, I barely recognize myself as the same woman who came to Chatemup three months ago. My necklace glitters in the bright lights, and I sigh inwardly. I don't think I'll ever forget the look in Declan's eyes when he told me what it says, or the pang in my chest as he said it.

Leaving is going to suck. But I refuse to think about that until I absolutely have to.

I grab my shampoo, and as I'm wiping the bottle dry, there's a knock at the door.

"I've got it," Declan calls out.

I hear him answer it as I zip my toiletry bag.

"Hey, Kenzie, come in."

"Hi, honey. Are you all set to go?" I ask as I come out of the bathroom. She looks cute in jeans and a cropped top, but her brows are pinched.

"Yeah." She folds her arms, then immediately unfolds them. "I'm meeting Connor in a few minutes."

"Are you okay?" Declan asks. "We can still drive you to the airport if you'd rather come with us."

"No, thanks. He's going anyway, and this way you guys don't have to waste your time." She looks at me pensively. "Mom, I need to talk to you."

"Okay. What's up?"

"I have a problem."

"What's wrong, honey?"

"I haven't exactly been honest with you about my classes."

Shit. Declan and I exchange worried glances. "What do you mean?"

"I've missed some of them."

"Why? You're not working. What could be so important that you've had to miss classes?"

"My yoga instructor got hurt, and I've been filling in for her."

"You missed classes to help with yoga?"

"Yes, and not just one or two classes. I've missed several—"

"Mackenzie, this is your *future* we're talking about. You can't just not go to classes."

"I'm going to give you some privacy and take our bags down to the car." Declan picks up our luggage and heads out.

As the door closes, I lose it. "How can you be so irresponsible? Do you know what it costs for me to send you there? Can you talk to your professors and make up the work?"

"Probably, but I'm not going to," she snaps.

"Mackenzie—"

"Mom, *stop!* I loved teaching the classes. *That's* what I want to do with my life. I hate school. It's not for me, and you didn't even go to college, so why should I?"

"So you don't have to work your ass off and scrimp pennies the way your father and I did. Jesus, Mackenzie. You know your father still lives paycheck to paycheck. Is that what you want for yourself?"

"I don't care if I don't make a lot of money! I knew you'd go ballistic. That's why I didn't tell you I didn't want to go back to school when I came to see you. It doesn't matter anyway. I've already dropped out."

"You *what?*"

"I quit school. You said I had to be more responsible with your money, so I dropped out before the last day to drop classes. I had to, or you wouldn't get your money back."

I pace, fuming. "How much did they pay you to teach those classes?"

"They didn't, but I'm going to get certified and—"

"Have you lost your mind? How could you make that big of a decision without talking to me first? Have you spoken to your father about this?"

"I'm an *adult*, Mom. I can make my own decisions."

I close my eyes, breathing deeply, trying to calm myself down, but it's like trying to stop a raging sea. When I open my eyes, her arms are crossed, and she has the same fierce determination in her eyes that she did as a kid every time she went against what I said. But I've had enough. "You're right, Mackenzie, you're an adult."

She lets out a relieved breath.

"And being an adult means you can pay your own way. I'm done. You'll have to find a job and figure out how to pay for rent and groceries and anything else you need."

Her jaw drops. "How am I going to pay for all of that? I still need to get certified to teach."

"You're an adult. Figure it out. I love you, Kenz, but I'm *done* being your doormat, and right now I'm so upset I can't see straight. I need time to process this."

"Whatever."

She storms out the door, and I stare after her, unable to believe what she's done.

Chapter Forty-Three

NICOLE

"I still can't believe Mackenzie dropped out of school," I say as Declan and I head into my cottage. I drop my bags by the door and walk into the living room. "Why do I feel like she was already careening down a hill with no brakes, and by cutting her off, I gave her an extra shove?"

"Because it's hard to let your kids deal with their decisions and face the consequences, but I'm proud of you." He draws me into his arms. "You did the right thing. She drew a line in the sand when she said she didn't need to consult you or her father before dropping out, and you're staying on your side of that line."

"But it feels awful." I lower my forehead to his chest.

He lifts my face and kisses me tenderly. "I know it does. But a wise woman once told me to stop being someone I love's life raft, and she was right. I'm sick over the idea of the intervention with my father, but I know it's the right thing to do, even if he fights us."

"I'm sorry."

"Don't be. I should have done it ages ago. It has to be done, and you need to let Kenzie grow up. If you keep fixing her problems, she'll never be capable of figuring things out on her own."

I sigh and flop down on the couch. "I know. I just hate it." Declan sits beside me and puts his arm around me. I put my head on his shoulder. "That's what she wanted to tell me when she came to visit before school started, but she said she knew I'd go ballistic."

"You knew something was wrong."

"A lot of good that did me. I have so much to do today. I should get started." I have to strip the guest beds, do laundry, and get the house ready to be closed down for the winter. At least packing should be easy. I didn't bring much.

Our phones chime with texts at the same time. I pull mine out of my back pocket and see a group text from Russ to all the members of the beach family. *The party is at six! Be there or be square.*

"I forgot about the party. I love Russ and Marlo for doing this, but I don't feel like celebrating."

Our phones chime multiple times as more texts roll in.

Aspen: *Wouldn't miss it, baby doll!*

Maggie: *There better be sophisticates.*

Marlo: *Russ already has the bar set up!* She added a wineglass emoji.

Russ: *Shaved ice, too!*

Marcus: *Ice? Is that what they call it now?* He sent an eggplant emoji. Several laughing emojis popped up.

Maggie: *We don't need to know about your manscaping, Russ.* A see-no-evil emoji pops up.

Declan holds me a little tighter. "You need to go to the party. They're going to miss you when you leave."

"I know. I'll miss them, too. I should start getting the house ready to close it down for the winter."

"Why don't you take a day to chill and leave Tuesday instead of tomorrow?"

"Because I won't chill. I'll write, and I'll be stewing over Kenzie, which means I'll write a fight scene for my characters. It's better to stew in the car and get it out of my system before I have to write again."

Declan's phone rings, and I see Lindsay's name flash on his screen. He tenses up, and I push to my feet, knowing he's going to be called away and even more annoyed because of it. "I'm going to start stripping the guest beds. Thanks for coming with me this weekend. I'm really glad you were there."

"Me too." As I walk away, he answers the call with a curt "What's up?"

I'm hurt and angry about Mackenzie, irritated with Lindsay for clawing at Declan every chance she gets, and so fucking sad about leaving him and my friends and this place where I've become whole and happy instead of a miserable shell of a person, I strip the bed with such force, the fitted sheet rips. I throw it in the trash, and as I bundle the flat sheet and pillowcases, Declan comes in looking miserable. My heart grows heavier.

"I know. You have to go help Lindsay." I walk past him, and he follows me into the laundry room.

"Sorry, babe. She's twenty minutes away, and her car won't start."

"She's the only person I know who can have car trouble every other week." I shove the laundry into the washing machine.

"I don't blame you for being mad."

I spin around, sure there's smoke coming out my ears from all my misdirected anger and from my heart that's breaking because it feels like he's choosing her over me, but then I see his loving, apologetic eyes, and my anger turns to acceptance. "I'm not mad, Declan. You told me your life was a hot mess from the start. I get it. This is who you are. Everyone's white knight." I force my voice past the painful lump in my throat. "It took me months to heal from my divorce and to not only find myself but to be happy alone, and as hard as I've fallen for you, as deeply as I care for you, I fell for *myself* first, and I'm not willing to go backward."

"What are you saying?"

"I'm saying I'm glad I'm leaving, because you were right. I deserve more than a man who'll ask how high every time his ex-wife says jump."

His jaw clenches. "Nic, you don't understand."

"Yes, I do, that's the thing. You say you want a relationship with me, but you're obviously not ready to move on. With Lindsay in the mix, I don't know if you ever will be." I walk out of the laundry room feeling like I can't breathe, and he follows me.

"That's *not* true. You don't know the whole story."

"Then tell me, Declan." My voice is shaky. "What am I missing? Because if any of my friends were dating a guy who showed up late for things because of his ex—an ex who cheated on him—and took off whenever she called, I'd tell them to run like hell."

His chest heaves, his shoulders rising. "Damn it, Nic. It's not that simple, and if you think I want her back, you're dead wrong."

"Then explain to me why you'd go to such lengths to keep her as close as she is." I cross my arms to combat the trembling.

He grits out a curse but holds my gaze. "You know I told you that my brother hit another car and killed the driver?" His voice is low and stern, as if he's forcing every word and needs me to hear them.

"Yeah."

"It was Lindsay's younger sister that he hit," he seethes. "She was sixteen. A fucking *child*. When I came home for Neil's funeral, I went out in the next town over, because I couldn't take hearing one more person tell me how sorry they were. I met Lindsay at a bar that night. I didn't know who she was or that we had that fatal connection. I was twenty, and she was twenty-four, beautiful, and drowning her sorrows. She told me she'd just broken up with an abusive boyfriend, which was true. It wasn't until I told her I'd lost my brother that we realized the truth. We were two broken kids just trying to fucking numb the pain. We hooked up that night, and then I didn't see her again. I never even told her my first name. I went back to the military, and I didn't think about her at all. Not for one second. And yeah, that makes me an ass-hole of epic proportions, but it is what it is."

A dull ache spreads through my chest. "It makes you a twenty-year-old who was grieving for his brother."

"That's a great excuse, isn't it? Then I got the call telling me she was pregnant. She got my number from my family. She was a mess, and she didn't want to terminate the pregnancy. She felt like the baby was a gift from God because her sister and my brother were taken away. It was my kid, and *God*, Nic, I wanted to believe that baby could take away my pain. I wanted that so badly, I'd have done anything. I married her, and her family blew up. They basically disowned her and have treated her like a pariah ever since *because* she married *me*. I called my parents and told them I was in love and they did me a solid. They took her in and gave her a home over the garage and helped with the babies while I was away. And I know damn well that every single time they looked at *her*, they relived losing Neil, but they never once complained. Her family still treats her like shit, and because she cheated on *me*, people around here shun her." He swallows hard, grief written all over his face. "So *yeah*, I go above and beyond for her."

Tears slide down my cheeks, for what they've lost, for his guilt, *and* for what we're losing. "That's a shame about her family, and I'm sure all of that is one more reason why it's been so hard for you to do the right thing by your father. You have more guilt on your shoulders than any one person should ever have to endure. But I met Lindsay. She's not helpless. She's a nurse, and a beautiful, confident woman."

"Who everyone treats like shit because she cheated on me," he grits out. "As if I'm someone special? I'm so fucking not, and I sure as hell don't want people being treated badly because of me."

"Maybe it's not just because she cheated but because the people in this town love you and don't like the way she's turned you into her puppet. It sucks that they don't treat her better, but that's not your issue to fix, even though you've probably tried. You're divorced, and Lindsay is a grown woman. She can choose where she lives and what kind of behavior she accepts from others."

"Nic—"

"Please don't rationalize it any further, Declan. This is really hard for me, too. I'm saying this as your friend, not as the woman you've been sleeping with." More tears spill down my cheeks, but we're not yelling. This isn't a screamfest; it's a heartbreak. "You're an amazing man who goes to great lengths to save everyone except yourself. How long are you going to put your own life on hold because you feel guilty? When is it going to be *your* turn to come first? It's no wonder Neil is commitment-shy. You've spent years showing him that even after a marriage ends, after you've both jumped ship, as the captain, you're never really off the hook." I swipe at my tears and force my legs to carry me toward the stairs. "You should go. Lindsay's waiting."

Chapter Forty-Four

NICOLE

I strip the rest of the beds, do laundry, clean the house top to bottom, and curse at every little thing—the sink for taking too long to drain, my feet for tripping over the area rug, the rug for existing, and the fucking sun for pouring in my windows. How dare it be bright and happy when my entire life has turned into a hot mess. I know I did the right thing with Declan and Mackenzie, but I feel like there's a gaping hole inside me, and *God*, it hurts.

I'm elbow deep in cleaning out the refrigerator, feeling like I'm going to explode. *I'm doing all the right things. Once I'm back in Virginia, it won't hurt so much, and Mackenzie can't hate me forever. Can she?*

I try to focus on the task at hand and not what's waiting for me in Virginia, but reality is hanging over my head like a noose ready to drop. I know every time I walk out the door I'll feel the oppression of my old life with Tim. Hell, I won't even have to leave the house to feel that. Bad memories linger in every room. His passive-aggressive comments float through the vents like ghosts. It'll be like it was at the wedding, only worse because Declan won't be there to have my back.

Fucking Declan.

What kind of spell did he cast to make me fall so hard for him?

He didn't even *try* to hide his red flags. He paraded them in front of me and warned me away. But did I listen? I can't even blame *him* for me falling so hard. His honesty and loyalty are two of the many things I love about him. He doesn't fake a damn thing for anyone, and from the moment we met, he cheered me on for who I am, appreciating me for *me*, not for what I do for a living or the awards I've won.

I touch the necklace, and that black hole spreads. Tears burn my eyes, and I throw a pint of half-eaten yogurt into the very full trash can so hard the canister opens and yogurt splatters everywhere.

"Shit!" Grabbing paper towels, I wipe the splatter from my shorts and legs and clean the inside of the fridge door. I don't want to think about Declan or his inability to establish boundaries with Lindsay. That's *his* life, his cross to bear, and I don't want it to be mine no matter how much I love being with him. No matter how much I love *him*. I don't want to be cleaning out this fucking refrigerator or closing the house for the winter, either.

I don't want to leave Chatemup.

I want to wake up and see the water and go to the coffee shop to write. I want to hear Claude gripe at me and see him smile when I give him a muffin. I want to eat Evelyn's cookies, which she brings claiming she made too many, when I know damn well she made that batch for me. I want to bundle up in sweats and take winter walks with Maggie and Aspen and listen to Maggie bitch about every step we take. I want to see her roll her eyes as Aspen spins those complaints into something positive. I want to sit around a bonfire with my friends and go on adventures with Declan.

My chest constricts.

Scratch that. This isn't about Declan.

This is about *me*.

I want the life *I* created here, in the place where I learned what life and love should be.

I throw soiled paper towels in the trash and lean my hands on the counter as tears run down my cheeks. I close my eyes, seeing Mackenzie's hurt, angry expression before she stormed out and a mix of those same emotions in Declan's eyes before I sent him away.

My own words come back to me. *Lindsay is a grown woman. She can choose where she lives and what kind of behavior she accepts from others.*

A virtual light bulb flickers in my angry brain.

When is it your turn to come first?

That damn pot-kettle thing hits me like a brick in the face.

It's no wonder Neil is commitment-shy. You've spent years showing him that even after a marriage ends, after you've both jumped ship, as the captain, you're never really off the hook.

It's no wonder my daughter doesn't ever want to get married. By staying in Virginia, where I was miserable, under the shadow of my failed marriage, I'm showing her the same thing.

I push from the counter, swiping angrily at my tears, as Mackenzie's vehemence sears from my own lungs. "I'm an adult. I can make my own decisions."

Gathering all my courage, I pull out my phone and call my mother. My heart races faster with every unanswered ring.

"Hello?" she yells breathlessly.

There's music playing in the background. "Mom? Where are you?"

"Hi, honey!" she hollers. "I'm doing Zumba with Janice."

"Hi, Nic!" Janice calls out, also breathless.

"It's an online class," my mom shouts. "We take it over Zoom."

"Oh." Totally thrown off, I say, "I'll call back." I can't even picture my mother doing Zumba.

"No, honey! I can listen and do it at the same time."

Janice laughs. "It's not like we do it right anyway. We just try to move!"

"It's okay. I'll call back when you're not busy."

"Hold on." She picks up the phone, breathing hard. "I'm here, honey. I need the break anyway. What's up?"

"I don't want to bother you while Janice is there."

"You might as well talk, honey. Janice is always here."

"Besties for life!" Janice hollers.

My mom has a bestie now? I close my eyes, debating backing out and calling later, but there's no good time to deliver bad news. I feel sick and imagine this is how Mackenzie must have felt before she walked into our hotel room. *Fuck it. If my daughter can do it, so can I.* I open my eyes, throw my shoulders back, and rip off the Band-Aid.

"Mom, Mackenzie quit school, and we had a fight. I told her she had to grow up and pay her own way, and I feel like crap because of it, but I didn't know what else to do. And now I'm packing up my cottage, but I've built a life here, and I don't want to come back to Virginia." My words fall fast and painful, and there's no holding them back. "I'm not coming back, Mom. I know that's selfish and I should be there taking care of you, but I promise I'll come visit between manuscripts, and you can come here for the summer, or whenever you want. I just can't live there anymore. I can't be in that house, or in that town, where I feel like I'm always hiding from the lies Tim spreads. I just . . . I can't do it, and I'm so sorry." I have a crushing feeling in my chest.

The line is silent save for the music and my mother's breathing.

"Mom?"

"I'm here, honey. I wasn't sure you were finished. Mackenzie called me about an hour ago and told me everything."

"I'm sure she hates me. I just don't want her struggling her whole life because of an impetuous decision."

"Honey, your life changed at eighteen from an impetuous decision, and look where you are now."

"But it was so hard getting here." More tears fall. "Remember Jay and I barely scraping by? He could have gone to college and made something of himself."

"You both could have, but life happens, and you can't live with regrets."

"I don't regret any of it. I just don't want Kenzie to face the same hardships."

"And I didn't want you to face the same ones I did, but we can't control our children. Mackenzie has needed to grow up for a long time, and the only way she was ever going to do that was if you took a step back and let her flounder. She'll find her footing just like you did."

"Why didn't you tell *me* that? I could have done it sooner, and maybe she wouldn't have quit school."

"Sweetheart, you've been a little busy growing up yourself these last few years, learning who you are and figuring out your own life. You knew in your heart she was floundering, and you did the best you could with the emotional energy you had available. If I'd hounded you, it would have only pushed you away from me. I guess I'm a little selfish, because after your father died, I needed you, too."

"And now I'm abandoning you. Forget it. I'll come back."

"Don't you *dare*. I've never seen you happier than you've been this summer. Every time we talk, you rattle on about the fun you're having. Why would I want you to come back to this place and be miserable?"

"Because you're there alone, without Dad."

"I did feel alone after your father died, but you were here for me in a way a daughter shouldn't ever have to be."

"You raised me. Of course I should be there for you."

"Honey, bringing a child into the world is an adult decision. Children don't owe us a damn thing."

"I didn't do it because I owed you. I did it because I love you."

"I know, and I'm telling you to stay in Chatemup because I love you. You weren't the only one building a life this summer. You've finally found your people, and I've found mine. You have a life now, sweetheart. It's time to live it. Enjoy those lovely friends and that wonderful beau of yours."

Tears of relief and sadness fall like rivers down my cheeks. "Thanks, Mom, but I'm not doing this for Declan. I'm doing it for me."

"I didn't think you were doing it for him, but I wouldn't blame you if you were. The way he looks at you reminds me of how your father used to look at me, and that's rarer than a purple unicorn."

I think that black hole just burned all the way through my back.

We talk for another few minutes, and I don't burden her with what happened between me and Declan. She's had enough big news for one day.

After we end the call, I realize she didn't react when I said Mackenzie probably hates me. Fear whips like icy wind inside me. I spend the next hour trying to distract myself from it by reorganizing what's left of the food in the refrigerator, putting away the laundry, and making the beds. But Mackenzie is too big a part of me to ignore the rift.

I take my phone out to the deck off my master bedroom and call her. It goes straight to voicemail. "Hi, honey. I'm sorry we fought. You caught me off guard. Call me when you can. I love you."

Emotionally drained, I lie on the lounge chair and close my eyes. The joy of knowing I'm staying does little to ease the pain of sending Declan and Mackenzie away.

I awake to my ringing phone and bolt upright at the sight of Mackenzie's name on the screen. "Kenz?"

"Hi, Mom." She sounds distant.

I guess I don't blame her. "Hi, honey. How are you?"

"Fine," she says curtly.

"Yeah, me too. Can we talk?"

"Are you going to yell at me and tell me I'm stupid?"

"*No*, and I didn't call you stupid. You took me by surprise, and I'm sorry if I reacted strongly. I'd like to understand how you came to the decision."

"Why does that matter?"

"Because you're my daughter, and I love you."

She sighs. "You won't understand."

"Maybe not, but I'd appreciate the chance to try. I know how much you love yoga, but I thought you liked school and your friends there, too. I'm trying to understand why it had to be one or the other."

"I like my friends, but I never loved school. I only said I did because you and Dad wanted me to go to college so badly. I'm sorry I'm not more like you."

"What do you mean by that?"

"You always knew what you wanted," she snaps. "Everything was easy for you. You had a path. You knew you wanted to be a mom and you knew you wanted to write, and you did it."

"Mackenzie, that's *not* true." I pace the deck. "I don't regret having you. I never have. But you know my pregnancy wasn't planned. I didn't want to be a teenage mother, but it happened, and I loved your dad, and we loved you from the second we found out I was pregnant, so we made it work. But we had to bust our asses just to keep you in diapers. While other kids our age were going to parties and getting degrees, we were staying up all night with a colicky baby and eating Ramen noodles because it was all we could afford. If I made it look easy, then *yay* for me. It's my job as your mother to protect you, and I never wanted you to feel like a burden or an obligation. So I guess I did one thing right. But there was no life path to follow, no career path laid out." I'm so upset, I have to take a minute to regain control and lower my voice. "If there was any kind of path, it was one of love and determination not to fail as a parent. I lucked into writing, honey, and I have worked tirelessly to make a living at it. You've seen how hard I work."

"I know you work hard, but you love it."

"Yes, I'm lucky to love what I do, but nobody wants to work seven days a week. Don't you remember after your dad and I divorced, how you and I went to live with Grandma and Grandpa until I could afford an apartment and childcare?"

"Yes, but that was fun."

"For *you*. Not for me. I love my parents, and I appreciated their help, but what twenty-three-year-old wants to move in with their parents?" I stop pacing and force myself to take another deep breath. "Honey, I'm sorry if you felt like you had to live up to some image of me. I never meant to make you feel that way. I just wanted things to be easier for you than they were for me. If yoga is your passion, then I support you in pursuing it."

"You do?" she said with disbelief.

"I want you to be happy, Mackenzie. But if you're not in school full time, you've got to pay your own way. Otherwise you'll never learn how to take care of yourself."

"That's what Grandma said."

"She told me you called, but I didn't know she told you that." It's good to know she agrees.

"I wanted to get her advice, but she was as mad as you were."

"We sound mad, but we're really just worried about you."

"I know. Grandma said if I want to be an adult, then I have to act like one, which I thought I was doing. But she pointed out that it would have been better to have a plan in place before dropping out, even if I didn't want to share that plan with you or Dad. So I've come up with one."

"That's great."

"Now that school is back in session, I'm hoping more jobs will be available. I'm going to talk to Rhea, my yoga instructor, and see if she needs any help while I get certified. *Paid* help. If she doesn't, she might know of another studio that does. I also talked to Dad, and after he yelled at me for quitting school, he said if I can't find a job here, he'll talk to his boss to see if I can come back and work with them while I get certified. Then I can come back to North Carolina and work with Rhea if I want to."

I'm glad to hear she is taking this seriously. "You wouldn't mind working in the auto shop again?" She helped them out on and off when she was in high school.

"It's not one of my top choices, but I really want to get certified, so I'll do what I have to."

"Tell me about certification."

She tells me about the different options and the types of yoga she's interested in and the certifications she's considering. "I have a long-term plan, Mom. I want to work in a studio while I build an online presence and eventually hold classes in person and online. I know you're worried about me making a living, but I can make twenty-five dollars an hour teaching in person, and there's big money in teaching online because your audience is unlimited. If I set up a studio in my apartment, there's almost no overhead except insurance and website costs. I'm sorry I sprung it on you, but I'm going to figure this out and make you proud."

"You already are making me proud. You have a lot to figure out, but it sounds like you're blazing your own path."

"I'm trying."

"Don't be surprised if a few trees fall along the way. All paths have obstacles."

"I'm realizing that, but I'm going to make this happen."

I hear the smile in her voice and hope my news doesn't upset her. "I need to talk to you about something else. I decided not to go back to Virginia. I'm staying in Chatemup."

"Seriously? What about Grandma?"

"Apparently Grandma has a bestie, and she does Zumba now."

"She told me. I'm glad you're not going back. I don't know why you stayed in Virginia for so long. That place is toxic, and everyone loves you in Chatemup."

Not everyone at the moment. "Yeah. I'm lucky."

"It's not luck, Mom. You're a fun person."

"Thank you, honey. I don't ever want you to think that if a relationship goes bad, you have to hide or live under the scrutiny of others. I want you to feel empowered to take control of your life no matter who's looking down on you."

"*Um, hello?* Isn't that what I did this morning?"

I smile. "Yes. I guess it is."

"Don't worry, Mom. I know why you locked yourself away for so long. Tim's a douche. But I would've sold the house right when he moved out and gotten out of there."

"Not if you had a daughter who was finishing high school, and then I was too swamped with work to come up for air."

"I guess that's true. But what are you going to do with our house now? Sell it?"

"Not right away. I want to make sure I like it here in the winter as much as I do in the summer."

"So . . . if I work for Dad while I get certified, can I live in our house in Virginia? I'll pay for my own groceries and stuff."

"It's your home, honey. Of course you can."

"Thanks. I want to ask you something else, but I'm worried you might get mad."

"Then ask yourself if it's worth that risk before asking me the question."

She sighs. "It is. Since I dropped out in time for you to get a refund on my tuition, if I get a job so you know I'm not going to be sponging off you, can I borrow the money to get certified? I promise to pay you back once I graduate and start working full time."

My heart says to give her the money outright, but I worry that will negate any lesson I'm trying to teach. "That sounds reasonable."

"Really?" she says excitedly.

"Yes, but not until you get a job."

"I will. Thank you!"

"I'm not trying to hold you back, Kenz. I'm trying to help you learn and grow up responsibly."

"I know you are. I'll let you know when I figure everything out."

A text rolls in. "Hold on a sec, honey." I look at the phone and see a group text from Russ. *If anyone wants to come early, my bride is ready for sophisticates!* I glance at the time: *5:20.* I can't believe it's so late. I try to ignore the sadness chipping away at me about Declan and focus on the positive. "Kenz, I'm sorry to cut this short, but I have to go. My friends are throwing a farewell party for me, which will now be a welcome-home party. I need to get ready."

"My how the tables have turned," she teases. "Now I know how it feels to be blown off for friends."

"I'm sorry. I can stay on. I'll just be a little late." Several more texts roll in from the beach family.

"I'm kidding. Tell everyone I said hello, and have fun. Give Declan a hard time for me. Actually, can you tell him we talked and we're not fighting anymore? I really like him, and I don't want him to think I'm a jerk."

"He doesn't think you're a jerk, Kenz." *He probably thinks I'm one.*

Chapter Forty-Five

NICOLE

I hear music coming from Russ and Marlo's backyard as I head down the hill to their cottage. I'm excited to share the news about staying in Chatemup, but it's clouded by anxiety about seeing Declan. Or worse, not seeing him, if he doesn't show up.

As I climb the porch steps, I see Russ through the screen door. He hollers, "She's here!" over his shoulder. I see Maggie and Aspen coming in from the backyard as Russ opens the door and hauls me into a hug. "The girls are so bummed about you leaving, you'd better check your trunk tomorrow. They might try to stow away."

"Actually—"

"Stop hogging the guest of honor." Maggie squeezes between us, lowering her voice conspiratorially. "I can't believe you're leaving me alone with these maniacs."

"Wait until you see the cake Evelyn made." Aspen takes one arm and Maggie takes the other as they lead me through the house and out the back door.

Candlelit lanterns surround the patio, and colorful balloons dance from long strings tied to the backs of chairs. A massive LATER TRAITOR

We'll Miss You banner hangs over two tables of food and drinks. The bonfire brings memories of my first real conversation with Declan, and I remember how engaging he was. He still is. Even more so now that I really know him.

I scan the yard for him as I'm passed from Marcus's arms to Marlo's and, finally, to Evelyn's, each of them telling me how much they'll miss me and asking where Declan is. I tell them he had to take care of something, and they nod, used to it.

Claude doesn't smile as he grumbles, "I'm going to miss those muffins."

I avert my eyes to the table in an effort to stave off the emotions swamping me and see the cake Aspen was raving about. It's shaped like an open book. Three tiny pink flowers with light green leaves border each corner, and *Our Beach Family* is written in pink script on the left. On the right are stick figures of each of us, and it's easy to determine who's who. Russ is holding two cocktail glasses, and Marlo is wearing a pink dress and a white veil. Above Aspen is a thought bubble that says *We'll miss you, baby doll*, and Marcus is looking at her with hearts for eyes. Maggie has a thought bubble above her, too, with *$&%@#!* in it, and then there's me and Declan, holding hands with hearts above our heads. I'm wearing my boots and cutoffs, with running shoes dangling from one hand, and he's wearing a white-and-gold cape and holding a white sword. There's no keyboard, pad, or pen. There's just *me*, and I love that as much as I love that Declan helps save people. But it makes me sad that they see that as who he is. It is part of who he is, but there's so much more to him. I would have drawn something to show his adventurous spirit and generous heart, like a ninja suit or a walking stick, and a big red heart on his chest. But our friends haven't experienced the adventurous side he's only shared with me.

Gratefulness for the friends who have become family battles with disappointment that he didn't even bother to show up.

Aspen moves beside me. "What do you think, baby girl? Didn't Evelyn do an amazing job?"

I refuse to let any man, even one as wonderful as Declan, ruin this night and look at my friends. I feel so much love for them, even with my inner turmoil, my smile isn't forced or half-hearted. "I came to Chatemup hoping to meet friends and find the pieces of myself I'd lost over the years. I never imagined finding warm and wonderful people like you, who would remind me what it's like to fit in and be part of a community, much less welcome me into the family you've chosen."

Tears sting my eyes. "I'm not sure there are enough words in the English language to convey how much your friendship means to me, so maybe this will. I love it here too much to leave. I've decided not to go back to Virginia. I'm staying to see if I can make a year-round go of it, or if you guys will drive me bonkers."

"Oh, baby girl!" Aspen throws her arms around me as everyone talks at once.

"Thank God," Maggie says. "I need you to slow down the wicked walker before she kills me."

"Best news ever," Marcus cheers, and there's another round of embraces and excitement.

"What did she say?" Claude asks.

"She's staying in Chatemup," Evelyn explains.

"Does this mean I'll still get muffins?" Claude asks, and everyone laughs.

The next hour is filled with good food, fun conversation, much-needed laughter, and making of plans for walks and dinners in the upcoming weeks.

"I don't know what Evelyn put in this cake, but I'm addicted," I say to Maggie, and shovel a bite of my second piece of cake into my mouth.

Maggie cuts herself a piece. "I guess it's a good thing Declan showed up now, before we eat the whole thing."

I spin around and see him closing the distance between us and nearly drop my plate.

Chapter Forty-Six

DECLAN

That's right, Bootsy, you can't get rid of me that easily.

"Hi," she says nervously.

"We need to talk." I take her plate before she drops it and set it on the table. "Excuse us for a minute, Maggie."

Taking Nicole by the arm, I head to the side of the yard, away from the others. Neither of us says a word until I stop walking, and then I say, "Nic," at the same time she says, "Declan."

"I'm sure you have things to say, but it's my turn," I say firmly. "First of all, I'm sorry I'm late to your party, but it's been a long day. I was pretty pissed when I left your house."

"I'm sorry, but—"

"Please don't rationalize it." Parroting her words earns an almost-smile. "What you said made a lot of sense, but it went against the person I've been for a long damn time. It wasn't until I had a little space to think that I realized the person I've been isn't the person I want to continue being."

Her brows knit. "Do you mean the person you want to continue being with me?"

"Yes."

She inhales a ragged breath. "I understand."

"No, you don't. You have no clue about the things I'll do for you. How could you when all I've shown you is who I've been?"

"That's not true. You made plans to help your father, and that was a big change."

"Yeah, a plan for days later. That's not who I want to be. I'm a man who takes action. I told you I knew how to move heaven and earth for the people I care about, and I care about *you*, Nic. I didn't fix Lindsay's car or give her a ride today. I told her that I was sorry that marrying me caused trouble with her family, and I was sorry about her sister, but I was done serving time for those things. I made it very clear that I will not be answering her distress calls anymore."

Shock rises in her eyes. "You really did it? Are you sure you're okay with that?"

"More than okay. Thank you for kicking me in the ass and opening my eyes to the chains that have been holding me down. Your ass kicking freed me."

"No, it didn't. You did that all on your own." Her eyes tear up, and she throws her arms around me. "I'm so happy for you."

I wrap my arms around her, feeling like I can finally breathe again. "Does that mean you don't want me to stay out of your life?"

"I didn't want you out of it before. I just couldn't stay in a relationship where your ex-wife was more important than us. I can't believe you really did it."

"Heaven and earth, baby. You'll never have to worry about that again." I lean in and kiss her. "I would have been here earlier, but after talking with Lindsay, I went out on my boat to clear my head, and for the first time in my life, I failed to check the gas gauge before taking off. I ran out of gas and had to call Chuck to bring me some."

"The savior gets saved," she says sweetly.

"He'll never let me live that down. While I was out there, I called Ethan about my father. We rallied the troops, pulled a few favors with the rehab center, and once I got back on shore, we held the intervention."

Her eyes widen. "You already did it?"

"Yes, but it didn't go well. He didn't go to rehab, and he's pissed at all of us."

"I'm so sorry."

"I'm not. It needed to be done. He can be a stubborn bastard. Where do you think I get it from? That's a messy situation, and it's likely to get worse before he gets his head out of his ass long enough to see the light and do the right thing. But we're not giving up. We love him too much to let him ruin the rest of his life, and I care about you too much not to get things right. And as you pointed out, *I* deserve more, too. I deserve *you*, Nic, and in order to earn your trust, and hopefully your love, I have to be the man *you* deserve. I know all those *deserves* probably hurt your writer brain, but just go with it."

She laughs softly and goes up on her toes, meeting me in a sweet kiss. "Thank you."

"*Wait.* I almost forgot. I made you a going-away card." I pull it from my back pocket and hand it to her.

Her brows knit. "Is this from my notepad?"

"Yeah. I forgot you were here and went up to your place. When you didn't answer the door, I figured you were still mad, and I went in to find you so I could grovel. Then I remembered the party, and I couldn't come to a farewell party without a card."

She reads what I've written on the front of the folded paper.

JOB OPENING: ADVENTURE BUDDY

AVAILABILITY: JUNE 1–AUGUST 31 (RECURRING ANNUALLY)

JOB DESCRIPTION: AN UNUSUAL AND EXCITING PERSON TO SHARE IN ADVENTURES

Her brown eyes flick briefly to mine before she opens and reads what I've written inside.

REQUIREMENTS: WILD HAIR, SEXY BOOTS, SKIMPY CUTOFFS

BENEFITS: HANDSOME CO-ADVENTURER, SNICKERS PROVIDED, CLOTHING OPTIONAL

OTHER CONVINCING FACTORS: IRRESISTIBLE DIMPLES AND THAT THING I DO WITH MY TONGUE

She presses the card to her chest. "I love this, and I want the position, but I've made some important decisions, too. I decided to stay in Chatemup instead of going back to Virginia."

"Are you kidding? Please don't be kidding."

She beams at me. "I'm not kidding."

"For how long?"

"Forever, unless I get sick of it, I guess. I already told my mom, and I had a talk with Kenzie, but I'll tell you about that later."

I pull her back into my arms. "God, Nic. Does this mean I get you all to myself?"

"If *to yourself* means sharing me with our friends, my deadlines, and Matt at the coffee shop, then yes."

"Fucking Matt. I can take him out." We both laugh, and I take her in a long, slow kiss, happier than I can ever remember being. "If this was one of your books, right about now is when the hero would get down on one knee, right?"

"Probably."

"In that case." I take her hand and sink to one knee.

Panic blooms on her face. "*Declan.* What are you doing? Get up. You know I can't . . . Get up. *Please* get up. We're not ready. You don't want to do this. Everyone is watching us."

"The hell I don't. Nic, you sexy siren. You lured me in with coffee stains and snarky conversations, and I have fallen hopelessly, desperately in love with you."

Our women friends gasp.

"What'd he say?" Claude asks.

"He said he loves her," Evelyn answers. "Shh."

Everyone laughs, and Nicole whispers, "I love you too, but please don't say anything else."

Fat chance. "Nicole Ross, we weathered our hot mess summer and came out better people because of it. Would you do me the honor of being my adventure buddy for fucked-up fall? And if that goes well, maybe we can progress to wet and wild winter."

Laughter tumbles from her lips.

I rise to my feet. "I told you I'd always have your back. What do you say, Bootsy?"

"I say *yes*, Dimple Dude. I would be honored to be your adventure buddy for fucked-up fall, and please don't mess it up, because I'd really like to make it to wet and wild winter."

"God, I love you." I tug her into my arms as cheers ring out around us, and I kiss the living hell out of her. Our friends converge on us, and Nicole is passed from one set of loving arms to the next as I get shoulder claps.

"Does this mean you're hanging up your white-knight cape?" Russ asks.

"No more helping army buds or anyone else who calls?" Marcus asks.

"I wouldn't go that far." I draw Nicole back into my arms and gaze into her beautiful eyes, seeing a future I'll do anything to protect. "But I'm going to be a little busy saving myself for a while."

Epilogue

I dig through the shopping bags scattered around my feet in the living room, fish out one of the cute dresses I bought for my book signing, and slip it over my head. It's the first week of June, and the book I wrote last summer releases tomorrow. I can hardly believe it's been a year since I first came to Chatemup. This has been the best year of my life. My mother is happy, my daughter has finally figured out how to be a responsible adult, and Declan and I have fallen into a love so deep and true, sometimes I have to pinch myself so I know I'm not dreaming. We have our moments, like any healthy couple, but I wouldn't trade this man for the world.

I zip the dress and twirl. "What do you think of this one?"

Declan whistles. He's sitting on the couch with his feet on the coffee table, legs crossed at the ankles. "Damn, Bootsy. You can't go wrong with that one. You look hot."

"You've said that about the last three outfits."

"Is it my fault you look great in all of them?" He flashes those devastating dimples and pulls me down to his lap.

"I have to choose one before tomorrow." I've been working so hard to finish another manuscript so I could take a few weeks off, I didn't have time to go shopping until today.

"They'll all look better on the floor, and you know how I feel." He runs his hand up my leg.

I wiggle my ass. "Enticing?"

"*Mm.* You little temptress." He pushes his hands into my hair and takes me in a toe-curling kiss. "You should be yourself, darlin'. Wear your cutoffs and boots."

"I can't do that."

"You can, and you should."

"I'm glad you love me in them, but it's my first signing here, and my editor is coming. I need to look professional." I push from his lap and grab another outfit. I whip off my dress, and he reaches for me, but I jump back, laughing, and put on the peach dress.

"That one will look better on the floor, too."

I plant a hand on my hip. "What are you doing here if you're not going to help me?" We're together every night, but we decided to keep our separate homes. Why fix something that's not broken? It's worked out well the few times we each needed a little space, and I have to admit, it's fun spending some nights here, some there, and an occasional night on his boat.

He pushes to his feet. "I came over because I have a surprise for you."

I swear between our adventures and his sweet and sexy texts, he spoils me rotten. "Why didn't you say something?"

"Because the second I walked in the door, you were like a whirl-wind. You threw me on your couch, told me to help you pick out an outfit, and started taking off your clothes. What'd you expect me to do besides sit back and enjoy the show?"

"Fair point."

"Not that I minded." He pulls me into another kiss. "Ready for your surprise?"

"Are you going to tell me that I'm rehired as your summer adventure buddy? Because I think I earned it." Last night I gave him a hands-on demonstration outlining the benefits of hiring me as his summer adventure buddy, and he snarkily told me he'd think about it.

"There's only you, Bootsy, but we need a new name for our summer, because we like our hot messes. What do you think about sinfully sexy summer? Or naked and naughty summer?"

"I think I love this surprise."

He laughs. "That wasn't your surprise. This is." He pulls a familiar black silk blindfold out of his pocket. It was a gift from Santa last Christmas, and we have made very good use of it.

"Oh my. It's *that* kind of surprise?" Shivers of heat riddle me with the luxurious thought of being loved by this man. "I'm more than ready." I close my eyes as he puts it on me.

He brushes his lips over mine, whispering, "That's a good girl."

"Well, hello, Dirty Dom." Anticipation burns through me. I love when he gets in this particularly playful mood.

"Here we go, beautiful." He takes my hand, leading me through the room.

I hear the patio door open. "We're going outside? In the daylight? That's a little kinky."

"Shh."

"I didn't mean kinky in a bad way. I like it. We just have to be quiet."

"*Nic*," he says firmly. "Shh."

"Sorry, Dirty Dom." I giggle.

He chuckles as he turns me by the shoulders. "When I take this off, I want you to look up."

"Yes, *sir*, but you know you're next, and Madam Boots is in a demanding mood."

"Jesus," he grits out, and takes off the blindfold.

I look up, and above the patio doors hangs a gorgeous distressed white wooden sign with intricate starfish and shells carved around the edge and raspberry letters that read My Happy Place. Kick off your shoes and join the adventure.

"Declan. It's gorgeous. Where did you get it?" We've spent months tossing around names for the cottage. Declan had suggested Bootsy's, Writer Girl's Retreat, and a hundred others, but My Happy Place just felt right.

"My old man and I made it together."

"That makes it even more special."

"I need something to keep me busy now that I'm not drinking."

"Rick?" I spin around and find Declan's family and mine, and Rachel and Dani.

"Surprise!" they all yell, and the girls rush in to hug me.

"Don't worry," Rachel says. "I covered Mackenzie's ears when you started to talk about Dirty Dom."

"Sorry, Kenzie."

"She'll live." Dani embraces me. "Have you called him Daddy Dom yet?"

"No! No more Dom talk." I pull my daughter into my arms, hugging her tight. I couldn't be prouder of her. She went home and worked with her father while she got certified, then moved back to North Carolina to work with Rhea. As a certification gift, I forgave her debt for the classes, and she was thrilled. She's been teaching yoga full time online and off, and she's really making a name for herself. "I can't believe you're here."

"I can't believe you called Declan Dirty Dom."

We both laugh. "Can you just delete that from your memory bank, please?"

"Nope. It's good blackmail material. I missed you, Mom, and don't worry, there's no hidden agenda, and I paid for my own airfare this time."

"I'm not worried." She's growing up and has even started reaching out to see how I'm doing from time to time. "I'm just glad you're here." I move to embrace my mother. "Hi, Mom." She seems more like her old self again. Having friends has been good for her, too. We've visited several times since the holidays, and she and Declan have gotten really close.

"Hi, sweetheart." She hugs me. "I missed you."

"We just saw you three weeks ago."

"I know, but Janice and I are taking a road trip to California, so I won't see you for a while."

"Holy cow. Really?"

"Life's an adventure. Live it or lose it." My mother looks at Declan and winks.

I make my way around the deck, hugging Neil and Eric and Ethan, Annie, and their girls. We see his family often, and the boys visit when they can. My heart is full by the time I reach Rick. It took two torturous months for Declan and his family to convince him to get help, and it was worth every moment. Rick seems happier and healthier, and it took a tremendous weight off Declan's shoulders. I've seen a big difference in the rest of the family, too. With every passing month, they gain more confidence in Rick's sobriety.

"Thank you for making the sign. I love it."

Rick embraces me. "I'm glad. I wanted to put a limerick on it, but Declan nixed that pretty quick."

"That's probably a good thing."

He glances at Declan talking with Neil and Mackenzie. "I wasn't sure I'd ever see my boy happy again after he lost his brother. Thanks for bringing him back to us."

I fan my face. "Don't make me tear up. I already embarrassed myself enough today."

"What's that, Madam Boots?" Ethan says from behind me.

Declan slaps the back of his head, and Ethan laughs.

Rick shakes his head. "That's one for the memory books."

Declan's gaze finds mine, and my heart stutters as he comes over and draws me into my other happy place, within the confines of his arms. "I can't believe you brought everyone here for the naming of the cottage."

"It's a big event, and a reason to celebrate."

"I'm surprised you didn't invite our friends."

"I—"

"Let the party begin!" Russ hollers as he comes around the side yard carrying a cooler, followed by Marlo, Aspen, Marcus, Evelyn, Claude, and Maggie. "The sophisticates have arrived!"

"Not me. I'm not sophisticated," Maggie calls out, and everyone laughs.

"Oh, yes you are, baby girl," Aspen says. "There are many different types of sophisticated . . ."

"Look what you've started."

Love brims in Declan's eyes. "It's our next great adventure, Bootsy. Just go with it."

"I'm going with it, and I'm going for it."

I go up on my toes, and as he lowers his lips to mine, I know I'll never get enough of this man who always speaks his truth and loves with his entire being or this place that has truly become my home.

A NOTE FROM MELISSA

I had a blast writing Nicole and Declan's story, which is loosely based on my own "hot mess" summer, and I hope you enjoyed reading it. I did not fall madly in love with my real-life adventure buddy. However, I do love him madly as a friend. Dating after divorce is interesting and complicated at any age. Dating after finding happiness within yourself and being afraid to risk that happiness by letting someone else in creates a whole different level of scrutiny of potential partners. I'm sure some people will wish Nicole and Declan had shacked up in the epilogue, but I always listen to my characters, and this was what worked best for them. That said, who knows what will happen after another season of co-adventuring!

If this is your first Melissa Foster book, you might enjoy my other funny, sexy, and always deeply emotional love stories. All my romance novels are part of the Love in Bloom big-family romance collection. They are written to stand alone and may also be enjoyed as part of the larger series. Characters from each series make appearances in future books, so you never lose track of engagements, weddings, or births. You can find more about my Love in Bloom series on my website (www.melissafoster.com) and download free reader checklists, series orders, and other free and fun book-related information on my Reader Goodies page (www.melissafoster.com/rg).

Be sure to sign up for my newsletter to keep up to date with my new releases and to receive an exclusive short story (www.MelissaFoster.com/News).

Happy reading!

~Melissa

ACKNOWLEDGMENTS

There is nothing quite like a sense of community among close-knit friends to keep you grounded, cheer you on, and pick you up when you fall down. This book has brought up many fun memories, and it's a joy to embellish and share some of them with the world. I'd like to thank my own beach family and my hot-mess adventure buddy for giving me so many cherished memories. Thank you for the sophisticates, bonfires, dinners, laughter, late-night talks, and for all your love and support. Single life would not be as fun without each of you.

I'd also like to give a shout-out to my friend and fan Danielle Skinner for allowing me to borrow her name for this story. I have been waiting to use the name Dani since I first met Danielle several years ago, and it fit Danielle Potter perfectly.

I'm forever grateful to my assistants, friends, and family for their generous support and endless patience. Loads of gratitude go to my wonderful editor Maria Gomez and the rest of the professional and talented Montlake team. My books would not shine without the editorial expertise of Kristen Weber, Penina Lopez, and my capable proofreaders.

If you'd like to get a glimpse into my writing process and to chat with me about my Love in Bloom big-family romance collection, please join my fan club on Facebook, where I chat with fans daily (www.Facebook.com/groups/MelissaFosterFans).

To keep up with sales and events, please follow me on Amazon and sign up for my newsletter (www.MelissaFoster.com/News).

ABOUT THE AUTHOR

Photo © 2013 Melanie Anderson

Melissa Foster is the *New York Times, Wall Street Journal,* and *USA Today* bestselling and award-winning author of more than one hundred books, including *Maybe We Will* and *Maybe We Won't* in the Silver Harbor series, and *The Real Thing* and *Only for You* in the Sugar Lake series. Her novels have been recommended by *USA Today*'s book blog, *Hagerstown* magazine, the *Patriot,* and others. She enjoys discussing her books with book clubs and reader groups, and she welcomes an invitation to your event. Melissa also writes sweet romance under the pen name Addison Cole. Visit Melissa on her website at www.melissafoster.com.